The Shards
GemQuest Book Three

Gary Alan Wassner

Windstorm Creative
Port Orchard § Seattle § Tahuya

Acknowledgments

I want to thank the many poets and lyricists who tell their stories so well and create such clear and distinct characters in just a few lines, particularly Joni Mitchell and Leonard Cohen. With their impassioned words and their poignant relationships, both of these brilliant ar'Tists captured my emotions a long time ago and they have imprisoned them with their magic for over thirty years now. So much of what they have written turns in my mind all the time. They have been a constant source of inspiration for me, easing the sorrows and enhancing the joys, and their words have helped to make countless moments in my life fuller and richer and more graspable. I cannot imagine my world without them, and I am so very grateful that they chose to share their most intimate emotions with us all.

The Shards
GemQuest Book Three

Gary Alan Wassner

Chapter One

Teetoo pivoted ever so subtly to the left and allowed the air to rush in under his right wing. As soon as he felt the gust lift him, he tensed the fine tendons that inundated the delicate filament and caused it to bend slightly. His wing caught the wind exactly as he had hoped, and he smiled as he was thrust forward and upward with an incredible burst of speed. He navigated the floes that propelled him with the precision of a master. While arching his back, he brought his knees to his chest and tucked his feet securely into his body. At the same time, he elongated his arms, stretching them out as far as they would go, and he pointed his slender fingers to his rear while holding them tightly together and cupping them. Finally, he bent his head down just a tiny bit and allowed the translucent inner lids of his eyes to descend protectively over his pupils.

Teetoo soared high into the afternoon sky. A wave of exhilaration swept over him as he masterfully manipulated the slightest of variations in the wind, dipping and diving, ascending and rocketing as he chose with only the gentlest flex or bend to the tip of the wing. He willed the blood in his veins to withdraw from his extremities, thus lightening the points of friction, and he rushed ahead at even greater speeds. His wings glistened in the sun as they absorbed its warmth and became even more buoyant and additionally flexible. For a few minutes, the Weloh allowed himself the luxury of free flight.

It had been so long since he had ventured into the heavens and his restraint had taken its toll upon him. He was born to fly, and when he was unable to do so due to injury or circumstance, he felt stranded, much as a human would feel if he was afloat at sea for an extended period of time. Teetoo had never wanted to develop his 'land legs' too thoroughly. The sky was his home and he reveled in the opportunity to abide there once again. He suppressed the fears and the concerns that plagued him these difficult days and he coursed through the air temporarily unburdened.

He curved the back edges of his wings fractionally and thinned the filament by elongating it at the point where they joined his hips, and abruptly slowed his momentum. He banked to the left and came up and around to an almost vertical position, as if he were standing upon an invisible platform in the sky itself. Slowly, he swiveled until he was staring downward at the city below.

As soon as the spires of Seramour came into view, his concerns rose like bile in his throat; bitter and unwelcome. His wings were full with air, and he hovered over the city, dropping only slightly as he gazed below. He opened his eyes wide, exposing them once again to the elements, and with his incredibly acute vision he scanned the Heights from one end to the next.

You did a good job, Premoran, my friend. The damage is minimal considering what the city faced only weeks ago, he thought proudly as he scrutinized the expanse of Seramour. With the memory of his companion fresh upon his mind, a wave of anguish rushed over him, and he fought back the trembling that ensued. *These days of doubt seem interminably long. Yet, time is ever the thief. It steals our tomorrows and turns them into yesterdays regardless of our perception of the pace. And still no news! How long can I live with this uncertainty? Must I fly to Sedahar myself for the answer I seek?*

These contemplations stripped Teetoo of the last vestiges of joy that had been spurred on by his flight. He tucked his wings into his sides, bent his head downward and began to fall. This precipitous descent was always so exhilarating for him, but today he barely noticed the sensations. His mind was preoccupied with other thoughts as he plunged toward the surface.

Alemar emerged from the doorway and stretched her arms wide. She was not yet accustomed to the warmth of the air, and her first sensations were ones of concern. The memory of Eleutheria on the verge of collapsing upon itself and disappearing into a river of melted ice was still vivid. She could not yet feel comforted by the sun's warmth without consciously reminding herself that the threat to her beloved city was no longer imminent.

She looked into the sky and envisioned the towers of her homeland glistening like crystals under the bright mid-day light, and she smiled. Out of the corner of her eye, she saw what at first seemed no larger than a speck in the sky. Her eyes locked themselves upon it, and she watched closely as it grew in size and approached the city at a tremendous speed. Carefully, she scrutinized the object as it came nearer and nearer.

Alemar stepped out from the shelter of the building and walked to the middle of the square without ever taking her eyes off of the plummeting body. No alarms sounded and no effort was made to defend against this seeming invader by any of the guards nearby. Rather, they too watched closely as it approached the surface of Seramour.

"A spectacular sight, is it not?" Queen Elsinestra said, as she emerged from the doorway to stand next to the Princess.

"It must be the most amazing feeling to be able to soar like that," she replied.

"To him, it is probably no different than walking is to us, though I know he enjoys it so."

"I suppose I enjoy a stroll through the hills of my own country as well, though I could not imagine ever being quite so exhilarated by it as he must be."

"Perhaps a brisk gallop through the countryside upon your favorite horse would be a more appropriate comparison."

"I suppose so," Alemar answered contemplatively while keeping her eyes glued to Teetoo's plunging silhouette.

Elsinestra walked up to Alemar and placed her arm fondly in hers. Together, they stood and waited for their friend to reach the surface.

"I fear that today there will be no joy in the Weloh's eyes when he finally joins us. His heart is aching ever more as each day passes."

"Has no news of Premoran of any sort reached the city?"

"No. None. And it is not for lack of an effort to attain it. Teetoo has been deep in contemplation all evening. When I last left him after supper, he was ascending the tower steps, and he did not come back down until early in the morning hours, the guards informed me."

"Have you spoken with him yet today?" Alemar asked.

"No, my dear. But I hope to shortly," the Queen answered as Teetoo neared the surface about twenty yards to their left. "Come. Let us at least show him some warm and friendly smiles. Perhaps we can ease his suffering if only just a little."

They both walked arm in arm over to the Weloh who had just landed nearby as delicately as a dove upon a pennant's mast. He settled himself quickly upon the ground, and his body seemed to alter in shape slightly. His skin began to redden and take on a less brittle appearance. His fingers stretched and flexed, and they lost their elongated mien as did his legs and feet. Carefully, he pulled the clasp from his hair and let it fall once more upon his slim neck. His facial features softened, losing their sharp, bird-like qualities, and resumed a more human appearance. Finally, he blinked his eyes slowly and deliberately until they were clear and blue once again.

They watched as his translucent wings virtually disappeared

beneath his arms as if they had never been there at all. Although he now looked almost completely human, both Alemar and Elsinestra could not stop staring at him. The Princess had never seen the transformation before, and even though it was subtle, it was complete. Teetoo had virtually shifted in shape before her very eyes, and she scrutinized him closely in wonder. Elsinestra had witnessed this many times before, though even she was still mystified by how smoothly he slipped from one form to another in such a perfectly calm and unpretentious way.

"Have I frightened you?" Teetoo asked Alemar with concern in his voice as they approached him. She had not been able to pull her eyes away from him, so awed was she by the change.

"Oh, I am so sorry," she exclaimed, embarrassed. "I cannot help it, but I am fascinated by you, Teetoo. How glorious it must feel to be able to fly that way. And though you really look the same as you did when you first alighted, you have changed completely! I watched as closely as I could, and even though everything about you has altered, you are who you are still!"

"I am who I am, Princess. That is true!"

"You know what I mean," she replied, blushing. "You joke with me, but you have no idea how incredible it was for me to watch you. Do you will the changes in your body?"

He thought for a minute as if the question was an unusual one.

"No. I do not," he finally said. "My body recognizes the change in the environment naturally, and I am not even aware of the 'transformation', as you so characterize it. Much occurs internally as well. My vision modifies too, as does my breathing and even the way I think. But, none of these changes are governed by will."

"Did you have to learn to fly as a child? Even birds, when they are first hatched from their eggs, must practice. Often, they fall from the nest and die because they do not know how to stay aloft."

"Learn?" he asked. "I honestly cannot remember. This ability is so much a part of what and who I am that I do not separate it in my mind as you do. I do not think of myself as having two personalities or two natures. I am a Weloh," he replied as if that was enough to explain everything. "And you my Queen?" he addressed Elsinestra. "Do you find me fascinating too?"

"Utterly! You could only imagine the extent, my darling Teetoo!" she replied, but her eyes were elsewhere.

The Queen of Seramour was intently watching her husband, Treestar, King of the Southern Elves, as he directed the reconstruction of their beloved city from his station upon the platform in the center of the massive square. In only four short weeks, the buildings that had been undermined by the wood-eating insects from Sedahar had all been torn down, and new ones were designed, the frames of which had already been constructed. The great avenues that crisscrossed the city were paved anew with enormous planks of Noban, hewn from the trees below, then sanded and polished as only the elves of Lormarion could do. The Chamber of the Stars which had suffered immeasurable damage during the attack, was in the process of being rebuilt exactly as it had been previous to the siege. One entire side had been burnt to a cinder, leaving not a trace of the remains of the errant elf, Ruffin, whose traitorous conduct aided Colton and his minions so greatly during the horrible battle. The tower would continue to remain the highest point in the city, and soon they would be able to ascend it once again in safety and gaze across the expanse of Seramour from its vantage point.

The fields and farmlands that sustained the people were plowed under and replanted. Though it was already fall, the Heights benefited from a far longer growing season than the lands below due to both the proximity to the sun, as well as the lack of much of the cloud cover that kept the surface cooler. The tunnels and shelters that were targeted by Colton during his attack were repaired and reinforced, and Treestar and his engineers sought better ways to penetrate the foundation trees without undermining their strength, thus providing even greater security for the youth, elderly and infirm of Seramour in the event of future aggression.

Elsinestra gazed proudly and lovingly upon her husband as he carried out his duties, and she knew how he had ached with each and every blow that the city suffered, as if it had been his own body and limbs that were being maimed and broken. She dabbed her brow with a silk handkerchief that she pulled from her braided belt, and smiled to herself.

"I must return to the castle. There are still so many wounded that I cannot afford to stand here and chat much longer, though I do so enjoy the opportunity. Will you accompany me, Alemar? Your ability to heal has come so far in so short a time that your presence has become invaluable to our people," the Queen said admiringly.

"Certainly, Aunt. I appreciate the chance to help. I know that you would do the same for my people if the circumstances were reversed," Alemar said.

"Henceforth, we must all recognize our commonality, though not just in the face of adversity. There is so much we can learn from one another."

"What you have taught me about healing I will proudly bring back to Eleutheria. I never knew that I had the ability before," the Princess said.

"Many discoveries in life are simply lessons we have not learned yet. The talent abides and awaits the right teacher," Elsinestra said.

Alemar contemplated Elsinestra's words for a moment, deep in thought, while her finger inadvertently traced the birthmark behind her ear as one might casually curl one's hair.

"After Uncle Bristar left to return to the mountains, I realized how much it meant to have us all together again. I must confess that I have been having premonitions though, and they grow more troublesome to me with each day that he is gone," Alemar said.

"Premonitions? Why have you not spoken of this before, Alemar? You should feel comfortable in confiding in me. Perhaps I can help you to decipher them," Elsinestra offered kindly.

"Oh, I am more than comfortable in telling you anything!" she professed immediately, not wishing to convey the impression of mistrust in any way. "I merely did not want to trouble you with some silly worries of mine when you had so many problems of your own to cope with. But now I fear that they are not merely unwarranted concerns."

"Tell me, my dear. What is it that torments you? What have you 'seen'?" the Queen asked.

"I have never been subject to visions before, and I was unsure as to whether my thoughts were projections of my distress or something more tangible and ominous. But the same visions have reoccurred repeatedly, and I cannot ignore them any longer," Alemar replied.

Elsinestra raised her delicate chin and looked at Alemar with deep worry etched upon her face. She did not speak, but rather she allowed the younger maiden to find the words herself that she required in order to express the visions. Alemar closed her eyes and focused her thoughts upon them.

Teetoo had been standing a short distance from them, and the expressions upon the faces of the two women drew his attention away from his own concerns. He walked over to them, stood beside Alemar and turned his gaze upon her as well.

"Colton has assaulted Pardatha. He has also attacked Seramour. Both times he was unsuccessful in his efforts to capture or kill the heir," Alemar began. "He almost succeeded in destroying Eleutheria without even sending a single warrior to accomplish that task. Uncle Bristar has already informed us that Silandre, the mountain that sustains the city of Crispen, seethes and broils from within, and that he now fears an assault on his own domain."

"Yes, dear, this is all true. But the heir still lives, Eleutheria is safe, Pardatha, as far as I know, thrives in the aftermath of Colton's attack, and Seramour has survived and will soon be as good as new. That leaves unresolved my brother-in-law, Bristar's homeland. Do you fear an offensive against Crispen? To what purpose?"

"I cannot say, but yes, Elsinestra. I am afraid that Caeltin is preparing to do something terrible in that realm. I have had these dreams, though they occur not only during my sleeping hours. They are like real experiences dancing before my eyes in a macabre and bloodstained way. I cannot see into the future, though it seems as if I am watching things that are yet to be," Alemar replied.

"What could he possibly want in Crispen?" the Queen asked.

"What did he want in Eleutheria?" Alemar asked. "That did not prevent him from trying to destroy us."

"He requires no reason, ladies," Teetoo joined in. "We cannot understand how he thinks. In some cases, it is clear to us what motivates his actions, particularly when it comes to the heir. He must stop the boy from finding the Gem of Eternity! There is no question about that. But, in his effort to bring the world closer to dissolution, we cannot always know why Colton chooses his battles as he does. His power is great despite his recent failures, and he is spreading it in many directions. It is possible that he does not know for certain what he wishes to find in each of his endeavors," Teetoo said.

"You speak as if you fear that he has already been victorious," Elsinestra commented.

"That he has defeated Premoran, you mean?" Teetoo inquired as he turned toward the Queen.

"Yes. It is at least conceivable that Premoran has prevailed, is it not?" Elsinestra asked.

"More than conceivable, I suppose," he responded somberly.

"Then let us not speak of the future as if Caeltin were the only one guiding the weave. We must continue to hope," Elsinestra said.

"I will never cease hoping, my Lady. Not until fact has replaced speculation, and I no longer have reason to wonder," Teetoo replied.

"Do you have suspicions, Teetoo? Can you sense anything? Would you know if the battle between Premoran and Caeltin has been won or lost?" Alemar asked.

"I am certain that I would feel it. I believe that many of us would know. When the earth is robbed of a great force, whether for good or for evil, it reacts. The weave is altered forever and the cloth must then compensate for the absence of a thread which had been so prevalent in the design theretofore. It would not occur unnoticed. You know what happens when one of the great trees departs," the Weloh said.

"Yes," Alemar replied, and she shuddered slightly at the thought.

"So you know that Premoran is alive still! And if he is alive then we have reason to believe he may still prevail," Elsinestra said boldly.

"No more or no less than before. When he went to confront his brother, he himself did not think it would be resolved quickly. They had much to discuss," Teetoo said.

"Do you think they will actually talk?" Alemar asked.

"They will talk in their own way," Elsinestra responded before Teetoo had the chance. "I do not know if verbal conversation will be the medium."

"They are brothers despite their differences. Once, they were close," Teetoo said, recalling poignantly Premoran's recollections of his brother before their separation.

"It is hard for me to imagine one so good as he being linked by blood to the Dark Lord," Alemar said.

"The circle goes around and around, my dear. And it is multidimensional. Where does evil end and goodness begin?" the Queen commented.

"Surely you do not believe that they are just differences in extremes?" she asked, aghast at the thought.

"You misunderstand me, my child. No. They are as opposite as anything could be; pure evil and pure goodness. It is just for the purposes of human understanding that we compare them at all. If we did not weigh one against the other, or see one in its relationship to the other we could not begin to make sense out of their meanings. They are truly of different kinds nevertheless," Elsinestra responded.

"Colton's evil is like no other. He is not simply bad, as one might characterize the actions of a spoiled and errant child. Neither is he immoral and cruel like a killer who disregards the value and meaning of life. He is amoral! He thrives outside of our concepts of good and evil. He wants life as we know it to end completely. If one were to characterize him more clearly, one would have to say that he is neither good nor evil at all. He is cruel simply because he has no regard for life, though he does not see his actions in the same light that we do. Cruelty requires malice and forethought, does it not?" Teetoo asked.

"I would think that the definition of 'cruel' implies that one enjoys or at least is aware that the actions that one commits are causing pain to someone. The word does suggest that there is evil intention," Elsinestra said. "So what you are saying is that his behavior is not cruel because he does not intend it to be so?" she asked perplexed.

"In his eyes, what he does is correct. Of course, we see it differently. But then again, the understanding of ethics has always been riddled with issues of perspective. We kill at times to preserve, while he kills to annihilate. Is the act of killing or the taking of life the issue here or is the defining characteristic the purpose?" Teetoo asked.

"You are confusing me," Alemar said, and she shook her head. "Evil is something tangible to me. I can feel it! And when something is good, I can feel that too."

"But it is not an object to be looked at and scrutinized as is a rock or a tree," Teetoo replied. "What is it that you really feel?" he asked.

"I feel the spirit of the earth! I feel the pulse of life!"

"And when you extinguish the life of your enemy to further your purpose, what do you feel?"

"Relief. Accomplishment. Satisfaction," she said thoughtfully. "But I also feel sorrow."

"That, my dear Alemar, is the entire difference between the moral person and the immoral person! You think about what you do, and you have reasons for what you do. You are convinced that there is a greater purpose that governs your values, and you try to be consistent in your quest. The immoral person enjoys the pain and misery that he causes, but most importantly, he recognizes that he causes it. Colton cares not about any of this. He is not immoral! He functions outside of this ethical hierarchy, and what he desires is not defined by its relationship to life."

"I have taken the lives of others many times," the Princess continued pensively. "But never frivolously or for sport. I believe that when there was necessity to kill it was to preserve."

"You are beginning to understand sacrifice, Alemar," Teetoo said seriously. "And all these words have meanings far greater and deeper than our ability to explain them. We are creatures of feeling and intellect, and we are thus so unique."

"It has been difficult to suppress my feelings at times though. Life is life, and the taking of it alters the weave for all time, though sometimes it is necessary nonetheless to strike," Alemar said.

"And now you begin to understand courage too, my Princess," Teetoo replied.

Alemar bent her graceful head pensively for a moment and considered the Weloh's words.

"I have doubts sometimes, Teetoo," she said sincerely. "I do not make these choices between life and death casually. I must do what I must do, yet I question my prerogative, and I suffer from the weight of the responsibility. Sometimes I wonder if I am worthy of making these decisions."

"And so the third lesson is learned," Teetoo replied smiling. "Humility. This is oft times the quality most lacking in people of action, though it completes the ethical triad. Yet, without it courage can be cruel and hard, and sacrifice can be misguided."

Alemar bowed her chin and considered the ideas Teetoo had just expressed.

"Could you begin to imagine the heart of a person who felt nothing but relief at most at the destruction of life? Our value system is defined by opposites, and it becomes clearer and clearer in relationship to the extremes that it incorporates. Caeltin D'Are Agenathea has only one goal, and everything that lives, be it good or evil, poses an obstacle to it," Elsinestra said.

"The heir must come to understand these things," Teetoo said more seriously than before. "He will be taught by Cairn of Thermaye, the scholar that Baladar 'called' to Pardatha some time ago. It is crucial that the boy realizes the difference between the evil that thrives among us and that which is totally apart from this world. This understanding will help him to combat it without wasting any of his own vital energy."

"Cairn is the right man," Elsinestra replied. "I knew it when I first met him. Though we had little time or opportunity to converse, I have complete confidence in his ability to instruct the boy."

"Davmiran must also have weapons of another sort if he is to prevail," Teetoo said. "And he must know how to use them."

"Robyn dar Tamarand will teach him what he must. That Chosen is stronger than even we imagined," Elsinestra replied.

Alemar lifted her head abruptly at the mention of Robyn's name, and both Elsinestra and Teetoo noticed the immediate change in her demeanor.

"They are a good team, the three of them. The warrior woman from Avalain provides the final link in the chain. Filaree is quick and certain in her movements and decisions. They seem quite attuned to one another. I have great faith in their abilities," Elsinestra continued. "Davmiran responds to them well. They seemed to have formed a strong bond in so short a time. Circumstances forced them to trust one another completely at the onset. They had little time to doubt."

"I have heard much about the bravery of Filaree of Avalain. Is she all that they say she is?" Alemar questioned.

"All and more, my dear, as are the others. I was impressed with her immediately," Elsinestra replied. "Perhaps you two will get the chance to meet them all one day. You are much alike."

"Robyn dar Tamarand and I are already acquainted with one another. He has visited Eleutheria a number of times. It seems that I was the only one who was willing to associate with him," she recalled. "My brother was mistrustful for so long of anyone and anything from the outside world. He had my father's ear then, and Robyn was never completely welcome in our land." Alemar's eyes were suddenly soft with sorrow. "Had Kalon been able to overcome his suspicions, they probably would have gotten along quite nicely. Despite his obstinacy, his heart was pure. My brother died well, did he not?"

"Quite nobly, I am told. My brother-in-law still speaks of his prowess, and he has never been an elf whose admiration was easily attained. Your brother rests eternally now with my nephew Adain, and all the others whose lives were cut short by our opponent. His name has been recorded in the books of legends, among the other heroes of our race."

Changing the subject so as not to become too morose, Alemar turned to Teetoo once again.

"Is the Lady Filaree as comely as the rumors suggest?" she asked.

"Her beauty matches her prowess, if that gives you an idea,"

Teetoo said. "They are all four a comely group, well suited for the tales that will inevitably rise around them. The Chosen and the Lady make a handsome couple. It is fitting that our heroes bear the qualities that people will respond to."

"A couple, you say?" Alemar asked tentatively. "I did not know."

The Princess was looking down at the ground distractedly, while considering the Weloh's words. A sharp pang of jealously pierced her heart momentarily, and the unbidden emotion made her exceedingly uncomfortable.

"'Our' heroes?" Elsinestra questioned Teetoo with a slight smile upon her finely drawn lips. "You just referred to them as 'our' heroes."

"Should I have said 'your heroes' instead?" he asked, embarrassed. "I have come to feel very much a part of this world."

"It is an honor for us all to be accepted by you, Teetoo. We have always felt the bond between us, you and I," she said, and she reached over and grasped his hand. Shyly, he lifted his face to hers, and with wide open eyes he stared deeply at the Queen. "Have you finally come to realize that your life and your fate cannot be separated from ours any longer?"

"I have know that all along," he replied. "But now that Premoran is no longer by my side, I realize that there is still so much that I can and want to do here. We have always worked as one, he and I. I often thought my allegiance was to my friend. But now I realize that it is to the earth itself, to my home," he said softly.

"Your home," Elsinestra repeated, and she squeezed his fingers tightly.

"When Premoran relinquished the shards to the boy," he began, remembering the moment, "I recognized how connected we all are. He had spent so long gathering them from each of the departed Lalas, and all of his efforts were not for his sake, but for everyone else's. I have often felt alone, being the only one of my kind left. But at the moment that he handed Davmiran the pouch, it occurred to me that we are each and everyone of us unique, and therefore in a very important way, the last of our kind. The shards represent what remains, and I represent what remains."

"There are some moments in each of our lives that bring so much else into focus," Elsinestra responded. "Once we have lived them, it is hard to remember how we felt before."

Alemar listened with one ear to the conversation, and it bothered her that she was unable to rid herself of the nagging feelings that accompanied the news about Robyn dar Tamarand. *Am I really jealous?* she wondered, unaccustomed to emotions of this sort. *The thought of him with the Lady Filaree makes me very uncomfortable. Perhaps it is just because he has always been so kind to me, but he is so handsome! Will they marry, I wonder? After all, they are both human. It would not have worked for the two of us anyway.* She scoffed at herself. *What foolish thoughts. There was never anything between us really. He never looked at me that way. What a fool he would think I am if he ever knew I felt this way. It is better that he love another of his own race.*

Elsinestra had walked over to the Princess, and she stood beside her while she pondered these matters. Alemar was so caught up in her own deliberations that she did not even notice the presence of the Queen. She placed her hand upon her shoulder, and Alemar lifted her head, startled.

"Forgive me, Aunt," Alemar said, blushing. "My mind was elsewhere."

"No need to apologize, my dear. We all have a lot to think about these days. But, it is now time for us to go. We have so much to do, and the morning hours are already behind us. Come. Let us continue your lessons in the infirmary," she said, and she took the girl's hand in her own and began to lead her toward the palace doors. Under her breath, so that Teetoo could not hear her words, she continued to speak. "You may fool a man, but you are not good at concealing your feelings from one of your own sex. Would you like to talk to me about it, Alemar?" she asked. "Though I have no daughter of my own, I am still a mother," she said sweetly. "And I too am deeply in love." Alemar's face colored an even deeper crimson once again at the Queen's words. Turning to face the Weloh, Elsinestra asked aloud, "Will you assist my husband again today, Teetoo?"

"Yes, your highness. I look forward to it. The busier I am, the less I think of the loss."

"We will hear something soon, I am certain," she replied reassuringly, though the air still hung with doubt. "We expect to see you at dinner tonight. Do not disappoint us, my friend."

"Until later, then," he said, and he bowed deeply as the two ladies walked away arm in arm.

Chapter Two

The snow was falling heavily upon the already frozen ground and it quickly concealed all the signs of his departure. He watched guardedly as each hoof print disappeared behind him. It made him feel as if he had never even been there, and he was disturbed terribly by that thought. The young elf stood up tall in his saddle, twisted his lean body around and looked behind himself anxiously, as the snow gathered upon his brow and the wind lashed his face and blew his auburn hair straight out behind his head, exposing his pointed ears.

While the path of his departure vanished even as it was created, his memory of the events of the last few months also began to fade into the recesses of his mind, and he began to believe that what had occurred had merely been a dream that he had just awoken from. He frantically grasped at the remaining images that danced before his mind's eye, and he tried desperately to bring them into focus, to crystallize them so that he would not loose them forever, yet he felt them slipping away despite his efforts, leaving him frustrated and discouraged. With a heavy heart, he battled both the harsh elements as well as his ravaged emotions simultaneously, and he grew more and more disoriented by the second.

It was difficult to see clearly through the heavy clouds of wet, swirling flakes, but his vision was quite keen, and in spite of the veil of white that shrouded him, he could distinguish more than anyone would have supposed. Dalloway squinted his lovely, almond shaped eyes, hoping to catch a final glimpse of the wondrous place he had just left. Even as he did so, he began to forget what he was searching for. He cocked his head to the side in a bewildered manner, and then he shook it back and forth in an effort to clear it of the confusion that was besetting him.

I am *going the right way,* he thought confidently to himself, feeling certain of that at least.

He continued to stare in the opposite direction from which he traveled, unwilling to simply turn his back and still unready to accept the fact that he had to leave. Like a child in fear of separating from those whose love and protection had succored him for so long, his heart grew heavy with each step that drew him further away, though he could now barely recollect enough to feel anything other than a muddle of vague, disassociated feelings of comfort and safety within the lapsing memory. The expression on his handsome face was addled and brimming with concern, for he could not understand what was happening.

Why can't I remember? he wondered. *The harder I try, the more difficult it is becoming.*

Sadness enveloped him unbidden, and he knew instinctively that as the distance grew between him and the place he just departed from, the more threatened he would feel. He was just not sure why anymore. He yearned to look backward and he succumbed to that yearning, but try as he might, he could hardly remember nay longer what lay hidden behind the curtain of swirling and blowing snow.

Vainly, he tried again and again to summon up the images from the depths of his psyche; the name and the face, the soft voice and the soothing touch. But all of the identifying characteristics were quickly dissipating. The slender fingers of his thoughts reached out painstakingly, but it was impossible for his mind's grip to remain firm, and they vanished like smoke in the wind, scattered even more quickly by his mental touch. Nevertheless, he continued to struggle to remember, loath to give up his efforts. He felt as if what he yearned for was still possible to find if he concentrated hard enough, and he sensed it lurking somewhere behind the distractions of the moment, within the endless morass of his unconscious mind.

Despite the accelerating downfall of snow, he was sure that he could see the outline of the delicate spire that marked the location of the portal behind him. He smiled to himself slightly as a rush of emotion flooded over him, swathing him in a prickly blanket of both joy and regret. But the feeling was short lived, and just as quickly as it enveloped him, he was perplexed as to why he was even smiling at all.

When he first left Eleutheria he had been so anxious to get back home.

How long have I been wandering? he wondered, the slate of his remembrance now wiped completely clean of the events of the past four months. He shook his head again in confusion, and looked all around. *What has happened to me? I feel like I am on the right path, but to where? I thought I knew only moments ago. I want to go back home, to Seramour, but I know that there is something I must do first,* he deliberated to himself painstakingly.

He tried to account for the time that had elapsed, but his memory was clouded and obscure. He sensed a passage, a rupture in the continuum between his departure from Eleutheria and now, and he grew frustrated with each effort to resurrect it. As each fleeting image of where he had been for all those days in between was about to come into focus, it slipped away forever, and no effort on his part could bring it back.

He had no trouble envisioning Alemar as she bade him farewell, and he was easily able to recreate the poignant moment when he walked his horse out through those marvelous and massive gates of ice. It was not difficult to picture her brother Kalon's scowling face as he peered down upon him from the high walls surrounding the city. He could even remember his first evening on the road and how he laughed to himself when he discovered the small package of carefully wrapped sugared cloudberries that Alemar must have slipped into his pocket before he left. He vowed then and there, as each of the succulent fruits burst upon his tongue, that he would return to his cousin one day and try to assist her in convincing her people and her father most of all, that it was time to rethink their position and to reevaluate their long held beliefs that isolation was the only path for them.

By the First, that brother of hers is such a bore! he thought. *And I am being polite.* The ends of his delicate lips turned down in a sour scowl as the scenes of his previous encounters with Kalon flashed before him. *If he were not my cousin too, I would have thrashed him myself. What I cannot understand is why uncle Whitestar tolerates him. I guess he is his son after all, but still! It is so obvious that he is only avoiding having to confront these problems. I suppose he is the King, and he has a right to deal with his subjects, including his own children, in whatever manner he chooses. But, Alemar's case is the better of the two. Why does he discard it so easily?* he continued to reminisce.

The ground was firm and the snow was thick and deep. It seemed colder to him than he remembered when he first left Eleutheria.

Why does it seem as if I have been away for so long already? he thought as he walked his horse carefully down the path. *The sun is awfully low in the sky for this time of year. Strange, I don't recall noticing that before.*

As he thought back on the days past, he grew confused once again. There were gaps in his memory, and he was troubled by them.

I feel like I have been somewhere and done something, yet I do not for the life of me know what.

Dalloway brushed his hair from his eyes and was astonished by its length.

How could it have grown this fast? I could have sworn that Alemar cut it just before I departed. I have never liked it hanging upon my shoulders. How odd this is, he thought.

He shifted in his saddle once again and looked back toward Eleutheria. Though he could see nothing but blowing snow, his skin tingled as he stared. He reached across his chest with his free hand in order to brush some snow off of his opposite arm and he felt something shift beneath his cape and tunic. Despite the cold, he removed his glove and stuck his fingers inside his blouse. His hand grasped a medallion hanging from what felt like a rawhide string.

When did I get this? he questioned himself, startled by this discovery. *Alemar must have slipped it over my neck before I left. Why did I not notice this before now?*

It was slightly warm to the touch as he held it in his hand, and to his great astonishment, he felt it pulse. He heard a distinct humming in his head and he thought for a moment that his ears were failing him. As it grew louder, he closed his eyes and leaned back in his saddle as his head slumped to the side. The reins fell loosely on his horse's withers. His hand remained firmly fixed upon the pendant as he fell heavily to the ground.

Chapter Three

"Do not seal the chamber yet," the silver haired man beseeched the others. "He will come. I know it!"

"How long can we wait, Tobias? It is dangerous enough without leaving ourselves exposed like this. If he was going to come, he should have arrived by now. Perhaps he has chosen not to join us," a high pitched, though clearly male voice replied.

"Or something prevented him from joining us," another said ominously while stepping forward to stand next to the other two. His hair was deep red like a fine ruby, and freckles played in patterns across his boyish face. "We cannot discount that possibility."

"Surely we can wait a little while longer, Harton. We have risked so much already, another moment or two will not make that much of a difference," the beautiful, black-skinned Blodwyn intoned, ignoring for the moment the concern that Connor, Chosen of Catalan, had just raised. "Without him, we cannot accomplish as much as we would like to."

"Blodwyn is correct, Harton. What matters another few minutes anyway? We are well past the point of no return. If we are found out, nothing will make a difference!" Liam remarked looking down at the stone floor beneath his feet. "I do not like the feel of this," he said, as he shifted his balance uncomfortably from leg to leg.

"Nor do I!" still another of the Chosen made his opinion clear. "This meeting was ill conceived. We should each have confided in our own. Concerns of this sort should not be shared unless the Lalas themselves choose to reach out to each other," Pithar, the bond-mate of Marathar said.

"The doorway is still open, Pithar. You are free to leave if you so desire," Dashiel, Nemaroe's bond-mate replied rather nonchalantly, and he pointed to the entryway. "That is, if Harton of Alklyn does not shut it in his haste." He lifted his regal head and tossed his thick mane of black hair back over his broad shoulders. Looking at the others from behind his serious, grey eyes, he extended himself to his full and impressive height. "I venture to say that this opportunity may never rise again. It would be best if we could all unite behind our good intentions. After all, it is with no malice that we gather together."

"I have come this far already, and do I suppose that the thread has already been set," Pithar replied with a sigh. "I cannot eliminate what I have done from the weave. It is there for all to see for evermore. My actions have surely altered the pattern by now. What good would it do to depart at this point?" he replied, shrugging his broad shoulders complacently. "I know that each and every one here has the other's best interests at heart," he agreed.

"Then reserve your disappointments for another time. We are all anxious, Pithar. This meeting is unprecedented. It is natural to be concerned," Blodwyn, the only female in the chamber said as she restlessly smoothed the folds of her shimmering tunic about her hips. "What is done, is done. As you yourself noted, our actions can no longer be taken back. They have surely become a part of what is and what will be."

"Well spoken, Blodwyn," Edmond, Chosen of Xia said. "When we first conceived of this gathering, it was already too late. Thoughts come to us unbidden it seems, yet their roots are hidden in the weave as well. We all embraced them, regardless of our doubts, and they have led us here. Save your regrets for those things you have not yet done, not for actions already taken."

"And for actions attributed to us as well, whether true or not?" Phero asked. "The rumors of Relamon's demise would be welcome if the horrendous actions attributed to him were true, and surely we would all regret them then."

"Aye. But were they true, nothing could be done to change them anyway," Blodwyn replied. "Sadly, it is a reflection on just how great the rift has grown between the trees and the people that something as abominable as what the Possessed one, Margot, concocted is being embraced as fact."

"The desire for the truth has never motivated the Talamarans. Let them believe what they will," Pithar scoffed.

"She has done more than persuade them. Even my appearance before the city walls would not alter their beliefs. Relamon has advised me not to attempt to set right their notions now and to dignify Colton's effort with a denial. It seems easier for my tree to live with this lie than for me," Phero confessed.

"This state of affairs is unspeakable!" Harton exclaimed in frustration.

"Ten Lalas have left us already. Our ranks have been depleted over the last three tiels to such a degree that communication has even become difficult between those of us who still remain. If not for this gathering, I would never have known that you, Carlisle, feared for your own tree or that the countryside if rife with gossip of your tree's alleged atrocities, Phero. Perhaps Relamon has a reason for wishing you to remain aloof from the situation, but I can understand how it must hurt you to do so. Wayfair tells me much, but it seems that even he cannot reach out to all the others as he once was able to. Until you informed me, I had no idea what had occurred in Talamar," Crea said.

"Neither did any of you, it appears. What dismays me the most is that these people seem so eager to embrace this lie and denounce the Lalas. Have they drifted so far from the trees so quickly?" Phero asked.

"We are all drifting upon these unsettled waters, my friend. You of all can imagine my plight," Carlisle responded, shifting his considerable bulk uneasily to his other leg. "My Lalas, Mintar, speaks less and less to me, and his melancholy is wearing my spirit out. I cannot help but feel abandoned at times, yet what am I to do? He professes that he is well, but he is troubled nonetheless, and I do fear for his health. My own welfare is not now my concern. It was a struggle for me to leave him even to come here. But since I made that decision, I would rather that we accomplish something so that I can return with hope in my heart," he said pleadingly. "By the First, may this venture not be in vain."

Blodwyn moved to the front of the assemblage and raised her wooden walking stick in the air. She brought it down heavily on the stone floor. The noise echoed throughout the chamber and drew everyone's attention to her immediately. Wrapped in a cape of brown velvet clasped tightly at her neck by a ruby broach, she was an imposing figure. A braid of thick, dark hair fell almost to the ground behind her, and her gloved hands held her stave tightly. Her face was smooth and ageless, dominated by large, black irises which nearly concealed the whites of her eyes completely.

"We await only one other of us. If he does not arrive within the next half hour, we have no choice but to seal the entrance and attend to our purpose," she said. "Each moment that we leave ourselves exposed increases the likelihood that we will be discovered."

"I agree!" Harton chimed in. "I wish to return home as soon as possible. Deceiving Farrow was difficult enough for me," he said, referring to his tree. "Had it not been for the fact that I know in my heart something has gone terribly wrong, I would never have come here to begin with."

"There is little here that could betray us. The cavern has been swept clean of all living matter, and the walls are hundreds of feet thick. We are so deep within the mountain that unless someone was followed here or let it be known where he was going, we are safe," Dashiel said. "You are all too nervous. Since when have the Chosen become so meek?"

"Since when have the Chosen gathered together behind the backs of the Trees?" Liam asked.

"Not one of us here could be happy that it has come to this!" Crea said, angered somewhat by the confessions and concerns of the others. "It is not necessary to profess your worries. We all share them!" he said to the group. "We are here in order to learn and perhaps to help one another. Our motives are noble, and we have no reason to regret our actions."

"What I regret is that circumstances have led us here!" Edmond replied. "We must all stay focused on the important issues. Our deception was necessary, though this necessity has not diminished the regret for anyone, I am sure. Nonetheless, we are here and we must therefore overcome our emotions."

A crackling sound caused them all to jump and everyone's eyes sought out its source instantly. Waves of power flooded the room, as each Chosen searched in his or her own way. In no more than a moment, they were all staring at the entrance whose shimmering portal appeared liquid like and fragile. The doorway stood before them, hewn into the stone in an irregularly shaped, upside down U. It was sparking now, and there was no doubt that someone or something was attempting to enter.

The eleven formed a semi-circle before the opening and linked hands as if on cue. Sparks flew about the chamber once the link was completed, and then from behind the doorway a light began to shine so brightly that those the Chosen had suspended from the ceiling in order to illuminate the interior paled in comparison. It grew in intensity until they were all squinting from its brilliance.

Blodwyn, standing at the left most point of the link, raised her wooden scepter with her free hand, and held it defiantly before her, unsure of who or what was about to intrude upon their congregation.

"Stand fast, everyone!" she said.

"Have we been found out so soon?" Pithar asked sadly.

"And if we have been?" Tobias challenged him. "What wrong have we done? We seek only knowledge," he replied, though a worried expression marred his strong and sharp features.

"Fear not. Our aim is true!" Blodwyn said.

"And if it is the enemy at our gate?" Liam asked.

The others all looked at him as if this thought had not occurred to any of them until he uttered it. They could all feel a distinct vibration penetrating the solid rock of the chamber floor. It rattled their bones and chilled their souls. The portal grew brighter and brighter, and the liquid appearance of its shimmering surface began to stiffen and grow cloudy.

"Prepare, my friends. Whatever it is that approaches is almost upon us," Crea warned.

"Be ready to seal the opening if we must," Pithar said.

The vibrations grew more intense by the second, and a loud crack pierced the still air. Sparks flew wildly everywhere, originating from the entrance and shooting in all directions throughout the chamber, then bouncing off the walls and falling upon the cold, stone surface upon which they slowly faded away.

Blodwyn raised her staff higher and a dome of bluish light descended protectively over the group of eleven. As they stood apprehensively behind it staring intensely at the opening, the toe of a booted foot became visible as it stepped through the opaque barrier.

Chapter Four

It was hard to tell for certain just how much time had passed since they carried Tomas into the shelter of the cave. For at least six days, he neither spoke nor even acknowledged the presence of the others. Preston sat diligently by his side all the while, convinced that Tomas knew that he was there. He insisted that he was going to be next to him when his friend needed him the most, and that meant whenever he was ready to speak. So, Preston planted himself and refused to move.

After another few days went by and the boy exhibited no signs that he was imminently regaining his cognizance, Prince Elion and Queen Esta helped Preston carry Tomas deeper into the cave and away from whatever it was that caused the boy to withdraw so fully into himself to begin with. Stephanie, Tomas' childhood friend, saw to his hygiene and made certain that he was comfortable and kept warm. She sat herself down beside Preston, and together they stood vigil over their troubled friend. There they remained until it was no longer prudent to do so.

Elion ventured back toward their point of entrance, but as he neared it, the stench of death assaulted his nostrils and the air grew putrid and acidic. It was difficult for him to breath, and he had no choice but to retreat once again. Before he would turn his back on what appeared to be their only means of escape, he fought the terrible burning whenever he took a breath and the stinging and tearing of his eyes, and he inched his way forward. As he neared the opening, he heard loud crashes of thunder, and he saw that the rain was pelting the ground with a violence that shocked him. Lightening illuminated the small doorway in a macabre way, casting streaks of blue and yellow light across the smooth, stone floor. But in the end, it was the odor that ultimately caused him to turn back. Never before had he smelled anything so bad. Even the dying gasps of the Valkor that blanketed the air at the battle of Pardatha were easier to stomach. Elion retched uncontrollably at this onslaught upon his senses, and he turned from the entrance is disgust.

When he returned to his friends, he reluctantly informed them of the situation on the surface. They had all believed that they would shortly be able to depart for Avalain once the immediate threat had passed. The disappointment when Elion told them that their escape route was no longer viable, hung in the air as if it was a tangible thing. Queen Esta was particularly saddened by the news initially, though she withstood it in her normally stoic manner and was, as usual, an example for the others. She merely dropped her regal head for a moment, and then moved on emotionally, accepting the situation without another hint of regret. Stephanie sighed deeply and then burst into tears, whereupon Preston leapt to her side to comfort her. He had been so anxious to travel to the legendary city of Avalain himself that it was arduous for him to ignore his own emotions, yet he did so quite valiantly nevertheless.

They were all fortunate that the young dwarf was so keenly aware of what type of rock and stone would provide them with a safe haven and of what type might present a danger to them all. He navigated the curves and bends of the tunnels that emanated from the small cave they first encountered when they entered as if he had been there before. He listened to the rock, smelled it, touched it and literally tasted it before he was willing to lead them deeper inside. In the presence of need, he shortly forgot that they were trapped here now, and he embraced the role that had inadvertently been foisted upon him.

Once they all realized that they could not return the same way that they entered, Preston took charge with a newly found maturity that lifted his esteem in all of their eyes. The frightened, run-away youth of only months ago had grown up in a very short time, and the others acknowledged this change by following him further into the cave with confidence, and without questioning his decisions either openly or within the privacy of their own thoughts.

As it turned out, the tiny opening that Preston espied on the fateful day of their departure from the woods of Pardeau, led to a massive labyrinth of passageways and chambers that twisted and turned endlessly it seemed into the depths of the earth. Fortunately for them all, there was an ample supply of fresh water that trickled and dripped constantly from the cold rock surfaces, and created a perpetual and soothing cacophony of sound. In addition to the all important water, various types of mushrooms grew everywhere in abundance, and Preston knew exactly which ones they could eat and which ones would get them sick. The very large, woody tasting ones that grew out of the crevices of the walls were the best, particularly when they roasted them until they were tender, while the small, button shaped fungi were to be avoided at all costs. Preston assured the others that a tiny taste of those would cause a violent reaction within minutes of their consumption.

The group took turns carrying Tomas as they ventured further and further into the cave. The air was fresh and abundant regardless of how deep they descended, and they could even feel the wind in places as if the cavern itself was exposed to the surface breezes. Long and narrow shafts rose from the ceilings out of which these zephyrs blew, though none was wider than a few inches, and it was impossible to enter any of them in order to escape to the surface.

In most areas, a fine powder of phosphorescent particles coated the surface upon which they walked, and this illuminated their way. The walls were also coated with the same material, and fortunately it was rarely difficult for them to see. Though the light was far from bright, the glow was warm and comforting, and certainly more than adequate. Elion smiled when he first noticed the material. He opened a small pouch that was tied to his belt and showed the others a similar stash of matter that the elves of Lormarion used to light the ground within the depths of the forest beneath Seramour. He showed the others how to sift through the dirt upon the floor in order to isolate these bright particles, and they all soon had their own supply tucked safely into their garments in the event that the tunnels eventually grew dark.

Though he confided in the group, Elion was reluctant to share with the others the last words Tomas uttered when he found him despondent and chagrined outside the entrance to this haven some three weeks ago. The idea that the boy's own Lalas could have betrayed him to Caeltin D'Are Agenathea, the Lord of Darkness, terrified him so that for the sake of his friends, he kept the news to himself. He would tell them all when the time was right, but it would be pointless for them to suffer needlessly now when the circumstances were so uncertain already. He had yet to reconcile the Lalas' actions himself, and unfortunately he had no opportunity to discuss the situation with Tomas before he collapsed.

"I wonder what they are thinking in Avalain," Queen Esta said aloud.

"Is there anyone there who knew where you were going when you first left?" Stephanie asked from across the broad chamber, as she pressed a cool, damp cloth on Tomas' forehead. She looked at his beautiful face, marred by worry and concern even in his inchoate state. Affectionately, she adjusted the blanket that lay atop his unmoving body, and then she walked across the cavern toward the others who had assembled by the small fire Elion was nursing.

"The Captain of the guard, Lord Markel, will figure out something to tell the people until he knows for certain what is going on, though I did not take him into my confidence. I regret my lack of foresight. It was unlike me to not anticipate that something might go wrong with my plan. Marne and I thought we would be back in only a few days. We were simply going to gather some information on my daughter, Filaree," she recalled sadly.

"How could you have suspected? Had you even a hint that you were walking into a trap, you never would have gone in the first place," Preston said, as he shredded some of the mushrooms with his pocketknife.

"And Marne would still be alive," Esta said regretfully.

"It is small consolation to think that we might never have all met if you had not ventured into the woods that day," Elion said, as he stole one of the slices from the dwarf and popped it into his mouth.

"The fabric weaves of its own will, Elion. Marne would yet be with us, but you Stephanie would still be subject to the dictates of Margot and her crusaders. Who knows what that might have lead to? It is not for us to question fate, though its heart can seem so cruel at times," the Queen replied.

"I am so grateful to you all, you cannot imagine!" Stephanie said. "I think that I would have died myself if I remained there much longer. I could not just go along with what they required any more. It was getting harder and harder to avoid doing the things they asked of me, and I would never have been able to support them and their abominable ideas. My days were numbered," she remembered.

The young girl shuddered noticeably and her hand shook as she lifted it from the boy's brow. Tears flowed involuntarily down her rosy cheeks.

"You are safe now, Steph. Although it might seem that we have led you into more trouble, I know it will all work out. You do not have to be afraid," Preston said tenderly.

He put aside what he was doing and moved so that he was sitting beside her. The girl sobbed quietly into her hand, and Esta moved to comfort her as well.

"Hush now dear," she said soothingly. "It certainly appears as if we have leap from the frying pan into the fire, but we will see this clearly to the end soon. It will all begin to make sense in time."

Stephanie dried her eyes with the back of her hand, and then she sat up straight. Elion too joined the others, as the three of them formed a tight circle around the maiden.

"I am not crying for myself. I could not be so ungrateful. You are all so wonderful to me," she said. " Nothing could have been worse than what I left behind. I just feel so awful about everything! I do not feel worthy of your attention. Marne is gone and I am here in her stead. She was so strong and so noble. I look at myself and I feel that all of you would have been better off if I had perished rather than she."

"Such foolish words!" Esta said forcefully. "Why make such comparisons. Each one of us has a role to play, and you will discover yours in time. Besides, you had nothing to do with her death whatsoever! Marne died in service to me! If anyone should feel guilty here, it is I. And believe me, my dear, I do! Had it not been for all of you, I would have perished as well. Now stop your fussing, and let us all be thankful that we have found one another."

Esta took the girl's hand and squeezed it firmly but affectionately, whereupon Stephanie sucked in her breath and dried her swollen eyes with her sleeve. The Queen put her arm around the girl's shoulder and hugged her to her side. Stephanie had not felt a motherly touch in a long while and she warmed to it immediately. She had almost forgotten just how much her circumstances had changed in only a matter of less than one year. Though it hurt her to recall the days when her father was alive and her mother was healthy, and Pardeau was a place where strangers were welcome and the citizens felt safe and secure, it also reminded her vividly of how fortunate she was to have discovered her old friend and his new companions. Stephanie smiled warmly at the Queen, and she returned the squeeze with a meaningful one of her own.

"When you ride the crest of the wave, the height can be exhilarating and the speed with which you travel can take your breath away. But beware when the wave breaks. And break it must, at some point. Marne knew the risks that she took, and she embraced them with the fervor of a true heroine," Esta said. "We shall grieve for her certainly, but we cannot change what has already occurred. It is fruitless to pine over it. We have so much else to do."

Esta and Preston hovered over the girl protectively, while Elion stood closely by, and each member of the group was moved by her emotions. They all harbored doubts and concerns deep within themselves, and her honesty and openness brought them to the surface. While comforting her, they assuaged their own feelings as well, and the bond between them grew firmer and more secure. All four of the companions felt it as if it was almost a physical thing.

"Lives are built upon moments like these," Esta said earnestly. "Whether our paths diverge in the days to come or whether we are all still together, I will not soon forget any of you."

It was bright where they had gathered and they therefore had no difficulty observing how emotional this moment was for each person present. Their facial expressions gave them away. The remainder of the chamber had grown dark, though no one noticed the change during this encounter. Elion was the first to realize that the area where Tomas lay was no longer visible.

"I had better attend to the boy," he said, a bit startled by the depth of the darkness.

The others all rose hastily and walked behind him across the floor. The light had gone totally out in the recesses of the chamber, and Elion disappeared into the obscurity before they could even catch up with him.

"Does anyone have any of the powder on them?" Preston asked.

"I do," Stephanie replied, and she reached into the pouch that hung from her belt.

As soon as she opened the string tying the top, her hand stood out in the darkness as if there was no body attached to it. Quickly, she retrieved a small pinch of the phosphorescent material and flung it in the blackness around them. As it made contact with the air the substance was activated, and the entire immediate area was swathed in a yellowish glow.

In the pale light, they could distinctly see Elion kneeling in front of them, beside the blanket that covered the boy. Elion turned to face the others with a grim expression etched upon his elfin features, and he rose slowly with the blanket in his hands. Something was terribly wrong.

"He's gone!" Stephanie exclaimed, dumbfounded.

Chapter Five

"Concentrate!" she admonished her friend. "Find what is common to it all. It is there, Angeline. You only need to sift through the particles in order to isolate it."

Tamara sat beside the slim and muscular woman and guided her as she attempted to start the evening fire. What had seemed miraculous to her only five or so weeks before was now routine, and the stout sister was a good instructor. Angeline stretched her long index finger, swirled it slightly, and the pile of dry twigs and leaves began to smolder.

"You've go it!" Tamara exclaimed, as happy with the other woman's accomplishment as if it had been her own success. "Now, just let it spread all by itself. You must learn not only how to begin the process, but when to back away as well. If you exert too much of an influence, the result may be far more extensive than you might wish. It is much harder to contain the energy once you have unleashed it. As it outstretches, it assumes a life of its own. You may not be able to control it so easily."

Tamara furrowed her brow, and with her right hand she directed a short wall of debris to form around the burgeoning fire. The material she used was just as flammable at the onset as what burned within the circle, but Angeline watched closely as it seemed to change in consistency with Tamara's urging. What had seconds before been dry leaves, dust and twigs was being altered at its core. The essential elements were being divided and diffused by the more experienced sister, and a new material composed of the same elements as that which existed before but now in a different configuration took shape before their eyes.

"How did you know what to change and what to leave as it was?" Angeline asked.

"I cannot answer that," Tamara replied. "I sense the essence of what I am manipulating somehow, and I think about the qualities that I need in order to accomplish the task that I have in mind. A lot of what I do is not directed by my will as you might think. Although I am conscious all the while, it is my spirit that guides the material to an extent. I have learned to feel with my senses much as I have done my whole life with my limbs."

"I think I understand," Angeline said. "When the fire just began to ignite, it seemed as if the pieces had just fallen together. It felt right somehow."

"That is how I would have explained it too," Tamara replied and she nodded her chin up and down. "It just begins to feel right. I believe that there is a symmetry to life and to each object that we see in nature. If we rearrange the elements and achieve that symmetry again, it seems correct."

"Have you ever found that what you created was wrong?" Angeline questioned. "Has there been a time when what you did turned out different than you wished?"

"Not in the end. Not yet, at least. There have been times during the process when I have been unsure of what the outcome was going to be. But there always seems to be something deeper, something other than my will and desire that guides me, and I have not yet been plagued by doubt about the outcome of what I have tried to accomplish. Remember though, sister that this is all quite new to me as well."

"What I cannot get used to is that it just seems so natural. Now that I look at things the way you have instructed me, I cannot imagine seeing them any differently. I spent my entire life unaware that my relationship with the world around me was so much more intertwined than I ever conceived. It seems as if a door in my spirit has opened," Angeline commented. "My eyes gaze upon the exact same elements as they did before, but they no longer look the same."

By this time, the small fire was burning brightly and it illuminated their faces, as well as the surrounding desolate landscape that seemed to stretch in all directions. Though it was still daylight, the hills cast a grayish pallor upon everything, obscuring the remaining sunlight, and many areas were concealed by almost complete darkness and shadows.

The two sisters had been traveling for about three weeks. When they first left the Tower of Parth, they were more than just a slight bit unsure of themselves. Although Tamara had only recently gone on a journey of her own before they had set out on this one and she returned unscathed despite some difficult circumstances, Angeline had not been away for many years. She was competent certainly, but in many respects she was quite sheltered, and her strength had never been challenged. The two women had always respected one another, though no one would have called them friends. Now, after only a few short weeks, the bonds between them had grown strong, soldered together by the importance of their mission as well as by the discovery that they had so much in common after all. They became true companions in a rather short while, due in no small part to the fact that both of them had such giving hearts.

The first week on the trail, their path had been clear and well defined. The roads that led away from Parth one would never have called well traveled, but they were distinct and easy to follow. The terrain was flat and wooded, but it was not difficult to traverse. Parth was constructed upon the intersection of the roots of many of the great Lalas, and the soil above it and around it was fertile and teeming with life. But, as they drew further and further away, the environment changed dramatically.

The few humans that they encountered during their first days on the road were respectful, though nervous when they saw the two sisters approach. They hesitated to talk to the women, and despite Tamara's ebullient personality, they were uncomfortable around them and seemed to desire nothing more than to be anywhere but in their presence. The sisters honored and respected these concerns and did not insist upon engaging them in conversation, although it did cause them to question this unusual behavior. The Sisters of Parth were never shunned before for any reason, and people everywhere usually felt safe in their presence. Things had surely changed in only a short while, Angeline and Tamara agreed. When evil stretches its dirty hands across the land, very little remains unsullied and unspoiled.

By the beginning of the third week, they had not seen anyone for days. Traveling became more difficult as they entered the hills. Shelter was harder and harder to come by, and the territory they covered was less forgiving. By the end of the third week, the hills gave way to rocky, dry mountains that were irregularly shaped and rose incredibly high into the cloudless blue skies. Though they were red in color, they were not made of clay but rather of layers of rock that seemed to have been placed one atop another like a stack of griddle cakes. These stacks dotted the sky in all directions and they had to maneuver their way around and between them in order to continue on. In some cases, they needed to climb these slippery sided peaks for it was impossible to find a pass, and the climbing was onerous and painstaking upon both the horses and the women.

Tamara nurtured the fire that Angeline had just started, and gazed upward at the top of one of the larger of the pinnacles that towered overhead. The afternoon sun was partially hidden behind it, and the shadow that the peak cast stretched nearly across the plateau upon which they sat. The sisters allowed their ponies to graze freely, knowing that they would find whatever they could to munch upon and never wander off too far, while they planned their course for the days ahead.

"If we continue on this way, it will take us much longer than we expected to reach the swamps," Tamara said.

"At least it is dry here," Angeline said, shuddering at the thought of what lay ahead. "Is there no other route we can take but through those wretched bogs?" she asked.

"You don't know that they are so awful, sister. More often than not, the tales that grow around places such as these are exaggerated and do not resemble the truth of the matter in the slightest," Tamara responded, seeking to soothe her companion's concerns, though her own were no less troublesome. "First though, we must pass through the Valley of Desolation. Right at this moment, that thought concerns me more than the bogs," she said. "Why must people name these places so? Are they not bad enough in and of themselves? If it were called the Valley of the Sun or the Valley of Heroes or some such more positive name I really think I could bear the idea of it better."

"It is just a name sister," Angeline reminded her, though she too found the title disconcerting. "As long as we have enough water and supplies, the idea of crossing through a barren valley no matter what it is called is much more appealing to me than wading through the swamps beyond it. I would rather be able to see what my feet encounter than have to imagine what it is that is brushing against my legs!" Angeline replied, and she shuddered slightly at the thought.

They sat upon a precipice overlooking what appeared to be a chasm perhaps one hundred feet in depth at the least. Tamara dangled her feet over the edge, while Angeline remained safely back a few paces from the precipitous rim. She found it very uncomfortable to gaze over the brink and it even caused her to cringe at Tamara's boldness and lack of fear.

The hole in the ground before them was somewhat regular in shape and about fifty feet in diameter. The massive rocks that lined it were broken in geometrical patterns, and it was obvious that the edges were continuing to break away and fall into the depths as the years passed. Much like the surface of an egg that is cracked inward in one spot and still stuck fast to the rest of the shell, the huge slabs of red rock hung suspended from the edge in straight edged blocks, while still others had detached themselves from the surface and had fallen down, forming gargantuan piles of stacked rocks upon the floor of the hole. Some of the boulders lining the rim had substantial cracks in them too, and it was almost possible to imagine which one would be the next to break off and career into the pit. Over time, trees and shrubbery had sprouted in the morass below, and at least two of these unusual, scraggly ones had reached high enough to break the surface with their topmost branches and leaves, twisting and bending maze-like as they headed for the top.

"What could have caused this area to cave in so?" Tamara asked, leaning over the edge precariously, casually unbothered by the sheer drop.

"I certainly do not know, and if I were you I would not venture so close. You may slip and then where would our quest be?" she asked nervously. Angeline was unsure of whether it bothered her more for Tamara to be leaning into the chasm than if she were doing it herself. "Please, sister, back away a bit if only to ease my mind."

"Does it disturb you that much?" she replied.

"Yes, you cannot imagine. For those who have no fear of heights, it is impossible for them to understand the feelings that one who does experiences. I practically swoon when you do that."

Tamara put her hands beside her and began to push herself backward, at least enough to relieve the tension in her friends expression. As she did so, she looked behind her to make sure that she was not going to slide her ample bottom onto anything sharp, and she noticed what looked to be a swarm of insects heading in their direction from the east. There was a dark cloud, irregular in shape, that was moving steadily toward them as she watched.

"Sister? Do you see what is approaching?" she asked Angeline calmly.

Angeline straightened her back and looked in the direction that Tamara indicated with her outstretched hand.

"I do, sister. It is too dark to be a storm could. It is pitch as night!" she observed, scrutinizing it as closely as she could.

"And it changes shape as it moves," Tamara commented, watching it closely herself. "Only a moment ago it was much more elongated. Now, it seems to be fattening up a bit."

"It is most certainly alive, sister! Or at least it is composed of things that are alive. No wind is causing it to assemble so," she replied, touching her index finger to her tongue to moisten it and then holding it up to the air.

"Yes, Angeline, I agree. And we appear to be directly in its path," Tamara replied as she looked around her for some shelter. "There does not seem to be anywhere we can go to conceal ourselves."

"We don't know that it is dangerous in any way. Maybe it will dissipate and not come this way at all," Angeline replied optimistically.

"Wishful thinking, my friend. I fear that we may be its sole purpose for being here to begin with," Tamara rejoined ominously.

"Why? Do you believe it to be more intelligent than the sum of its parts? It looks to be a swarm of bees or flies or the like."

"Here? An innocent swarm of flies so thick that we can see it from this distance? I think we had best assume otherwise, sister. What we carry with us will surely be desirous to others as well. We cannot sit here and wait to find out!" Tamara said, and she rose from her sitting position as if she was a lightweight young maiden.

Angeline did not need another warning to follow. She too stood up on her long, muscular legs, shouldered her bow and arrows and began to scan the horizon for an alternative to where they now stood unprotected. But alas, her sharp eyes could spot nothing either that would afford them a means of protection.

"We appear to have wandered to a place that is the least conducive to hiding, sister," she said calmly, although her body was poised for action.

"Yes, sister. It seems that we have indeed," Tamara replied calmly, though her insides were churning.

They both watched with growing interest as the cloud approached them, hoping upon hope that it would pass them by, and quite unsure as to how to defend themselves against it if they should actually be its target.

"We can conceal ourselves by stirring up the dirt and debris around us," Tamara said. "But the ground is so barren and rocky, I am afraid that there is not enough of anything loose upon it to hide even one of us successfully," she observed with a slightly more desperate tone in her voice.

Angeline had moved even further away from the edge of the pit that bothered her so, while Tamara had done just the opposite. She realized that the hole in the earth was perhaps the only place they could hide, and she was walking slowly toward it to see if there was even one edge that they could step down over without careening into the chasm.

"I cannot, sister!" Angeline shouted as if she had guessed what her friend was contemplating. "You would have to blindfold me and knock me out before I could get even as close to the edge of that as you are now!"

"What choice have we, sister?" she asked as she paced the perimeter carefully. "I would rather take my chances down below than up here. Whatever that is..." she said, pointing to the approaching darkness, "...it is surely coming our way. And I have a very bad feeling about it!"

"Sister, I am petrified! I cannot do this," Angeline replied. "Is there no other option?"

"None that I can see," Tamara responded, searching all the while for the best place to begin their descent.

"You must help me then," Angeline said, struggling to reconcile herself to the idea . "I am embarrassed that I am behaving this way sister, but truly I would not be if I could help it. Heights are my greatest weakness," she confessed abjectly and solemn.

"No one of us is perfect, sister. I have so many weaknesses that I could not even claim one to be my greatest," Tamara replied humbly. "Now come to me and do not look down. I think that I have found a place where we can safely step," she said reaching out her hand in support.

Angeline moved carefully toward her and clasped her friend's outstretched fingers tightly. Together they approached the precipice.

"Look! Over here, as I suspected. The surface is soft where the vegetation grows and I can dig my boot into it. We can also use the branches to hold on to. They seem securely anchored in the earth," Tamara said as she tugged upon the protruding twigs with her free hand. "I will go first, but you must not resist when I call you. Wait though until I am certain that the ground will hold me. If it can sustain my weight, you have nothing to fear," she said smiling, despite the circumstances.

Angeline took a deep breath and then released Tamara's hand reluctantly. The sky had darkened considerably in the last few minutes, and both women were sure that they could hear a buzzing sound in the air though it did not sound exactly like any insects they recognized. The noise chilled them both to the bone, and that made it easier for Angeline to gather the courage to confront her fear. There was something so menacing in the air that she could practically reach out and touch it. By now, she had no doubt that this horror was coming for them, and the chasm before her suddenly loomed quite clearly as the better of the two alternatives.

"There seem to be many crevices down here into which we can step. It is far better than I hoped!" Tamara shouted from just below the surface. "Come now. Use the same places that I used. They are no longer slippery and your feet are smaller than mine. You should have no problem," she urged confidently.

Angeline slowly but surely inched her way toward the edge. She crouched down and used both her hands to stabilize herself as she backed one leg over the side. Tamara's strong hands grabbed her foot and placed it securely onto the first footing, wedging it deep into the soft but solid soil.

"The next one is just below to the left a bit. You can do it, Angeline! It really is not as difficult as it seems. Just don't look down," she urged.

"I am alright, sister," Angeline replied. "If you could see what I see now, I think you would understand that down here is the where I would rather be!" she said, as a heavy and unnatural darkness quickly enveloped the entire area, shutting what was left of the sunlight off almost completely. "We must hurry now, sister. The noise up here is almost unbearable!"

Tamara needed no further prodding in order to increase her pace. Quickly, she reached with her leg for the next crevice and stepped firmly upon it, and Angeline followed as deftly as a mountain goat, surprising herself and her friend as well. The two maidens disappeared into the depths of the hole, obscured by both the safety of the darkness reaching out to them from below as well as by the blackness that menacingly descended upon them from above.

"Step lively Tamara," Angeline urged as the more sprightly maiden scurried down the sheer wall of the pit almost on to the head of her friend.

"You seem to have regained your nerve, sister," Tamara replied, while at the same moment she searched the wall for another place to insert her toe.

"The darkness is both a boon as well as a fearful enemy, sister. The dread of it propels me downward while it conceals the precipice that initiated my concern."

"Do not be too thankful, Angeline. The noise grows louder. Even in this gloom we may not be able to evade what hunts us down," she said balefully.

In fact, the buzzing sound was increasing in volume although it was impossible to see or feel anything other than the cool air wafting upon them from below. There was no question that the noise was descending faster than they were, and at their current pace whatever was causing it would soon be upon them.

Tamara continued to step as quickly as she could without even thinking about where this drop might ultimately lead them. It was their only option and she chose it willingly. Now though, it occurred to her that the darkness that cloaked them coupled with their enemy's pursuit might be more than they had bargained for. She could see nothing whatsoever either above her or below her, and the only sound she could decipher in the gloom was the incessant droning of the enemy.

A shudder coursed through her body unbidden, and Tamara suddenly grew terribly worried.

"Are you with me still, sister?" she called up to Angeline. Her call was greeted by silence. "Angeline? Can you hear me?" she asked again, hesitating in mid stride this time, but only the sound of buzzing reached her ears in response.

Tamara frantically began to claw her way back up in search of her companion.

"Where are you? You must be here or I would have felt you pass me by. What is it that prevents you from answering me?" she cried.

She heard a scraping sound just above her head and she stretched out to touch it believing that it must be her friend's foot, but her hand came in to contact with something thoroughly repulsive, something totally unexpected, and she withdrew it in fear and disgust. Her hand felt as if it was on fire. As she retracted her arm, an abominable odor reached her nostrils causing her to wretch momentarily in response, and she could feel her fingers sticking together, coated by a slimy substance that would not yield to her pressure when she attempted to separate them. Panic began to grip her and she forced herself to breath deeply and relax, though her heart was beating twice as fast as normal. She held on to the wall precariously with her free hand and she dug her feet deeper into the crevices in the wall.

Tamara knew how important the scroll that she carried was, and for a fleeting moment she hesitated before reaching out again. She could suddenly feel the parchment against her body, and it struck her instantly that her awareness of it was generated by the object itself as if it had a mind and spirit of its own. But in her heart, nothing was more important than life after all, and she could not sacrifice her friend even for this. Tamara fought the impulse to protect the map, and she refused even to reach her hand inside her tunic to touch it, though it seemed to beckon so saliently. She climbed up another notch and held fast to the wall with her clean hand. She then turned her concentration inward. Using the same power that she used to conjure a glowing orb out of the surrounding air, she caused a great heat to rise in her fingers, though it neither hurt nor burnt her skin. Within seconds the slime that had adhered to her fingers began to sizzle and fall away in liquid-like droplets. The instant her fingers were clean, she turned this energy into light rather than heat, and her hand glowed as if it was illuminated from within, and it cast a cleansing radiance upon the entire area. She was unconcerned at this point if she revealed her own position. Angeline's welfare was at stake!

She squinted in the semi-darkness, hoping to avoid the temporary blindness that she feared would accompany this blaze of light, and what she saw through her half opened eyes horrified her. Angeline was coated from head to toe by a seething cloak of muck that oozed and churned all over her. It glistened as her light reflected off of its iridescent surface, and it seemed to withdraw from the touch of the light as if it was being attacked by it. The surface area closest to her glowing hand thinned considerably as she watched aghast, though Angeline's skin remained coated nonetheless.

Tamara could see that her friend was breathing beneath this repulsive cocoon, and she was grateful for that at least, though it provided her with only a moment of comfort. Frantically, she considered what she could possibly do, and the frustration that she encountered as she realized just how limited her experience was in this regard almost paralyzed her completely. When Angeline's eyes locked upon her own and she saw the fear and the plea for help in them, all of her thoughts receded and her instinct took over.

With the fury of a Moulant protecting its own, Tamara allowed the light to fade abruptly. She no longer needed it in order to see what was before her. Suddenly she became conspicuously aware of the soil that she clung to with her other hand, as if the life within it was calling out to her. She manipulated the organic matter in ways she did not even understand, and it coalesced at her mind's touch. Changing shape and structure at her command, the particles realigned themselves and formed a sheathe of a coarse though giving substance that draped the sheer wall directly in front of her. This fabric-like matter beckoned to her senses, and she responded as if she had done this a thousand times before, instantly recognizing an affinity that now seemed to have been there all along.

Tamara kneaded it with the fingers of her free hand, not knowing entirely why, and it began to elongate and thin out like the dough of a bread. She could barely see anything in the darkness, but within her head she was certain that the image she focused upon was as accurate as any visual impression could possibly have been. Having only the use of one hand, since the other held her fast to the wall and prevented her from plummeting into the depths below, she was growing impatient and anxious, not to mention fatigued. Fortunately, the material that was coagulating before her was surprisingly receptive to her touch and incredibly buoyant. She spun it around as if it was a child's toy top, using her fingers to bat at it and thus increase its velocity. It began to spin and spin, faster and faster. Within seconds, it started to fan out in a funnel shape, narrower at the bottom while it grew wider at the top, and swiftly it rose upward, first covering Angeline's slime encased feet and then inching its way deliberately toward her head.

As soon as the spinning matter came in to contact with the foreign substance that had enveloped Angeline, the buzzing sound increased exponentially, and Tamara squinted her eyes and scrunched up her face in the blackness, trying to shut her eardrums without the benefit of a muffler of any kind. The sound was deafening and she had no means of protecting her ears from it. But, her discomfort was soon mitigated by what was unfolding before her. Everywhere that this new matter encountered the old, a reddish glow resulted and the immediate area surrounding her captive friend began to gleam brightly. The enemy churned and seethed in response to her magic. For the first time, she could clearly see just how thoroughly encased in this abhorrent wrapper her friend was, but she also saw that Angeline was still breathing even though her entire body, from head to toe, was enveloped. Tamara looked on in relief as the gooey mass began to dissolve into great gelatinous gobs and fall in heavy, viscous drops from Angeline's legs to the gloom below.

She craned her neck in order to look upon her sister's face once again, and she blinked her eyes quickly, certain that what loomed before her was merely an illusion. Even though what she had created was having a greater effect upon their attacker than she could have dreamed, she was shocked by what confronted her now.

I should not be so surprised. Evil is as evil does, she thought quickly as the particles surrounding Angeline coagulated and reformed as she watched.

The image of that odious woman whom she had encountered in the woods on the way to visit Liam and Oleander was staring down at her, imbedded in the web that encircled Angeline. It was three dimensional and as real as could be. This was no mere phantasm! Margot's long black fingernails reached out menacingly toward her and the grimace upon her sharp features was one of sheer fury and unbridled rage. From her precarious position, the sister could do nothing but gape. Fortunately, the manifestation began to fade as quickly as it personified itself before her, succumbing to the power brought to bear against it. Tamara knew in her heart that this would not be the last she would see of the venomous Lady Margot. Twice thwarted, she would be deadlier the next time. Tamara could virtually feel the malevolence in the air as the smothering mass that Colton's loathsome crony had unleashed upon them was quickly overcome by her own unseasoned efforts. Much to her relief, her friend's body was almost completely cleansed of the abominable slime by this time.

Tamara's foot slipped slightly, but she was reluctant to look down and risk losing her concentration. With her toe, she searched determinedly for a crevice in which to insert it once again, but the wall of the pit was swiftly becoming coated by the slippery liquid that showered down upon everything from above. She jabbed her foot into the wall repeatedly but to no avail, and then she felt herself losing her grip. At the same moment, a large droplet of slime fell upon her forehead and adhered to her skin. It immediately began to burn painfully. The feeling was so revolting to her that her hand went instinctively to her face in order to brush it off as quickly as she could. Unfortunately, having already lost her grip with one leg, the abrupt movement coupled with the slick coating caused her other toe to slide from its foothold as well, and she began to fall backward and away from the wall. She reached out for something to grasp, but alas there was nothing there to take hold of, and her descent accelerated.

Angeline's face was fully exposed now, and the last thing Tamara heard was her friend's anguished gasp. Angeline's features rapidly faded from view as Tamara careened uncontrollably down into the gaping jaws of the dark and forbidding pit.

Chapter Six

Four hundred dwarves stood solemnly, two by two, beside the steep wall of rock that abutted the forest of Crispen, led by Maringar, eldest son of Brimgar Daggerfall of the Thorndar Daggerfalls. Each one wore a jet black leather jerkin that covered him to the knees, crisscrossed with bold red stitching as was their style, and decorated everywhere there was a tiny bit of space with sharp silver studs. They carried upon their backs picks and an axes, at right angles to one another, and secured by straps of red rawhide, the fringes of which hung down behind them at all different lengths, marking their age and experience. The tips of their picks glinted and sparkled in the morning sun, as each one had a finely cut diamond set into the point, the hardest of stones, capable of penetrating the dense rock of the Thorndar's coupled with the skill and immense strength of these powerful men. No implements were better for mining than those forged by the dwarves in the furnaces in the depths of the mountains.

Their skin was white as snow and their hair was pitch as coal, a fitting contrast for these multifaceted people. Each and everyone squinted his small, black eyes in response to the assault of light upon them from the bright, cloudless sky above. The dwarves disliked the sunshine and they rarely spent any extended periods of time out in the open. They preferred the cool darkness of the caves and tunnels when they were not in their underground city. And they detested water! The dwarves of the Thorndars avoided the lakes and rivers like the plague, and they never, ever went near the ocean either to fish or for the purposes of travel. There was not a single dwarf known who could swim worth a darn. But their skills were second to none when it came to mining and stonework.

Many of the men had long braids of thick hair that hung on either side of their rather large ears, in the front rather than the back, and secured with bands of intricately tooled leather sewn together by threads of the finest silver. Upon their broad heads they wore skullcaps of leather, studded too with silver and fearsome looking. Some had horns attached to them that looked as if they were growing through their helms straight out of their heads. Their feet were shod in heavy, thick soled boots laced to just below their jerkins. Their fingers were short and strong, and covered in calluses, as were their large hands which hung ape-like from long, stout arms.

They were all quite short compared to the elves. Only Maringar stood out from the rest in stature, more because of his extraordinary musculature than for his height, though he was taller than the rest of his countrymen. His skullcap was entirely crafted of silver, though it was far simpler than those of his companions, and his clothing was unadorned aside from an insignia emblazoned across his broad chest. His axe hung from his hip rather than across his back and he carried no pick. Instead, a wide dagger protruded noticeably from his belt, sheathed in a scabbard of red, embossed leather.

At the request of Baladar of Pardatha, Brimgar instructed these, the most skilled of his miners, to march from the safety of their homes northward and to lend their knowledge and experience to the Mountain Elves in this time of crisis.   He entrusted the leadership of this mission to his eldest son, and Maringar rose to the occasion. Though the dwarves had not actively allied themselves with the elves in thirty tiels, both peoples recognized need's dire plea, and they rallied to the cause.

Baladar's entreaty required little persuasion. After the defeat of Colton dar Agonthea at the gates of Pardatha, in a large part due to the alliance that was struck between Brimgar's son Preston, Prince Elion of Lormarion and the Chosen Tomas, the twin to the fabled heir, such cooperation was eagerly embraced. The dwarves departed their homes with no reluctance, and the elves of Crispen welcomed them with open arms.

The elves lived high in the mountains in a city carved out of the bedrock of limestone and quartz, on a broad plateau at the southern base of Silandre, the tallest of Crispen's peaks. Above the tree line, the air was naturally cool and fresh, and the water was among the purest in all the land. It ringed the city to the north creating a crescent shaped wall of liquid as it crashed down into the multitude of pools and lakes that abutted the fields and quarries of the city. These spectacular falls issued forth from great fissures in the mountain making it appear as if the mountainside itself was alive. The melting snows added to the great volume of the flow, which resulted in countless fonts of blue-white water that pooled and gathered everywhere, manipulated and directed by the prodigious skills of the elves. It cascaded down from the heights above and ran through the streets of Crispen channeled by elaborately engineered canals, cleansing and revivifying the city continuously, in addition to providing the people with an endless source of fresh and pure water for all their needs. The rushing sound could be heard everywhere in the city, and for the elves, it was one of the most comforting ones they could hope to hear.

Bristar stood beside Maringar, flanked by the elite of his troops; fifty of the best hunters and fighters in Crispen. The two leaders were a study in contrasts! With his long white beard, sharp features and blue eyes, the Elfin King was the exact opposite of his ally, yet they felt an immediate kinship under these trying circumstances, or perhaps due to them. The pure waters of Crispen were heating up alarmingly of late, and the efforts of the elves to cool them had been rebuffed completely so far. Though the liquid flow was still fresh and pure, it had risen many degrees in temperature, and that rise was accelerating!

Maringar flipped his braids behind his shoulders, first the right one and then the left one, in a smooth, natural motion, where they finally hung almost to his thick waist, weighed down by silver beads woven throughout. His eyes were bright, though dark as night, and they sparkled beneath heavy brows of dense, black hair. He sniffed the air with his broad nose, which invoked an image of an animal carefully hunting its prey in Bristar's mind, and that image was strangely comforting. Though young, Maringar exuded an air of confidence and purpose that rippled through the air and infected all of those who stood near him.

"We should not linger too long here. The wind carries upon its wings the scent of evil," Maringar said.

"Is it the wind alone my son that brings the Dark Lord to our gates?" Bristar replied rhetorically. "I have felt his presence in our water for a few months now. And in the caverns as well. There is little in Crispen he has not touched," he said sadly.

"The hearts of your people remain pure, my Lord," Maringar said. "I sense that it will take much more than this to infect them."

"You sense well, young man. And I thank you for the observation. The people of Crispen are a seasoned lot. We have not lived here for a thousand tiels without challenges. But the waters of Silandre have always been a source of renewal for us. Water is like life itself. It has its identity which it maintains over time, yet it is never the same from moment to moment. It is within time, not outside of it, as are we."

"Does anything physical remain the same from instant to instant?" Maringar asked in his deep, resonant voice.

"I suppose not," Bristar answered, shaking his head. "Only good and evil never change. They manifest themselves in everything that lives, and for them, our world has stability."

"Colton's evil brings stability?" Maringar asked, astounded by the thought.

"Colton's evil is outside of the world we know. He manipulates what exists to further his desires. His evil brings only death and destruction, as he wishes. He reanimates the evil out of the past and he generates new horrors from the loose threads that society sloughs off," Bristar said, and a slight shiver coursed through his body. "It was a metaphorical stability that I was referring to," he continued after a moment's silence. "Good and evil are ideas, extremes, opposites perhaps. Even though we seem to feel their presence in things, the things themselves are neutral. Warm water may be a boon to a traveler stranded in the frozen north, though it is a fearful threat to us when we do not expect it. Death is death, yet when it is the enemy lying upon the cold earth with his blood spilled, we rejoice."

"Intent determines the action, and a thing that is used for evil purpose is not necessarily evil in and of itself," Maringar agreed.

"Yea. As I said, only good and evil do not change. What bodies they inhabit and the actions those bodies take are the things that change."

As they spoke, a rider approached from the cliffs above. His long auburn hair flew out behind him as he rode down the hill. His horse was a magnificent creature with an auburn coat and mane too, like his rider. It was hard to distinguish where the warrior's braid ended and his horse's tail began. As he approached, one could see that he rode without the benefit of a saddle or a bridle, yet his horse ran straight and true. His left hand clasped the thick mane of his mount, while his right was raised high in the air over his head. In his fingers, he clenched a long, delicate bow.

Bristar lifted his head when the movement caught his eye, and the expression of pride and admiration upon his weathered features was unmistakable. He abruptly broke off his conversation with Maringar and strode out to meet his son.

"Hail, father!" Beolan shouted enthusiastically. "I see our guests have arrived," he said, pointing to the assembled dwarves.

He leapt from his horse and onto the ground while the animal was still in motion. His voice was youthful, unburdened by the weariness of life's responsibilities, though it rang with a tone of soothing confidence rather than with the arrogance of youth. Bristar moved quickly to embrace him. The affection between them was obvious. Maringar stood respectfully in the background and did not move to interrupt this reunion between father and son.

"Let me introduce you to Maringar, son of Brimgar," the elf said with his arm still around the shoulders of the young man. "He and his noble men are prepared to enter the mountain on our behalf."

Beolan immediately raised his right hand out to the visitor and they clasped each others palms tightly. The elf appeared to be much younger than the dwarf he now stood beside. Beolan barely had a whisker upon his smooth face, while Maringar's beard hung low before him, emanating from his stark, weathered skin. But both of them were young men in the reckoning of their own people, and their eyes sparkled with the light of youth. They bonded instantly as their gazes locked upon one another.

"Welcome, brother!" Beolan said, honoring Maringar with that appellation.

Rarely did an elf welcome a dwarf with such a greeting.

"You ennoble me with your salutation," he replied graciously while bowing his head. "My men and I are proud to offer what help we can."

"And it is well appreciated! Whatever has infiltrated the heart of Silandre is beyond our knowledge. It has begun to infect the waters that flow throughout Crispen, and we cannot locate its source. It is good of you to offer your assistance," he said, and he bowed low to the dwarf leader.

"The battle we fight, we fight together. The time has passed when what happens in Crispen is of no consequence to the events in the Thorndars. If our enemy has done nothing else, he has solidified his opponents," Maringar replied.

"Well said," Bristar interjected.

"Aye!" Beolan concurred. "It is unfortunate though that we could not have met under more favorable circumstances."

"Need has reached out to us all. That we can recognize her calling gives us all hope," Bristar said. "What did you find within the cave, my son?" he then asked apprehensively.

Beolan dropped his chin to his chest and shook his handsome head back and forth slowly. When he raised it once again, he stared deeply into his father's eyes.

"It is as we suspected, father. I could barely proceed more than a hundred yards before the heat overwhelmed me."

Bristar tried to mask his concern, but it was obvious that he was deeply disturbed by the news his son brought him.

"It is fortuitous then that our friends have arrived more quickly than we had expected," he replied.

"What is it you suspect is causing the temperature to rise so?" Maringar asked. "The waters flow from both within and without Silandre. Are all the well springs affected?" he asked, as he squinted his black eyes and gazed upward toward the towering peak.

"What comes to us from the melting snow is still cool and fresh. But, once it merges with the floes from the heart of the mountain, it quickly rises in temperature. Clearly, the warm water is the stronger of the two," Bristar commented.

Maringar turned his eyes to Beolan expectantly. A concerned look overcame the Elfin Prince's features, causing him to appear tiels older than he did just moments before. He took a deep breath, and then he began to speak.

"I entered the cavern just above the falls over there," he said, pointing to a massive spout of water that seemed to burst straight out of the side of the cliff before it crashed into a large pool of blue liquid about two hundred yards beneath it. "You can see the small opening if you look closely," Beolan continued.

Maringar's eyes were not nearly as sharp as Beolan's in the daylight, and he squinted and strained them in an effort to locate the area that the elf was referring to.

"At first, I thought it was the earth itself that was preparing to erupt as I ventured deeper, even though Silandre was never alive in that way before. But now I have other suspicions. The heat is not constant. There were moments when it seemed not to be in evidence, but as I walked further into the cave entrance, it reached me in vapid spurts that cascaded outward. I had to take shelter behind whatever outcropping of rock I could find in order not to be overwhelmed. But, just as quickly, the bursts of heat passed and I was able to proceed, though not very far. Then the noise began..."

Bristar gasped audibly as Beolan spoke, but his voice remained silent.

"We know that Colton's hand is upon this activity. We just do not know what manner of abomination he has unleashed against your city. He is capable of manipulating the physical world as easily as he does the spirit world," Maringar replied.

"As I walked, I could have sworn that the walls of the cavern were expanding and contracting. They seemed to be alive, as if the mountain was breathing," Beolan remarked. "The air wreaked with the odor of death and decay. I could barely breath it in. In addition, all the surfaces were coated with a vile slime that burned the skin upon contact. I even found it difficult to maintain my footing. Bones littered the area, some quite large in size, and all of them were picked perfectly clean as if the flesh had been boiled off of them."

"Great temperatures can cause such things to occur," Maringar said.

"Aye, they could at that. And I am sure that much of the destruction within the caves was caused by the fires and heat," he agreed.

"I have witnessed a sundering of the bowels of the earth by quakes within my own land, and in some cases liquid fire has erupted from the cracks and crevices. It can be so intense that it melts the rock itself!" Maringar said.

"It is no mere quake that disturbs the foundation of Silandre," Beolan said. "Quakes do not howl and quakes do not screech," he said gravely. "Quakes do not leave a putrid residue behind. Whatever is threatening our land is alive, I am afraid. Something horrendous has taken up residence in the bowels of our beloved mountain!"

Bristar took a deep breath and expanded his chest. He raised his head high and cleared his throat, causing the other two to cease their conversation.

"He has awoken the beast!" Bristar whispered to them. The old King's eyes were now focused and bright.

Both Beolan and Maringar stared at him keenly.

"The beast, father? What beast do you speak of?" Beolan asked incredulously. "Why have you never mentioned this to me before?"

"I dared not mention it. Those who are old enough would sleep ne'er more if they suspected. We have not spoken of it in tiels," he replied, still in a hushed voice though no one except the two young men was near enough to overhear his words. "It can be none other than the beast of legend, the creature that was exiled from the underworld itself!" he said, wringing his hands unwittingly. "He has resurrected the Armadiel, the bane of life, the demon of demons. In the deepest chambers of my heart, I feared that such was the case. When the reports first began to reach me, I refused to accept the possibility. But now, I am certain," he said forlornly. "Think back, Beolan. You will recall the tales from when you were a child, though you may have chosen to forget them."

"The Snake of Recos?" Maringar asked astonished, recognizing the reference.

"The same!" the King replied. "And may the First protect us all!" he exclaimed.

Beolan had never seen his father so anguished. He seemed to be growing older right before their very eyes. Bristar's demeanor grew more humbled and more circumspect with each word that he spoke, his head bowing slightly lower and his shoulders stooping deeper and deeper. The vibrant, healthy elf suddenly looked timeworn and frail.

"The great books speak of the archfiend," the King said in a weaker voice than before. "There was a poem about this monster that as a child chilled me to the bone. It does so still. My father recited it to me in order to teach me a lesson one day," he smiled an ironic smile as he remembered that moment so many ages ago. Immediately thereafter, his face became stern and troubled again. "To this very day, I can recall the effect it had upon me. Listen closely now," he enjoined the two young men, and then began to recite in a subdued and serious voice.

"His body seethes, it does not breathe,
His soul is black and cruel.
He sits upon his throne of tears,
and contemplates his rule.
No living things dare go too near,
Their fear is strong and true,
For he is the bane of life itself,
All fear him but the fool.

The Armadiel has come to dance the dance,
To spread his hands and challenge chance,
To cleave the thread of happenstance,
To cast his net upon the sea,
To gather the souls of the brave and free,
Too blinded by the light to see,
Salvation's secret silver key.

For those of you who think you know
What evil is, where hatred grows,
Where pain begins, when pity dies,
The transgression that you recognize,
The broken vow, a trust decried,
The anguish of loss, your love defied,

What suffering means when hope has died,
The difference between truth and lie,
Beware the beast!
He comes for you,
And all of those whose aim is true,
Your world to sunder,
Your heart to still,
To gather the cloth in his hideous hands,
To rend the weave 'till nothing stands,
And all that is alive, to kill....
And all that is alive to kill!

When he was finished speaking, he bowed his head and did not gaze at either his son or Maringar. His breath was unsteady and he suddenly looked ancient, standing before them shriveled and small. Beolan was shaken by his father's reaction, and although the words of the poem disturbed him too, his father's transformation unsettled him even more.

He walked the few paces between them and placed his arm around Bristar's shoulder. He spoke to him in a soothing and comforting tone, and as he did so, he sensed a subtle change in the fabric, a passage of sorts, from one phase to another, and it caused him to stumble upon his own words for an instant. He no longer felt like a child before this great man. The roles he had accepted since he was a young man had shifted in a matter of moments. Simultaneously, he felt a great burden descend upon him like a mantle of steel, but his body tensed and strengthened in response. His heart began to beat faster as he stood beside the King.

"Father?" he whispered. "It will be all right! We will conquer the beast!" he said to him confidently. "The dwarves know how to find it, and Maringar and I will journey at their head. Together, we will purge our land of the Armadiel!"

Bristar shook his head slightly as if to awaken himself from the nightmare he had become preoccupied with.

"Yes, my son. Yes," he replied, and he lifted his bright blue eyes to meet those of the strong young man who stood before him. "I am certain that you will," he said, though his mind was clearly elsewhere still.

"Come, father. Let us return to the palace. We have been standing here for far too long. You need to get some rest now," he urged him. "We will discuss our plans later, after you have had an opportunity to lie down and refresh yourself."

The young Lord briefly turned to the men waiting expectantly before the sheer slope of Silandre, and signaled for them to stand down. Facing Maringar next, his eyes bespoke all that needed to be said, and he merely saluted the stalwart dwarf respectfully.

"Shall I join you, Beolan?" Maringar asked, not wanting to intrude upon the moment yet anxious to assist in any way that he could.

"I would be honored if you would," he replied, bowing his head slightly in his direction.

Maringar tersely whispered something in the ear of his aide before approaching the two elves.

"If I may?" the dwarf asked, as he placed his stout arm around Bristar's hunched shoulders.

"Certainly," Beolan responded warmly.

Together, the two fast friends supported Bristar and guided him away from the assemblage of warriors toward the city gates.

Chapter Seven

"Make haste now! We are almost there," Robyn urged.

They could see the plains spreading out in the distance just beyond the trees as they spurred their horses anxiously ahead in the early morning hours. Calyx bounded out of the nearby hedge and joined Filaree, Robyn, Cairn and Davmiran. With the elder Chosen in the lead, they left the shelter of the forest and made their way cautiously across the open fields that led all the way to the gates of Parth.

After escaping the horrors in the forest beneath Seramour, Robyn dar Tamarand led his companions to an abandoned shrine midway between Seramour and Parth that had been their home for the past three weeks. Warded and vigilantly protected by Robyn, the crumbling building served their purposes well. Not a person had visited it in two tiels before they arrived. The Lalas to whom it had been dedicated had died quite some time ago, and the people in the surrounding towns and villages avoided the entire area due to the grievous memories that the place invoked, as well as the fear and anxiety that close proximity to the remains of one of the great trees caused.

The sadness at the passing of Adones, one of the first of the Lalas to depart the earth, was pervasive and exacting. After more than two tiels, anyone who knew the tree or even knew of it, was still overcome by melancholy whenever he or she neared its former abode. The air itself hung heavily with gloom, like the moss that drapes the weeping branches of the ferion trees in the southern marshes. It was so obvious that one could practically see it, and the effect it had on any passerby who unwittingly stumbled into the area was so profound that the entire vicinity was scrupulously circumvented.

The shrine itself was sundered and in ruins, but beneath it lay a small living area that was still completely intact. Robyn had visited this particular shrine a number of times in the past, and he was aware of the existence of the subterranean chamber. It was actually a small complex of rooms that had been constructed many tiels ago for the Chosen who came to pay their respects and spend a few days or weeks or months in contemplation. When the Lalas died and the shrine fell into disrepair, the rooms below remained undisturbed. Few travelers ventured near such unwholesome spaces as this one.

They departed the shelter of the shrine upon the rising of the sun a day ago, and they rode all day and all night long. As they neared the border of the woods, they made camp if only for a few hours. They all believed it would be better to approach their destination during the new morning hours, rather than under the cover of darkness. They waited until the light of the moon and the burning embers of their campfire ceased their competition, and finally surrendered to the supremacy of the rising sun.

"It will be wonderful to sleep in a bed once again," Filaree said

The group had been riding for only a few hours on this day, though they had been on the road for a long time. Already, the trees were thinning out and the ground beneath their horse's hooves was becoming flatter and easier to traverse. What appeared to be a path, though not a well worn one, meandered through the woods, and they followed it.

"And I was just getting used to my pallet," Cairn replied sarcastically.

"Yes, I am sure you were," Filaree quipped. "I could tell by how easily you rose each morning."

"Was I that obvious?" he smiled.

"It was not the stretching and groaning as much as it was the stomping of your feet to begin the circulation that gave you away," she said.

"I was unaware that I had an audience. Should I be flattered or mortified?" he questioned.

Calyx growled affectionately at Cairn, and the scholar leaned over and kneaded the Moulant's thick fur with his fist.

"So you agree with Lady Filaree, I suppose?" he asked his massive friend. "Have you won him over too, my Lady, as you have the rest of us?"

Before Filaree could respond, Davmiran abruptly stood high in his stirrups and pointed to the vague outline of a tower far in the distance.

"I have seen this place in my dreams," he said quizzically.

"Could it be that I have described it to you so clearly that you think you saw it whilst you slept?" Robyn asked as they continued to walk.

"No. It is too perfect a resemblance. Though I do not question your prowess as a teacher, no one could have planted such a complete image in my mind without reverting to magic," the boy answered.

"I would have told you if that had been the case. Besides, there was no reason for me to do so," Robyn said.

"There may have been a reason for another to have done it, though," Cairn interrupted. "Had Mira ever been to Parth?" he asked.

"I do not know," Davmiran replied.

"I do!" Robyn said. "Of course she was. It was a long time ago when she was a young woman, but I remember the sisters mentioning it once. She visited the Tower with a contingent from Gwendolen who were on their way to a gathering of the Lords."

"A gathering of the Lords?" Filaree questioned.

"Tiels ago, when the network of Lalas was strong and unbroken, the leaders from all of the lands got together once a year to discuss matters of state, to solidify alliances, and primarily, to reiterate and confirm their commitment to all that is good, and to the wisdom of the First as disseminated by the Lalas. It was a joyous day, and people traveled to it gladly. It was an honor to be chosen to attend along with your Liege Lord. All of the races were represented, and it was also an opportunity for them to spend some time with one another."

"When did this stop?" Filaree asked. "I do not remember it at all."

"Before you were born, my Lady," Cairn replied. "Surely your father attended a number of times, though."

"The last gathering was just before the great Lalas Ishdomar departed the earth," Robyn replied sadly.

"Was he the first to go?" Filaree questioned.

"No. He was the third. But at his demise, people began to realize that something was seriously wrong with the balance," Robyn said.

"And after Ishdomar was gone, the network was significantly weaker. For the first time, the chain was broken," Cairn continued. "The city folk and townspeople began to withdraw and become frightened. The great depressions began, and everything was unsettled."

"Why is it that I have never heard of these meetings?" Filaree asked, surprised.

"Your mother and father must have decided to withhold this part of history from you. Perhaps they thought to protect you from the sadness of it all," Cairn guessed. "I was studying government at Thermascon when I first learned of them. They were really more pageantry than politics, but a number of memorable pacts and covenants did ultimately result from them over the span of time."

"Few people discuss the gatherings any longer. They were part of a time gone by, a time when people felt safer and more comfortable. It is hard to remember. Even for me," Robyn replied with a far away look in his eyes. "Things seemed so certain then."

"How old are you, Robyn?" Filaree suddenly asked.

"Older than you may have suspected," he replied. "Though not so old as you might now be imagining. My father used to tell people that I must have Elfin blood flowing through my veins, since I seem not to age like the rest of his line," Robyn laughed.

"You did not answer me," Filaree repeated.

"No?" Robyn said again. "I thought I had."

"Look! Over there!" Davmiran interrupted. "I can see the silhouette of the tower now quite clearly in the distance."

They all turned their attention in the direction that Davmiran pointed. Sure enough, high in the northern sky rose the Tower of Parth, an important piece of history by anyone's reckoning. What they all saw was an unadorned spire that rose, practically windowless, straight and true. Despite its simplicity of structure, it was like a beacon, and it drew all the wayward travelers who inadvertently stumbled upon it. They would be welcomed to a one by the sisters, fed, given a warm bed for the night and then sent on their way. For those visitors who had no particular destinations and arrived in Parth nonetheless, but were merely like seeds cast upon the winds of fate, the sisters tried to offer them guidance of a more spiritual type. These visitors were also sent upon their way hastily though. No one remained long in the Tower without having come by specific invitation, and those invitations were dispensed quite infrequently and extremely selectively.

No one except the sisters themselves was really sure what went on in the Tower. Rumors spread across the land from the day the Tower was constructed, but the certainty of purpose lay solely within the Tower itself. Built upon a convergence of power, a crossroad so to speak of the roots of the great trees, Parth was protected, and when one approached its lands, one clearly felt the energy that emanated from the soil itself. It coursed through the bodies and souls of everyone who neared it, and for those who advanced upon it with ill intentions they were quickly persuaded that they were entering the wrong domain.

The sisters of Parth built no walls around the Tower. They had no physical defenses aside from those possessed by the few women who had arrived with particularly good combat skills before their initiation into the sisterhood. No one had ever attacked Parth, and even the idea of such an assault was hard for most people to imagine. Besides, there never seemed really to be a reason to invade the area. The sisters provided succor and support to anyone who required it, regardless of their political orientation. They showed no favori'Tism. They neither asked for nor expected any compensation for their efforts, and they made no attempts to persuade their guests to change whatever perspectives and affiliations they arrived there with, no matter how disagreeable or contrary to their own they may have been.

"Do you see the sunlight reflecting off of those windows?" Davmiran asked the others. "It is so intense that it seems like it is originating from within the Tower as opposed to from without."

"It is like a beacon, even during the daylight," Filaree said.

"An apt description," Robyn commented. "Though the sisters would probably disagree with that portrayal. They have never wanted to draw attention to themselves or their work."

"Yet the power in this place is so strong, how could they not expect it to attract whatever enters this realm?" Cairn asked.

"My skin is tingling," Filaree observed.

"Mine too," Davmiran said. "What an incredible feeling!"

They all dismounted and let the horses graze momentarily without taking their eyes off of the tower in the distance. The sensations they all were experiencing distracted them and disrupted their equilibrium for just a few seconds.

"Is everyone alright?" Cairn asked, concerned now that the feeling had passed.

"I am fine. Just a bit dizzy," Filaree responded.

"Yes, I am okay too. I just feel a little weak, but it is nothing to be worried about," Davmiran answered, though his voice was unsteady.

Robyn did not seem to be paying much attention to his companions' words. One of his arms was raised above his shoulder, and he extended his long, slim fingers until the tips were arched and curved like the supple bows of the elves. A ripple of power surged through the air around them all. Filaree gasped. Calyx hovered protectively over Cairn and Davmiran who was standing beside him. He stood high upon his hind feet and bellowed in the air. Robyn remained perfectly still.

"The image of the Tower has grown blurry. Do you see it too?"

Filaree asked.

"Yes. I can barely make the spire out any longer," Cairn responded, squinting his eyes in the direction of Parth.

"What do you suppose it is? Only a moment ago, it was as clear as could be," Filaree asked.

"What do you think that was that rushed by us?" Cairn asked, more concerned at the moment for their own safety and security.

"Robyn?" Davmiran called. "What do you see?"

"There is a shield of sorts around the Tower. I cannot decipher its origins. It feels like nothing I have ever experienced before," he replied to the boy with his eyes still closed. "Join me here," he beckoned to him. "Take my hand, Dav," Robyn said, and reached backward with his free hand outstretched.

Davmiran walked over to him and clasped his strong hand in his own.

"Close your eyes, son. Tell me what you feel."

The boy shut his eyes tightly and concentrated while the others joined them, standing in a semicircle facing Parth.

"It comes from the Tower, whatever it is," the boy said after a moment, his voice having regained its strength.

"Yes, I know," Robyn replied quietly.

"It is almost solid in feeling. I cannot penetrate it very far."

"Odd, is it not? " Robyn said as if to himself. "It is full of the earth power, organic in nature, but no Lalas has placed this barrier here. I know of no Chosen who would barricade Parth. I wonder..."

"It seems to come from within the Tower, not without," Dav said.

Calyx growled defensively, and another rush of power cascaded by them, causing each one of the group to sway slightly and seek out each other for support.

"What was that?" Cairn asked after they all regained their footing.

"Something powerful is probing the Tower, and we just happen to be in its path," Robyn said.

"Probing?   Who would ever do such a thing?   To what purpose?" Filaree asked.   "Does Colton's reach extend this far north?   What of the convergence here?   I thought this area was protected."

"It is. Or it was," he said with concern in his voice. "But protection need not stem from the trees themselves in all cases," Robyn replied thoughtfully. "The taint of evil is unmistakable, though it is well concealed," he continued, as he opened up his senses to the passing currents of power that continued to wash over them.

"If we are not the target of this delving, I hope we do not become its victims," Filaree said in warning.

"Should we conceal ourselves?" Cairn asked. "We are quite exposed here, standing and talking like this."

"We are safe for now," Robyn said confidently. "Our problem will be how to penetrate the barrier around Parth, not how to avoid this reconnoitering."

"Maybe Parth is not the best place for us to seek shelter at this time. We should gather the horses," she said, disturbed by the uncertainty that had so suddenly overtaken them.

Dav was standing next to Cairn and he rested his graceful arm on his friend's shoulder. Softly and quietly, with his eyes half closed, he began to recite out loud,

"Tomorrow's wind, a premonition,
through the trees it blows.
Upon its wings, fate doth travel
with the breezes, to and fro.

Must we join the fray so soon?
Must the sunlight fade to gloom?
Must the singers change their tune?
Must the darkness shroud this moon?

Those of you who bear the weight,
the disquiet that will not abate,
the memory of pain and hate,
an urgency that cannot wait,
with courage still to challenge fate,

Walk down the road that none dare tread,
the path of conscience, the single thread,
as you watch the darkness spread,
without the fear and burning dread,
of what it is that lies ahead,
but heed the words your father said,
should you alone survive the dead."

"Where did that come from?" Filaree asked, as Davmiran opened his eyes and looked at the others with a dazed and confused expression on his face.

"I do not know. Honestly, the words just started to flow by themselves," Dav said a bit dumbfounded. "I cannot recall ever hearing it before or reading it."

"I cannot place it either. Do you remember the words still?" Cairn asked.

"I think so. I could repeat them if I tried," the boy responded, tilting his head in a quizzical manner.

"Why did it come to you now?" Robyn asked, not expecting the boy to answer. "What must we garner from it?"

"It should not be that hard to decipher. Perhaps you three are looking into it too deeply," Filaree said. "It is the last line that concerns me the most. The rest seems quite understandable."

"You may be right, Filaree," Cairn replied. "Though I wish I knew its derivation. Are you sure you cannot place it anywhere?" he asked both Davmiran and Robyn.

"My memory is limited," Dav said. "You know I cannot remember anything prior to my reawakening!" he exclaimed. "Could it be Mira speaking through me once again?"

"It is possible. She was a wise woman and more connected to the trees than anyone ever realized. It would not be unlikely that she would have recited poems such as this to you as a child. She knew you Dav, and she knew what you were destined for. She gave her life for that," Robyn reminded them.

"But still her legacy is strong!" Cairn said, squeezing the boy's arm reassuringly.

"In order to understand this, we must know whom the words refer to. It cannot be you, Cairn. You never did know your father, did you?" Filaree asked.

"That is true. No, it cannot be me," he said somewhat sadly, recalling momentarily his lonely childhood and solitary upbringing.

"My father was always reminding me of my obligations," Filaree continued. "He was a wise man and he had so much to teach."

"My father too, could be the one to whom the words refer," Robyn echoed.

"And mine?" Davmiran asked. "Did any of you know my father? I cannot remember him at all," he said, his smooth forehead creased with the strain of recollection. "All I know is what you have told me until now."

"I knew of him, as did we all. But we had never met. During the last years of the kingdom there was little contact with the outside world. Not much news escaped," Robyn said. "Mira was one of the few who communicated regularly, and that communication too ceased by the final year."

"Everyone knew of him, Dav. He had accomplished so much. I even remember when my mother told me that something was tragically amiss in Gwendolen," Filaree said, musing on those moments. "We were sitting in the chamber above the Great Hall. It has a huge window that overlooks the courtyard. We would often sit there and talk. You feel as if the entire world is at your feet in that room." It was evident on Filaree's face just how much she missed Avalain and her mother. After a moment, she continued her narrative. "We sat in complete silence, as we often did. It was so peaceful, and after my father died, my mother needed those private moments more frequently. I was fortunate that she included me," she smiled. "My mother laid her hands upon mine and looked me deeply in the eyes. The only other time she did that quite so intensely was the day my father died. Immediately, I was concerned. She told me that great changes were overtaking our world, and that the kingdom of Gwendolen was now shut off from the rest of us. She said that the King had sealed the borders and ceased all communication with the outside world. She also told me that she suspected that the Dark Lord's mark was upon this occurrence and that it boded ill for us all. Mostly, I remember shivering in response. The chill that crept across my skin was the most unwelcome feeling I had ever had," she said, as she felt a shiver run down her forearms now too, causing goose-bumps to rise unwittingly.

"I lived alone," Cairn said suddenly, and drew everyone's attention. "I had so little contact with the outside world at that time, you would think that these events would have passed me by. I too knew precisely when Gwendolen succumbed to Colton's advances. I felt the change gradually, though I was unsure of exactly what its origins were in the beginning. When your father, the King, finally cut off all contact with the trees and the Chosen, I was sitting before the stream by my cottage. There are some moments in my life that I could never forget," he said shaking his shaven head. "Calyx howled. He knew it even before I did. Then I felt it too. The water seemed to stop flowing and the wind ceased to blow. The woods grew perfectly silent and still. No one told me what was happening, but I knew. The stain of evil was upon everything. And the air felt empty, as if its essence had been withdrawn and only a deathly vacuum remained. The feeling has never fully passed since that day," he said, and he stared sadly at the ground.

"The effect of his loss upon us all is a telling indication of how important he was, though it unfortunately tells you nothing of what kind of a man he was," Robyn said. "But Dav, I believe that it is he to whom the words refer. Think of the final line. Were you not in fact the only one to survive when the kingdom finally yielded?"

"It is a warning, though, to 'heed the words'. Dav has already 'survived the dead'. So, what are the words he now needs to heed?" Cairn asked.

"If he listened to his father's words then, and if Mira listened as well, he would not have survived. The King's spirit and soul had been compromised by the deceptions and trickery," Filaree said.

"And by the manipulations of the witch who so successfully worked her way into the very heart of the circle surrounding the royal family," Robyn said.

"So how is this ever to be helpful? " Davmiran asked perplexed. "I cannot remember anything!"

"But you did recall the poem," Cairn said. "Now you just have to recollect what it was that your father tried to tell you."

"Cairn is right. This poem perhaps is the trigger that will eventually release the memory from the captivity of your mind," Robyn said.

"I think we should talk about this at another time," Filaree said ominously, and the others all raised their heads to gaze in the direction that she was already staring.

The energy that had surged through the woods had finally come into contact with the wall of power that surrounded Parth. The area of impact was beginning to spark and glow dangerously. They could also hear the various and disparate sounds of impact, none of which were comforting.

"Gather the horses," Filaree said to the others. "We had best be gone from here soon."

"Yes," Robyn agreed. "This may be our one opportunity in a while to make our way into Parth," he said, and his words caused the others to stare at him incredulously.

"Into Parth?" they all repeated at once.

Chapter Eight

"Be still! You gain nothing by speaking," he said, and then he snapped the chains taught.

Unlike ordinary metal links, the irons that bound him were forged within the mind of the most evil of beings, and they reacted to the master's moods as if they were extensions of his limbs. He needed only will it and they responded. They pulsated and slithered around his wrists and ankles, and around his throat as well, making it impossible now for him to do anything other than gag.

He was so weak that he could barely keep his eyes open. He knew though that if he closed them, he may never open them again, and so he fought the impulse to surrender and allow sleep to overtake him.

What are these chains made of? he wondered. *If I could only pierce their surface I could find a way to loosen them.*

Premoran drew whatever power he still retained into his right wrist, knowing full well that doing so would weaken the rest of his extremities beyond the danger point. He waited for his brother to turn away from him, and then he quickly probed the links. A shock coursed through his entire body, and his head thrust backward sharply and involuntarily. He could feel the warm blood dripping down the back of his neck, but he could also sense that he had utilized the exact amount of force needed to penetrate the ingeniously woven fetters that were being used to constrain him.

That was worth the pain, he thought, and he blinked back the tears that had filled his red and swollen eyes. *Their derivation is of the earth as I suspected. So my brother could not stop himself from utilizing it still.* He smiled slightly and took a deep breath. *It is so sad, so tragic for us all. If he was not so deadly, then the irony would almost be heartbreaking.*

He hung from the stone wall, partway up from the floor to the ceiling. Nothing visible shackled him to the wall, suspending him thus. The chains bound his arms and legs and caused him pain and discomfort, but they did not help to hold him in place. When his brother entered the room their ends sprung toward his hands like iron to a magnet stone. The air around him was buoyant, though dry and stale, and it felt lighter than it should have. It was the air around him that kept him from falling to the surface of the chamber. Colton had infused it with a resilience that the prisoner could not pierce.

When Premoran awoke what now seemed like weeks ago, the first thing he saw was his brother's enraged face peering at him from below. He thought he was dreaming still, for in reality, he never expected to survive the battle that he entered into when he left his friends in Seramour. All that concerned him was that the boy, the heir, was given the time and opportunity to escape his brother's madly obsessive pursuit. In that respect he succeeded, and as far as he was concerned, victory was his. Colton's efforts were once again thwarted. But he knew fully well that he would pay a great price for that.

It would have been easier for me if he had killed me, he thought, as excruciating waves of pain washed over him, compelling him to search deeply for the light of salvation within his soul. *But, with life, there is hope,* he reminded himself.

"You could stop this at any moment, brother," Colton said to him, though his voice was not audible to the ear. It echoed across his numbed consciousness. "As allies, we would be unstoppable," he hissed.

Premoran resisted responding to him, but in his weakened state, he could not control himself as he would have wished.

"So you realize that you are stoppable now?" he asked.

The chain around his neck constricted immediately, making it impossible for him to speak another word.

"You are a fool! You insist upon provoking me still? What have you to gain, Premoran?" he asked, knowing that his captive could not respond. "I am winning already, and you are aware of that too. It will just take time. No one can defeat me. They have rebuffed my assaults up until now, but with each blow that I deal them, they weaken and I grow stronger. I care not for the losses I incur. You know that," he said. He turned his back on Premoran nonchalantly and allowed the chains to relax just enough so that he could breath more comfortably.

There was a subtle hint of doubt in Colton's voice though he tried so hard to conceal it, and Premoran noticed it immediately. He looked at him through half opened eyes, and it seemed almost as if his image was fading slightly. The wizard shook his head and squinted his eyes in order to clear them.

Thank the First, I can at least move some part of me, he thought. *Why is he keeping me alive? I was certain he would have killed me this time as soon as he had the chance. Is it still so hard for him to sever the ties completely, I wonder? How can I use this to help us all?*

Premoran searched the chamber perfunctorily, as his weakened physical condition did not allow him to do anything more thoroughly. And, as he suspected, he discovered no obvious weaknesses in structure of his prison.

"What did you expect to find?" Colton asked sarcastically.

"You have already surprised me, brother. I am alive," he replied.

"Do not think you are alive because I still harbor some affection for you," he hissed back. "There are things you have not yet revealed to me. I wish to know them before I terminate your life," he said matter-of-factly. "And there is something I need you to do."

Does he reason still? I expected him to be far madder than he appears, the wizard thought.

"You must see what I have accomplished here," Colton said to him, as if he was a visitor coming to Sedahar for the first time. "When you and your 'friends' forced me to leave, your disdain was so obvious. Surely, had they lived, they would marvel at me now! What a shame that they cannot share this experience with you."

He cares even to this day. He has not overcome his rancor. I must turn this weakness to my advantage.

"Calista would not have been surprised," Premoran replied.

Colton's head snapped around at the mention of the Lady of the Island, but he kept silent. It was obvious that he had touched a sensitive nerve, and he wanted to probe it further and determine the depth of his concern.

"She always believed that you were destined for great things," he continued despite the dryness in his throat and the incredible pain. Even as a young man, Colton could not conceal his need for praise.

"You tease me, brother. Do you think that silly compliments will gain you mercy?" he asked. "Harbor no such illusions. They will only frustrate you."

"Mercy? Why would I expect mercy from you? I would kill you this instant if I could myself."

"Still so honest. Time has not changed you?" Colton asked.

"I remain constant. It is you who cannot find your peace amidst the changes."

"And so you understand! Soon, things will change no more. The fabric will cease to weave," he said in a far off tone.

"I am tired, Colton," Premoran said, and he closed his eyes. "You have neither been strong enough to change things, nor to cope with things as they are. Indeed you must suffer all the time."

"Are you trying to provoke me?" he replied, turning abruptly to face the captive man. "You will die when I decide to kill you and no sooner, so it is unnecessary to waste what little strength you have left on my behalf. You shall not force me to dispatch you sooner than I choose."

"I have known you all of my life. I expect no compassion from you. But I will not be grateful to you for my life. My work is done. The boy is free and the fabric weaves of its own will once again. Do not your failures ever cause you to question your strength?" he asked provocatively.

Colton laughed a hideous laugh that echoed off of the stone walls interminably. He rose into the air so that he was face to face with his brother.

"The trees have forsaken him," he hissed through his full, blood red lips. "I thought you would have known by now that they conspire with me?" he said, and he stared deeply into Premoran's eyes.

Premoran felt as if he had been hit with a battering ram. Colton allowed his brother to probe his mind briefly, as he knew that he would. The result was even more devastating.

He speaks the truth! Premoran thought, astounded. *This cannot be. They would never do that. But I saw it in his mind! I heard them speak to him!*

He gasped for breath, and he felt his heart beating very quickly within his chest. Suddenly, the pain became almost unbearable, and he realized just how close to the limit his physical self was being stretched. He looked at his brother's face once more, and then he immediately regretted it. Colton floated before him, and the corners of his mouth were turned up into a horrifying smile. The Dark Lord bent his head toward him and leaned in close until Premoran could feel his hot, rancid breath wafting over him.

"The end is near. It is inevitable now," he said quietly. "Will you share the final moments with me?" the Dark Lord whispered in his ear.

Chapter Nine

Caroline lay upon her back on the blanket and stared up into the night sky. She had first spread her mat on the soft snow that shrouded the entire field before placing the woven covering down. The warm wool coupled with the tight mesh of the mat kept the chill from radiating upward, and she remained warm and comfortable despite the freezing temperature.

The stars were as bright as ever, and she searched for a shooting one, a sign of good luck, but the heavens did not oblige her this evening. During warmer times, she would lay here for hours on this soft and sheltered knoll until she fell asleep, waking with the dawn. Then she would return to her house, the beautiful cabin that her father constructed stone by stone and stick by stick, and begin her morning chores. Unfortunately, the winter seemed to have arrived much earlier this season, and the snows and winds were heavier and stronger than she had ever seen before.

This evening was no different than the multitude of others that preceded it the past few weeks, but Caroline had no complaints. Though her life was simple and quiet, it was never boring. She had the trees and the animals to communicate with, and thus she never lacked for companionship. She also had her father, and she adored him, everything about him! He was noble and strong, honest and wise, and brave and gentle. He brought a smile to her delicate and flawless face whenever she thought of him.

Caroline was merely two tiels and four, though she had the look of a far more mature woman. She carried herself with dignity, always holding her graceful head high and proud, though without the slightest hint of haughtiness or arrogance. Her hair reached almost to the ground, and it flowed down her back in waves of glistening auburn, and her eyes were bright green. They always sparkled, just like fine emeralds do when they are illuminated by bright rays of light. She had a small, slightly turned up nose and ruby red lips that stood out markedly against her porcelain skin. No matter how often or for how long she lay in the sun, her skin color remained as white as new snow, seemingly immune to the effects of nature.

Father must certainly think that I am a dolt! she thought. *I sit here for hours staring up at the sky. Perhaps I am!* She laughed. *But it is so beautiful. I cannot imagine that anything could be as beautiful as the stars.*

Her father never stopped her from indulging herself in this way.

He rarely told her what to do anymore. After her chores were done and the animals were tended to, she was free to wander and weave, read and play as she wished. She loved him dearly; he was the world to her. Caroline never knew her mother, nor did her father ever speak of her other than guardedly and briefly, and she never questioned him about the woman, though her interest was growing steadily as she grew older. She often wondered now why he hardly mentioned her, why it appeared to pain him so when the subject came up, but she respected his silence. She trusted his judgment, and she believed that the moment would come one day when he would be able to reveal to her what yet seemed so hard for him to disclose.

They never traveled very far. Conrad, her father, told her that they lived in the most beautiful place in the entire world and so there was no reason to leave it. He provided her with anything she wanted, though her needs were few, and they never lacked for food, despite the snow covered ground and cold, cold weather during the fall and winter months. He also told her that she should avoid contact with people at all costs; that they were dangerous and always to be avoided. In fact, she had never even seen any other beings like herself and her father for more than a brief second or two, and then only from a considerable distance. Her father kept them well away from her those few times anyone wandered into their realm.

She kept herself busy with her animal friends, perfecting their skills at communication and studying the heavens and the stars. She maintained a small garden of healing herbs and flowers, she grew vegetables when the weather permitted and she sang; she so loved to sing! Occasionally she would learn about the world outside from a bird or a fox that had chanced upon other creatures during their travels or migrations. But, as her father had warned her many times before, others who resembled herself were feared and loathed by her animal confidants, and so she too developed a natural and instinctive suspicion of anything human or human-like.

Lately, nevertheless, Caroline was growing inquisitive about what lay beyond the perimeter of her wanderings despite all of what she had learned of the outside world second hand. Her father had insisted that she spend every night in the cabin or upon the grounds nearby, so she never roamed too far during her daily travels. At sixteen years of age, her curiosity was growing steadily now, but her father turned a deaf ear to her pleas for an opportunity to journey with him on one of his many trips away from home. In fact, as she grew up, he grew more and more adamant about her staying close to home and far away from any contact with the world outside of her own small and confined one. When she questioned him as to why, he withdrew and his face took on a horrid and ugly expression as if he had tasted the most sour of fruits, and her interest waxed in direct proportion to his increasing reluctance to discuss it. She knew that he would not cave in to her requests in this regard, so she ostensibly accepted his restrictions. But, she could not suppress her longing to learn more about exactly what he was so indisposed to reveal.

As she lay flat upon her back, she heard a rustling sound in the distance and she let her mind's voice reach out to it.

Who goes there? Is it you, Feala? Or you Amak?

The sound continued, though the animals she called out to did not respond. Rather, a strange mix of cryptic half-words, images and emotions flooded her mind. She was certain that whatever responded to her inquiry had never conversed before. Caroline had learned over the short span of her life that speaking in words was not natural to anyone but those sentient beings who customarily communicated out loud. She had to teach her animal friends how to understand her and how to reply. Though they uttered things all of the time, the sounds served as no more than self-expression, a commentary of sorts on how and what they were feeling, until she showed them the way to organize their thoughts and recall their images after the fact. The sounds she just heard were like those of her friends before she taught them properly.

It is most definitely a horse that I hear, she thought. *The noises are unmistakable. He does not yet know how to speak,* she giggled.

Caroline stood up and looked in the direction that she suspected the babble had originated from, and sure enough, in the distance she could see the silhouette of a riderless horse, saddled and laden with packs with its reins hanging down .

A human's captive! What is this animal doing out here? I wonder what happened to the rider, she thought, cautiously looking all around her. Her heart began to beat double-time. *The horse seems unconcerned. Maybe he left him behind a long while ago. Could a human really have wandered all the way here? People never come here!*

She walked over to the standing animal and rubbed her hand tenderly down its mane, flipping the thick hair over to the other side. At the same time, she spoke to it silently and soothingly. It immediately lifted its nose to her face in recognition and whinnied in a startled response. Caroline had become adept at the art of communication in this manner, and she knew to proceed slowly so as not to frighten the animal. A horse's mind was limited, and though she was perfectly able to 'speak' with it in her own way, horses usually cared only about a few things. Their perspective was narrow, despite their tremendous affections and sense of loyalty. Some good, fresh grass, water, a comfortable girth and saddle and a rider who did not constantly jab them in the belly were their primary concerns. She did encounter a great war horse once whose sense of self was quite elevated and different from all the others she had met. He even spoke to her of his accomplishments on the field of battle as she guided him through his past as best she could, and Caroline was immensely impressed with his magnanimity and his regal demeanor. But for the most part, horses had little to say and less to argue about, though they were almost always gentle and friendly nevertheless.

She learned from this gelding that he had a strong affection for the one who had harnessed him, and she found that very odd. It did not make sense to her that the horse could like a human! Whenever she listened to her other friends speak about men, they did so with loathing in their hearts. This animal was actually fond of whomever it was that lead him here, though he was content nonetheless to graze.

Caroline spoke to him silently, slowly inserting her thoughts into his stream of consciousness, and she began to develop a picture, though proportionately quite different from her visual reality, of what the absent human looked like. Through the horse's mind, the images barely looked human, but she knew from previous experience with others of his kind that objects appeared to be much larger to him than they actually were. Still, she could see the image of a face that was not unbecoming; a man's face, though his ears were sharp and pointed and his eyes slanted upward, unlike her own or her father's. His hair was auburn colored and rather long, and he wore clothing like nothing she had seen before.

She urged the animal to tell her something more about him, about his personality and whether he was as dangerous as her father had always led her to believe that strangers were. Caroline immediately felt pangs of guilt for doubting him, but she could not help but ask. The impression of the rider that she was receiving bore no hint of evil, no sign of peril in the slightest, and she had come to know that animals did not lie. Some species were far more sophisticated than others, but none had ever communicated anything but the truth as they saw it, and it was up to her to interpret their intuitions. Cruelty and meanness were always evident immediately, as were kindness and tenderheartedness, though often good traits were confused with bad ones if the beast was hungry and the rider or master was in a rush to get somewhere. Caroline needed to exercise her discretion often lest she be mislead by inaccurate motives. But, in this case the message was clear and uncomplicated, and she quickly grew fond of the man that this horse recalled in a jumble of feelings and images.

Is he alive still, I wonder? The animal's memories are yet fresh and clear. It can not be that long ago since they were separated.

There were some things animals could not tell her, and an understanding of the future or where people and things were when they were not directly within their view was one of them. Horses particularly, were weak at 'speculation.'

She perused the ground around the young animal and began to follow his footprints in the snow. Luckily, no new flakes had fallen in almost an entire day, so she could spot the hoof prints easily. She traced them for sometime until she finally saw a crumpled body lying sideways upon the frozen ground up ahead. She ran to catch up to it in order to see if the person was hurt badly, for surely he did not fall and remain there voluntarily, but she hesitated abruptly.

Father has warned me so many times. Should I be doing this? she thought. *Perhaps I should go back and tell him and bring him out here. But, what if the traveler is hurt? What if I have discovered him just in time to save him? I must try to help. Besides, his horse cares for him too much for him to be dangerous!*

Caroline walked cautiously up to the prone body and slowly knelt down beside it. His face was far more beautiful than the horse's distorted image conveyed. His eyelids were closed and his exposed skin and all of his clothing were lightly covered in soft snow. There was no sign of blood on the ground, though his clothing could have concealed it, but it was clear that he was not merely sleeping. It was also obvious that he had not been lying there for all that long. She saw a bow lying upon the ground nearby, and the sight of the weapon made her heart beat faster.

He is a warrior, I suspect, she thought. *Could he have been felled in battle? Are there others?* she wondered and grew concerned that some more dangerous humans might be lurking about nearby.

She quickly perused the ground all around searching for a sign of a fight or the footprints of others of his kind, but there were no markings but those of his own and his steed's. She breathed a bit more easily for the moment, and she continued to look at the handsome man. Carefully, she reached over and pushed a lock of his hair off of his face and behind his ear. As she did so, she realized with a start that his ears were quite pointed, so unlike her own and her father's.

"An elf!" she said aloud, shattering the silence with her unexpected words. "Father has mentioned these beings to me!"

As she continued to gaze upon him, she began to feel things that she had never felt before. When dealing with animals, she had always had to coax them to remain consistent and organized in their 'thinking', to guide them so that she could participate in their images. In this case, entire streams of images began to flood her mind, though they were fuzzy edged and disordered; uncontrolled and unguided by a wakeful mind, like in a dream. In addition, she seemed to feel the joy and the sorrow of his recollections much more intensely than she ever did in her previous encounters with animals whose capacity to retain the past was so much more limited than this elf's was.

Caroline fought to keep her eyes open, but she was being overtaken by the images flooding his brain. She knew that something dangerous and daring was happening but she could not control it. His thoughts consumed her and drew her in so quickly that she was unable to put up even a semblance of a defense. She collapsed beside him and her head fell upon his chest, swollen with his dreams. She was being drawn deeper and deeper into his reality, losing herself within his visions, while becoming no less than a part of his unconscious thought process, and she could do nothing to prevent it. She felt herself slip away so unexpectedly as if all the breath had been suddenly sucked from her body, and she could not move even a muscle. In an instant, the conscious entity that had been Caroline was gone entirely.

"Caroline? Where are you?" her father called from a distance, but she could no longer hear his voice. She had already lost herself inside of the silent visitor's mind, and another's memory guided her. "Caroline! Daughter!" he yelled anxiously, seeing the bodies lying upon the ground ahead, near where the stranger's horse stood grazing.

As he approached as rapidly as he could, he grew more and

more agitated. By the time he reached her side and saw her closed eyes and limp body he was frantic with concern.

"Caroline! Look at me, child!" he screamed. "This cannot be happening. I cannot lose another to this accursed power." He lifted her in his arms. Carefully, he separated her from the stranger's body upon which her head lay. "Speak to me! Say something! Come back, my darling. Come back to me!" He removed his gloves and rubbed snow on her unresponsive face. Tears ran down his cheeks and froze in thin, opalescent streaks.

"Why did you not listen to me? You cannot be near outsiders! I told you that! Your power is a curse! It will kill you as it killed her!" he sobbed.

Conrad turned to the motionless stranger and kicked him in the leg.

"Wake up! It is your fault. You cannot die! If you die, I will lose my daughter forever just as I lost her mother!" he yelled harshly.

He placed Caroline gently over the saddle of the nearby horse and returned to the stricken elf. The distraught man lifted him up as well as if he was weightless, and hoisted him over his own shoulder.

"Keep breathing!" he said in the elf's ear as if his will alone could keep him alive.

Holding the horse's reins in his free hand, and with the elf hanging limply across his strong back, he swiftly lead the animal bearing his unmoving daughter through the thickening snow and toward their cottage.

Chapter Ten

"Wake up, Princess," a soft voice whispered into her ear.

Alemar opened her eyes immediately. How someone could have entered her chamber without her knowing it, even though she was fast asleep, disturbed her initially. But as soon as her vision cleared and she was able to focus in the dim light of the new morning, she was immediately at ease.

"What is it, Teetoo? Have you news?" She sat up and drew the covers around her bare shoulders.

"He is alive, my Lady! Premoran lives!" he sighed with relief, though there was a hesitant and tentative quality to his tone. "I could not fully decipher the message, but it most definitely was from him," he said calmly, yet consternation marred his graceful features.

"You were right after all. You knew it all along," she smiled and laid her hand atop his incredibly delicate fingers.

"I suspected. Now I am certain!"

"Do you know where he is? Is he free? Was he victorious?" she asked excitedly.

"He is his brother's captive," he replied sadly.

"But he is alive!" she joyously declared, ignoring the obviously dire circumstances surrounding his survival.

"Yes, he is alive," he said, and he bowed his graceful head.

Alemar lit a small candle that sat upon the table beside her bed. In the light of the flame, she could see that the Weloh's round eyes were filled with tears. She slipped from the bed with the blanket shrouding her, sat beside him and placed her arm around his stooped shoulders.

"This is good news, Teetoo," she said soothingly. "Is this not what you were hoping to hear? He lives!"

"We must help him, Princess," Teetoo said quietly without lifting his eyes from the floor. His brow was furrowed and his voice was stern and determined.

"Can we?" she asked, as if speaking to herself. The thought of having to come to the aid of one as powerful as Premoran had not occurred to her heretofore.

"I do not know. But we must try," he answered glumly.

"Of course we must," Alemar agreed. Her mind immediately began to assess their options. "Have you a plan?" she asked.

"A plan, my Lady?" he inquired as if this was a strange question.

"Do you have any idea as to how we can rescue him?" she elucidated.

"Rescue him?" he replied, looking at her like the word had no meaning to him.

"Yes, rescue him," she said, eyeing the Weloh oddly. "Teetoo, you are confusing me. You just told me that we must help him How else can we assist him?"

"We must kill him, Alemar," Teetoo said quietly with his features frozen in a tragic grimace.

"Kill him? What are you saying? Why would we kill him?" she asked incredulously.

"Because there is no other way to save him," he answered. "This is what he would want us to do. He must be suffering beyond reason, beyond our wildest imagination."

Alemar was unaccustomed to problems without solutions, and she was totally unwilling to accept her friend's analysis of the situation.

"Listen to me, Teetoo," she said, taking hold of his limp hand once again and looking him in the eyes. "We will find a way! If he is a prisoner of Caeltin's, then we can free him. If he is alive, then there is hope."

"He is in Castle Sedahar," he said sullenly. "We cannot enter Colton's domain. It would be suicide. We have no choice but to end Premoran's life ourselves or somehow provide him with the means to do it."

"Why? Why do you say that? Caeltin would never expect us or anyone to attempt to sneak into his castle, so we would benefit from the element of surprise. Besides, how do you know that we could not penetrate his home? Has anyone ever tried to before?" she asked.

"Not that I am aware of," he replied, less downcast than a mere moment before. "And that in itself is a lesson we should heed ."

"I see no lesson in that! It merely means no one has had enough reason to attempt it. It does not mean that it cannot be done. There is a chance that we could do this, and if there is even a chance, then we must try. We are strong! We are resourceful! And you can fly, Teetoo! You can go anywhere you want to," she said.

"The Dark Lord will see us coming. His eyes are everywhere," he said, skeptically.

"Then we must hide from them very carefully. I am an elfin warrior and you are a Weloh! My ancestor was the Ice Princess, and her father rose from the dead and came to our assistance right here only weeks ago. Anything is possible, Teetoo! That much I have learned. Caeltin has thrice been defeated already. A new tree has sprouted and thrives in Pardatha! Premoran lives! What more could we ask for? We can do it, Teetoo. I know we can," she implored him.

"Your words give me hope, Alemar. But they are just words," he said glumly, and he turned away from her. "Sedahar is a quagmire of vileness and decay. It is unlike any other place on earth. Assuming we could even gain access to his home, we could never escape again. We are not strong enough to stand up to him."

"Even with Premoran at our side?" she asked.

Teetoo raised his sad eyes to the ceiling, and a lone tear ran down his pale face and hung for a moment from his graceful chin. As the smile turned the corners of his lips upward, the tear fell to the floor silently.

"Perhaps, Alemar, perhaps. But we do not know what condition Premoran will be in, even if he is still alive when we get there," Teetoo said. "He will be weak at the least. And in pain, I am certain. The Dark Lord is a cruel master, and an even crueler brother. We should not count on Premoran's assistance in any capacity. Why Colton has kept him alive this long is baffling me. We may find that he is already dead by the time we get there."

"Then you agree to try?" she asked, and she turned her beautiful face beseechingly toward him while pointedly ignoring his reservations.

He hesitated before responding to her. After raising his chin high, he gazed across the room and out the small window on the other side. The sun was rising in the east, and it cast a soothing glow across the sleeping city. After another moment of silence he moved to Alemar's side once again.

"How can I not?" the Weloh replied, and he grasped her hand tightly. "He is my friend. I love him like a father. Besides, you present a very good case. Or should I say, you make a weak case sound convincing," he smiled.

Alemar let go of his hand and walked to the dressing table on the other side of the room. She opened the drawer and removed a small pouch from it. Pulling softly on the worn strings, she opened it and stuck two of her fingers inside. Carefully, she withdrew a folded and ragged piece of parchment and began to spread it out on the bed. It was covered with faded writing, ancient letters and runes, and at the bottom there was a simple line drawing.

"What have you here?" Teetoo asked, unsurprised that the Princess seemingly pulled something out of her hat once again.

"Just a little item that I though might be useful at some point," she replied, grinning. "My uncle gave it to me before he departed for Crispen. It belonged to my mother, he said. I thought at first that it was simply a memento. But now I realize that it is much more than that," she said while beckoning to Teetoo to lean in closer and have a look for himself.

"Can you read the writing?" Teetoo asked, looking closely at the letters.

"Yes, in fact, I can," she said. "My father always believed that knowledge of the old ways was important. I learned as a child to understand much that has practically been forgotten by most people. One of the things that he insisted that I study was the old language of my people."

"You are a very deep and complicated woman, Alemar," the Weloh responded.

"Not really. Just disciplined, I think. I worked hard as a child to make certain that my father respected me after my mother died. I was afraid that he would forget that I was his daughter after he remarried. I could not bear the thought of losing both of my parents."

"I am certain that your father respects you. If I were he, I would feel nothing but pride in having a daughter like you."

Alemar laid her hand on Teetoo's arm and looked at him earnestly.

"Thank you. That means a lot to me," she said. "I miss my home, and I miss my father. Having you by my side has made it so much more bearable."

"What do the letters mean, Princess?" he asked after a brief moment.

"Sedahar," she replied simply.

"Is the drawing a map?" he asked.

"I think it is a route of sorts into the dreaded place. It certainly is not a detailed map. I do not even know if it will be helpful, it is so vague and cryptic. Sedahar purportedly changes all of the time itself, but the bedrock upon which it is built endures. It seems to me to be more like a way to navigate a maze than a drawing of a path, but it seems almost useless it is so elementary," she said, looking at it more closely. "It appears as if some water has marred the surface. I hope it has not ruined it."

Teetoo bent down and ran his smooth fingers over the parchment. "May I?" he asked her.

"Of course," she replied, stepping back a pace.

He began to rub the surface lightly with his index finger, causing just the slightest bit of heat with the friction of his hand. Almost instantly, a soft powder rose into the air. It began to sparkle and glitter as it spread out over the paper, and it clouded the space with a fragrant odor.

"My eyes see things slightly differently than yours," he said, staring at the parchment.

"Does your nose smell things differently as well?" she asked. "The odor of Lalas is unmistakable!" Alemar commented, and she breathed in the wonderful bouquet as deeply as she could.

"It is marvelous for me, too," he replied, though his concentration did not
waver.

As they stared intently at the paper before them, what heretofore appeared to be indefinite and simplistic began to transform before their very eyes. Within an instant, an intricately detailed map appeared in front of them, almost three dimensional in mien. Colors swirled and settled upon the paper, defining the areas even more exactly. It was clear that the route it charted originated in the dead remains of a once mighty Lalas and that it followed the massive tunnels and caverns that were left when the tree's roots decayed and disappeared, straight to the outskirts of Castle Sedahar itself.

"This is amazing!" Alemar exclaimed. "I would never have done that in fear of damaging the parchment."

"A fortuitous gift," Teetoo said. "It appears that we have found our way into Sedahar after all!"

"As usual, the fabric weaves of its own will," Alemar replied. "I had no idea that any of the trees ever grew that close to his domain. What a great Lalas it must have been to have had a root structure so extensive and elaborate. Now we have no excuse but to rescue Premoran!"

"It will not be easy, Princess. Even though this has presented itself to us, we must realize the tremendous risk that we take."

"Is there no risk to be taken by not trying?" she asked.

"As usual, you are right. In fact, doing nothing could result in an even greater peril for everyone. There must be a reason why he has kept Premoran alive for this long. He needs him for something."

"Is it possible that he is merely toying with him; languishing in his victory? In any case, we cannot allow Caeltin to use him, even if it is only for his self gratification," Alemar replied menacingly.

"No. If we find we cannot save him, we must put an end to his captivity in some other way," he said seriously.

"I understand, Teetoo," she said sadly. She put her arm around the Weloh and he embraced her in return. They hugged each other tightly for a moment before separating.

"We are going to succeed, you know," she commented without the inflection of a question in her statement. "We must. Fate has brought us together, and together we will face whatever obstacles get in our way."

"I could not imagine a more formidable ally than you, Princess. Your optimism alone could topple the Dark Lord."

"I believe in the efficacy of thought and faith," she said earnestly. "And I also believe that what we are fighting for is good and right. We will prevail."

"By the First, I hope so," he responded. "May the Gem of Eternity illuminate our path through the darkness," Teetoo said solemnly.

Chapter Eleven

The silhouette of a slim figure cast a shadow across the polished stone of the floor, illuminated by a brilliant light that emanated from somewhere behind it. Sparks continued to fly in all directions, silently and soundlessly bouncing off of the roughly hewn rock walls before burning out and floating to the ground in soft, grey snow-like flakes. The bluish aura that surrounded the semi-circle of Chosen flared brightly for a moment and then was extinguished as if it had been sucked out of the room by a powerful exhaust. The doorway sealed itself with a hiss as soon as the visitor was fully within the chamber, leaving behind only a faint line upon the wall where it once was and some billowing steam which rose slowly toward the ceiling before disappearing into the darkness above.

Blodwyn released the hands of her companions and stepped forward with her staff held high in front of her. The other nine Chosen looked on with mixed expressions upon their faces. Some were shocked at how young Tomas appeared to be, while some of the others were simply relieved that he had finally arrived, and they breathed a bit more easily for it. Still others were paranoid and discomfited by the entire proceeding, and the distress was almost tangible. Though they stood together without breaking their formation, the tension was unmistakable.

"What is this place?" Tomas asked. "Who are you all?" the boy inquired with no fear in his voice, but merely surprise.

Blodwyn stepped forward once again and assumed the leadership of the group in the absence of a formal hierarchy.

"We are all, each and everyone, Chosen of the trees," she replied.

"Why are you here, and why have you summoned me?" he asked suspiciously, as he looked all around the room.

"Have you no intuition?" Dashiel asked.

Tomas gazed at each of ten people standing in a semicircle before him, lingering momentarily on each face and bonding with each in his own way. He felt their doubts, their fears, their insecurities and he also sensed the hope that welled up within their souls. Some resisted his advances, while others welcomed iand embraced it. He did not force himself upon anyone, but lay his spirit open beside their own and waited for them to invite him in. Eventually, even Pithar accepted his overture.

"Is Robyn dar Tamarand not here?" Tomas asked, knowing full

well the answer already.

"We thought it best not to involve him in this," Blodwyn replied.

"He has his hands full with the heir," Connor said. "Besides, if we do not accomplish anything, we lose very little. His presence here would be too great a risk for him."

"We do not even know where he is," Liam admitted.

"You knew where I was?" Tomas asked.

"No," Blodwyn responded immediately. "But we hoped that we could reach you with our call. And we were correct."

"We elected not to attempt to contact the Chosen of Promanthea. Our methods are not foolproof. The correspondence could have been traced. We could not jeopardize the heir," Edmond said.

Tomas considered these comments for a minute.

"Should I feel elated by your concern for my brother, or slighted by your lack thereof for me?" he asked seriously.

Crea, Chosen of Wayfair, stepped forward at that remark.

"We could not accomplish much without one of you, Tomas. We had to make a decision and we chose you. Were we wrong to do so?" he asked.

The boy bowed his head and closed his eyes. He stood silently for a second or two.

"No. You were not wrong. I understand. I would have done the same thing." He raised his chin high and looked at the group once again. "To involve my brother in this conspiracy would have been dangerous," Tomas said.

"Conspiracy, you call it?" Blodwyn asked, her head cocked to the side in question.

"Is there another way to describe this meeting?" Pithar inquired, agreeing with the boy's characterization. "We meet in complete secrecy. We seal ourselves within a chamber that no thoughts can penetrate."

"We seek to make things right again!" Liam pointed out. "We do not seek to do harm to anyone or anything. Secrecy was essential. Is not the term 'conspiracy' rather harsh?"

"I apologize," Tomas said. "I did not wish to impugn your motives. It is just that I have learned to question many motives these days."

"The fabric weaves of its own will. We had few choices left," Edmond said. "You are here, are you not?" he said to Tomas.

"Of course he is here, Edmond. What does that prove?" Harton asked.

"Why must you quarrel, Harton? Edmond simply made a point. If we were not all meant to be together, than the boy would not have arrived before the chamber was sealed," Liam said.

"Have we no control over anything anymore?" Crea moaned.

"We do. And we can still effect change. We are not separate from our bond-mates, just apart," Carlisle said. "I wish only to come away from here with hope."

"And you will, Carlisle," Blodwyn said. "We all will."

"Hope? I want explanations. I want information. Hope is merely a feeling. I need a reason!" Tobias intoned.

"Have you all been betrayed as I have?" Tomas asked bluntly. His words took everyone off- guard and caused a hush to descend upon the entire room.

"Betrayed?" Blodwyn repeated. "How were you betrayed, and by whom?"

They all stared at the boy intently, dreading his next words. "By Ormachon, my bond-mate," he replied so quietly they could barely hear him. "I was traveling with my friends, and he gave away my location to one of the Possessed, an evil woman whom we had encountered earlier in our journey."

"How do you know it was the Lalas?" Liam asked, shocked by the boy's revelation.

"I know," was all Tomas said. His eyes grew dark and pensive as the memory resurfaced once again.

"Was the woman called Margot?" Liam asked.

"Yes," Tomas replied not surprised that at least one of the Chosen knew of her.

"She entered the woods where I live and attempted to kill a sister from the Tower. Needless to say, her efforts were thwarted," Liam explained.

"By the Lalas?" Tomas asked.

"No. By Premoran. The sister from Parth was coming to convene with me and with Oleander when she was waylaid before she arrived."

"I have also heard of her," Harton said. "She has taken charge of the Duchy of Talamar."

"It is no surprise that the spineless son of the dead Duke has relinquished his authority to Colton. I have had my doubts about him from the day he was born," Carlisle sneered.

"She has also raised a considerable army whose sole purpose is to relieve the trees of their authority. She has somehow convinced the people the Lalas have turned against them," Liam continued.

"Somehow?" Pithar said. "We raise the same questions. Is it a surprise that those less familiar with the ways of the trees doubt their motives at this point, particularly when they are being urged to these sentiments by one as 'qualified' as she is in the art of persuasion?"

"She insists the trees have commit such a series of vile and horrific acts! No Lalas could ever do the things she claims. It can only be the work of one of Colton's servants." Liam said.

"The Lalas have allowed the seeds of doubt to sprout in many minds," Blodwyn said.

"They must have a reason for what they do," Edmond said.

"To what purpose?" Dashiel asked, stone-faced. "Why would they encourage these sentiments?"

"Would that we knew," Connor said, perplexed.

"Is it that they are encouraging the feelings, or are they unable at this time to alter them?" Harton asked.

"Neither choice you offer is a good one," Tobias commented sullenly.

"Why would your bond-mate beguile you in such a way? It is unthinkable!" Pithar asked.

"His purpose eludes me. I cannot imagine why Ormachon would wish to confuse you so," Crea said.

"There must have been a reason," Blodwyn said quietly, furrowing her brow. "If you are so certain that it was Ormachon who gave your position away, then he must have had a reason. This would not be the first time we did not understand the motives of the great trees," she continued, seeking to turn the mood of the group away from such depressing analyses.

"Never have I heard or read of one sacrificing a Chosen in such a way," Harton said.

"You omit one thing, my friends," Carlisle said, and the others all turned their attention to their comrade. "The boy is here!"

"Good point," Connor said.

"A crucial point!" Dashiel echoed with emphasis.

Carlisle smiled and said, "How did you escape from the Dark Lord's lieutenant? If Ormachon intended you to be captured, do you not think that you would be in Sedahar this very moment?" Carlisle continued. "What miracle saved you from Colton?"

"I collapsed and I have no memory of how we evaded the storm that descended upon us. I only just awoke when you summoned me," Tomas replied.

"So, you did not resist the onslaught?" Carlisle asked, and Tomas shook his head in agreement.

"I was unable to. I do not know how I ended up where I awoke. I assume that my friends saved me and carried me inside this shelter."

"It is no coincidence you took refuge in the very same cavern that we chose to convene this gathering in?" Blodwyn asked, sweeping her staff around in a broad circle. "I do not believe in chance. There is a greater plan at work here."

"Could Ormachon have known? It is possible that he sent this evil one after you so that you would leave your path and seek the shelter of this mountain?" Harton asked, stunned by the thought.

"He could have spoken to me. He could have told me," Tomas said quietly. "When last I was with him, there were things that he withheld from me; information, thoughts. I felt as if he was pushing me away, and I could not understand it then."

"I felt the same thing the last time I was with Wayfair, as kind and good as he is," Crea said, recalling the rejection vividly.

"As did I!" Edmond echoed.

"The trees are keeping things to themselves, it seems. I too have felt the distance recently," Liam said.

"The world is unstable. They are dying! Are they seeking to preserve themselves in ways that they have not attempted before?" Connor asked.

"Or are they seeking to protect us from the pain that they are suffering?" Tobias asked.

"Perhaps. Their reach has been truncated of late. We all know that. They cannot simply pass on everything that they would like to as easily as they could have previously. We do not know just how hampered they are," Harton said.

"It is possible that Ormachon had no other option but to frighten you into this shelter," Crea said.

"Why did he not tell me when I was in his presence only a short while before?" Tomas asked, unsatisfied with the possible explanations that had just been given.

"I am convinced that they have a plan!" Blodwyn repeated. "If Ormachon wanted you dead or captured, you would be dead or captured now! You would not have found refuge and you would not be here telling us this."

"She is correct, of course," Tobias said knowingly.

"By revealing your position to the enemy he could have confused them as well," Pithar speculated.

"What do you have in mind?" Blodwyn asked, and they all turned their attention to the Chosen of Marathar.

"Were you attacked? Did the enemy in fact seek you out?" Pithar asked.

"Yes, I felt the approach and I saw the skies darken. The smell upon the wind was unmistakable."

"They took the advice of a Lalas and sought you out based upon what Ormachon told them?" Pithar asked.

"Yes, most certainly," the boy replied.

"Does that not strike you all as strange?" Pithar asked the group. "Why would one of Colton's Possessed ever heed the words of a Lalas unless they were words of warning concerning their own welfare?"

"It strikes *me* as strange," Blodwyn said emphatically.

"I did not have a chance to even think about this," Tomas said. "I only just regained my senses. The last thing I remember is the horrid, sickening feeling that engulfed me after I realized that the enemy was informed of my whereabouts."

"And yet, though you fell to the ground senseless, you were not overcome? You ultimately escaped and found your way here?" Pithar continued.

"Yes, all that is true," Tomas said. The terrible feeling of loss and abandonment that had not left him since that fateful moment was slowly abating somewhat. "You think that Ormachon gave my position away for a reason other than that he has forsaken me?" the boy asked with his green eyes wide and pleading.

"Yes, I truly do. There is no other explanation for why you survived, and for why you are here with us now," Pithar said.

"Do you think that Ormachon knows of this meeting?" Harton asked abruptly.

"If he does, than they all do!" Crea responded chillingly.

"I doubt that the trees know we are here. They would not have needed to resort to such deception in that case. They could have simply advised each of us that we needed to find Tomas and bring him here," Connor said.

"Well then, we are facing one of two choices," Blodwyn summarized. "Either the betrayal was real and Tomas escaped regardless of his Lalas' desire to see him captured."

Tomas visibly paled at that comment, and Liam went to his side to offer him support and comfort.

"Or," Blodwyn continued, either unaware of the boy's discomfort, or simply unmoved by it. "this was planned, and he sought to drive the boy into the mountain for some other purpose."

"What other purpose than meeting us could the Lalas have had in mind?" Dashiel asked.

"Why did we choose this place to gather?" Crea asked, and the others looked at him immediately as if he said something terribly important.

"We chose this cavern because it is a place that is sheltered and protected from the outside," Harton said.

"Exactly! Is it not sheltered from both the trees as well as from Colton?" Crea inquired.

"I believe we have our answer!" Blodwyn said emphatically. "Ormachon knew that he could direct Tomas here and that he would be safe within the caves. At the same time, by accurately revealing the boy's whereabouts to the enemy he has garnered their trust, so to speak. He must have needed to do that for some reason."

"Colton must be elated thinking that the trees are starting to break ranks and offer him assistance. In his arrogance, he probably blames the woman he sent after you for not capturing the boy, and he has not even suspected the greater plan," Liam said.

"You are so certain that there is one?" Pithar asked.

"I will hope and pray to the First that there is," Liam responded.

"When has there not been?" Connor asked. The others nodded in agreement, though Pithar's expression remained stoic.

Tomas listened intently to all that was being said around him, and he felt much calmer and much more at ease as the speculations of the Chosen unfolded. What they were saying made perfect sense to him, and though he was still hurt by Ormachon's secrecy and deception, he no longer suffered from the terrible pain that his initial suspicions had caused him. He remained silent while the others continued to analyze the situation.

"What must we make of that ominous passage in the Tomes that refers to the 'Chosen?'" Dashiel asked.

"'The Chosen shall die in the darkness alone, bereft and far away from home,'" Blodwyn recited.

"Yes, that one," Dashiel confirmed.

"It seems that one or all of us must perish," Harton replied.

"Must?" Tobias asked.

"Will. Must. Shall--it is all the same in the end," Harton said.

"Perhaps not," Crea said, looking quite serious. The others turned toward him now and waited for him to elaborate. He recited:

> *"Who shall choose, and who shall be Chosen?*
> *The fabric weaves, the fabric is woven.*
> *The First to come, the last to go,*
> *The rivers run from the melting snow.*
> *And all of those who deem to know*
> *What purpose belies this unwholesome show*
> *Are surely wrong,*
> *They need not guess.*
> *Who is so noble to pass this test?*
> *Who will bond with the very best?*
> *Who will breathe a dying breath?*
> *Who will remain after all the rest?*
> *Who, my friends? Who?*
> *Can you guess?"'*

No one spoke for a few moments, as they contemplated the words.

"Why do you think this section sheds any more light upon the previous one?" Dashiel asked.

"I am not sure. It seems though that the Tomes are trying to tell us that the answer we are seeking is far removed from what we might expect. I am accustomed to riddles, but the tone of these words is quite different from what I am used to hearing in the great books, as if the writers were toying with the reader," Crea replied.

"Will there be a new one Chosen? Do you think then that it is neither really one of us nor all of us after all?" Connor asked.

"I suspect that we shall not be able to figure the riddle out yet no matter how hard we may contemplate. Nevertheless, there is enough doubt for us to believe that the outcome anticipated is by no means certain," Crea summarized.

"The Tomes write about what will be, not what has been. Of course they are uncertain," Pithar said.

"However we wish to interpret the many passages referring to the Chosen, we can be sure of some things at the least. We can be sure that the Chosen will play a significant part in whatever develops. Thus, either one of us, all of us or someone not yet bonded will be a material component in what will be," Liam said.

"There is a new tree in Pardatha," Tomas suddenly said.

"The boy makes an interesting point," Carlisle replied. "Soon, presumably, it will choose."

"We must watch carefully how this unfolds," Blodwyn said. "I propose that we organize ourselves in that regard."

"A very good idea, Blodwyn," Harton said. "Why should we not act in concert when we recognize situations that merit our attention?"

"Shall we vote on this, or is a simple 'Aye' sufficient?" Connor asked.

"A voice vote is fine with me," Liam said.

"And with me as well," Crea echoed.

"Harton? Would you be so kind as to systematize our approach to this observation? You have the most experience at statesmanship and delegation amongst us all," Edmond asked.

"It would be my pleasure," Harton replied, flattered. "That is, if everyone agrees?"

All of the others agreed that a formal vote was not necessary, and they quickly and without hesitation sounded their unanimous approval.

"We must have a more efficient means of communicating with one another in the future. The method of summoning this time was much too cumbersome," Blodwyn said.

"Yes, and we must keep in contact more often," Connor emphasized.

"We can no longer leave it up to the trees to inform us," Dashiel said sadly.

"The balance has shifted. We must face that reality," Crea said reluctantly.

"The trees are fighting a battle of their own," Liam said. "There will be much in the days to come that we will not understand, I fear. We can support one another during these dark times, as we did today."

"I am grateful for all of your words," Tomas said humbly to the group. "I would have been unable to see my way clearly through this alone."

"This meeting was a success if only for that reason We must make certain we can always assist each other when crises arise."

"No longer can we afford to allow our communication to be governed so tightly by the trees," Tobias said. "Sadly, they are withdrawing more and more, as we have all become aware. It is time now for the Chosen to act."

"He is right! We all know it. We must continue to meet and to converse. The battle that the Lalas are fighting may not be one that we can participate in now," Blodwyn said.

"They must exclude us from some of what they are going through. I cannot imagine how difficult it must be for the trees to suffer the continued losses of their own. We can only begin to feel what they must feel. If they require distance, we must give them that distance," Dashiel said.

"It is so hard to do, nevertheless," Edmond said. "I care not if I die anymore. I just want to die with hope in my heart."

"We have reason to hope now. We have done something unprecedented, which has generated much anxiety and trepidation. But it was necessary. We have forged a new union, the need for which the times have thrust upon us. May the First forgive us if we are mislead by the signs all around us. Of this we are certain; our hearts are pure," Crea said.

"The trees conceal from us what they must. We conceal from them what we must," Tobias said cheerlessly.

"If we work in concert, perhaps we can serve the people better than we did before this gathering," Blodwyn said.

"The people and the heir," Crea exclaimed.

"And Tomas here, too," Liam said, laying his arm tenderly on the boy's shoulder and reminding all of them that he was as crucial to the future as was his brother.

"We shall help you whenever and however we can," Blodwyn said to Tomas. "But, we must be careful not to reveal too much, even to one another. Secrecy is your best protection. The more knowledge you disclose about your whereabouts or your destinations, the more you increase the chances of that knowledge falling upon the wrong ears. Traitors are rampant upon the land in these times."

"Your friends are strong and loyal. They will assist you on your travels too," Edmond said.

"The dark clouds are amassing everywhere. Colton is thwarted in one city and he then attacks another. The disbelievers grow in number as the Lalas' influence wanes. We must do whatever we are able to. It is our duty," Liam stated. "Today, we have trod upon a new path. Need has beckoned to us. Know that we will be with you wherever the weave takes you."

"Our method of communication with each other must be secure and it must be foolproof. We cannot depend upon the trees to spread the news as easily as they did in the past. Besides, we have a different agenda now," Harton said.

"How shall we contact one another in the future? We all agree that the means we utilized this time are not ideal," Dashiel agreed.

"Has anyone something better in mind?" Crea asked. "Secrecy is essential. We have few choices if we wish to conceal our contact with each other from both the trees and from the Dark Lord."

"If we cannot keep this cooperation secret, than its efficacy will be impaired," Connor said.

"I know of no way other than the method we used. It seems that everything else we might avail ourselves of requires a Lalas or a relic or vestige thereof," Liam said.

"Neither do I. I have never needed to contemplate a means that would bypass the awareness of my bond-mate. And now that I do, I am at a loss. I thought this day would never come," Pithar said regretfully.

"None of us anticipated such a need. It is time though that we attempt to function independent of the trees. They must know this even as we do it," Crea said.

"Do you think, Crea?" Tobias asked. "Do you really think that they would understand?"

"I would hope that in their beneficence they would recognize what we are trying to do. They cannot stop the losses. The trees still die. Should we all just die with them?"

"Was that not something that we all accepted when we embraced the bond?" Harton asked.

"Yes, but not at the expense of the world. Did you anticipate then that Colton could bring the trees to their knees?" Dashiel asked.

"Is that what has happened?" Pithar asked, exasperated. "The Lalas are dying out of fear? Marathar is not afraid of the Dark Lord," he said adamantly. "If he chooses to die, it will be for reasons other than cowardice and defeat."

"I meant no disrespect, Pithar. We all feel the same way. But the trees are dying! That is a fact. We must do what we can to help those who remain. If we can assist the heir in finding the Gem perhaps this tragic episode will come to an end," Dashiel replied.

"And in order to assist the boy, we must be able to communicate," Blodwyn said. "We have come full circle once more, and we are no closer to a solution than when we began. How can we comport with one another if all out methods are linked to the trees?"

"Does no one here have any ideas?" Crea implored them.

"I do!" Tomas said excitedly, and he stepped forward as he spoke. Before anyone even asked him to reveal it, he pulled the ring out from beneath his tunic and held it before them all to gaze upon. "There is no question that we can communicate through this," he said.

The silver ring hung from the original piece of rawhide that he had stung it through the day that he retrieved if from the sapling beside the charred remains of his Aunt and Uncle's house in the woods of Pardeau. It seemed for a moment as if a hundred tiels had passed since that fateful moment when Cairn of Thermaye wandered into the glen and so fortuitously stumbled upon him. That was the very first day the darkness touched his soul so thoroughly. The images of his friends passed quickly across his mind's eye, and he was comforted by those memories as much as he was repulsed by the others.

"This is the twin to my brother's golden ring, though as with he and I, they differ in some minor ways," he said.

"Minor?" Harton asked. "His is gold and yours is silver."

"The color is not significant," Liam scoffed. "It is the power that ties them together."

"I said it was the twin. They are not the same, nor do they serve the same purpose. They are similar," Tomas explained.

"Do you know what purpose they do serve?" Blodwyn asked seriously.

"No," Tomas replied without hesitation. "But, I am learning. I know that it will provide us with a means of communication. It reacts to my thoughts sometimes as if it was alive," he said in a dream-like voice. "When I speak of it, I speak with certainty."

Tomas bent down and laid the ring on the stone floor before his feet. Immediately, a high pitched sound flooded their minds, though it was soft and tender and not harsh or unappealing in any way.

"Come," the boy beckoned. "Gather around," he extended his arms and grasped Liam's hand with his left and Blodwyn's with his right.

Without hesitation, the others stepped forward and formed a tight circle around the pulsating ring. The sound reached deep inside the mind of each of the Chosen standing there. It seemed to emanate from within rather than without, and it felt so natural and so soothing. Though it was rather shrill at first, it very quickly found the level of thought, the pulse of each individual's life, and it harmonized with it so completely and so totally that it soon felt as if it belonged to each and every participant from the onset. Smiles crossed everyone's faces unbidden, and they all swayed in harmony with the inner vibrations.

The ring itself began to spin, and as it accelerated in speed, an audible music began to flood the chamber, though subtly different from the previous pitch. They each felt a deep yearning and a brief sadness. Those emotions quickly transmuted into an inexplicable joy and lightness of spirit as the beautiful chords and notes struck their minds. The sensation was not dissimilar, though still distinct, from that which each Chosen experienced when in close proximity to a Lalas. The noise from within did not cease as that from without grew in volume. Rather, the two rose to meet one another within the minds of the Chosen. As this union of essences was consummated, a new level was attained, one which combined the individuality of each participant with that of the ring and with the souls of one another. Briefly, they all floated in a sea of bliss, far removed from the troubles of the world.

Tomas was the first to speak. All of the others still seemed quite mesmerized by the interaction which had just taken place.

"I must return to my friends," he said softly. "They are worried about me." He thought for a moment and then said as if he knew this all along, "You need only invoke the memory of the ring and the Chosen you wish to contact in your mind's eye and the link will be enacted."

"And we must each return to our lives as well," Blodwyn spoke for the group, as she raised herself out of the ecstatic stupor into which she had fallen. "It will be difficult enough to conceal our movements from the trees. The longer we are apart from them, the more likely they will question us."

Soon, the entire chamber was once more filled with individuals, separated by their own unique consciousness, and no longer united in the manner that they were only moments before.

"And if they do?" Pithar asked, now fully cognizant.

"We will answer in the best ways that we are able to. We cannot lie, but we need not say more than is necessary. Our silence can reveal as little or as much as we choose it to," Connor said.

"Remember! We do this out of necessity. There is no trickery here. There is no ill intent. We have begun to weave a new pattern into the fabric, and we shall not be able to see its shape or contour for quite some time. But the threads have been set and there is no way any longer to sever them without destroying the cloth within which they are imbedded," Tobias said.

"May the First guide us and keep us all," Blodwyn said, as everyone nodded in agreement.

Slowly and reluctantly, they let go of each other's hands, but the bond that they created that day would never be released. Though the Chosen had always had much in common, until that fateful day it had been the Lalas themselves who maintained the links. They all knew that much had changed with this gathering, and regardless of the reluctance and concern they all initially felt, the world was not the same as it had been even a scant month ago. The fear of being abandoned by the trees was still paramount in each one's mind, but the structure of support that they solidified here felt right, and it consoled each and every one of them in this, their time of need.

Tomas was much relieved by the realization that he had come to by virtue of this gathering. Though sleep had mercifully spared him from constant restlessness and despair since the moment of the 'betrayal', the debilitating feelings had now abated, and hope once again replaced fear. Even Harton the skeptic, was comforted now and thankful that he had attended this unusual convocation.

Blodwyn stepped forward with her staff once more held high in front of her. She traced its tip along the faded and barely visible outline of a doorway in the rock wall. A slight hissing sound could be heard by them all, and then a bright, blue light flickered and flitted across the hard, solid surface. Shortly, the edges of the former opening began to emerge more clearly until a well defined exit was visible. She hesitated for a moment and then looked back at the group that had assembled anxiously behind her.

"Are you ready?" she asked. Each of the Chosen nodded in agreement. "Let us go forth then," she said, as the doorway swung open before them.

Chapter Twelve

Frightened faces could be seen everywhere, peeking timidly and cautiously through the notches of the high walls surrounding Talamar. They were meticulously careful not to expose themselves to the assemblage below. They scurried and squirmed, dashing from one crenellation in the stone to the next like rats in a cage, gaping at what they perceived to be the enemy at their gates. The Knights of Avalain sat motionless astride their enormous war horses with their weapons sheathed, though that did not detract from the formidable impression that they made upon the inhabitants of the city.

Parsifal remained silent and stern as he led his steed slowly up and down the ranks, never allowing his gaze to falter, never relaxing his focus upon the center of the balustrade above the great gates. He watched as the soldiers upon the blocks ran back and forth in a disorganized and undisciplined manner, peering out between the great stones carefully and fretfully at the columns below. He made no overture to those above. He sent no words of greeting; no messages and no supplications. The presence of the Knights alone was enough to engender a response from within the darkened city.

When he had first approached the outskirts of Talamar, the change in the appearance of the area struck him profoundly. The roadways were scabrous and in disrepair. The walls of this trading city, formerly impressive and well maintained, had been marred by letters and symbols scrawled across them, blatantly proclaiming the inhabitants' new allegiances in graphic and disrespectful ways. The gates were closed and sealed, and the polong trees that had always ringed the city walls in precise geometric formations one hundred meters deep, were charred and hewn, and their precious oil was clearly no longer being harvested. What had been Talamar's pride and joy, as well as a continuous and renewable source of income, was now a graveyard of ruin. As far as the eye could see, the land surrounding the city had been reduced to a lifeless, sickly tangle of decimated and abandoned debris, intermingled with felled trunks and scorched branches. But, this ruination paled beside the horror of the rows of human carcasses hanging like slaughtered farm animals within meters of the city walls.

Parsifal reunited with his men after riding practically nonstop from county Pardeau all the way to Talamar. He left Queen Esta in good hands and he was confident that her companions would protect her in his absence. As he neared the gates of the city, he saw his noble troops assembled before them. They sat tall in their saddles with their armor gleaming in the sun and the white flag of truce hanging limply in the still air before them. They did not break formation in order to welcome him. They simply accepted him back as if he had never been gone, but the joy in their hearts upon seeing him before them once again was recognizable upon all of their faces.

He took charge immediately, regretting instantly upon his arrival the constraints he had placed upon his men in the days prior. In the absence of their leader, and much to their disgust and chagrin, they were forced to allow the stakes upon which the rotting corpses were suspended all around the city walls to remain standing. They would not interfere with the affairs of Talamar no matter how painstaking that restraint might prove to be until Parsifal had arrived, as they were so instructed. Now, stone faced and rigid with shrouds tied tightly around their faces, they methodically toppled each of the wooden poles, withdrew the shafts that pierced what remained of the barely recognizable decaying bodies, and buried each of the men, women and children in separate graves besides the walls in full view of the soldiers above. As they did so, the remains of what was supposed to have been living trees piercing the bodies of the citizens of Talamar fell away completely. It was no more than subterfuge, a clever bit of macabre trickery, and it must have been obvious to the people above for quite some time now that the cause of their deaths was from a source other than they had been led to believe. The abiding semblance of bark and branch crumbled to dust at the Knight's touch, revealing roughly cut spears and shafts beneath the artificial surfaces; weapons clearly produced by the hand's of man, not the Lalas.

What Queen Esta and Marne had suspected from the onset had in fact proven to be true. The Evil One's mark was upon this deception, and his lies were the foundation of its birth. Sadly though, even after they knew the truth, the cowardly people of Talamar allowed this detestable evidence of treachery and treason to remain before their very eyes, unhampered by any efforts on their part to mollify their wrongs by providing an honorable burial for the innocent victims. Parsifal vividly recalled the arrival of Sir Etan at Castle Avalain, and his horrific retelling of the Lady Margot's account of the betrayal at Talamar and the great 'crime' of the Lalas against mankind. He spat upon the ground in disdain, as he replayed the troubled visitor's words in his mind.

I was certain that the Lalas would never behave in such a way, he thought to himself. *How is it that these people accepted such a version for so long? Can they not clearly see that what they were told is untrue? Did they never question what she said to them? What manner of people are these?* he wondered, looking up at the frightened faces above. *The Dark Lord's servant has turned them all into ignominious cowards, and she has stripped them of their consciences. I grieve for them all. May the First forgive them,* he thought.

The Knights' activity went unchallenged by the gaping figures above, though the contempt of the noble soldiers below was so mighty that it was almost tangible. They performed their duty methodically, yet with an abiding tenderness for the innocent victims of this horrendous charade. As the sun set upon the first day of their muster, no one had yet appeared to address them and officially acknowledge their presence. Nevertheless, upon the completion of their sorrowful task, they resumed their vigil before the walls. Darkness did not deter the Knights, and they stalwartly maintained their position straight through the evening and on into the new dawn.

With the morning sun, a more frenetic level of activity could be seen on the walls above. Soldiers had replaced the citizens who had been standing there, and rather than scurrying from one vantage point to the next, they appeared to have taken up more permanent positions. Parsifal remained as still as a statue, standing before his men upon his horse, and it was clear that he and the Knights had no intention of relinquishing their position any time soon. They made no gestures to the troops atop the walls. They made no overtures and no appeals. They were prepared to stand there forever, it seemed to those within the tarnished and beleaguered city. By mid morning, a crier appeared on the balustrade with a parchment in his hands. He stepped forward cautiously as the soldier by his side raised a horn and blew one sharp note. Lifting the scroll before him, he began to read in a surprisingly meek voice.

"It is with great regret that his Lordship, Duke Kettin of Talamar, cannot address you personally. He is bedridden and has not the strength to rise. He has instructed me to greet you and to apologize for not doing so sooner. He was unsure of your motives in approaching the city in such a manner, and he wished to assess them by observing your actions before he conversed, however indirectly. He asks that you state your purpose in coming here under arms. Furthermore, he asks that you advise him as to who sent you, and under whose auspices you march upon his city."

Parsifal listened carefully to the words of the crier, unmoving and silent. When the envoy was finished speaking he stepped forward slowly, removed his helm from his head and secured it upon his saddle. After removing his silver gauntlets and carefully tying them to his belt, he then dismounted, ceremoniously dropped his steed's reins, and then slowly stepped forward a few paces. His presence on foot was no less impressive than it was when he sat high in his saddle, though without his helm his imposing features were even more striking. Parsifal exuded honor and virtue, whether he spoke from the back of a lowly mule or that of a majestic stallion. Slowly and with determination, he raised his noble head so that the sparkling blue of his eyes was staring directly into the beady black hollows of the Duke's messenger.

"I am disappointed the Kettin is unable to participate directly in this exchange," he said, his deep, melodious voice sincere in tone. He was markedly unwilling to bestow a title upon the absent leader of Talamar. "What I have to say should be said directly to the one responsible for the welfare of this city."

He waited another moment before he continued.

"Talamar is not the place that I remember it to be," he said, sweeping his arm in a broad gesture before him. "Much has changed since last I was here as a guest of the Duke and Duchess, and it is for that reason we are here now. Her highness, Esta, protectress of the Knights and Queen of the Kingdom of Avalain has charged us with the task of persuading the citizens of Talamar to return to the fold and forsake the path that they have recently chosen or been compelled to walk upon."

Once again, he paused and permitted his words to sink in to the minds of all of those who listened. His presence alone engendered hope, and his powerful voice and forthright manner began to elevate the spirits of these despondent people, many of whom had almost given up before the Knights' arrival.

"You have all been the victims of deception and evil purpose, though it is clear to me that the ruse that seduced you initially had been exposed long before our arrival at your gates," he said, making it obvious that he was nevertheless disturbed by the fact that they tolerated that abomination for so long. "What is done is done! Actions committed are etched in the fabric and cannot be unwoven and sewn again differently," Parsifal said solemnly. "But the Lalas are great and magnanimous, and forgiveness is theirs to bestow. If it be fear that held you back from your righteous course, you have no reason to fear any longer. If it be cowardice, then you can choose whom you would rather contend with; the Knights of Avalain here and now or the Dark Lord's envoy when she returns. There is a battle to be fought and you all have another chance to choose what side you wish to be on when it is waged. If your hearts cannot lead you in the correct direction then perhaps your fate lies with Colton dar Agonthea and not with the trees after all. But you will have to contend with us first!" he said and he turned his back upon the gaping throngs.

Slowly, he walked back to his horse and with one easy motion, he hoisted himself upon its back. "The Knights of Avalain take their responsibilities seriously," he said, and he walked his mount as close to the walls as he could while still being seen by those above, and no one would ever have doubted his sincerity. "But, you must choose freely. What shall it be?" he asked, looking up at the crowds above.

During the entire time Parsifal was speaking, the people of Talamar slowly began to mass upon the walls. The crowd had been steadily growing, and by this time, there was barely an inch of space inside of which another body could squeeze. They poked their heads through the gaps in the wall, pushed their way to the edges of the balustrade and climbed atop the thick stone in order to be able to see and hear more clearly. In a steadily growing frenzy, the formerly cowed and frightened subjects jockeyed and squirmed, and desperately fought their way to the front of the lines as if their salvation awaited them below. Every now and then, in their ardor to be able to see the famed and illustrious Knights and amidst all the pushing and shoving, someone would fall headlong from the wall to the soft grass below and find themselves unable to re-enter the city. Yet, they righted themselves and remained attentive nonetheless.

The city guards were trying hopelessly to keep the people back, but the flood of citizenry was too overwhelming for them to stop unless they wished to resort to physical restraint. In the absence of Lady Margot, and with the Duke ostensibly bedridden and unable or unwilling to provide leadership, the army gave way to the thrashing and pummeling of the crowd. They retreated to the background and let the mob rule the day.

The arrival of the Knights of Avalain opened a floodgate of passion within the hearts of the people of this besieged city. Strangled by fear and the threat of death, many reluctantly swore allegiance to Lady Margot in the weeks past. Everything had deteriorated so rapidly after the arrival of the Dark Lord's first emissary, followed so soon thereafter by the death of the Duke and Duchess. Kettin was never the people's choice, and when the strong and stunning Lady Margot assumed control during his time of weakness and mourning, the citizenry welcomed her. Talamarans always preferred having their choices made for them, rather than making choices of their own. They were negotiators and compromisers; primarily traders and bargainers by nature. Margot knew this of them and she reorganized the city immediately, offering them just enough to entice them. She ruled with confidence and surety, as well as with a cruelty that they understood and respected, and the people feared her immediately but they admired her as well. In fact, there were those who still did admire her, but their allegiances were all too easily bought and sold.

When suddenly they awoke to find trees sprouted before the walls, with their friends and relatives of all ages and sexes impaled upon them, they were aghast. They accepted her explanation without question or thought, and rallied quickly to her side. Fear and self interest drove them, and though it could never truly rule their hearts, it obscured their memories and weakened their already limited and now exhausted resolve. Everyone knew that the Lalas were dying, and many truly believed that in their death throes they were losing their compassion for the citizens of Talamar; a compassion that many never candidly felt they deserved to begin with.

By the time the truth began to surface, most of the inhabitants had already committed themselves fully and completely, and there seemed to be no turning back. Margot surrounded herself with enormous Ogres and horrid smelling, evil trolls who violently and mercilessly dealt with any who thought to resist her authority, though few did even from the onset. They were not a courageous people to begin with. They turned upon one another in order to garner favor, and they readily gave up their neighbors in order to save themselves; a sad and an ignoble lot. Under these trying circumstances and the lack of internal leadership, all thoughts of opposition faded as quickly as they arose in even those few with the strongest of characters.

Two weeks ago, early one grey morning, Lady Margot rushed out of the gates on her jet black steed with her minions in tow, leaving only Kettin and the Talamaran soldiers she had trained in charge. She left in such haste, trampling anyone or anything that happened to be in her and her troops pathway, that all believed something truly alarming was transpiring in the world beyond the gates of the city, yet they felt relief nonetheless. It was the first time in a long time that the city was free of its recent leadership. The oppressive feelings of anxiety and dread that hung over them every moment of every day that she ruled Talamar were exhausting. In addition, the fear that grasped them with its sharply clawed hand was wearing away at them slowly but surely. In her brief absence, it felt to many as if the sun had risen after weeks of darkness and gloom.

Out of sight, out of mind! The people of Talamar had short memories and even shorter measures of loyalty. The Knights of Avalain with their confidence and impressive appearance, represented an alternative to the depression and joylessness that Margot brought with her. And they offered protection! They were strong and magnificent, and fearless and righteous; a combination of all of the qualities that so few Talamarans embodied themselves. Parsifal offered them a chance, a ray of light, and it began to appear as the better alternative to what they had recently been living with. Weak people make weak decisions. Whether they choose good or evil, their motives determine their worth. Greed and self interest often obscure the honorable path, and these were the emotions and concerns that precipitated the decisions that the people of Talamar made.

The soldiers could do nothing to prevent the people from storming the closed and sealed gates. In fact, many of the armed men themselves sought anonymity in the crowd of desperate citizens, until total chaos prevailed within the square inside the city walls. Screaming and crying could be heard everywhere, as children lost sight of their parents, husbands were separated from their wives, and families and alliances of all kinds were ripped asunder in the desperate frenzy that ensued as so many tried to escape from what had been a virtual prison for weeks now.

High up in the tower chamber of the castle, Kettin stood at the leaded window and carefully scrutinized the scene in the street below. He ignored the persistent banging on the door and the shouting, and he repeatedly pressed his hands to his ears in an effort to block out the unremitting sound. He could see the Knights assembled beyond the walls, and at first he thought that the people were gathering in order to attack the columns of soldiers who had arrived at his doorstep the previous day. But as he watched, he soon realized that they were seeking only to flee the city, not to defend it.

"Where are you, Margot? How could you leave me here like this? What am I to do without you?" he beseeched the stone walls that surrounded him. "My people are abandoning me! You told me you would protect me!"

He watched helplessly as the guards who stood before the gates in their new white and green tunics with the trees emblazoned across their chests, were throttled and pummeled and pushed out of the way by the mob. He observed as their ranks collapsed and they gave way to the frantic population. He saw the surge of the masses as they rushed to escape the confines of he city. Kettin gasped as the heavy wooden bars, reinforced by the iron that encircled them, were lifted by the unruly crowd and tossed to the side like a child's play-sticks. He pulled the curtain halfway over his face and left only his eyes exposed, as the enormous gates of Talamar were flung open wide and the throngs of people virtually collapsed upon one another in their rush to flee. From his vantage point, he could see the Knights step casually to the side and form two lines perpendicular to the walls, between which the crowds stumbled and scurried and fought their way out of the city.

"What do you want?" he finally yelled to whomever was buffeting his door. "Leave me alone! I do not wish to be disturbed!" he cried, panic stricken.

Through the thick wood, he could hear someone shouting.

"My Lord?" Fobush yelled. "You must let me in! I have to speak with you!" his councilor insisted. "Time is running out!"

"What is it you need from me? I am not well. I need to rest," Kettin pleaded.

"Open the door. There is nothing wrong with your health. It is your soul that is sick. This door cannot protect you any longer!" he replied angrily. "The witch is not here to stop me now!"

"I am sick! I am weak! I am not hiding. Cannot someone else help you? What can I do?" he cried.

"Be a man for once!" Fobush shouted furiously. "Face the situation that you are responsible for creating! If you do not open this door, I will bash it down myself if I must."

Kettin heard a loud banging on the door, much more violent than before. He could see the hinges bulging and the dust flying all over the chamber as the thrashing increased. Slowly, he moved away from the window and sat down in the corner farthest from the doorway. He drew his knees into his chest and grasped them with his arms. Finally, he bent his head, buried it in the flesh of his forearms and began to sob uncontrollably. Through partially concealed eyes swollen with tears, he saw the wood give way, and filled with dread, he watched as it shattered and splintered into a thousand pieces and fell all over the thickly carpeted floor.

"Get up from the ground, Kettin!" Fobush said in disgust as he moved toward the cringing Duke. "The time of reckoning is upon us!"

Chapter Thirteen

"Ouch!" Tamara exclaimed as she hit the surface with a dull thud. She blinked her eyes over and over again in an attempt to determine if there was any light down here at all. Sitting up, she rubbed her legs with her hands to try and bring the circulation back. Apparently her fall did more damage than the pain indicated, for she could barely feel her own ankles they were so numb.

Propping herself up with one hand, she leaned heavily onto the floor of the pit. It was covered in a spongy, moss-like substance that was not offensive at all to the touch. As she grew more accustomed to the space, she thought she could see some sort of illumination in the chamber, though it was certainly dim. It did not emanate from any one direction but seemed to come from everywhere at once, as if the substance upon which she sat was itself iridescent. Though she tried as hard as she could to look around her for a sign of Angeline, she could not see far enough into the distance to serve her purposes.

"Angeline?" she called cautiously. "Are you here? Can you hear me?"

Her words were greeted with silence.

Could she still be up there hanging onto the wall? she wondered. *Her fear of falling may be sustaining her,* Tamara supposed, but before she could even finish her thought she heard a scraping sound coming from above her head.

"Is that you, Angeline?" she called out in the semi-darkness.

"Thank the First you are alive!" she heard her friend say from somewhere above her. As she spoke, her voice became louder and clearer as she quickly scrambled down the wall. "I watched you disappear into the darkness and then I heard you hit the ground. I counted the seconds between those moments, and at least I knew you hadn't plummeted too far a distance. Are you hurt? What did you land on?" she asked, almost at the bottom now herself.

"I am not sure. But it is not rock. I am thankful though that I still have some extra padding on my bottom," she said, though her body was beginning to ache somewhat by this time.

"Can you stand? Is anything broken?"

"I do not think so," Tamara replied, scanning her body, searching for serious injuries. She stood slowly in the semi-darkness and stretched her limbs one by one. Though they were stiff, none were immobile, and her movements were not accompanied by any serious pain. "No. Nothing is broken. I was lucky."

"You certainly were!" Angeline said, and Tamara felt the comfort of her friend's hand on her shoulder. Her silhouette was vaguely outlined beside her in the dark. "Where are we, do you think?"

"I have no idea," Tamara replied honestly. "Are *you* okay?" she asked, remembering her friends close encounter with the enemy only moments ago.

"Yes, thanks to you!" she answered gratefully. "By the First, Tamara, I was scared! What a horrible feeling that was. I could not breathe at all. And the voice inside my head was just awful! It was laughing and beckoning to me dreadfully, coaxing me to relax and give in to it. You know, I almost did!" she said, shuddering at the memory. "It all happened so fast."

"I saw her face," Tamara said quietly.

"Whose?" Angeline asked.

"Lady Margot. The woman who attacked me when I first went to visit Liam and Oleander. We seem to be destined to confront one another," Tamara said thoughtfully.

"How did you do that before?" Angeline asked, referring to her rescue from the ghastly slime that had enveloped her.

"I really do not know. At least, I could not tell you in words," Tamara said. "But, I saw her face materialize before me as I worked. She was not happy!"

"Did you expect her to thank you? That was my job. Thank you, Tamara. Thank you so much!" she said sincerely.

"There is no need to do that, Angeline. You would have done the same for me, I have no doubt," Tamara said humbly.

"I would have certainly if I could. You speak as if what you did anyone could have done. Tamara? Do you realize what power you have?"

"Power?" she asked, surprised. "I merely did what I had to do."

"Well sister, would that we all could do it as deftly as you!"

"It was a natural response to the circumstances," she said.

"I am in your debt, sister," Angeline said humbly.

"And now you can repay that debt, sister," Tamara said smiling. "I am a bit stiff in the leg. Would you help me to straighten up?" she asked.

"Of course, sister," Angeline replied.

Angeline helped Tamara to stand, and she massaged her right ankle and calf vigorously.

"That helped," Tamara said, as she put her weight upon the

sore leg and pressed it into the soft surface. "Oh my!" Tamara exclaimed as her foot sunk about four or five inches into the ground. "This is quite unstable, is it not sister? I am glad that I did not sink even deeper." She pulled her foot out of the downy matter and shook it off. "What do you suppose we should do now?"

"I was hoping that you would have some ideas, sister," Angeline replied.

"Well, I imagine that it would do us no harm to look around. It seems safe enough down here. At least that awful woman did not follow us any further," Tamara replied, and then she looked suspiciously around herself.

"Are you thinking what I am thinking?" Angeline asked, as she inched closer to her friend.

"I believe so, sister. If she was afraid to follow us down here, maybe there was a reason."

"Maybe. I too was wondering that."

"Let us be careful then," Tamara said, taking her companion's arm in her own.

Together, they began to walk cautiously in the dim, iridescent light in the direction that they happened to be facing. The ground was littered with rocks of all sizes and shapes, and Tamara tripped upon one in the gloom.

"Ouch!" she cried. "That hurt. Careful where you walk."

When they reached the stone and mud of the wall, they followed it to their right and continued pacing out the perimeter of the chamber. Tamara stood closest to the wall and Angeline walked beside her. The stout sister allowed her fingers to gently graze the surface as they moved, and she tried to understand its composition by concentrating as hard as she could upon its feel and texture. It was moist and smooth, though their were indentations every so often that she hesitated at first to stick her hand into.

After walking almost one hundred paces Tamara stopped. Angeline could she that she was perplexed by something.

"What is it? What have you discovered?" Angeline asked.

"Walk back with me to where we started," was Tamara's reply. When they had retraced their steps, Tamara let go of her friend and knelt down. Placing one of her hands on the juncture between the wall and the floor, she proceeded to measure upward in hand lengths as she would a horse in the stables, until she reached the first indentation that she had felt previously. She then walked about five paces to the right and knelt down again. Once more she measured the height from the ground up until she reached the next hollow. Nodding her head as if she was reaching some understanding, she continued another five paces to the right and repeated the procedure again.

"These holes are not here by accident!" she exclaimed. "They are precisely the same distance apart from one another and the exact same height from the floor. Someone or something arranged them so," she proclaimed, satisfied with her analysis. "And none of the rocks, no matter how broad they are, stand higher than the holes. Could this be mere coincidence?"

"The holes certainly not. But the rocks? To what purpose, do you think, if not by chance?" Angeline asked. "They seem natural enough."

"I have no idea. But maybe if I reach inside one of these cavities I will get some answers about them at least," Tamara replied and swiftly stuck her hand into the one closest to them. She was surprised to find that it was actually quite deep and that her fingers barely felt anything. Her arm was not long enough to reach the hollow's end. "I cannot imagine what these are. They are so uniform in size and shape, but I cannot feel anything inside."

"Did you hear that?" Angeline said, startled by a hissing sound coming from above their heads.

"Yes, sister. Unfortunately I did," she replied, and she abruptly withdrew her arm from the wall. "We may have spoken too soon about Margot not following us down here."

"Is it she, do you sense?" Angeline asked, and she hastily drew her bow from her back and notched an arrow.

"It can be none other than she. I am certain. Come, quickly! We must find a place to hide!" Tamara said, grabbing Angeline's arm once again. "I do not know what more I can do to keep her away from us."

Tamara conjured a small orb of light, just enough to illuminate the area in front of it, but not strong enough to expose them to their enemy, though in the semi-darkness it was a risk nonetheless. They quickly ran to the wall of the pit and began to search for an opening large enough for them to conceal themselves inside of. But, all the indentations were of equal size and shape, as Tamara suspected they would be, and none were nearly wide enough for either of them to climb into. They continued to look regardless, as the whooshing sound grew louder and the air grew hotter and more humid by the moment. Margot, it appeared, was being more cautious this time, and she was descending into the bottom of the pit more slowly than during her previous attack.

"Have we put the fear of the First in her, do you think?" Angeline whispered hopefully.

"I doubt she fears anything other than Colton's retribution, sister. She wishes only not to be caught off guard again, I presume," Tamara replied. "Hush now. She approaches. Stay close to me," she said softly.

Tamara extinguished the light, and both women crouched down low against the wall and drew their capes over them in an effort to conceal their location. She felt the scroll pressing against her body and it seemed to throb in anticipation. In response, Tamara quietly slid it out of its case and placed it in the nearest hollow in the wall where her hand had just been only moments before.

Leaving the scroll down here might serve the same purpose as dropping it down the well in Odelot anyway. Who would ever find it in this pit?. At least if we are captured, Colton will gain only our lives.

In the darkness, even Angeline could not see her movements though she was right beside her. Tamara concealed the empty case in her robe once again, and then she backed away from the wall a pace or so. As the noise grew louder she thought she heard a very slight grating or scraping sound coming from somewhere behind her, but it was impossible to focus upon everything at once, and she needed to concentrate upon the descending enemy. She scanned the surfaces once again with her mind, but it was hard to find anything that responded to her touch.

What can these holes be for? she wondered, as her awareness continued to brush over them.

She probed the one nearest them as deeply as she could, but her examination yielded nothing, so she shifted her attention to what she hoped would be more productive. Tamara focused her thoughts upon her friend and herself, seeking only to conceal their position, but she really did not know what to do. Her experience was so limited, despite the fact that her power was strong. The only things that responded to her manipulations were the dust and debris that covered the soft surface, and they served only to make her want to sneeze as they rose from the ground in small swirls and zephyrs.

Suddenly an image of a woman whom she did not recognize appeared in her head, and an idea came to her almost simultaneous with the appearance of the vision. She manipulated the flurry of dust until it coagulated into a domed shaped, rock-like substance. Though it looked heavy, it was as light as the eddies of dust, and she willed it to settle down around them with its broadest side resting flat against the cavern wall. It was not perfect, but it served its purpose. They were now concealed from the enemy to some extent. Margot would see through the ruse eventually, but it would give them a little more time to think and plan.

Whose face was that I saw. She looked so sweet, but so full of anguish. Was it she who planted this idea for a shelter in my mind?

Tamara had not another moment to wonder, for as soon as the rock surface settled around them, so did the enemy. She could hear movement outside of the covering and both she and Angeline held their breaths so as not to make the slightest sound. The noises were muffled by the overlay, but sounds could still be heard nonetheless.

"Sweep the area!" Margot ordered. "They must be here somewhere. There is no place for them to go!"

The sisters could feel the surface pounding with the footsteps of those who accompanied Margot. It was no small number that had descended with her in order to find them.

"Whoever finds them will have the privilege of killing them!" they could hear her shout.

Tamara was tiring from the effort of maintaining the illusion that was protecting them. She knew that she could not keep them hidden forever. Fortunately, there were many rocks strewn all around and the one she had created looked no different than any of the others. The odds of them discovering this one were slim, and they had not even begun to suspect the deception yet. They would search the chamber from top to bottom first, and then maybe consider the other options. Nevertheless, they could not remain hidden here indefinitely, and the prospect of Margot giving up before she found them was not likely.

Angeline tapped Tamara softly on the shoulder and tried to get her attention without making her lose her concentration, but she was so preoccupied with her thoughts that she ignored her completely. After another attempt and another rebuff from Tamara, Angeline grew more persistent.

"Sister!" she whispered. "I have something to tell you. You must listen to me."

"Hush now, Angeline. It must wait. I cannot waver in my attention to what I am doing," she replied, and she continued her focus upon the shield and the enemy.

"It cannot wait," Angeline said, and with both hands she physically turned Tamara's head toward her.

Tamara gasped as she found herself gazing into the eyes of a being, the likes of which she had never seen before. It took all of her strength to not drop the ward completely and expose them all to the enemy. Behind the glowing, bulbous eyes of this odd looking creature was a tunnel that seemed to wind endlessly outward from the cavern.

In a high pitched though tender voice, the creature spoke, "Come! Quickly!" It beckoned for them to follow it, and it reached out one incredibly thin and almost opalescent arm to Angeline and another to Tamara. The tips of its exceedingly long, knobby fingers ended in round suction cups, and Tamara felt one adhere to her skin upon contact. "You have nothing to fear," it said in a sweet, convincing though very strange voice. "It is the others who should beware," it continued, though this time the tone of voice was totally different than just a moment before, and frighteningly malevolent. The creature was as tall as they were, though much, much thinner. Its clothing fit it so close to its pale skin, with the exception of a colorless, filament-like flapping cape, that it could have been wearing nothing at all, and even so, it was almost amorphous to their eyes.

In a bit less light, it would be practically invisible, Tamara thought.

As they shuffled their way to the opening in the wall, half bent over and half on their knees, Tamara remembered the scroll.

"I must go back for a moment!" she said, and she tried to pull her arm away from the visitor's grasp.

In her anxiousness to regain the parchment, she relinquished her focus and the rock surface that still concealed them began quickly to dissolve into dust once again.

"Oh!" she gasped as she realized their hiding place had rapidly crumbled around them. Before she had a chance to attempt anything more, the strange creature pulled her sharply into the gaping hole.

She struggled against it but it was extraordinarily strong, and the suction was impossible to break. Headlong, both she and Angeline were hauled through the space. As soon as they stepped off of the spongy surface and onto the stone floor of this newly exposed tunnel, the chimera that had hidden them in the cavern disappeared completely. Margot turned immediately toward them and caught Tamara's eye with her own vicious gaze a scant moment before the sister vanished into the darkness beyond. Instantly, Margot charged after them, maddened by the realization that she had been fooled once again. But, before she could take even three steps, dozens of round, shiny shafts shot out from the holes in the cavern walls at an amazingly high speed, the ends of which were sharpened to fine points and glistened menacingly. They extended from one side of the chamber all the way to the other, and instantly thrust themselves neatly into the holes on the opposite sides.

"Jump!" Margot yelled when she saw what was happening. Deftly, she leapt and grabbed a root sticking out of the wall above her head, thus saving herself from being savagely impaled on the end of one of these deadly beams. Her troops were not as quick as she was, nor were they as agile or as lucky. At least ten of the ponderous ogres were skewered like pigs on spits by the thrusting rods. The remaining seven escaped this initial attack only to find themselves trapped beneath the bars upon all fours as if they were behind a prison gate. They were crouched down awkwardly under this impenetrable maze of obstacles, and to add to their predicament, the spongy surface cover beneath their heavy feet was giving way rapidly around them, rising over their thick ankles and coating their legs as their great weight drew them deeper and deeper into it. They growled and grunted loudly and thrashed around, banging frenziedly on the obstructions above them.

Margot was furious. She screamed at her men to break the bars, but they could barely budge them no matter how hard they tried. She hurled yellow fire at the rods, but it only served to ignite the soft, pulpy matter beneath them. Rapidly, the fire began to spread, and it sent a caustic, green smoke upward toward the angry woman perched precariously above it. The ogres screamed in fear and pain as the fire gained in intensity all around them. In the limited space within which they were trapped, they could barely reach to their own feet in order to snuff out the mounting flames. The sounds that Tamara and Angeline heard from within the safety of their newly found shelter were monstrous and gruesome

Without another thought for her troops trapped below, Margot raised her free arm and began to ascend toward the surface above. Thwarted once again, she sought to abandon this failed gambit as quickly as she could, and well before the smoke engulfed her as well. The sounds of the ogres burning to death in their prison below did not bother her in the least. Her only concern was for her own escape and for the reaction this failure would engender in Colton, her unforgiving master. She had no grief for the dead and dying that she left behind in her haste to escape. She barely heard their ghastly cries as she rose out of the pit. Her thoughts were immediately consumed by an overwhelming dread at the prospect of facing the Dark Lord once more.

Tamara leaned close to Angeline's ear and whispered, "I left the scroll in one of those holes that the posts came out of."

"Oh my!" Angeline replied, and she covered her mouth with her hand. "Why did you do that? What are we to do now?"

"I thought it would be better if we were not captured with it in our possession. When this creature appeared, I had no time to retrieve it," she replied.

"Maybe it will burn up in the fire," Angeline said.

"Our instructions were to drop it in the well at the world's end," Tamara said.

"Do you think it will matter? It will be destroyed either way."

"I thought that before when I placed it there. It seemed the better alternative than to have it make its way back to Colton if it was discovered on me. But now I do not feel quite the same about it," Tamara replied.

The strange creature was leading them carefully down a dark passage. They were so relieved to have escaped Margot once again that they barely considered where they were going and who was leading them. He or she, they could not tell for certain, was not listening to their conversation and seemed to have little interest in anything other than getting to where it wanted to go.

"I must go back, Angeline," she said. "I cannot leave without knowing what has happened to the map. It was my responsibility."

"The place is in flames! Besides, the smoke itself would disable you before you even got there. I can smell it from here and my eyes are burning. Maybe you can go back later after the fires die out."

Tamara considered her options.

"Do you think it is safe to follow him?" Angeline asked.

"He saved us for certain," she replied. "Besides, I get a good feeling from him. Do you have a name?" Tamara said to their host. "Mine is Tamara, and this is Angeline," she said, pointing to the other sister. "We did not mean to trespass," she explained before it even had a chance to answer. "Where are you taking us?"

The creature turned its face toward Tamara, and its eyes were so deep in color and so lovely that a smile crossed her face unbidden.

"I am Etuah. I am taking you to our home," it replied softly.

"Are there others of you down here?" Tamara asked.

"Many."

"Do your people have a name?" she continued.

"We are the Drue."

"Drue? I have not heard of you. You are quite different from us in appearance," she said.

"As we expected."

"You knew we were coming?" Tamara responded, surprised.

"The moment you entered the hills, we followed you. Your charge is a crucial one. Our assistance was necessary."

Tamara and Angeline looked at each other in shock. The last thing that they expected to hear was that their fall into this horrid pit was anticipated by anyone. What if they had not survived the initial plunge? What if Margot had captured them before Etuah rescued them? So many things could have happened. Besides, Etuah knew why they were traveling in the first place. Who could possibly have given this creature that information?

"Are you friends of the trees?" Tamara asked boldly.

"Friends? Yes, in a manner of speaking we are friends. We maintain the hollows."

"The hollows?" Angeline asked. "What are the hollows?"

"The spaces that they have abandoned after the shards have been removed."

"Shards?" Tamara repeated. These words were unfamiliar to her, and she was becoming more and more confused by the moment. It also disturbed her that Etuah did not proclaim her allegiance to the Lalas when she had the opportunity. "You speak of things that I do not understand. But do you not revere the trees nonetheless?"

"Revere? Most certainly!" she replied as if the question itself need not even have been asked. "You have much to learn, sister. But first, we must reach our destination. We are almost there," it said sweetly.

"May I ask you one more question?" Tamara reluctantly found the courage to say.

"Certainly."

"I do not wish to offend you in any way. You have been so helpful to us. The First knows what would have happened to us had you not arrived when you did and had that chamber not been equipped as it was." She hesitated again.

"What is it you wish to know?"

"I am a female, if that is what you were wondering," she replied nonchalantly.

"How did you guess?" Tamara asked.

"Female intuition," she said, and they all laughed heartily.

It felt like a tiel has passed since they had smiled, let alone laughed out loud, and this moment served to break the ice between them all. Etuah's large mouth and thin lips opened nearly as wide as her entire face as she continued to chuckle, and her suction tipped fingers grasped the two sisters more tightly and tenderly than before. With her free hand, Tamara reached forward and squeezed Etuah's incredibly thin arm in response.

"Thank you, Etuah," she said earnestly as the Drue led them further into the depths of the mountain.

"It was my pleasure," she replied. Etuah reached behind her and grasped the unusual cape that now hung limply at her back. She seemed to wring it in her hand as if she was squeezing liquid out of a rag. Something fell upon the ground at her coaxing and she lifted it up and handed it to Tamara. "I retrieved it before the conflagration," Etuah said.

"The map!" both Tamara and Angeline cried at once.

Chapter Fourteen

"Is there more you can tell us father, about this beast of legend?" Beolan asked King Bristar.

Beolan, Bristar and Maringar sat around a beautiful table of polished Noban that had been gifted to them many tiels ago by his brother, King Treestar. Alongside of Bristar sat his wife, Queen Aliya, an elf whose beauty rivaled that of Queen Elsinestra herself, though it was quite different to gaze upon. Her hair was strawberry blonde, streaked with a silvery white, and it hung nearly to the ground behind her in a thick, woven braid. She was rather diminutive in stature, though she did not give the appearance that she was frail in any way. Her eyes, uncharacteristic for an elf, were green and they sparkled and shone against her whiter than white skin. Aliya's gown was made of a pale white silk, woven with silver threads, and it draped her body loosely. It was cinched at her mid-section by a solid braid of silver. Her waist was so small that it appeared as if a single one of her husband's hands could have encircled it entirely.

Other than these four, the room was empty. After having spent the previous evening acquainting their guest with the marvels of Crispen late into the night and then relaxing as best they could, they each met the new dawn with a sober and dedicated demeanor, and they each arrived here as planned, exactly at the appointed hour. Beolan closed the door and set the seals at his father's request after they had all entered. Bristar did not feel it was prudent to alarm the people of Crispen with rumors and tales about the beast yet. It would do no good for the citizens to lose sleep over something that they could do no more than anguish over at this point, so they talked until the moon was high in the evening sky and gave the citizens the impression that they were relaxed and confident.

"So much is changing all around us. Monsters of legend return to plague and torment us. The Lalas die and we cannot understand why. What is even more disconcerting is that they provide us with no explanation of their own," the King began, finally able to express his true concerns behind these closed doors.

Bristar reached out his hand and grasped his wife's tiny palm in his own before continuing. He was sadder than usual, and his normally confidant voice was slightly weaker and less robust in tone. Aliya noticed it immediately, and she looked at him with consternation marring her delicate features. No one else interrupted the King as he spoke. They waited patiently for the older man to complete his thoughts.

"The races have united," Bristar said, and he tipped his head to Maringar who acknowledged the comment by saluting him with a hand upon his heart. "And, furthermore, my brothers and I have overcome the obstacles that kept us from recognizing our mutual interests for so long. Our kingdoms are now open to one another, and we welcome any and all advice and assistance. Colton has made many attempts to thwart us, and we must harbor no illusions that his setbacks of late will deter him from continuing his efforts to destroy us. But, for all that has occurred, for all that has been lost, much has also been gained. The heir is awake! And he has a twin whose impact upon the fabric of our lives has already been significant. We can assume that in time his influence will grow concurrent with his power. On the other hand, Premoran's fate is as yet unknown. As the last of his kind, the last of the guardians, his loss, should that be the case, will be significant to us all."

As Bristar recapped the events of the past year, his strength seemed to return somewhat. His eyes perked up, and they began to sparkle once again. He seemed to sit straighter and taller in his chair, and his voice regained the fullness and confidence that had characterized it in the past. But then, as he mentioned Premoran, a cloud seemed to pass over him once more. His eyes grew dark and his expression was pained.

"What is it, my husband?" Aliya asked.

"There is something I have not told you all," Bristar said gravely. "Now that you have confirmed that the beast is within our midst, I cannot keep it to myself any longer."

"Tell us, father," Beolan urged.

"The Armadiel is most definitely alive. I dreaded the possibility, but now I am certain that it is true. If we do not destroy him quickly, he will bring Crispen to its knees within weeks," he said gravely. "The monster must be stopped! We cannot allow him to grow and expand his power. None of you know the nature of this beast. He is like no other living thing. His strength lies in his ability to infiltrate the very essence of the objects around him. They become like him--rock, water even the air we breathe. He transforms the character of things and turns them into extensions of his own evil and destructive power."

"How can you be certain that it is the snake of Recos who has been unleashed upon us?" Maringar asked.

"My son described the walls in the cave as if they were breathing, as if they were alive! That was when my suspicions were confirmed. I had misgivings before then certainly, but no hard evidence to support my concerns. I did not want to allow my fear of what might be to color my interpretation of what really was. There were other signs as well, but they were more subtle. I visited the hillock and listened to the earth numerous times of late, and I felt the pain of change everywhere. But until today, I was unwilling to commit to its cause," he said sadly. "Now I regret not accepting the counsel of my suspicious mind. If indeed the rock of Silandre has succumbed so soon, we are in more imminent danger than even I suspected. And that is not the worst of it."

"I am not sure, father, if the walls of the cave were shuddering because they were possessed or because they were resisting. It just seemed to me that they were active and alive."

"Rock is of this world. Though it is dense and less mutable, and certainly not sentient, it is as actively involved in the fabric of our existence as are the streams and forests. Anything that participates in nature is susceptible. Some elements resist naturally while others resist consciously. But make no mistake about it, all things resist for as long as they can. The Armadiel is stronger than anyone could imagine, and his strength lies in his ability to find the one weak link in the chain of life and attack it relentlessly, until its essence becomes raw and pliable," Bristar explained.

"Why has this monster been let loose upon us?" Aliya asked. "Other than to thwart the alliance and hinder our ability to assist our brethren in the quest, why Crispen?"

"The answer to your question is what I have been leading up to, my dearest," Bristar replied. "Before we left my brother in Seramour, I met with Premoran briefly. He came to me in the woods of Lormarion. At first, I thought it was a dream. I have told no one of this until now," he related. "He told me that deep within the core of Silandre a key had been placed thousands of tiels ago. He told me that we must retrieve it now for it is the only thing that will unlock the gates to the chamber that they must reach in the dead city, and that we must deliver it to the bearer of the map in Odelot. Without this key, another quest cannot be accomplished, he warned. He said that the consequences of that would be most dire."

Bristar hung his head heavily, and Aliya put her arm around his broad back and hugged him tightly.

"I sent you into the mountain fearing the worst, and you

confirmed it," he said to Beolan. "I had intended to tell you this and have you go in search of the key. But, I waited too long, and now the Dark Lord has taken advantage of my negligence."

"'Twas not your fault, husband," Aliya said. "You have only just returned home. The beast you speak of did not arrive here yesterday."

"Yes, I know. But nonetheless, I could have been quicker in responding to the wizard's request. We should have gone for the key immediately. Now it is too late. The beast may already have it," he said forlornly, and he hung his head as if he had been defeated in a great battle and the weight of the loss was bringing him to his knees.

"No, father. It is not too late! If the key we seek is in his possession, then we must kill the beast first, that is all!" Beolan said vehemently. "And if it is not, then we will find it."

"How does one fight such a monster?" Maringar asked. "Tell us and we will rid the hills it!"

"I do not know. I fear that there is no way. He is the nemesis of life itself," Bristar said forlornly, shaking his head.

"Surely father, we can find a way. We cannot just give up!" Beolan said.

"Husband!" Aliya said sternly. "What has come over you? Do you think that you would have this key in your pocket right now had you jumped from your horse and ran to Silandre the moment you returned? No! The Monster was surely there before you even entered the gates of Crispen! I do not mean to criticize and compound the hurt that you are inflicting so aptly upon yourself. But, be reasonable!"

"I need you, father! We all need you now," Beolan said. "Mother is right! What we must do is find a way to defeat this enemy so that we can do as Premoran instructed. The battle is not over. It has only just begun! We will find this key, and Maringar and I will carry it to Odelot ourselves. I promise you that!" he said as Maringar aggressively nodded his agreement.

Bristar looked at his son and smiled.

"Forgive me," he said. "Forgive me, all of you. What a fool I am being, feeling sorry for myself at a time like this."

Aliya sat up straight and put her delicate hands upon the table. "So, husband! Where do we begin?" she asked.

"We must search the archives," Bristar said, as his color returned to his cheeks. "Perhaps we will find a clue amidst the old parchments. But we must do so quickly. We have no time to waste. He has already started upon his path of destruction and no doubt, Caeltin has done more for him than merely unleash him from his prison in the bowels of the earth."

"With Maringar and his men to assist us, at least we will be able to penetrate the areas that would have been impossible for us to enter alone," Beolan said gratefully.

"Aye, that is true," Bristar agreed. "Without the Daggerfalls an their people, it would have been the Armadiel who did the seeking. We are fortunate that our friends have lent us their support," Bristar acknowledged. "And Caeltin could not have anticipated this."

Maringar accepted the compliments humbly, in keeping with his character. But he knew, as did the others, that the dwarves did not march for totally altruistic reasons. He blushed nevertheless, and his large nose and white cheeks turned red more easily than he would have expected himself.

"You need not have come here solely to assist us," Aliya said, sensing his discomfort. "Your actions are honorable even if they have a dual purpose. We accept the fact that the peril to us is a peril to all. The world is no longer as separate and apart as it was."

"Was it ever separate truly?" Maringar asked. "Or did we simply accept it as such? The trees held us together despite our reluctance to recognize our commonalities."

"Well said, Maringar. And now we must assume those responsibilities ourselves," Bristar said.

"Some of them, my dear," Aliya replied. "The trees have not abandoned us entirely," she reminded them.

"No, but they fight a war of their own now," Beolan said. "They are embroiled in battles we cannot observe."

"As was always the case, son," the Queen replied.

"Then why has the balance seemed to change so?" he asked.

"I do not know," she said solemnly. "Therefore the quest for the Gem has become paramount. The heir of legend, Davmiran, will find the answers for us all. If the light is withdrawn from this world, everything will die. Why the First would deprive us of our sustenance, I cannot begin to fathom."

"If Caeltin seeks the Gem as well, perhaps the First is merely protecting it from the Dark Lord's iniquitous grasp by shielding it," Beolan speculated. "If it does not radiate it would be harder to locate."

Bristar, Aliya and Maringar all looked at Beolan as if he had solved the riddle of the universe. It had never occurred to any of them that this privation could have been planned.

"What an interesting thought, my son," Bristar said, as he bent his head in contemplation.

"Quite interesting!" the Queen agreed.

"At the least, it is a more hopeful way of assessing the situation," Maringar said.

"It merely makes sense, that is all. Surely someone has speculated in this direction before me," Beolan replied.

"Frankly, it never did occur to me that this could be a defensive measure," Aliya said. "I have always assumed that the light was being withheld from the world against the will of the First."

"The consequences are grave regardless of the reason" Beolan said. "Due to this deprivation, the trees are dying!"

"A sacrifice perhaps?" Bristar asked.

"That would be in keeping with what we have come to expect of the Lalas," Aliya said.

"They must suffer the loss of the Gem's radiance too," Beolan suggested. "The First must be aware of these consequences though."

"Is it the price that must be paid? Perhaps they suffer even more than we suspect," Aliya added.

"Could it be that the Gem's light sustains them as the sun sustains ordinary plant life?" Maringar proposed.

"And that without it, they cannot thrive?" Bristar continued on this train of thought.

"Emotionally or physically?" Beolan asked his father.

"Maybe both. The First's role, as we have come to understand it, is to harbor and protect the Gem. The Gem is like the sun, but it nourishes the soul and the spirit. Caeltin knows this too, and he knows that if he can find the Gem of Eternity and destroy it, then life will cease altogether. We cannot survive with hearts as cold as stone. And the grass and trees and wildlife cannot survive if their spirits are stilled. The essence that defines them is nurtured and maintained by the Gem's light. If the Gem ceases to shine, then dissolution will result," Bristar explained.

"But, father, if the First in its wisdom is protecting the Gem by concealing it and therefore the Lalas die, will not the world be more vulnerable in the end anyway? And won't Caeltin then be even stronger?" Beolan asked.

"It would seem so, my son. I cannot fathom the logic."

"The fabric weaves of its own will," Aliya said. "New alliances are being created by virtue of theses changes. The heir has been revived and he too seeks the Gem. A twin to the heir has revealed himself! Change is afoot everywhere and it has been precipitated by what we have just described; by the First's choice to withhold the Gem's radiance from the trees and from the world."

"A crossroads," Bristar said soberly.

"More than that, father. A new age!" Beolan said.

"That will come after the final battle is fought," Bristar replied.

"The heir must find the Gem before Colton does," Maringar said. "There will be no other age if the Dark Lord prevails in that regard."

"Thus, we must triumph here against the Armadiel! The obstacles Caeltin continues to place in our way and in the way of our friends and allies can only serve to distract us from his true desire and his true goal. We must defeat the beast, and then focus our attention upon retrieving the key and continuing the Quest," Bristar said.

"The longer we are forced to defend ourselves, the less energy and time we will be able to devote to helping the boy," Aliya agreed. "Surely he knows that."

They all sat in silence for a short while, contemplating what they had just discussed. Though it was mere speculation, it was beginning to appear to them all that such a situation was most likely prevailing. And in the wake of this possibility, the imminent threat loomed even greater upon their horizon, for every moment that they had to devote to eliminating it kept them from assisting the heir more directly.

"I will get the Tomes and we must ponder them closely," Aliya finally said, and she rose from the table and walked to the large wall of books that stood nearby.

Her movements were so graceful that it almost seemed as if she floated across the carpeted floor. She grasped a delicate ladder that hung from a bar that ran the length of the wall and she slid it to a point midway across the room. After climbing to the very top rung, she reached up, still some distance from the uppermost shelf, and she clasped a heavy book in her small hand. She then laid it carefully on the ladder and opened the thick cover. The lettering inside was bold and thick. After perusing it quickly, she nodded her head, and then with both hands, she lifted the volume and backed down the ladder carefully, step by step.

"Join me," she said as she brought it to the table. "Together maybe we will find something that will assist us here. This is the volume that describes the beast's last encounter with our people."

"I have read it too many times," Bristar said. "And each time I feared that this moment might come. It is as if the future has already occurred and I am just reminding myself of what happened."

Aliya began to turn the thick pages while the others looked on over her shoulders and read along with her. She scanned the lines quickly, searching for something that might be useful.

"Stop mother!" Beolan said. "Turn back one page and read the last two lines for us," he instructed her.

She read:

> *"A snake it is not, a snake it is,*
> *A strength? A weakness?*
> *What claim is his?"*

"What do you make of those lines?" Beolan asked, clearly having something in mind himself.

"It seems merely to be a description of the beast's nature," Bristar answered. "What strikes you about them?"

"You have taught me, mother, that nothing in the Tomes is gratuitous. If the Armadiel is likened to a snake, then what are its vulnerabilities? Why bring up the issue of strength and weakness if not to reveal information?" Beolan said.

"Thus," Maringar continued, "it may draw both fortitude and exposure from its likeness to a reptile. We must then determine when a snake is most strong and when it is most vulnerable."

"In all the other passages that mention the monster, it is described quite differently. I had never imagined it to resemble a serpent," Aliya said.

"Even as a child," Bristar recalled, "I was led to believe that it was more like the human species than a reptile."

"Need it resemble a serpent in looks in order for it to share a reptile's characteristics?" Beolan asked.

"In my land, we always referred to it as the 'Snake of Recos'. I always assumed it resembled the reptile species," Maringar said. "It is strange that you never did," he said to Bristar and Aliya.

"Read the next line, mother, if you would."

> *"Renewal is its gift to keep,*
> *What harm it sustains, pain so deep,*
> *Gone with the old,*

No time to weep,
Who fathoms well the depth of sleep?"'

"What is renewal for a snake?" Beolan asked excitedly now.

"Birth? Egg laying?" Aliya suggested.

"Mating?" Maringar offered.

"Shedding its skin!" Beolan cried.

Bristar, Aliya and Maringar all looked at Beolan expectantly.

"Keep reading, please," he said to his mother with a renewed urgency. Aliya continued where she had left off.

> *"'To end the pain and begin again,*
> *A moment simply,*
> *A sly refrain,*
> *What looks like slumber may not be such,*
> *A lapse perhaps,*
> *A formative rush,*
> *Be quick, be strong,*
> *Be bold, be tough,*
> *A time to ply the killing touch. "'*

As soon as she read the final word, Beolan slapped the table once more with his open hand. "You see?" he asked. "It could not be clearer! When the Armadiel sheds its skin it can be killed!"

"By the First, I think you may be right!" Bristar concurred, and he grabbed his son around his shoulders and hugged him tightly.

"Regardless of whether it resembles a snake in its appearance, it renews itself by losing its outer layer. Thus it can slough off what harm may have been inflicted upon it and constantly return to battle as if it had never been injured. Do you remember the stories that terrified me the most when I was a child, Father?" he asked Bristar, recalling now what he thought were merely folk tales, and the King nodded. "I had nightmares about the Armadiel because it seemed so impossible to me that no matter what was thrown against it, it prevailed. It was burned in fire, blasted by magic, its skin was frozen under tons of ice and snow, it sustained arrow after arrow and blade after blade, yet when it came back to battle it appeared as if it had never been attacked at all. Its battle scars were gone completely!"

"I too, feared this monster for similar reasons. But the fact that it could pervert nature by robbing it of its natural affinities disturbed me even more," Bristar recounted.

"There are things we believe we can rely upon," Aliya said. "When our beliefs are shaken in such a manner by evil, it is difficult to maintain a steady course. Caeltin D'Are Agenathea upsets the balance that we all take comfort in. He disrupts those things we hold most dear. By reanimating the Armadiel, he has once again brought our nightmares to life."

"Yes," Maringar said. "But he could not account for those things that have changed prior to this. He has set many things in motion, and he has attempted to thwart the very flow of life itself, but in so doing he has also precipitated alterations in the fabric that he never anticipated. He know what he seeks, but even he cannot predict the future. Some things are not in his control." The young dwarf stared hard at Beolan. "He could not predict that we would unite. He could not predict that his calumny would lead us to a new brotherhood." Maringar clasped Beolan's wrist with his powerful hand. "Though he has unleashed upon us a monster, the likes of which we have never fought in our lifetimes, he has also effected the birth of an alliance, the likes of which he could not begin to understand."

"Your words lighten my heavy load," Bristar said with sincere gratitude.

"We fight for a joint purpose," Maringar reminded him.

"Yes," Aliya agreed. "And it is high time that we all recognized that! Those noble of character rise together in times of grave trouble. We will conquer this beast!"

"We must strike during the moment of its rejuvenation. If we can believe that the Tomes are literal in their description in this case, then when the beast appears to sleep, if only for a brief second, it will be vulnerable to our attack," Beolan said.

"Then we must first injure it enough for it to require renewal," Maringar said.

"Yes, and we shall do that in concert, you and I," Beolan replied. Aliya and Bristar rose up together and reached out for each other's hand. They approached the two younger men thoughtfully.

"So much is at stake," Aliya began. "But I have a profound feeling of calm and comfort knowing that the two of you are as one in your understanding. Only a day ago, I feared the time might soon come when grief would replace my pride in my son. Yet now I am at peace. You two boys shall not disappoint me," she said boldly and with conviction.

"I too am confident. I had felt the weight of the world upon me and it nearly struck me down. Things may appear so unclear and unsettled at times, and then within moments, clarity replaces confusion. I believe that you are correct in your interpretation of the passage in the great book. Now, I could read it and garner no other meaning," Bristar said.

"Please, refresh yourselves and then join us in the banquet hall. We shall have a final supper together and toast you both," Aliya said, and her eyes sparkled. "It should be no other way!"

"I agree," Bristar concurred. "The spirit of victory is with us now. We must welcome and nourish it this evening, so when you depart on the morn to confront the beast, it illuminates your path and puts the fear of the First in your enemy's hardened heart."

They reached out their hands toward Beolan and Maringar. The young men grasped them willfully and then clasped each other's free, outstretched palm, thus completing the circle. They stood there for a few moments in profound silence before releasing their grips.

"We have reason to be hopeful," Aliya said. "The Tomes have provided us with possibilities that we were unaware of until now. As usual, the great books lead us to the water. But the task of inflicting harm upon the Armadiel is a treacherous one, and one that will not be easily accomplished. Though the two of you know what you must do, the distance between awareness and execution is nonetheless substantial."

"Much will depend upon how completely the beast has infiltrated Silandre's structure. You must be able to get close enough to it in order to be effective," Bristar said chillingly.

"My men will help us break through whatever barrier has been constructed to bar our way," Maringar said confidently.

"This monster shall not destroy Crispen so easily, father. And he will not keep us from doing what Premoran requested of us. He may have the ability to recover from the wounds we inflict upon him, but during one of those efforts, we shall surely strike him dead!" Beolan said. "Though he proceeds against us with the confidence of Caeltin burgeoning within his soulless body, he will die all the same just when he believes he will be born once again.

"He is formidable beyond measure all the same, my son," Bristar cautioned. "May the First guide you both and protect you."

"Crispen!" Beolan said as he thrust his fist into the air.

"Crispen!" the others shouted in response, and the word echoed off of the stone walls of the chamber until it faded away and left them standing in contemplation amidst the silence of expectation.

Chapter Fifteen

"Quickly!" Robyn urged them. "I can see the opening forming."

The four humans and the Moulant were standing together barely inside the shelter of the woods. The noise around them was almost deafening, and Robyn was shouting just in order to be heard. Though the leaves upon the trees scarcely stirred in response, the air was alive with power.

"Over there!" he pointed ahead to a bright spot on their left. "Can you see it?"

"Yes!" Filaree replied. "It looks as if someone has taken a knife and slit the air open."

"It is clear beyond it. The blurriness is gone," Cairn said.

"That is a good sign indeed," Robyn replied.

"I hope we can make it through before it closes again," Cairn said anxiously.

"It must be there for us to try to enter through. Why else would it have appeared in our time of need?" Filaree asked.

"We must go quickly!" Robyn said. "I do not think this opportunity will reveal itself to us again so soon."

The air was crackling and sparking all around them now, and great bolts of silent lightening streaked across the sky, illuminating the landscape eerily. The power that surged from the south behind them struck the shield around the Tower of Parth at its top directly in front of where they stood, and then it proceeded to sizzle down in yellow-white rivulets to the ground where the earth absorbed it. Dust was rising from the surface as the clash stirred up the debris, and it created thick clouds around the walls, making it hard to see where the shield met the earth.

"Is it wide enough for us to get in?" Cairn asked.

"Yes, I believe so," Filaree responded, surveying the area to the left and to the right of them. She had drawn her sword, and she crouched over her horse's withers apprehensively. "I will go last. Robyn, you lead the way. Guard the boy's back, Cairn. I will follow once Dav is safely inside." Filaree pressed her horse forward, and exposed herself to the light of day beyond the tree line. She waited for Robyn to emerge.

"Let's go!" she shouted. "We may not have much time!"

Robyn stepped forward with Davmiran close behind him. The boy had spoken nary a word in the last few minutes, but it was not fear that kept him silent. His body was listening to the surges all around him, and his senses reeled in response. He was trying to understand the power as it flooded over him.

"Stay close to me," Robyn said. "Once we start running, we must not stop until we are safe within the walls of the Tower."

"What if the space closes?" he asked, surprising Robyn and the others with his words.

"Have you had a vision?" Cairn asked, disturbed by the question.

"Is there something you want to tell us before we commit to this?" Filaree questioned.

"No," he replied honestly. "But if we are unable to enter by the time we get there, we should have a plan."

"We do!" she answered. "We run for our lives back to whence we came!"

"And we hope and pray that we make it!" Cairn added.

"Are you ready?" Robyn asked, interrupting them. They were. "Here we go then!" Robyn said, and he spurred his horse sharply forward.

The big animal reared and then lurched ahead. Davmiran said something into the ear of his mount, and it sped out of the woods behind Robyn. Cairn followed and Calyx kept pace with the boy at his side. Filaree waited with her back to Parth, watching the woods.

It was perhaps five hundred meters or so that they needed to traverse before they reached the opening that they sought. As Robyn approached it at a full gallop with Davmiran close behind, he turned to see if the others were all there as well. To his surprise and chagrin, Filaree still stood at their point of embarkation with her sword held high in the air.

"What is she doing?" Cairn said as he reached the other two.

"I am not sure," Robyn replied, concentrating his gaze and attempting to see her more clearly. "But, you had better step inside while you can," he said to Dav and moved slightly to the side.

The opening was shimmering brightly and the edge was smooth and rounded. It did not appear to be a breach for it was not jagged edged or darkened. It was just wide enough for both the boy and his horse to slip through.

"Go ahead, Robyn," Cairn said. "Calyx and I are fine. Stay with Dav."

"Will you wait for Filaree?" he asked, the concern clear upon his voice.

"Yes, I intend to," Cairn replied. "Hurry! Don't leave him

alone."

Robyn hesitated for a brief moment and then followed the boy through the narrow passage. Cairn turned his gaze back upon Filaree who was still standing by the forest's edge.

"What can she be doing?" he asked Calyx. "I am sure she can see that Dav is safely inside by now."

Calyx growled from deep in his throat and bounded out toward her. Cairn did not protest. He continued to watch as the Moulant approached Filaree with tremendous speed. As soon as he reached her, a flash of orange light enveloped the two of them, and it blinded him temporarily. The scholar shielded his eyes vainly with his hand, and he attempted to rub the shooting stars out of them. When his vision cleared a moment later, both Filaree and Calyx were nowhere to be found!

Without thinking, he kneed his horse sharply and they shot forward, though he almost lost his seat in the process. The opening in the shield was still there and he glanced at it apprehensively as he left it behind. Within moments, he was standing where the others had been only a short while ago, but there was no evidence of their presence. The ground was singed just outside the tree line and a number of the branches lay broken and splintered and scattered all around. Cairn plunged into the forest as panic gripped him.

"Filaree! Calyx!" he shouted. "Where are you?"

His shouts were greeted with silence. As he followed the path back into the depths of the woods that they had only recently traveled, he heard a branch snap on his left. Swinging his horse around sharply in the narrow space, he saw Filaree lying on the ground, and her body was glowing strangely. She was not moving, and he rushed over to her and leapt from his horse as agilely as a young buck, reaching her side in seconds. From deeper in the woods, he heard a violent thrashing followed by an earsplitting screech that was not human.

Cairn lifted Filaree's limp body up and laid it over his horse's withers. The noise surrounding him grew louder and closer, as he mounted his horse behind the unmoving woman. He was reluctant to leave without knowing where Calyx was, but he had no choice. He jerked his horse's head fervidly around and spurred him forward. As soon as he emerged from the shelter of the trees, he saw a bolt of orange light streak over his head and smash into the shield surrounding Parth. Upon contact with the barrier, it fizzled and sparked wildly before dying out. When the bright light faded, the shield was still intact, but there was a large, dark blotch upon it. Cairn also noticed that the opening into which his friends had slipped seemed just a tiny bit narrower than it was moments before.

He raced for the opening as another bolt of energy sped by him just to the left, and once again hit the barrier. The opening seemed to shrink once more in response to the attack.

"We are almost there," he whispered into the horse's ear, bending over nearly to the animal's head, and protecting Filaree's body with his own at the same time. "Where are you, Calyx?" he said aloud, more anxious now for his friend than even for himself.

Cairn jumped from his mount and grabbed the unconscious warrior in almost the same motion. He turned toward the forest to take one last look before slipping through the opening while leading his horse in behind him, but he saw nothing. Once inside, his eye caught some movement at the perimeter of the woods, and a split second later, Calyx' massive body was loping toward him. Vivid streaks of iridescent fire were unleashed from somewhere amidst the trees, and they singed his back and caused him to roar in pain and anger. But the giant Moulant did not falter in his path. He continued to run toward Parth, and to deftly dodge the deadly barrage.

Cairn laid Filaree upon the ground, and before he could abandon the safety he had only just attained in order to assist his friend, Robyn stepped in front of him and disappeared through the opening. Once more outside, the Chosen raised his right hand with his palm facing the ground, and it appeared as if he the surface of the soil lifted in response. Dirt and debris, rocks, pebbles and branches all rose in the air and sped toward the source of the attack against the Moulant. A dense cloud of tiny, concentrated missiles flew in the direction of the woods.

Calyx meanwhile, had reached the opening to the Tower but it was now too narrow for his huge body to fit through even when he stood sideways. Orange fire bolts were repeatedly hitting the shield in many different areas, and although it remained intact and relatively unscathed, the slit that provided entry to him and the others moments ago was growing smaller and smaller. The defensive effort that Robyn unleashed was partially effective and it seemed to slow the attack somewhat near where they stood. He continued to concentrate upon the area that appeared to be the point from where the attack stemmed, and he drew upon the earth for assistance. The cloud of particles grew denser and darker. It began to swirl and gurgle, generating within itself both large and small whirlpools of darkness that stirred up the soil even more, and obscured them from the sight of the enemy.

Meanwhile, Robyn backed up toward the Moulant, while never lowering his arm for a moment, and he placed his other hand against the wall. A bright white light formed around this hand as he pressed it against the shield. The edge of the opening seemed to grow soft and pliable with his touch as the glow spread from the top to the bottom. It drooped and sagged as if it was made of wax and it was melting. Davmiran quickly grabbed the softened skirting of the slit and bent it inwards, peeling it back like the skin of an orange, enough to allow Calyx to slip through. Robyn quickly dropped his arm and passed through himself. As soon as he was inside, Davmiran released his hold on the shimmering portal, and the opening closed completely, accompanied by a powerful whooshing sound. Robyn watched until there was no trace of it left, then he allowed his chin to drop to his chest and he closed his eyes.

Chapter Sixteen

"Why must you play games with me?" he asked. "Are we not all beyond that? You seek my help, and I seek yours."

I have not the need you speak of, the tree replied.

"Yet you have chosen to confide in me? What motivates you then?"

Some sacrifices are necessary if we are to preserve what we can in the face of the inevitable.

"You have realized then how hopeless the situation is for them all? And for yourselves as well?" the deep voice asked. "The outcome has been foreseeable since the beginning of time. It is no surprise to me that self interest now governs your actions."

We have the larger picture to consider. We must survive beyond dissolution, though life upon this earth may not.

"You are no different than I am! And all these tiels I have felt no kinship with the great Lalas," he scoffed. "We should have been allies long ago. So much needless and enduring suffering could have been avoided. Now that you see what is to come, you have chosen to forsake those so devoted to you? How different are we really?"

Your sense of what we must do is far different than ours. Our vision extends beyond today. You would be wise not to perceive us as allies.

"Is this a threat that I hear?" he laughed. "What you choose to do after time has stopped for the rest of us, I care little about. I can think of no other word than 'ally' to describe you. Would you prefer the appellation, 'traitor'? Is that a more apt description?" he asked malevolently.

Call me what you will. I have given you enough information. Now take it and be gone! the Lalas said, and the words exploded in Colton's mind.

"I am grateful, Ormachon. I will use it well, believe me," the Dark Lord said in a mocking voice before his image vanished from the glen.

Chapter Seventeen

Conrad bent down and dumped Dalloway's unmoving body on the doorstep of his home as if it was a sack of potatoes he had brought home from one of his trading trips. He then rushed back to the horse that stood obediently nearby, and gently and tenderly he lifted up his unconscious daughter.

"I should never have let you wander alone. How could I have been such a fool?" he cried, tears streaming down his cheeks.

He kissed her on both of her eyelids as if she was a small child, and he carefully pushed back a lock of her auburn hair that had loosened itself from the long braid that hung down to the ground around his feet as he carried her inside the cottage. He placed her softly upon the bed in the corner, covered her with a soft blanket of goose down and then quickly lit the fire in the large hearth. Grabbing a kettle from the table nearby, he pressed once upon the pump handle next to it and allowed the water to fill the pot almost to the brim. Taking it with him to the cabinet above the hearth, he removed two large leaves from the drying bin inside. Conrad stuffed the leaves hastily into the water, closed the cover tightly and then promptly hung it from the hook over the growing flames.

While the Lalas tea brewed, he went back outside and picked up the elf. Reluctantly, he brought him inside as well, knowing that his daughter's fate was now inextricably bound to this stranger from the other world, the world that was so incredibly dangerous to her health and well being. He laid him roughly down upon a mat before the fire and turned his back upon him almost as soon as Dalloway's body hit the floor.

I must keep him alive, he thought. *Sophia died because I failed to keep that other one alive. I will not fail this time.*

After making sure that Caroline was breathing steadily, he returned to the prostrate elf. It was hard for him not to hate the stranger, simply because if it was not for his trespasses, his daughter's life would not now be imperiled.

He does not look like an evil warrior. His face is gentle and he bears no battle scars. What felled him, I wonder? Ach! I should not trifle with worries about him! That will not bring Caroline back to me.

The kettle began to rattle and spit, and he turned away from Dalloway and rushed to the fire. Using a long hook, he removed the pot from the flame and poured the liquid carefully into two large mugs on the long table.

"Ouch!" he exclaimed, as he scalded his lip tasting the steaming liquid. "I left it on the fire too long. Now I have to wait for it to cool. Darn it all!" he lamented. "She needs this tea! What more can I do wrong?" he railed.

The ice was melting off of Dalloway's clothing and forming a small pool of water all around his body. His hair was disheveled and straggly, but he was still handsome nonetheless.

He is noble looking. Regal too despite his youth. Why would he intrude upon our lands? I will have to recheck all my wards. How could he have breached them without me knowing? he wondered. *What could have brought him here? There is nothing here anyone from the outside could want.*

He touched his lips to the tea once more and then nodded his head, satisfied with the temperature at last. Carefully, he raised Caroline's face to the cup and opened her delicate mouth. He let the liquid drip slowly down her throat.

This has to help her. The brew is potent. It will clear her head.

After he had made certain that his daughter had swallowed as much as he thought she could do safely under the circumstances, he walked once again over to the intruder. Roughly this time, he opened the elf's jaw and dribbled some Lalas tea down his throat as well. Rubbing upon his Adam's apple, he caused the silent visitor to swallow involuntarily, and then he nodded his head in acknowledgment once more. He repeated this process a number of times until the tea was running down Dalloway's chin.

His skin is so cold, almost as if his body is frozen. I wonder how long he was out there. It is unnaturally cold though, despite the warmth in this room.

Conrad pushed the intruder's sleeve up in order to feel the pulse.

It is strong! He does not seem to be injured or ill. But he is freezing still! He should have warmed up a little by now, no matter how chilled he is.

"Stay alive now," he admonished. "My daughter's life depends upon you!"

You are so much like your mother, he thought, gazing upon his daughter's lovely face. *You will not share her fate though! I will not let this man die. I know better now. He will survive and so will you!* he promised. *What could be wrong with him? Something has pushed him into this deep sleep. It is not natural. How can I awaken him?*   A f t e r making sure that both the elf and his beloved daughter were breathing comfortably, he stepped outside the door of the cottage and sat upon the front steps in order to contemplate the situation. He always thought better out of doors.

Unnaturally cold. Why is he so cold? Perchance if I warm him up, he will come to his senses, Conrad thought. *Maybe someone put a spell upon him and froze him. He appears to be healthy and he has no signs of injury. He is breathing steadily, his heart is strong and his color is good despite the temperature of his skin. Maybe all that is keeping him benumbed is this intense cold. If Caroline had not stumbled upon him, surely he would have perished by now. He would have died and no one would have been the wiser. If he was ever found, it would have seemed as if he simply succumbed to exposure. Someone planned this!* he began to believe. *Someone wanted him dead and they wanted it to appear as if he died naturally.*

He rushed back inside and opened the heavy lid of the trunk that sat in the corner. From inside of it, he pulled out two thick blankets of a soft wool-like fiber and brought them back to where Dalloway was lying. With both hands, he flung one open and spread it over the prone elf. As he went to tuck the sides in around him tightly, a medallion on a leather thong fell out of his shirt and dangled upon the welting of his jerkin.

What is this? Conrad thought, and he lifted it carefully. Despite the elf's intensely cold body temperature, it was warm to the touch. *Not an ordinary elf, this one. This token bears the ancient runes of Sidra. He could not have stumbled upon such an artifact. Things like these do not get misplaced. No. It must have been given to him, or he stole it! But it would take quite a thief to lift a token from Sidra's cache. She is not one to be easily fooled, especially by an elf. Her affections have always been reserved for humans. Could she really have given it to the likes of him? Why would he be so worthy in her eyes?*

He placed the medallion back inside Dalloway's tunic, and then he finished wrapping the first blanket around him before grabbing the other blanket and doing the same with the second cover, leaving only his head exposed. The floor was already wet with water from the thawing of his clothing, and it quickly seeped into the blankets. He walked over to the fire and placed some large pieces of wood upon the embers. He then fanned the small flames until the new wood caught. Shortly, the fire was raging once again and the room was heating up quickly, drawing the moisture more rapidly out from the elf's apparel.

A token from Sidra. She never gave me anything like that, he was almost jealous at the thought. *He must be an important elf. More the reason to awaken him.*

He quickly checked that Caroline was comfortable before picking up a wooden stool and carrying it to Dalloway's side. He sat upon it and watched the elf, hoping his body temperature would return to normal naturally. But, though his face grew rosy and his hair stuck to his forehead and cheeks as the water seeped out of it, his skin remained icy cold. The room was so hot now that Conrad had to remove his shirt so that he would not pass out himself.

I wonder about that medal. He must have it for a reason. Maybe I can make some use of it here.

He reached inside the intruder's shirt once again and grasped the pendant in his hand. It was still warm and his fingers tingled slightly as he held it. He rose quickly and walked over to the fire. Conrad picked up a small pot filled with hot water that had been sitting upon the flames, carried it back to the side of the insensate visitor and then sat down again. Without removing the thong from the elf's neck, he extended it as far as it would reach and let it hang into the pot of boiling water. It sizzled and steamed as soon as it came into contact with the liquid, and within seconds, it began to glow.

As I suspected, he smiled.

The medallion seemed to absorb the heat, to suck it in, and Conrad watched as the leather string that was looped through it began to glow as well. The heat was radiating down the cord on both sides of the medal toward the knot that secured it behind the man's head. Once the circle was complete, a brilliant light burst from the center of the token and spread quickly over the elf's entire body. Conrad jumped back a pace or two and almost fell over backward on the chair. He could feel the heat and he panicked for a brief moment wondering if he had unleashed a power that was going to harm him even more. He watched anxiously, poised to withdraw the cauldron of hot liquid if the elf seemed to suffer as a result.

Sidra? Are you with me now? Is it you who has caused this elf's stupor or will you be my daughter's savior? he wondered anxiously, hoping that he would not regret this gamble.

The light grew brighter and brighter as it continued to envelop the elf's body. The air around him grew moist and steamy, and a small cloud of mist hung over him. Conrad could hear a slight hissing sound as the moisture evaporated. The cloud grew thicker and it soon appeared almost solid, as if he could grab it and move it in chunks. Beneath its surface he could see tiny whirlwinds and zephyrs playing upon the elf's skin, rushing and spinning frenetically up and down his body, his arms and his legs.

He withdrew the now empty pot and pushed it to the side, thus allowing the medal to hang freely once again. His skin tingled as it came into contact with the thick fog that surrounded the elf, and two or three of the mist-like whirligigs skirted speedily up and down his arm before leaping playfully back into the cloud and disappearing in the larger mass. The hair upon his arm stood up in response, and he ran his hand across it involuntarily. It was warm to the touch, and he smiled broadly in response. Just as quickly as it began, the illumination went out and the room took on an eerie glow. The vapor still shrouded the elf's unconscious body but it was now as still as could be, and it appeared more like a heavy mantle that lay immobile upon him. Conrad leaned in as close as he could and he fanned the air with his hands in an effort to dissipate the cloud of moisture so that he could gaze upon the man's face.

He was no more than six inches from Dalloway's face when the elf abruptly opened his eyes. Both men jumped, startled, but Conrad continued to hover over him. "Do not try anything!" he warned.

"Who are you?" Dalloway asked feebly.

"I will ask the questions," he replied gruffly. "Who are you? And how did you get the medal?" he asked, pointing to the token that hung upon his shirt. *Thank the First he is alive!*

"My name is Dalloway and I hail from Lormarion. The last I remember, I was leaving Eleutheria, the home of my uncle, Whitestar," he began to explain as honestly as he could, though it was clearly difficult for him to recall. "What medal are you referring to?" he asked perplexed, and he looked down to where the older man indicated. "I never saw this before," he said, as he touched the medallion weakly. "You did not place this around my neck?"

"It belongs to Sidra. Look, her mark is right there on the back, as plain as the day is long!" he said, turning it over and showing the runes to Dalloway.

"Sidra? What is Sidra?" The elf looked more and more bewildered by the minute. He tried to rise, but his arm gave way as he propped himself up, and he collapsed to the floor again.

"Sidra is a she, not a what, and don't you move just yet, young man," Conrad warned him. "You are still not very strong, and I do not want you to hurt yourself."

"Thank you for the concern," Dalloway replied.

"It is not you for whom I bear concern."

Dalloway was so thoroughly exhausted that he found it hard to think clearly, but he was grateful nevertheless for the blankets and warm shelter within which he now found himself.

"I do not know who you are or how I got here, but I thank you humbly for helping me," he said weakly. "You have nothing to fear from me, kind Sir."

"I have plenty to fear!" Conrad shot back. "Stay put while I see to my daughter." Conrad walked over to the bed in the corner where Caroline lay, but he kept his eyes on the elf all the time. "Do not try to escape. I will be upon you in a second!"

Dalloway closed his eyes and lay back once more. He was exhausted, and the only thing he wanted to do was rest and regain his strength.

Conrad sat next to the girl on the very edge of the bed and turned his head for an instant in order to look upon her face. To his astonishment, her eyes were open and she was smiling at him.

"Caroline!" he exclaimed. "You are alive! Can you hear me?"

"No need to yell, father. I am right next to you. My hearing is very good, remember?" she replied affectionately though weakly.

He was so relieved that for a moment he forgot all about Dalloway. He smoothed out her hair gently and tenderly pushed it off of her face.

"Is he okay?" she asked.

"Fine, though reluctant reveal much," he said disdainfully.

"He speaks the truth, father. He has no recollection of what has happened to him. He is not concealing anything intentionally."

"Do you know that, my child? Or are you just smitten by his innocent look?"

"I am certain," she whispered. "Go to him. We must help him. He was felled by the most evil spell, and it compelled him to forget something very important. We must assist him in regaining that memory. Sidra's mark is present upon him. He cannot be bad!"

"I wondered about that myself, Caroline, but I am still reluctant to trust him. He must leave as soon as he can regardless. You cannot be near him."

"Why, father? What are you keeping from me?" she asked.

"You are like your mother, Caroline. You cannot be among outsiders. I have told you that before. It is dangerous."

"That was not an answer, father. Why can I not be near this elf?" she repeated.

"Because you cannot!" he exclaimed, as if he was speaking to a small child.

She placed her hand atop his and looked deeply into his eyes.

"You must tell me the truth," she insisted.

"Why must you know? You are safe, now. I will take this elf to the edge of our lands, and send him on his way."

"Father, please," she pleaded.

"Because you will die!" he finally shouted. "Just as your mother did! You are an empath, Caroline, you will become lost in his mind and in his pain. I will not lose you as I lost your mother!" he cried.

Caroline lay back upon the bed and closed her eyes. *So this is what he feared for so long. Surely I will not die from this. I felt his fear and I felt his confusion, and I am certain that I was stricken by the magic that held him in its grip, but I am alive.* "But, I did return, father," she said soothingly. "I was drawn into his consciousness, I must admit. But I am fine now," she explained.

"If he had perished, you would have too. You were his captive, his prisoner, and his fate became yours. You cannot control this. It is beyond your power," he said.

"I speak with the animals and they do not control me. I enter their minds as I did his, and I feel and see what they feel and see. Did mother do that too?" she asked.

"No. I do not think that she could. The thought would have frightened her. She never even mentioned it. And after a point, your mother kept her distance from all living things other than me. Even with me, if I suffered, she suffered. There were times when I would have a nightmare and she would wake up screaming. For the last tiel of her life, she saw no one and spoke with no one besides me. At least until...." he hesitated.

"Until what?" she asked.

"Until she had no choice! Until it was impossible to avoid. Until the day she died!" he cried.

"Please, father. Tell me what happened. It is time."

Conrad sat down upon the floor and crossed his legs and arms. He lifted his head and looked hard and long at his daughter before he began to speak. "Your mother always waited for me before she went into the garden to gather the vegetables for the evening meal, but this one night, I was delayed. I had fallen asleep up on Heather Hill, and when I awoke, the sun was already setting. She was terribly afraid of being in the dark alone, and when I realized how late it was, I rode as fast as I could.

"I had a terrible feeling that something was wrong. And as soon as the house came into view, my worse fears were confirmed. I had not yet warded the perimeters of our land, and a stranger had come upon the house..." His face took on a far away expression. Caroline could tell just how difficult this was for him. She squeezed his hand lovingly, and he looked at her again with so much pain and so much love in his eyes that she could barely keep herself from weeping.

"You were nowhere in sight. A horse I did not recognize stood before the porch. I panicked. At first, I thought that someone had come to rob us or steal from us, but as I dew closer, I saw the horse was well groomed and the saddle was finely tooled and immaculately kept. It was not the mount of a thief! But there was blood upon the animal, the saddle and the blanket. I thought the poor beast had been pierced by a spear or something! I jumped from my Pater's back and searched for the wound, but it was nowhere to be found." He voice caught and tears fell. Caroline gently wiped them from the rough skin of his face.

"Then I saw it! A trail of bright red blood leading into house. I raced inside. Panic gripped my heart. I threw the door open, but—" He broke off. Caroline waited for him to regain his composure. When he spoke again, his voice was flat, exhausted. "It was too late. Sophia lay upon the floor next to the warrior. He had been pierced through the heart by an arrow. Your mother's hand was upon it. He had come here for help, and your mother tried to save his life. But she had been drawn into his pain and into his soul. He died so quickly--before she could do anything for him. Or for herself. She died with him, at the very same moment."

Conrad was exhausted from having related this instant to his daughter. Although he was distraught from the memory, he felt as if a great burden had been lifted from him. He reached out to Caroline and they hugged each other tenderly.

"She died because I was not there to help her," he cried, anguished. "And I vowed that very second that I would never allow this to happen to you!"

"Why do you think I will succumb to the same fate? I have survived, father. The elf is alive and so am I," she said calmly.

"If he had died, I would have lost you forever!" Conrad cried out.

"I am not mother," she said quietly. "I have learned how to protect myself. The animals draw me in too, father. They have pain and they die, but I am able to separate myself from them. I have learned!"

"How do you know what you will be able to do?" he replied, still fearful and anguished. "You have never been among men, Caroline."

"I have now," she said seriously, and they both looked at Dalloway who was still reclining on the floor in the middle of the room. "No, father. I am not like mother."

The elf was sitting up and staring at them. He had obviously been listening intently to the story that Conrad just related to Caroline. His face was stricken with sadness that could only be genuine, and Caroline was certain that she saw a drop of moisture glisten in the corner of his eye.

"And our visitor is not a dying warrior," she continued.

Conrad looked at Caroline and then he quickly looked at Dalloway. They were both staring at one another like two children mesmerized by a spinning top. Stepping between them and breaking their line of vision, he began to speak to the elf.

"What brought you here? How did you find us? What were you doing in Sidra's domain?"

"I cannot answer any of your questions, I fear, even if you asked them of me a hundred more times," Dalloway replied. "My memory has been stolen from me," he answered, but even as he spoke, his expression was confused and perplexed. He shook his head quickly as if he was trying to clear it or wake himself out of a stupor. "I remember something," he began to speak again. "but it seems more like a dream than anything else. "Every time I try to bring the recollection into focus, it disappears. I was leaving a very strange and beautiful place," he said dreamily. "but I cannot remember it well. It seems as if the image I seek is right here before me, but a barrier of fog obscures it each time it begins to solidify and I start to envision it."

Caroline stood up and walked over to Dalloway, and Conrad jumped in response, frightened that she might get too close, frightened by the unknown, by fear itself. She looked at him reassuringly, and her gaze calmed his beating heart.

"There is something important, very important, that I must do," the elf strained to recall. "Some instructions that I was given." His eyes were shut tightly and the effort to remember was plain on his delicate features. "I was to go somewhere, to find something." Finally, he sighed deeply, and his head lolled upon his chest. "That is all that I can remember," he said.

"I can help you to remember," she said calmly. "Will you let me?"

"No, Caroline! It is dangerous," Conrad pleaded.

"If it is unsafe for you to do so, then you must not try," Dalloway said.

"It is safe," she replied. "I know that it is safe, and I know that together we can bring back your memory," she said confidently. "I too bear some of your past within me already. And I too see the path that you have been attempting to return back down. It is obscured for me as well, but it beckons."

"How can you be certain?" Conrad asked. "What if you are wrong and you become lost forever?"

"I am not wrong, father. I was meant for this," she said with conviction. "Mother's legacy is strong within me, and I have had the opportunity to learn about myself these past few years. My animal friends have taught me well. Trust me," she beseeched him.

"Would that I could be as sure as you, my darling. I could not bear it if you were mistaken and if I willingly allowed you to try this."

"Trust me," she said again in a mature and ineluctable tone.

Conrad finally nodded his head, and squeezed his daughter's hand tightly.

"I would welcome your effort if you two are agreed," Dalloway replied graciously.

Conrad stared at Caroline with a look that brimmed with love and concern, and she stared back reassuringly.

"Do not worry, father. I know what I am doing," she said with confidence. "I am not afraid." She then sat down upon the floor next to her and took his hand in her own. They looked into each others eyes. "Relax and let me in," she said to him. "I will teach your mind to speak just like I do with the animals," she smiled.

Within seconds, both pairs of their eyes closed, both of their bodies went limp, their heads lolled upon their necks trance-like, and Conrad could do nothing more than helplessly gaze upon the two of them as his heart began to beat within his chest faster and harder than it had ever done before.

Chapter Eighteen

Teetoo and Alemar joined Elsinestra and Treestar just as the sun began to rise over the far horizon. The Princess stared out across the quiet city, now slightly illuminated by the rays of light, and sighed deeply. She backed away from the tower wall and turned to face the others who were still seated at the large table in the center of the thickly carpeted floor.

"Such a beautiful sight," she said. "I feel as if I am in the heavens themselves. Is this how thing look to you all the time?"

"It is a different perspective," Teetoo replied. "Looking down upon the tops of things, I see what others do not," he acknowledged.

"It seems so calm," Alemar commented. "Why would anyone want to destroy this?"

"What feels calm to you is torment to him," Elsinestra replied. "A lost and unsettled soul can find no peace."

"Are there no other choices for him?" the Princess asked. "Need everything be destroyed in order to still his pain?"

"It is a pain we cannot understand," Treestar said. "He is not one of us."

"I am alone in this world too," Teetoo said reflectively. "I am the last of my kind. There is something so frightening about being the last."

"Do you think that it is fear that drives him?" Alemar asked.

"In part. Fear drives us all at some point. But we all react differently to it. Fear of the unknown, fear for those we love, fear for those yet unborn. There are many kinds of fear, but it cannot rule the heart," Elsinestra said.

"He has no heart," Treestar remarked. "He is motivated by anguish and hate."

"Is there no way to appeal to him?" Alemar asked.

"He is beyond our help," Treestar replied with certainty.

"There was a time once," Teetoo said. "Premoran is of the same blood. And there is none as good as he. But alas that time has long passed. Colton is no longer of this world."

"It is so tragic. Look at the city," she said, and she rose and pointed to the horizon. "Is there anything you can imagine that could be so beautiful? How can he not see the simple beauty in life?"

"Do not try to understand his mind, my dear," Elsinestra said.

"It will only frustrate you. There is no good in him to find."

"He is beyond good and evil," Teetoo said. "He does not live within that perspective. In his mind, what he seeks is not wrong. He needs to escape this world and he cannot do so if this world continues to exist. There is no other way for him."

"So we must destroy him first," she said contemplatively. "It is ironic, is it not? Could he not simply kill himself and end his own torment?"

"How can you annihilate a soul?" Treestar asked. "It would remain a part of this world as long as the world remains. The only way out for him is dissolution."

"And if we do kill him, then what? If we cannot remove his evil spirit from this earth even through his death, then how can we prevail?" Alemar asked.

"We buy ourselves time, my dear. A respite," Elsinestra said. "The quest for the Gem of Eternity must continue. If the boy can find it, perhaps your questions can be answered."

"Yes. First things first. Besides, what is the alternative?" Treestar asked. "We must confront him at every juncture. His desires are not new. It is only recently, since the trees have begun to die, that he has become so aggressive. They kept him in check before, when the Gem radiated freely and the world was safe."

"'Twas no safer then than now," Elsinestra said, and she placed her palm atop her husband's hand. "The danger has always been present. But Caeltin has truly become bolder."

"Why do the trees not come to our aid? Are they all waiting to die?" Alemar asked.

"The fabric weaves of its own will, Princess. I am sure that they are doing what they can and must, though their actions may not be visible to us. You have communed with your own Lalas in Eleutheria. Did he not seem vital and strong? They do what they do beyond the scope of our vision and knowledge. Surely, they have only enmity for the Dark Lord. He is their enemy as much as he is ours. He wishes to witness their demise as readily as he does ours. It is inconceivable that they would stand idly by, or simply withdraw from the fray during our time of need," the Queen said.

"If they do not oppose him actively, then they encourage him all the more," Alemar persisted.

"We cannot know what the Lalas think. All we can be certain of is that they would never conspire against us, that they are truly our guardians. We must have faith," Elsinestra replied.

Teetoo was unusually quiet during this exchange, and Alemar looked at him questioningly. He turned his gaze away from her, and a hurt look involuntarily spread across her face in response.

"What is it Teetoo?" she asked. "Why are you so sullen?"

He was silent for another moment before looking at her once again. His saucer-like eyes were tinged with sadness.

"This discussion reminds me of one that I had with Premoran many times before. He had been tormented for tiels now about this very subject. He had been concerned about the Lalas' role in the wake of Colton's waxing power, and sadly he did not have the opportunity to mollify that concern. He gathered each and every shard, and he always hoped that in its death throe, one of the great trees would address his incertitude."

"And I too wonder," Alemar said. She looked out over the wall, placed both hands upon it and then leaned forward. She then breathed as deeply as she could. "The air here is very much alive. It is hard to accept that our world is so imperiled," she said sadly.

Elsinestra began to recite softly.

"What if the air were pure as gold and the water to stone should turn?
What if the birds were free and gay and the heavens commence to burn?
What if the sun did shine so bright and the oceans doth seethe and churn?
Why do we need to understand what is beyond our power to learn?

We ask the questions and search for the truth.
We encumber the earth with the burden of proof.
But we are no more than dust in the wind,
We come and we go like ripples in a stream,
In the eternity of time, we are but a dream,
A wisp, a sparkle, a moment, a beam,
A smile, a look, a feeling, a scene,
A touch, a gaze, a memory, a scream,

Here today and then no more,
a wave upon a distant shore,
the sand that through the sieve doth pour,
a yearning to unlock the door,
so fleeting, so transient,
so ephemeral, so brief,
so momentary, so short-lived,
a vanishing thief,

we yearn for the answers
we tally the score,
we shuffle our choices,
we pound on the door,
we cannot still the voices
that cry out for more,
for need's a profligate and wicked whore.
we crave so much more...
always, yet more...
Forever, still more..."

They all remained still and quiet for a moment or two after she finished speaking.

"That is so sad," Alemar finally said, breaking the silence.

"I always thought so," Elsinestra replied. "But it is also comforting in its own way. We cannot always know everything. Must we always try to? What need drives us so?"

"If knowledge can help us, then how can we not try?" Alemar asked.

"One day not too long ago, Premoran and I were having just such a discussion," Teetoo said. "I was also melancholy, and I yearned to know my place in this world," he recalled dreamily. "Premoran reminded me that everything lives on in that which survives. Nothing passes from this earth completely. He told me this because I was afraid that when I die, the legacy of my race will perish with me, as I am the last of my kind. He made me see that once a living thing has been born, it can never truly die, since it has set into motion so much simply by being alive. The results of its actions and interactions cannot be wiped away short of dissolution, and its trail shall lead into eternity. The trees know this. They will not allow the Dark Lord to prevail if it is in their power to prevent it," he continued. "We must have faith. Elsinestra is correct, Princess. We cannot know everything, and it is not even necessary that we do. Truly, the fabric weaves of its own will, and even the great Lalas cannot control the path of every thread and filament. Their perspective is different than ours, as much so as a bird's is from a man's, and I know that for a fact," he smiled.

"The lesson to be learned, my dear, is that we must continue to oppose, continue to resist, continue to fight and continue to search until we find the means to halt Caeltin's advance. The struggle will never end as long as time marches on. The twins are free! We could not have made that claim a year ago! We did not even know that Tomas existed," Treestar exclaimed.

"The Quest has truly begun," Teetoo said solemnly. "The prophesies have become reality once again. You and I, Alemar," he said, turning to the Princess, "must now fulfill our own destinies. We must find a way to free Premoran from Sedahar."

"And may the First protect you both!" Elsinestra swore, as they made their way toward the stairway.

"I am afraid that we must learn to protect ourselves," Alemar said dolefully. "At least until the Gem has been found," she replied, gazing once more over the balustrade and the tops of the buildings northward.

"Do not underestimate a power you cannot fully comprehend. Though many battles are being fought simultaneously, we cannot determine to what ends," Elsinestra responded, as she walked down the winding stairway.

"The trees will not forsake us," Treestar said, bringing up the rear.

"Nay, Princess. They have taught us the meaning of honor. They could never betray us," Elsinestra said confidently. "We must trust in their wisdom," she concluded, as they stepped out into the courtyard where the horses awaited them.

Alemar smiled affably at the others, but her heart had begun to ache and she knew not why. A terrible, nagging feeling had crept silently and secretly into her soul, and she felt the desperate need to weep. She maintained her composure as they all made their way to the platforms and bid each other a final farewell. She suppressed the doubts that were threatening to overwhelm her as she mounted her mare, but the anxiety remained even as she and Teetoo boarded the lifts and commenced their slow drop to the forest floor below. The Princess looked up and saw Elsinestra and Treestar smiling down at them, silhouetted by the now bright sunshine beaming out from behind, and she raised her arm in salute. For a brief moment, their bodies blocked the light, and she felt a dark and ominous shadow descend upon her. It quickly obscured their smiles and muted the beautiful song of Seramour.

Chapter Nineteen

"Are you alright?" Cairn called to Robyn from about ten yards away. He was once again crouched over Filaree's prone and unmoving body.

"Yes," Robyn replied. "I need only a few moments to regain my strength," he said, though he looked far weaker than he claimed.

"When you are ready, it would be helpful if you could come over here," Cairn said apprehensively.

Davmiran walked to Cairn and Filaree, and he squatted down beside them. Without speaking, he lifted the woman's hand and pressed it between his own.

"She has been stricken by the Dark Lord's power," he said almost at once. "I sense it in her blood. We must purge her of this or she will die," he said as calmly as if he was telling them that she had a slight cold.

"What are you waiting for then?" Cairn asked, his agitation obvious. "Can you do it, Dav?"

"I do not know," he answered honestly. "But I will try."

"Robyn? Perhaps you should help us out here if you can," Cairn urged.

"I still need some more time, I am afraid," he replied in a frail voice. "I am too weak to be of much use just now," he said with his eyes only half open.

"How much time does she have?" Cairn asked the boy, who had already began to hum to himself strangely.

"Yes, it is grave," Dav said. "The power is spreading like a virus in her bloodstream. If it reaches her heart before I can stop it, she will surely perish."

Calyx, who was standing guard behind Cairn, began to growl, though not in an angry tone, but the others were too preoccupied with what they were doing to notice him. Cairn watched Filaree and Davmiran as closely as he would a viper poised before him, ready to strike, and Robyn had slumped to the ground and sat there with his head lolling upon his shoulders. Davmiran had his eyes tightly closed and he appeared to have entered into a deep trance. They did not even notice as the two strange women hastened over and kneeled down beside them.

"Fetch Dahlia," the dark skinned one said. "Make haste, Rose," she urged. "We have no time to waste." The younger girl turned and sped off.

Cairn snapped his head around and stared at Emmeline. She smiled back reassuringly, and he was immediately put at ease. She laid her hand upon his, and he relaxed even further.

"Welcome to Parth," she whispered. "Would that it were under better circumstances. The Tower is secure, but it seems no longer to be safe as in the ages past," she said regretfully. "My name is Emmeline," she said, squeezing his hand affectionately.

Cairn looked at her quizzically but he did not speak. He was far more worried about Filaree than he ever imagined he could be. His heart pounded with each passing moment that she lay senseless before them. Calyx nuzzled the small woman who stood beside him and she laughed in response. The Moulant seemed to have taken to her immediately and that served to further put Cairn at ease.

"The boy seems to know what he is doing," Emmeline said as she watched Davmiran closely. "Has he had much training? He is quite young still."

"It comes naturally to him," Cairn replied, though his eyes were once again upon Filaree and Davmiran. "Can you help?"

"Me?" she asked as if the question was a very odd one. "I am not the best of our healers. But one of the other sisters has found her calling in this area. She will be here momentarily."

Even as they spoke, a middle aged woman came running from the other side of the wall behind which they were crouched. Cairn could see her head bobbing up and down as she sped toward them and he watched her brown braid rising and falling in the air as she moved. In seconds, she was beside Emmeline and she wasted no time. She stooped down next to the boy, placed her left hand upon his and she put her right palm on Filaree's forehead. With her eyes tightly shut, she began to hum in a high pitch. As if that was a cue, Davmiran followed her lead and he too was soon humming again, now in harmony with the sister.

In the meanwhile, Rose too had returned carrying a flask of kala sap and another of Lalas tea, the smell of which was unmistakable. She bent down next to Robyn and offered it to him. The Chosen took the syrupy kala first with a smile, and drank some of it. He then greedily poured the tea into his mouth and drank heavily until the container was empty.

"Thank you, sister," he said when he was done, and his voice was already sharper and more steady than before. "That has helped me beyond measure."

Rose bowed her head in acknowledgment and blushed.

Davmiran and Dahlia were swaying slightly in harmony with the sounds and within an instant, a white light began to spread around Filaree emanating from where the sister's hand lay upon her. It grew in size rather quickly at first, and then it seemed to stall and hover silently for a moment or two. Suddenly, another zephyr of spinning light formed above her feet and rapidly swathed her entire body, consuming the original light in its greater intensity. It did not take long before the stricken warrior was barely visible beneath the shimmering blanket of luminosity. The brightness encircled her like a multicolored cocoon, and it sparked and crackled as it wove a healing web around her. Just as quickly, she began to stir. Her fingers moved involuntarily and her knees rose up slightly. Her body began to convulse and rise and fall with her movements.

"Assist them," Robyn instructed Cairn. "She could hurt herself if she is not restrained," he said painstakingly as he was still not fully recovered. "The poison is being drawn out from her veins."

Cairn immediately sat beside her and as gently as possible, he pressed his weight against her, though the upheavals were growing more violent and difficult to still. He had to lay almost across her entire prone body in order to keep her from thrashing around. The light flowed over him as well as he lay, pressing down upon her, and it relaxed him immeasurably as he fought to keep her from further injury.

Dahlia shuddered from head to toe suddenly, and Dav swooned beside her, blacking out, or so it appeared to those watching. Filaree let out a shriek that put the fear of the First in the others momentarily, and then she just as quickly opened her eyes. The thrashing about stopped and she looked around suspiciously at first, seeing the strange sisters gathered beside her. She then noticed Cairn atop her and she shoved him hard.

"Is this really necessary?" she asked him, as a slender smile crossed her lips.

Cairn sat up abruptly, and then he turned as red as a ripened beet.

"It is good to have you back, my Lady," he said, regaining his composure. "But if you are not careful, I will ask Calyx to replace me the next time my services are requested," the scholar laughed.

"Would you do that for me?" she asked the Moulant who was standing protectively nearby.

Calyx bellowed affectionately and stood up as tall as he could, dwarfing everyone else.

Davmiran and Dahlia had also both opened their eyes and were apparently back to normal, though fatigue and surprise showed upon both of their faces.

"How did you weave that healing blanket?" Davmiran asked the sister.

"I thought you were the one who did it. I was simply adding what power I could to the mesh," she replied, rather stunned at the boy's question.

"No, it was not my doing." Turning to Robyn, he asked, "Was it you?"

"No, it was not me either, though I would love to take credit for it. It was a beautiful casting, full of the earth power," he replied.

Emmeline was crouching still in the background beside Rose and Robyn. She let her gaze fall to the ground and she said nothing.

"Sister?" Robyn inquired of her. "How did you do that?" he asked, realizing suddenly who was responsible for the event.

Emmeline was reluctant to lift her head and answer the Chosen, though shyness was never a component of her character.

"I have been practicing of late," she replied. "I did not think that I would be strong enough. These things are new to us all here in Parth."

"The method was quite unique. There is much power here and you drew upon it well," Robyn complimented her. "Have the other sisters developed their skills as well as you two have?" he inquired.

"We have all been studying hard and practicing even harder. Some have the gift while others seem unable to discover it yet," Emmeline explained.

The expression upon Rose's face grew sad and the sister fidgeted uncomfortably. Emmeline noticed her discomfort, and she reached out her hand to console her.

"Though it is new to us all, it comes more easily to some," she said.

"For many, the path to discovery is like walking through a maze. Not all who enter reach the end at the same time," Robyn replied. "It is indeed a gift notwithstanding, but as with all gifts, it creates an obligation too. In some cases, a gift can become a burden. Tread carefully, sister," he warned.

"Thank you for the advice," Emmeline said gratefully. "It is still so new to us that we have yet to understand the responsibilities that come with the power. We have embraced the study wholeheartedly, and we have adopted our new purpose humbly. We have much to learn. Perhaps you may be of assistance to the sisters during your stay in Parth?" she asked, and her pale grey eyes sparkled against her dark skin.

"It would be my pleasure, sister, though I have other pressing responsibilities as well," he replied, and he dipped his chin in Dav's direction. "Perchance we can assist one another?"

Emmeline bowed her head humbly. "It would be an honor, Robyn dar Tamarand," she responded, flattered by his charm and magnanimity.

"We should all return to the Tower now. Though we are safe behind the shield, I am sure you are all tired and weary from your travels. You can refresh yourselves and we can discuss the future," she said, no longer shy.

"The future," Robyn echoed. "Yes, we can discuss the future."

Filaree had risen slowly from the ground, as had the others who had gathered around her. She thanked each of the people who had helped her; Cairn with an affectionate squeeze; Calyx by standing upon her toes and kissing him on his furry chin; Davmiran she hugged warmly; while Dahlia she shook hands with rather formally but respectfully. She saved her gratitude for Emmeline until last. The older woman projected an unassuming aura that she took to immediately. In fact she reminded her of her mother in more ways than one; her humble attitude coupled with a noble demeanor, her silent strength and her underlying confidence all mirrored Queen Esta's character.

"I am thankful that you have been 'practicing', as you so stated a moment ago. I do not know what would have become of me had you not been present in my hour of need," she said gratefully.

"Do not thank me, my Lady," Emmeline said, bowing her head. "We are all merely dust swept away by the same wind. Those who can, must assist whenever and wherever they touch down."

"I thank you nonetheless," Filaree replied. "Gratitude need not be excluded simply because we all face the same peril. I acknowledge your effort and commend your skill."

"Luck, perhaps. Skill? I am merely a novice. You have a true master in your entourage," she said, deferring to Robyn. "We all hope to learn under his tutelage."

"Are we welcome here then?" Robyn said jokingly, and they all laughed a hearty laugh. "The barrier you have constructed around the tower seems quite impenetrable. It would tax even my skill, I imagine, if we needed to break through it in order to escape."

"No need to think of escape. You are most welcome! You may remain here as long as need requires you to," Emmeline replied.

"The sisters have somehow managed to unearth some manuals that have aided us immeasurably in understanding all that is occurring. Perchance you will peruse them yourself when you find the time," Dahlia added.

"Yes, by all means," Emmeline concurred. "We have only just touched their surface."

"I welcome the opportunity, sisters. Cairn?" he addressed his companion. "Did you hear what the women said? After all, you are the most studious of the group."

Cairn had been busy poking his finger in and out of the barrier, much like a small child who had been handed a new and mesmerizing toy. It was pliable and it stretched in response to his prodding. He turned abruptly when his name was mentioned, and once again, the usually somber scholar blushed deeply.

"No. I am sorry. I did not. I was quite fascinated with this wall here," he replied. "It is amazing! Is it meant to keep you in or the enemy out?"

"We are unsure," Emmeline replied, thinking to herself how fortunate it was that Tamara and Angeline departed before the shield manifested itself.

"Did you not erect it in defense?" Dav inquired.

"We did not erect it at all," Dahlia answered.

"No, it was not of our making, my son," Emmeline continued. "We thought at first that it arose in response to something from without, yet there was no apparent threat at the time. Now we see that our suspicions were correct. We certainly are grateful for it now. But it was a product of the earth, not the sisters of Parth."

Robyn looked upon it with renewed interest after Emmeline spoke and Davmiran cocked his head in consternation.

"Whatever its source," Filaree proclaimed, "I am happy to be behind it now."

"Aye to that!" Cairn agreed. "We have been running for long enough. The time has come for us to settle in and get on with our charge."

"Your purpose and ours may yet coincide," Emmeline replied. "It is good to have you all here. Shall we proceed to the Tower?" Emmeline asked them, and she extended her arm toward the imposing stone building in the distance.

Chapter Twenty

Tomas walked down the narrow stone path in total darkness. He required no illumination to find his way back to his friends in the cavern below. The ring hung heavily around his neck, and a comforting warmth emanated from it and spread quickly throughout his entire body. He reached into his shirt and grasped it with his fingers. It was surprisingly cold to the touch, despite the heat that it seemed to generate all around it.

It must come from somewhere within it, he speculated. *The warmth is real. I feel it on my skin, but the object itself is ice cold!*

Tomas continued down the dark corridor until he reached a V shaped juncture. Without hesitating, he followed the left most fork and descended a narrow, winding passage. He could see where he was going irrespective of the almost total darkness. Even with his eyes closed, the path he needed to follow was obvious to him. He proceeded without bumping in to the hard, cold walls and without tripping upon the loose rocks that littered the floor of the cave, until he found himself near the chamber within which his friends still lingered.

During the time that Tomas had been gone, Elion, Esta, Preston and Stephanie took turns reassuring one another that he was safe. They were all so intricately bound together emotionally and in other ways as well that they seemed even to share the fears and the doubts which first surfaced in one of the group and migrated to another and another in turn.

"I know in my heart that he will return to us," Stephanie said as they sat around a small fire and shared a meal of mushrooms once again.

"I hope he does so soon," Preston replied. "I don't know how many more days I can eat these things," he commented, trying to lighten the gloomy atmosphere.

"Thank the First for them!" Esta remarked. "We would have had to have left here by now if it was not for them."

"He would still find us no matter where we were," Stephanie said confidently. "Anyway Preston, how can you be concerned about food when Tomas is missing?"

"It is depressing enough in here already, Steph, without me adding to it. I meant no harm," he apologized, and the girl smiled understandingly back at him.

Elion sat pensively beside the others, but he did not join in the conversation. He appeared to be lost in reverie, though by his expression, the memories or thoughts he contemplated could not have been fond ones. They had all grown accustomed to the dim illumination provided by the phosphorescent particles that lay abundantly in the crevices and cracks of the walls and floors, and it was easy now to see each other despite the semi-darkness.

"What troubles you?" Esta finally asked the young elf.

He had been contemplative and quiet for most of the day now, and though Elion was never as lively and quick to enter into conversation as Preston, he was always affable and polite. Elion raised his head and stared into the darkness before him.

"Until now, I too had been confidant that Tomas would return to us within a matter of minutes. Now that the minutes have turned into hours, I am not so sure," he admitted.

"What has changed?" Preston asked surprised. His confidence had not yet wavered. "Why? It really has not been that long since we discovered him missing. We all know that he is a very independent person. He always does things on the spur of the moment, inspired by things I do not even understand."

"Exactly," Queen Esta agreed. "He is quite whimsical in his own way. For him to wander off without a word is not all that surprising."

"What is disturbing you, Elion?" Stephanie asked, her intuition piquing her curiosity and infecting her own mood. "What exactly is bothering you now?"

"I cannot tell you for certain. But since this morning I have had this odd feeling that we are not alone here," he admitted. "In fact, since we arrived here, I have sensed another presence, but I was too concerned with other things to focus on it. Since Tomas disappeared, this issue has prayed upon my mind much more, as you can all imagine."

"I know that your sensibilities are far more attuned than any of ours to such things," Esta remarked. "Is it anything specific that has triggered your concern?"

"No evidence, if that is what you mean by specific. I have seen no one nor have I heard anything. But I cannot help but feel that there are others present in this mountain."

"Could Tomas have known that? Do you think he went to find them?" Stephanie asked. "I think that you know more than you are telling us, Elion," she said. She was growing more concerned by the moment.

"Was he spirited away whilst he lay unconscious? Is that what you think?" Preston asked ominously. "Do you know something we do not know?"

"Taken from us as I took his brother outside of Pardatha?" Elion asked, addressing his first question.

"Yes, exactly," the young dwarf replied.

"No, I do not believe anyone or anything has either kidnapped him or taken him against his will. And I have this sense that he was awake and in control of his faculties when he departed."

They all sat there perplexed and bewildered. It was disconcerting enough when they first discovered Tomas missing, but to now discover that Elion harbored suspicions that the premises were inhabited by creatures other than the five of them was even more disquieting. Elion appeared to be deep in thought, and he hung his head pensively.

"I have not told any of you this yet for fear of disturbing you unnecessarily," he said, breaking the silence. "Since there was nothing we could have done with the knowledge that would have helped us or Tomas, I have kept it to myself since we arrived here."

"Speak, Elion," Esta said anxiously. "What is it you wish to tell us?"

They all leaned in closely in order to hear what he was going to reveal.

"The seconds before Tomas collapsed just prior to when I carried him in here, he said something to me," Elion began to relate to them. He raised his head and looked first at Esta and then at Preston and finally he rested his eyes upon Stephanie's young face. "He exclaimed that he had been betrayed," Elion said gravely.

"Betrayed? Who by? Was he referring to one of us?" Esta replied, shocked at the implication.

"Never!" Stephanie exclaimed, shaking her head back and forth. "That's impossible!"

"It cannot be!" Preston reiterated, taken aback by the thought.

"No," Elion said. "'Twas none of us, my friends," Elion replied quickly to their concern. "Though I cannot say which would have been worse."

"Who then?" Preston asked apprehensively.

"I find it hard even now to say it," Elion said, and he stared down at the floor.

"Please do not make us suffer any longer. Tell us," Stephanie beseeched him. "Why would anyone other than the Dark Lord or one of his kind want to hurt Tomas?" she asked astounded.

"It is difficult to say this," Elion stumbled.

The eyes of the other others were glued on Elion's face, and they waited in silence now as he gathered the strength to speak. His anguish was almost tangible.

"Ormachon!" he uttered quietly and quickly.

They all gasped simultaneously and shook their heads in denial.

"You must have heard him wrong!" Esta exclaimed. "That is inconceivable!"

"He is his Chosen, his bond-mate! There is no way this can be true!" Preston said.

"I will not believe that!" Stephanie said, and she hugged herself tightly with both her arms while she shook back and forth animatedly.

"But it is what he said nonetheless," Elion repeated softly and seriously. "I heard it myself the moment before he fell unconscious. If I was not absolutely sure, I would never make this assertion."

"I am frightened," Stephanie said suddenly. Preston moved to put his arm around her comfortingly.

"What could this mean?" Esta asked. "There must be some other explanation. A Lalas would not do such a thing."

"I have spent the past few days asking myself that question too, my Lady," Elion said, and he bent his head down sadly.

"Is there any chance you are mistaken, Elion?" Preston asked. "Could it be that you misheard his words?"

"I wish that were the case," the elf replied sadly. "But I unfortunately am quite sure of what he said. I heard the words as clearly as if I said them myself."

"Is the presence you sense here and evil one?" Esta asked, returning to Elion's initial concern momentarily. "I feel suddenly quite insecure," she admitted, and she looked around suspiciously.

"No, Esta. It does not feel so to me," he said reassuringly. "I do not think we are in any danger from it. The feeling is quite powerful though."

"I am beside myself!" Stephanie admitted. "What is happening to our world? This is so awful." She began to weep softly.

"We must renew our search for Tomas," Esta said determinedly, as she stood up and began to pace across the stone floor. "The poor boy!"

"Betrayed by his own tree," Preston repeated to himself. "How horrible! No wonder he would not awaken. How could he face such a situation?"

"For us all, it is a dismal thought," Elion said. "For us all, Preston."

"I will not believe it until I speak with Tomas once again," Stephanie said vehemently. "There will be some other explanation. You will see," she said to them all.

"I hope so," Esta replied from somewhere in the darkness. "By the First, I truly hope so."

Elion was poking at the fire and attempting to keep it alive without having to rise at that moment and retrieve more wood for it. Preston sat there with his arm tightly around Stephanie's shoulders, simply shaking his head back and forth, and Queen Esta paced and paced.

"I cannot stand here any longer," Esta said frankly. "Preston? You are adept at navigating this sanctuary. We must find him immediately! We have not come this far just to give up now. We cannot sit here any longer waiting for him to return. He could be in danger. How awful he must feel!"

"You are right, my Lady!" Preston replied. "We must begin to search at the least. I feel so for him. He must be so sad!"

"And frightened!" Stephanie added. "Tomas is courageous, and he has suffered so much already. But I know him, and this must have been devastating to him. I cannot bear the thought of him wandering these caverns alone with this knowledge. Elion, I wish you had told us before." Elion hung his head woefully.

"Alas, so do I now. I thought only to save you all from worry. It was a mistake and I apologize for it."

"I did not mean to criticize," Stephanie said quickly. "It would have made no difference really. You were only being kind."

"From now on, I will not presume so," Elion replied.

"Suffer no regrets, Elion!" Esta said boldly. "Your motives were honorable. Besides, it would not have changed things for us had we known sooner. It would have caused us all only more anguish. We would not have guarded him any more closely than we did. He would have slipped away nonetheless."

"She is right, of course," Stephanie said sheepishly. "I spoke too soon, Elion. It was selfish of me to say that. I am just worried, that is all."

"But you are correct regardless. I had no right to withhold this from the group," Elion said downcast.

"We are wasting time. What is done, is done!" Preston interrupted, though with no bitterness in his tone. "We must find him as soon as we can. If he is despondent and frightened, he could wander anywhere. He needs us now more than ever!"

"There are three passages that lead out from this chamber," Esta said. "One would return us to the place through which we entered, and the other two head deeper into the mountain. How do we choose which to pursue?"

"Do you think he went to find Ormachon?" Stephanie asked.

"That was my first thought too," Preston said.

"It would have been mine as well, if I did not sense some other presence here," Elion said. "I am sure Tomas felt it also."

"He must have! His sensitivities are so acute. He must have gone to find out what it is. But which tunnel would he have chosen?" Esta asked.

Preston walked to one of the openings, the floor of which inclined upward slightly. His eyes were already accustomed to the semi-darkness, and a dwarf's eyes were far more suited to seeing in the dim light to begin with. He got down on all fours and began to sift through the powdery, sparkling fragments which lay upon the surface, slowly making his way toward the passage, when all of a sudden the others heard him gasp loudly and they rushed to the source of the noise.

Elion had drawn his dagger, as did Esta, and Stephanie raised her arms protectively in front of her, brandishing a stick that she lifted from a pile next to the fire.

"Tomas!" Preston exclaimed, his voice infused with both surprise and relief.

Tomas walked into the room with his friends, and they all quickly embraced him. Stephanie was weeping with joy, Preston was pounding him on the back, Esta was standing behind him smoothing his hair as if she were his mother, while Elion stood by smiling.

"Why did you do that Tomas?" Stephanie asked as if she was angry at him, though relief was clearly motivating her. "You could have told us you were going somewhere. No one would have stopped you."

"Are you all right?" Preston asked. "What happened?"

Tomas seemed relaxed and untroubled, and his mood surprised them all. After what Elion had related, each of them expected that when they finally did find each other again he would be despondent and uneasy, if not totally anguished. But he was smiling and casual, as if he had gone for a simple morning stroll.

"Yes, I am fine," he replied. "I thought not about what I was doing at first. It was as if I was in a trance. By the time I was aware of what was happening, it was too late to return and advise you all," he explained. "I am sorry for causing so much concern."

"What is more important," Esta began, "is that you are all right. Elion informed us of your revelation," she said forthrightly.

The boy's eyes opened wide before he hung his head for a moment, but he quickly lifted it again and looked at Esta's face

"Be not concerned, your highness. I have come to grips with it," he replied.

"What are you talking about?" Stephanie burst out. "How could you possibly come to grips with something like that? You must be devastated!" she continued, and immediately regretted her impetuousness once again. She covered her pretty mouth with her hand as if she had said something terrible.

"It was not as it seemed," he explained. "There was purpose to Ormachon's behavior."

"As I suspected," Esta said, nodding her head.

"None of us believed it could be true," Preston added, as he gazed knowingly at Elion.

"It is a complicated story, and I have no facts to support my belief, but I am convinced that the 'betrayal' was necessary," Tomas said.

Elion stood in the background listening intently to every word Tomas uttered. He was still smiling, but his worry had not fully abated.

"Elion?" the boy said to him, realizing that he had not joined in the conversation along with the others. "Are you not happy to have me back too?" Tomas asked, jokingly.

"More than you could imagine," Elion said seriously. "But I know there is much you have to tell us, and I am anxious to hear it. Who else abides in this mountain?" he asked bluntly.

"Elion is convinced that we are not alone here," Esta explained. "It has been troubling him since you disappeared."

"Tell us, Tomas. Where were you? What happened to you?" Stephanie asked.

Tomas walked toward the fire that still burned in the middle of the floor, and he beckoned the others to join him around it. When they had all finally sat down once more and they could each look upon one another easily, Tomas began to speak.

"Yes, Steph, I was stricken beyond measure by Ormachon's actions," he related. "My mind was overwhelmed by the revelation. I must have collapsed, because the next thing I remembered I was lying in this very room, and my head was pounding."

"You did. I carried you back here to the cave Preston discovered just before the storm hit," Elion explained.

Tomas smiled at his friend.

"It seems that without you, my brother and I both are unable to take care of ourselves," he laughed. "That was no ordinary storm, Elion," Tomas replied, and his demeanor changed dramatically with those words.

"We suspected so," Esta said. "But the cavern sheltered us sufficiently from it. Preston spotted it in the nick of time," the Queen nodded to the dwarf warmly.

"The mountain is shielded," Tomas said. "'Twas no coincidence that you found it when you did, Preston. Thank the First that we met one another," Tomas said gratefully while simultaneously grasping his friend's arm.

"The fabric weaves of its own will," Esta said. "Have you something to tell us, Tomas?" she then asked. "As we said a moment ago, Elion is convinced that we are not alone here. Are you of the same mind?"

"I have sensed the presence of others since we entered this shelter," Elion confirmed. "Though now the feeling seems to have abated," he said curiously.

"Your instincts were correct, Elion, and they are correct once again," Tomas reasserted. "When I awoke it was not entirely of my own volition. I was 'called', much as my brother's teachers were 'called' to Pardatha by Baladar. I knew not why at first, but I suspected from whence the summons came. Even in the darkness, I knew just where to go. In a semi-conscious state, I walked to a chamber that had been warded and concealed deep within the heart of this mountain. There, I met with others of my kind, Chosen, who had gathered here for a number of reasons," he related to them, clearly unconcerned about revealing the events to his friends.

"This is quite unusual," Esta said gravely. "I have neither heard nor read of any other such meeting."

"These times are not like other times," Elion said. "But, would you or I or anyone other than a Chosen have been privy to this type of gathering had it ever occurred before anyway?" Elion asked.

"You make a valid point, Elion," the Queen agreed. "Though my dear husband was a Chosen too," she reminded him.

"But it was unprecedented regardless," Tomas said. "Quite unprecedented!"

"Have they all been betrayed by their trees?" Stephanie asked anxiously.

"Some have in other ways," Tomas said candidly. "But perhaps 'betrayed' is no longer the proper word to use to describe what was happening. The Lalas in their infinite wisdom are simply keeping things from us all. For what reasons, we do not know, nor will they tell us. But the others have convinced me that Ormachon gave away my location only to force us into this shelter from which, by the nature of the rock and the convergence of power herein, even his vision has been blocked."

"This mountain is impervious to both the Lalas vision and the Dark Lord's intrusions?" Elion asked.

"It seems so, Elion," Tomas replied. "That is why they chose this site to convene."

The others drew closer to Tomas, and their eyes were now glued upon the boy.

"Had we not been pursued by that storm, Preston would never have searched for the entrance and we would never have taken refuge here," Tomas explained.

"And you would not have found the others," Esta completed his thought.

"Exactly!" Tomas agreed. "We would have continued on our way to Avalain, and I would not have had a chance to meet with the them. The Chosen could not have summoned me as they did whilst we were roaming the open land. Their summons could have been overheard or detected, and they could not risk that."

"Why could not Ormachon simply have told you or instructed you or whatever it is he does when he communicates with you? Why did he have to reveal to Colton where you were?" Stephanie asked.

"He gained a confidence by so doing, one that was extremely hard to earn. And he has surely confused Colton enormously as well. This is what we all surmise," Tomas related.

"Correct me if I misstate what you are trying to say," Elion said. "Ormachon advised Caeltin of our whereabouts in order to frighten us into this cave so that you would then be summoned by the other Chosen? Is that not a bit farfetched, Tomas? I realize that it must be hard for you to accept what Ormachon has done, but regardless, this seems so unlikely, does it not?"

"Unlikely as it may appear, I believe it to be true," Tomas said honestly. "Something is preventing the Lalas from telling the Chosen what they are doing. But, surely they have a master plan that motivates their actions. We know they are dying, slowly, one by one," he continued. "We do not know amongst us why or what we can do to help them. What we hope is that the Gem of Eternity holds the key, and find it we must if we are to have any chance of saving ourselves and maybe even the remainder of the trees."

"Colton wants to find it as well, I guess," Stephanie said. "If he finds it first and destroys it what chance will the rest of us have?"

"Little or no chance, Steph," Preston said. "Don't the trees know where it is? Why can't they just direct your brother to it?"

"The location of the First who harbors the Gem is known to no one," Elion replied. "It has been so since the beginning of time."

"Not even to the other Lalas?" Stephanie asked.

"No. They do not know either, though they are bound to it in many ways," Tomas responded. "That was the only way to insure its safety. That is also why the First has never bonded with anyone."

"Why is it that now the light is being withheld? Does the First not know the effect such a masking is having on the world?" Esta asked.

"Caeltin has grown powerful. His reach has extended beyond his realm and he may be close to discovering its whereabouts himself. The shielding of the light may be a devastating but necessary result of that," Elion surmised.

"And so the Chosen agree," Tomas said. "And they believe that the weakening of the Gem's radiance has resulted in the continuing demise of the trees. They cannot or will not live in the absence of the light."

"So the conclusion brings us right back to the beginning once again," Esta said. "We must find the First and thereby the Gem before that evil beast does. And the longer it takes us, the more trees will die and the more our world will suffer."

"Exactly!" Tomas agreed. "And Ormachon did whatever he did in accordance with a plan that we may never fully know or realize."

He paused for a moment while everyone digested all of what was said.

"They fear for the first time in thousands of tiels," Tomas began to explain. "And we may therefore not understand all of their actions any longer."

"That is nothing knew to me," Stephanie remarked.

"Me either," Preston concurred with her.

"It does seem logical after all," Elion agreed. "I was very skeptical before, but there is a consistency to what we have said that rings true."

"Yes, it certainly does. But why would Ormachon want Colton to think that he is helping him?" Preston asked, still confused about that point at least.

"He would only want that if he wished the Dark Lord to think that he has given up on us," Stephanie said casually.

"That's it!" Elion almost shouted. "What you said makes perfect sense, Stephanie. It will certainly cause his confidence to flourish after his recent defeats. If he thinks that the trees have forsaken us and accepted dissolution as our inevitable fate, he might be thrown off guard, if only for a moment."

"Perhaps a crucial moment!" Esta said. "And that could give Davmiran and the rest of us just the advantage that we need."

"It could also generate a trust that the trees could use to their own advantage later on," Elion added.

"What must the Dark Lord be thinking?" Esta mused. "He knows that the Lalas have no more knowledge about the whereabouts of the Gem than he does. And now he thinks the trees, either one or many, are assisting him in preventing us from finding it ourselves. Thus, he must be convinced they have reconciled themselves to the conclusion that he has been pursuing since he first was exiled from the others."

"A natural conclusion considering that the trees really are dying!" Preston noted.

"And the best way to assure him of this would be to sacrifice you, Tomas!" Esta said.

"Or Dav," Elion added.

"Or both!" Stephanie said, and gasped once again. "Oh, I hope your brother is safe if his whereabouts have been revealed as well."

"Davmiran is safe," Tomas said convincingly. "That much I know for certain!"

"That is a relief to hear," Esta said. "I understand now why you are not quite so disturbed as you were before, Tomas. Reason and hope combined can be a potent elixir for an uneasy soul."

"When hope alone will not suffice," Elion added. "And in this case, we all required more than wishful thinking. But there is still so much we do not know." "We can speculate forever about this and we will be sure of no more than we are now," Preston said. "I say we start moving again and talk on the way. We will have plenty of time to ponder all of this."

"I agree," Esta said. "We should return to Avalain as we planned."

"Though I have always dreamed of Avalain, I have never wanted to go to it more than I do right now!" Stephanie said. "Do you think it is safe for us to leave here?"

"The storm has passed," Tomas said. "Colton has turned his attention elsewhere for the moment since he lost our trail. He seeks other things now. It is safe."

"Have the others all departed as well," Esta asked of the Chosen with whom he met previously.

"Yes. They have all returned to their homelands by now," Tomas replied. "We have agreed to keep in contact though."

"Oh?" Elion asked. "This is an encouraging disclosure."

"A council of sorts?" Esta asked.

"You could describe it so," Tomas replied. "Circumstances have made it ineluctable." Stephanie looked at him strangely, and he smiled. "Necessary, Steph," Tomas clarified. "That means necessary," he repeated, and she blushed in response to his words.

"Do the Lalas know of this?" Elion asked.

"No," Tomas answered. "That is the pattern of secrets, is it not? One leads to another. They have theirs and we now have ours," he said somewhat sullenly. "Though it will be most arduous to keep this from them, hide it we must." "Ineluctable?" Stephanie asked, smiling.

"Yes, exactly," Tomas replied and he grinned back at her.

The ring felt hot against his chest, but it was a comforting feeling, not at all a disagreeable one. Stephanie walked over to him and squeezed his arm affectionately, and he kissed her lightly on the forehead. Preston too sidled up to him as well and patted him sharply upon the back. Esta and Elion looked on approvingly, and then they too walked up to Tomas. They had all inadvertently formed a tight circle near the waning fire, five strikingly different silhouettes casting long shadows upon the wall of the cavern. They stood together in silence for a moment or two, with their heads bent and their eyes closed, and then as if on cue, they simultaneously separated. Without any further words, they all began to gather their belongings and prepare for the journey to Avalain.

Chapter Twenty-one

Tamara carefully placed the scroll back in the leather container that she had removed it from when capture seemed so imminent just moments ago. Gratefully, she sealed the case and slipped it into her blouse once again. Muttering a few words of thanks to the First under her breath, she followed Etuah as she led them deeper and deeper into the mountain. The strange woman did not question her about the scroll and she did not offer any explanation herself.

The rough hewn walls became smoother and smoother as they advanced, and the surface upon which they walked also grew less hazardous to traverse. Though many more tunnels appeared which led off of the one they walked through, Etuah did not waver for an instant in the direction in which she moved. The entire passage was curiously luminescent despite the fact that they had left the pit into which they had originally plummeted far behind. That had been open to the sky and therefore lighted by the sun from above regardless of its depth. Now though, they were deep into the rock where no illumination from above could reach any longer, and yet they could see with no problem. Tamara and Angeline both found this odd, and they scanned the walls and ceilings for torches or glow lamps, but there were none to be found.

"How is that we are able to see so clearly?" Tamara asked finally while still checking all around her for the answer, and Etuah looked at her with her enormous, platter like eyes and simply smiled.

"I wonder why she did not answer you," Angeline whispered in Tamara's ear. "Do you think she wishes it to remain a secret?"

"I do not know, sister. But if you have noticed, the light seems to accompany us as we walk, as if it turns on at our approach and turns off behind us as we advance. Look back. It is dark," she observed.

Angeline turned to look behind her, and lo and behold, it was pitch as night.

"Etuah carries nothing in her hands," Angeline said.

"No. I see that. It is curious," Tamara replied, pondering the situation.

They walked and walked for a long while in silence, following behind Etuah closely. It was hard to tell if they were descending or not, though the air seemed a bit more fragrant and certainly no thinner than before. The odor was musky but not unpleasant at all. In fact, it seemed to be refreshing as they breathed it in.

"Would you care for some water?" Etuah asked them suddenly.

"That would be wonderful," Tamara replied, not realizing how parched her throat was until the Drue mentioned it.

"In a moment then, we will stop for refreshment," Etuah said. "There is a spot just ahead."

They rounded a bend in the passage, and as they entered what appeared to be a chamber of sorts, they could hear the dripping sound of water echoing off of the walls. It was becoming easier and easier to see despite the fact that there still seemed to be no obvious source of illumination. The area that they had just moved into was not very large, and in its middle stood a pool of utterly still liquid. The pool itself was a perfect circle in shape, and the water came right to the top of it making it seem as if you could walk right across it without breaking stride or falling in. From the center of the ceiling hung a long and thin stalagmite that stopped about ten feet above the surface of the pool.

As Tamara watched, a single, thick drop of water fell heavily from the pointed stone into the pool below, and it caused the surface to ripple from the center out in a perfect rhythm, until the waves reached the edges and the water became still once again. The sound that the droplet made when it hit the main body of water was so beautiful that both of the women gasped in response. It was almost musical; high pitched and resonant.

Once they had all entered this chamber it became clearer to them that the light was coming from Etuah herself, for as she walked further into the open space, they could no longer see the areas behind her as clearly, while those before and around her suddenly became visible.

"You carry no light with you, Mistress," Tamara said. "Yet, your presence illumines the area around you. How is it so?"

"As guardians, we Drue are endowed with certain gifts. Our skin is unlike yours," she replied. "We retain what light we gather when we have the opportunity. It will fade with time."

"So you are the source?" Angeline asked.

"In a manner of speaking," she said. "A vessel, perhaps, would be a better description."

Etuah bent her long, thin body at the waist in an incredibly graceful manner and stuck the end of one suctioned finger into the pool. Scooping the liquid into it as if it was a cup, she pursed her thin lips and sucked it in loudly.

"Come," she beckoned to them. "Drink of the pool."

Tamara and Angeline gratefully walked to the edge and crouched down. Each of the women cupped their hands and dipped them into the water. It was cool to the touch, and it refreshed them even before they brought any of it to their mouths. Tamara gazed into the perfectly clear water and she saw Etuah's reflection looming behind her. Something caused her to turn around sharply and look at her face. The Drue woman was staring at her intently with a curious expression spread over her broad, flat countenance.

"What is it, Etuah? Is there something about me that disturbs you?" Tamara asked self consciously.

"No. Not at all. It is just that I sense a power within you that has been absent from the places we habituate for a long while. We are the guardians of the space left behind. Rarely are we fortunate enough to have a Chosen amongst us."

"A Chosen?" Tamara gasped. "Oh no! I am not a Chosen," she stammered as she stood up abruptly and faced the slender figure before her. "You are mistaken, Etuah. I am merely one of the sisters of Parth. Never would I presume to be a Chosen!" Tamara apologized for the Drue's error, and she shook her head vigorously in denial.

"Disclaim what you will. I sense a Chosen nonetheless," she replied, dismissing Tamara's protestations.

"I would surely know if I was a Chosen, would I not?" she asked rhetorically, embarrassed by their host's words. "I am so far from being one, that it is laughable. But I am most flattered by your misconception. Would that it were true," she replied, and she continued to look down at the ground humbly. "A Chosen," she muttered to herself. "Me, a Chosen!" she scoffed at the thought.

Etuah nodded her head knowingly, but said nothing more about it. In the meanwhile, Angeline was still stooped over next to the pool, gazing pensively into the still water. Tamara looked away from the Drue, anxious to change the subject which still caused her some discomfort. She walked over to her companion and crouched down next to her.

"Something has caught your eye, sister?" she asked.

"Have you looked into this water yet, sister?" Angeline replied.

"Yes," she answered. "But all that I saw was Etuah's reflection. Why? Is there more I should have seen?"

"The pool is so deep, yet it is clear nearly as far as I can see. Though nothing disturbs the stillness of the surface, there is movement in the depths of it. With each new drop that falls, it changes completely," she replied.

Tamara stared into the water too, and this time she immediately saw what Angeline was talking about. It did not seem like water any longer as she gazed deeply into it, but more like a portal into another world. It was hard to see at first, but the images became clearer with scrutiny. But, just as she felt she was beginning to discern figures and shapes amidst a heavily wooded background, a heavy drop of water hit the surface and caused a ripple to emanate from the center to the edges. As if this was a book she had been reading and a page had been turned before she was finished with the previous one, the entire scene before her eyes shifted. Once she was able to focus again, the scene she stared at was totally different from that of just a moment before.

"Curious, sister. Did you see that too?" she asked Angeline.

"Yes, I did. I have been watching this for a while longer than you, sister. It has changed with each new drop of liquid that falls from above."

"What is it that we are witnessing?" Tamara asked Etuah, turning away from the pool and looking back at the Drue.

"Bits and pieces," the woman replied. "The water is infused with life. It expresses itself as it wishes."

"Oh!" Tamara said, as if she understood what the woman was saying. "Is this the future or the past we see before us?"

"Is there a difference?" she asked, confused. "It is what it is."

"Certainly there is a difference between what was and what will be," Tamara said.

"For you perhaps. Not for us. We are the guardians of what is; of the void that is out of time. Here, nothing will ever change again," she said sadly. "There is no future and there is no past for us. Once the shards have been removed, these spaces no longer exist in the fourth dimension. Only the water renews itself and it brings to us concurrences. It matters not to us where they stand in time."

Tamara looked at Angeline to see if her friend understood this any better than she did herself, but it was clear from her expression that she was perplexed as well. They both sipped of the water nevertheless, and then they rose and stood beside Etuah. It was incredibly refreshing, and the two sisters smiled at one another involuntarily after swallowing some of it.

"We must go. You cannot remain with us for long," Etuah said, beckoning them to follow her.

Tamara was unsure if the Drue meant that because they had other pressing matters to attend to or because it was dangerous for them to stay here, but she heeded her guest's words without any further questions and hurried to follow. They walked down the stone path and kept as close behind their host as they could. The passage that they walked through seemed more and more like a roughly hewn tunnel as they drew further away from the point in which they entered. Those passages that extended off of the main one that they traveled were of varying widths, but most of them were certainly not wide enough for a human to traverse. They veered off in all different directions in no discernible pattern.

"Did your people create these burrows?" Tamara asked, as she rushed to keep up with Etuah.

"No. They are what remain," she answered questioningly, as if Tamara should have already understood this.

"I am sorry for my stupidity," Tamara confessed. "Was there something here before that is no longer? Shards? What exactly are shards?"

"When the great tree died, it left these spaces behind," Etuah explained. "The wise one came and collected the shards, the essences. After that, we arrived."

"You said you were the guardians of the hollows. Are the hollows what we call the forbidden spaces?" Tamara asked.

"Forbidden to all but the Drue," she replied, bending her long neck in acknowledgment.

"Yet we are here now?" Tamara said.

"Yes," she said meaningfully.

"Is it wrong that we are here? Are we in danger?" Tamara felt compelled to ask by the ominous tone in Etuah's voice.

The Drue opened her eyes wide and they seemed to cover almost her entire face.

"You are here because you must be. The Evil One has forced this confluence," she replied. "Where is there no danger these days?" she then asked. "Here in the hollows, it is only more conspicuous."

A shiver ran down both of the women's spines with that response. Neither expected an answer like that. But before they had a chance to ask anything further, the passage widened considerably and it appeared as if they were nearing its end.

"I will protect you as best as I can," Etuah said suddenly. "Take a deep breath, each of you, and take my hands," she instructed them, and then she offered each her long, oddly shaped fingers to grasp. "Do not look into their eyes," she warned.

The two sisters glanced at each other in fear and wonder, as they hurried to follow Etuah's directions, wondering who she could be referring to. So far, they had neither seen anyone else nor heard anything other than their own voices. Both Tamara and Angeline reached out anxiously and clasped the Drue's hands. The suction tips adhered to their wrists immediately in response, and they each felt a rush of energy flow through them. It was as if they had just awoken from a long and restful sleep, and just in time it seemed. As they walked into this more open chamber at the end of the passage, they could hear sounds that practically caused their blood to freeze in their veins. Muffled screams and agonizing moans echoed off of the walls and assaulted their senses mercilessly. Pleas for help from both ancient voices as well as youthful ones could clearly be distinguished among the horrible sounds that flooded their ears. Shadows seemed to cross right before their eyes, causing them to flinch and jerk protectively, and they could feel rushes of damp, stale air blow across their faces.

"We are crossing the nethers, the barren spaces where the lost souls are stranded. Stay close to me," she warned, and she gripped them even more tightly with her fingertips. "They will not harm you whilst I am here." Etuah lifter her head and flicked it to the left and to the right as she spoke. "Be gone! Leave us be. These humans cannot help you." Her tone of voice harbored no hint of anger, but rather a profound sadness inundated her words. She turned first to Tamara and then to Angeline, while blinking her bulbous eyes slowly. Her lashes were unusually long and when her eye lids closed, they reached nearly to the middle of her cheek. "They will remain here forever. It is our charge to insure that is so. Careful now, do not be lured into their grief," she warned the women.

Tamara thought that remark strange, considering how sorrowfully she spoke to them moments ago. Etuah seemed so kind, it was odd for her to wish suffering upon any creatures.

"Who are they? Why would you want them to abide so? They are in pain, are they not?" she asked.

"They have given themselves to the Dark Lord. There is no way out for them save dissolution. If they should be released from this confinement it could signify only one thing!" she replied sharply. "Sympathy for them I have, as I would for anything that suffers. But, if the day comes when I find they no longer haunt my days and my nights, it will mean the end of time for us all."

Tamara recoiled immediately at her remarks. The thought of these spirits doomed to eternal pain and suffering caused her to wretch involuntarily. Angeline's eyes brimmed with tears and she struggled to clear her vision and continue on.

"Why are they here?" Angeline asked. "Are they alive?"

"No. They are quite dead. They are here because they have no place else to go. They have committed crimes against the living that cannot be forgiven. Their souls are eternally lost and their spirits are drawn to those places where they believe the weave is weak or torn in the hope of escaping their torment. The hollows are closer to the void than anywhere else on earth. When the Lalas die, they leave only emptiness in their wakes. The lost ones are drawn to the spaces left behind. It is the closest that they will ever come to the nothingness they seek!" she explained as they walked. "All those who have given themselves to Colton throughout history cannot return to the earth like the rest of us. All that is organic refuses their entreaties. They have forsaken their rights to be a part of the cloth, and the fabric weaves without them. Their spirits have no place to go. They are exiles in time, and they must remain so eternally. Their freedom would mean our death; the ultimate death that would come with dissolution," she continued as she led the women across the stone floor. "It is the job of the Drue to keep the hollows secure. Though our realm would afford them no real refuge, they seek it nonetheless. What compels others to stay away, lures the lost ones in."

"What will happen if they breach your defenses?" Angeline asked.

"It would mean one of two things; either Colton has won and dissolution is imminent, or the Drue have simply failed to carry out their charge," she said. "The hollows would be the first to collapse if the Dark Lord should be victorious, as they are the closest to the edge," Etuah explained. "But neither will ever occur," she said confidently.

The screams had grown louder as they walked and the two sisters found themselves ducking their heads continuously in order to avoid things that they could not see and objects that they were not sure were even there. The ground was covered with a thick dust that scattered with their steps and clouded the air as they walked. A smoky mist clogged their noses and burned their eyes. Tamara covered her mouth and nose with her shawl and Angeline did the same. The pale light coming from Etuah's body illuminated the immediate vicinity, but it could not penetrate the thickening fumes.

"We are almost across now," she said. "Heed my words! When you pass this way again, do not look them in the eyes!" Etuah warned.

"Must we go through this awful place once more?" Angeline asked, cringing at the prospect.

"There is no other way," Etuah answered.

"Other way?" Tamara questioned.

"To Odelot!" she replied, as both Tamara and Angeline looked at each other in shock.

"You know where we are headed?" Tamara asked, stunned.

"Yes. We have been told. And we will assist you as much as we are able. You can no longer travel the routes that you had hoped to. Though it was never safe, it is less so now. We will teach you to navigate the hollows and they will lead you close to your destination," she explained.

"Who informed you of our journey" Tamara questioned the Drue.

"The Lalas know and thus, so do we," she answered.

"It seems that others knew as well," Tamara said, recalling vividly their most recent encounter with the Lady Margot, but Etuah did not respond to her remark.

"Stay close to me," she said instead, and she gripped them more compellingly with her suctioned fingertips. "It is just a bit further now."

Chapter Twenty-two

It is rare when evil manifests itself so abruptly and unexpectedly in the world. For most, it is painstaking to conceive of a wickedness that knows no mercy and a hate that is blind and rabid and altogether corrupt. To understand the mind of a beast to whom the pain and suffering of the innocent is unimportant is often too much to ask; just the thought of such a one overwhelms the senses. Such iniquity and depravity is and should be incomprehensible to the vast majority. Yet, there are moments in time when just such a savage rears its vile head and imposes itself upon us all; moments that will forever stand out as reminders that the righteous battle must always be waged, and that vigilance and peace go hand in hand. The creature must be confronted whatever form it has assumed and whatever guise it has chosen with which to seduce and destroy. When it strikes at the very heart of life and shakes the foundations of all that is held dear in the world, it must be met with by a force equally as committed and equally as determined. Evil cannot stand unchallenged lest it infects and poisons every living thing around it until they too come to accept its lies for truth, and they too begin to forget what it means to be merciful and compassionate and earthborn.

The Armadiel is such a beast; iniquitous and ungodly, perverted at its core. Its heart is no more than a cold stone within its chest, that lacks even the propensity for feeling. Though it has been unleashed by he whose nature defines wickedness and turpitude, the beast lives by its own rules and forges its own profane battle against all that exists in the shadow of the First. Its unholy alliance with Colton dar Agonthea serves them both. The Evil One resurrected it once again in order to remind his enemies of his power. But, as with any force not reckoned with, it alters the weave forever as soon as it steals its first breath from the very same air that gives it life. Though allies in their wicked resolve, Colton and the beast are not nor never will be friends.

Maringar, Beolan, Bristar and Aliya sat around a heavy wooden table in the depths of Castle Crispen. Spread out before them lay the maps of the mountain, with its tunnels and caves and chambers crisscrossing the parchments like the webs of a hundred spiders intertwined. Their hearts were heavy with concern for their people and the people of the entire world, but they were also encouraged by the sense of community and common purpose that the surfacing of the Armadiel had generated in them all. Aliya stood up in order to replace the charts as the two younger ones prepared to leave the room and begin their righteous crusade.

"Your men await you," Aliya said with her back to the other three.

"They look to you for inspiration," Beolan remarked.

"And to you for leadership," Bristar replied, clasping his son's arm firmly. "Your mother was not addressing me, my son," he remarked, as he glanced over his shoulder at is wife.

Beolan nodded solemnly in response, though he was not willing to accept this fully yet.

"Your support emboldens them so profoundly," he said to Maringar, changing the subject. "I can sense their comfort at your presence."

"At times like these, we must all find solace where we can. Uncertainty, though a common state, does not feel as menacing when there is no threat before us," the dwarf said. "It abides peacefully beside all our other emotions, and only plagues us when we are reminded of our vulnerability."

"It is your job to reassure," Bristar said to the two younger men. "The torch of leadership is passing even as we sit here. You must assume the mantle of responsibility, though it is a heavy one and one that you must bear for many tiels to come."

Aliya returned to the three men who had assembled in a small circle by the doorway to the chamber as they spoke.

"Each moment we delay, the beast grows in power and confidence. The time to strike is now!" she said calmly though with a piercing determination.

"She is correct, of course," Bristar agreed. "Your horses await you before the gates. It is time to ride. You will join us at the gates, will you not?" he asked his wife.

"Did you think that I would remain here by myself, my darling?" she asked affectionately.

Bristar smiled at her despite the gravity of the moment, and he put one arm around her narrow waist. He then encircled Maringar with his other, drawing him in close. Aliya raised both of her arms as well and firmly grasped Beolan with her right and the elfin King with her left. As a unit, they departed the room and walked somberly down the dim hallway toward the courtyard and the assembled troops who anxiously awaited them outside.

As they emerged from the huge, double doors of the castle

onto the cobblestone courtyard, a colossal cheer arose from the body massed before them. It cleaved the silence and echoed off of Silandre, the beautiful mountain to the north. For a brief and fleeting instant, the world felt safe again amidst the fervor of the preparations and the patrio'Tism and exuberance of the population. Beolan embraced his mother in front of the applauding throng and kissed her hand tenderly. He then bowed humbly to his father who returned his gesture by raising him up and hugging him tightly to his chest. Bristar then grabbed Maringar's arm and raised it high in the air with his own, while the soldiers cheered and cheered.

"Let them feel the spirit before they march into darkness," the King said quietly to the other three. "It is our responsibility to provide them the joy of these moments whilst we still can."

Bristar stood by as the two handsome leaders mounted their horses, and then he stepped aside into the background with Aliya close beside him. The two elder monarchs poignantly felt the passing of power concurrently, and they each held the other's hand tightly as the shade of the building enveloped them. At that very moment, the sun pierced the thick cover of clouds in a striation of brilliant rays that illuminated both Maringar's silver helm and Beolan's polished Noban bow exactly at the same time, causing them to shine so brightly it appeared as if the Gem of Eternity had manifested itself in their very midst.

"A sign if I ever saw one," Bristar whispered to his wife.

"Surely this bodes well for them," she concurred. "It is their moment," she said solemnly.

The soldiers saw the phenomenon as well, and the elfin warriors all pulled arrows from their quivers and rubbed them against the strings of their bows as if they were lutes, causing a great and musical sound to rise from their numbers. The dwarves of the Thorndars joined them in praise and recognition of their two leaders, and they drew their axes and picks from their backs and banged them together loudly and unceasingly, which soon required both Beolan's and Maringar's combined efforts to settle them down. When the soldiers of Crispen and those of the Thorndars were still once more, the Elfin Prince urged his horse forward a few feet.

"My brother and I..." he began in his clear and sonorous voice as he pointed to Maringar.

Before he could utter another word, an earsplitting outcry erupted from the throng once more in response. He waited a few minutes for the silence to settle in again and then he continued.

"My brother and I are united in our purpose. We know what we must do, and it is not a simple task that lies before us. Until yesterday, we were uncertain as to what scourge had been loosed within our mountain. We were unsure of what poisoned our waters and caused the very rock and soil of Silandre to rise in temperature. Alas, we now are clear," he continued, and a total hush fell over the entire assemblage. "It grieves me to tell you that the Snake of Recos, the beast of legend, is alive once more. He has been resurrected by none other than the Dark Lord and sent to Crispen in order to deflect us from our path and split the alliance that has been newly created between these good and free peoples of the world."

A nervous murmur rose through the crowd at the mention of the Armadiel, and Beolan allowed it to continue this time without attempting to still it. Most of the younger elves did not recognize the appellations, and as with Beolan himself initially, they needed to be apprised of the significance of his declaration by those in the multitude who knew more intimately of the histories. Soon, a troubled and more anxious quiet settled upon the people as they awaited their young leader's next words.

"We cannot allow this disease to spread!" he shouted. "Together, we and our allies are prepared to enter our blessed mountain and eradicate this pestilence from our land!"

Once again, the populace burst into applause, motivated by Beolan's confidence and strength, though an edgy tension still hung in the air nevertheless. He sensed it and addressed it as forthrightly as he could.

"We will succeed! This evil will not stand!" he shouted. "Though our battle may be a costly one, it is a righteous one and we shall prevail!" he said confidently. "We will purge the mountain of the beast!" he exclaimed without a hint of doubt in his voice.

Maringar had slowly urged his horse forward until he was standing alongside Beolan by the time his friend finished speaking. He raised the elfin Lord's arm high into the air again and he shouted in a clear and steady voice, "Crispen! Crispen! Crispen!" Beolan gladly took up the cheer with him, and together they shouted, "Crispen!" until the entire population joined them. The crescendo quickly rose until it reverberated off of the mountain's rock surface and flooded the entire valley with the chant, "Crispen! Crispen!"

Beolan and Maringar walked side by side across the paved courtyard and to the front of the assemblage of warriors from both nations. The young elf glanced quickly backward and caught the eyes of both his mother and father before pressing his horse forward into a trot. Maringar spurred his mount in pursuit, and the magnificent black stallion replied with a loud whinny as he rose on his hind legs and pawed the air with his massive hoofs. Within moments, both Beolan and Maringar disappeared through the huge gates of the city as the armies of both races eagerly fell in formation behind them, while they all still chanted fervently in unison.

"It is a new dawn," Bristar said to Aliya over the din as they retreated into the shadows of the castle and watched the men file out four abreast.

"A moment to mark time by," she replied.

"By the First, may it last for more than one brief morning!" he said anxiously and he squeezed his wife's hand.

Chapter Twenty-three

"I awoke one morning not too long ago and it was there, all around us! I must admit that I was quite surprised."

"Surprised? You were dumbfounded," Emmeline corrected her. "Your jaw was hanging almost to the ground!" she kidded the gray haired woman sitting in the high backed chair next to hers. "I have never seen you so out of sorts, Gretchen."

"I confess that I was taken aback at first," she blushed. "After all, this was not an occurrence that I had ever expected or anticipated. Were you any less shocked than I was?"

"Oh no, sister! I reacted exactly as you did," she replied. "You asked me when you first arrived if the barrier was erected to keep the enemy out or to keep us in," she said to Cairn. "Initially, I asked myself that same question. Though it did not feel wrong to any of us, I was uncertain in the beginning," Emmeline said.

"As was I," Gretchen concurred. "It was not until the first bolt of power struck it that I understood its reason for being."

"And then you appeared," Emmeline continued. "Rella was the first to spot your movements. Her eyesight is particularly good," she said admiringly of the sister they had been introduced to earlier. "We did not know who you were then, but it was clear to us that you sought out Parth for refuge in the face of this assault, and we decided to try to provide you with a means of entry."

"None of us knew what the shield was composed of or how to manipulate it. In fact, we did not think that we could alter it at all at first. But Emmeline here is quite extraordinary, and her efforts proved fruitful," Gretchen said with a slight smile.

The dark skinned sister bowed her head humbly in response to the words of her friend.

"The opening you created was more than sufficient for us all," Robyn acknowledged gratefully.

"We saw if from the forest edge and we hoped that it would remain open long enough for us to enter. Our concern was that after we committed ourselves to the attempt, it might close and leave us stranded and exposed," Filaree related.

"We had no way of sending you a message, though we would have so liked to. Our talents are quite limited," Emmeline said.

"They are greater than you take credit for, sisters," Robyn replied honestly.

"We are learning every day," Gretchen said, and Emmeline

nodded her head in agreement.

The large room was illuminated by the early morning sun that streamed through the high windows of the tower. No artificial light was necessary as it flooded the entire chamber from one end to the other. Cairn and Robyn sat across from Filaree and Davmiran on either side of the table, while Gretchen and Emmeline sat at opposite ends.

"How many sisters are in residence here now?" Robyn asked.

Gretchen hesitated for a moment and looked at Emmeline before responding, who nodded barely noticeably in response.

"We are nine in all," Gretchen said.

"And the other two?" Robyn inquired further. "Where have they gone?" he asked.

"You know much about us, Chosen. But perhaps we should learn more about you and why you are here before we reveal all of our secrets. After all, these times are strange indeed," Emmeline replied.

"Strange indeed," Robyn concurred. "I am sorry if I have offended you with my presumptuousness. But you have nothing to fear from us. In fact, I respect your desire to be cautious," he replied, seemingly sa'Tisfied.

"It is not fear that motivates me. And it is not for lack of trust that I hesitate. But, sometimes knowledge can be dangerous, and we do not wish to jeopardize any of you by telling you things that others might be desirous to know."

"Nor do we wish to jeopardize any of our own," Gretchen added.

"It is best if we do not know," Davmiran said suddenly. "That they are no longer here is sufficient," he said in a strange tone of voice.

The others all looked at him curiously. He had barely uttered anything up until this statement, and the expression on his youthful face was troubled and confused. Filaree leaned over and laid her hand on top of his.

"What is wrong? What is it that you see?" she asked him gently. "Is there something you wish to tell us, Dav?"

His face was drawn and uneasy, and it seemed as if he was trying to recall something that kept eluding him.

"The two sisters are gone. I cannot feel them any longer," he said, concentrating deeply.

Emmeline and Gretchen looked at each other gravely.

"Gone, young man?" Gretchen questioned. "In what way are they gone?"

His eyes were now shut tightly and he appeared to be struggling hard to ascertain something.

"They carry an object that many want, but none need," he said after a moment, as if in a trance.

"Dav," Robyn said in a hushed voice. "Be careful what you say," he warned him softly.

"None need save one," he continued, ignoring Robyn's advice as if he did not hear him at all.

"Did you not say to the sisters only a moment ago that knowing that they are gone was enough?" Cairn asked. "What has changed in these few minutes? Are they imperiled?"

"If they are in danger we must know," Emmeline commented, her voice now full of concern.

"A moment ago, I saw nothing. Now I see much," he answered. "Their threads have vanished though they have not been severed. They have stepped beyond the weave."

"I think it would be best if we let the boy rest for a while now," Robyn interrupted, and he rose and walked to Davmiran's side. "Come," he said to him, clearly trying to stop him from continuing to disclose these things to the others.

"Let him speak, Chosen," Gretchen said boldly. "He has not been coerced into revealing anything. What do you fear? You asked the very question of us that he is addressing now."

"There are things that are best kept hidden, that is all," Robyn said evasively. "I asked of you something that I hoped you would not answer and if fact, you responded as I had hoped. Now our sentiments are reversed."

"Robyn!" Filaree exclaimed. "What could you possibly wish to keep from us? Are we not equals here?" she asked, somewhat affronted by his attitude.

"She asks a legitimate question," Cairn agreed. "Let the boy continue. If there is something that he knows and that you know, it should be shared amongst us all."

Robyn sat down again heavily, and he shook his head back and forth.

"I only wished to spare you all some of what a Chosen must endure. If it is necessary for you to know it all, then so be it!" he said. "But the boy need not tell you. I can just as well."

Davmiran opened his eyes again and looked at Robyn, as a

single tear rolled down his pale cheek.

"I am sorry, Dav. It is a painful vision, I know," he said to him tenderly. "I hoped I would not need to speak of it so soon on our quest," he said to the group.

"We are strong of heart, sir," Emmeline said. "Just tell us the truth, whatever it may be."

"Yes, Robyn. Tell us. We can handle it," Filaree said stalwartly, as she poked her chin out and up.

"If your words reveal to us a situation that already is, then you will merely be opening a window for us that we have not yet been able to gaze out from. It will change nothing," Cairn said.

"I agree. Please do not keep us in the dark any longer," Emmeline said, anxious to know the fate of Tamara and Angeline.

"It could change more than you might imagine, Cairn," Robyn said to the scholar. "But, so be it! The fabric weaves of its own will. I have tried and I have failed. Now, we shall all suffer the knowledge," he declared, and he drew in his breath in preparation for his next words. "There are some places on earth that none dare venture into; some places so disturbing and so disheartening that it would be impossible to emerge from them unscathed if at all. No one chooses to tread there, yet some must. Premoran is one such person, and his strength is well known to us all," he explained. "I have been there once as well," Robyn said clearly recalling moments that he dreaded and then he paused for a brief second. When he began to speak again it was obvious that the words weighed heavily upon him. "The pouch you carry with you Dav, is filled with the shards from the hollows."

As soon as the name was mentioned, the room became totally silent. It was not so much the word itself but the way in which Robyn uttered it that caused the reaction. Even though the two sisters from Parth had only met him a short while ago, it was clear to them too that this was not a subject that he spoke lightly about.

"The hollows?" Filaree questioned. "I am unfamiliar with the place. Where is it?"

"I have heard the word before. There are writings that speak of it," Cairn said, and he was clearly profoundly concerned.

"Then it is by virtue of the pouch that Premoran entrusted to me that I learned of the sisters?" Davmiran asked Robyn softly.

"Yes, it is," Robyn replied. "They are what remains, and within them they carry the souls of the trees from which they came."

"Where is this place?" Filaree asked again.

"Alas, there are many such places. They exist wherever a Lalas was and is no longer," Robyn answered.

"The Forbidden Places?" Emmeline asked.

"Yes, sister, the Forbidden Places," Robyn acknowledged, and he immediately saw the recognition spread painfully across her face and those of the others. "You know of them?" he asked, only slightly surprised.

"Yes, Chosen," Gretchen answered. "We have studied the Tomes often enough. There is reference made to these dreadful spots, though it has always been unclear as to their derivation and to their location. Are you certain that Tamara and Angeline are in one of these 'hollows' as you call them?" she asked.

"There is no doubt, sister," Davmiran replied immediately. "Of that, I am sure."

Gretchen bowed her head sullenly and appeared to be deep in thought.

"Do not grieve for them so quickly," Robyn said. "There is no reason to assume that harm has yet come to them. The hollows can actually provide sanctuary for some," Robyn explained.

"Sanctuary? How could such places protect anyone? Are they neither here nor there? Do they not take a part of your soul the moment you trespass within them? Is it not true that no mortal has entered and returned?" Gretchen asked.

"I am here," Robyn said quietly. "I have been there and back. Premoran too," he continued.

"But you are Chosen, Robyn dar Tamarand," Emmeline replied. "Tamara and Angeline are merely untrained sisters who have some affinities like most of the rest of us here in Parth it seems. What defenses could they possibly have?"

"And why would they be there to begin with? What would lure them into the Forbidden Places?" Gretchen asked.

"The sisters of whom you speak are quite capable. Was Tamara not the one chosen for the pilgrimage to Liam and Oleander? And did the tree not speak with her and entrust her with an important task? I cannot know what is going on in the hollows. It is beyond my reach. But it has been known to be a place of refuge for those who are strong enough to endure it," Robyn explained. "If they have entered by invitation, then perhaps they are still safe."

"Invitation? They are dead places! Who or what could have offered them refuge there?" Emmeline asked.

"The hollows are junctures between the living and the dead. As

I said before, they are the places between. Yet, they still harbor the remnants of the power that once was present there. And they need always to be protected," Robyn said.

"Are you telling us that despite what we have all been led to understand about the Forbidden Places that people reside there?" Cairn asked.

"Not people, exactly," Robyn replied. "The guardians; the Drue."

"Drue? That is a name which is unfamiliar to me," Cairn replied.

"I have not heard it before either," Gretchen concurred and Emmeline nodded agreement.

"You will find only a scant mention of them in the Great Books," Robyn replied. "I am uncertain whether the even the other Chosen know of their existence. I had hoped not to burden you all with this secret."

"We in Parth are accustomed to keeping confidences. You have no reason to be concerned that we will reveal this to anyone," Emmeline assured him.

"It is not your intention that I am concerned about, sister," he replied.

"Be not concerned at all then, Chosen!" Gretchen said. "We are strong of character here. There is little that can be taken from us against our will."

"You believe that our dear sisters have taken refuge in one of these places with the consent of these beings?" Emmeline asked expectantly.

"They have most definitely," Davmiran answered for the Chosen. "They have crossed over and thus they are beyond, but they are being guided by the Drue."

"You know this now for certain?" Filaree asked.

"The shards are communicating with me in their own way, though words are not their medium. I cannot see into these places, but I believe that your friends are safe," Davmiran answered.

"What made you so reluctant to tell us about the hollows, Robyn?" Filaree questioned. "There is nothing so shocking about this, yet you feared that it would disturb us or be dangerous for us to know about them."

"What more have you not revealed?" Cairn prodded him, determined to learn the entire truth at this point.

"The hollows are a battlefront, so to speak," Robyn continued, his former reluctance now gone from his tone. "They are protected by the Drue because they are closer to the void than any other places we could ever encounter. The vacuum that is left behind when a Lalas departs the earth can never be reconciled with the world of the living. They are beyond dead, and Colton dar Agonthea is drawn to them unremittingly, as are all the stranded souls from time untold," Robyn explained.

"The Dark Lord wishes to enter these places?" Gretchen asked, confused.

"Yes. And all of those whose souls he has taken also desire to, for they have no place to go once their physical forms have perished. They seek out the hollows as places of refuge from their suffering. They think of them as their bridge to dissolution."

"A means by which they could overcome their anguish and pain," Davmiran added. "A stepping stone to their ultimate release."

"So why not let them have these places? They belong to the earth no longer," Cairn asked.

"That would be the most dangerous thing that could happen. If control over the Forbidden Places were to be relinquished to the Evil One, it would provide him with a formidable web of tunnels and passages right here on earth from which he could wage his war against us all; places of refuge for him and all of the lost ones. As long as these forsaken creatures are suspended between the living and the dead, they cannot harm us. But if they were to infiltrate the hollows, then they would be both here and gone. They would gain the ability to once more interact and influence the living. The hollows could be a staging ground for their assaults against us," Robyn explained.

"Are there many such places?" Filaree asked. Her concern was mounting steadily.

"With the departure of each tree, they grow more expansive. They extend as far as the roots of the Lalas did, throughout the network that once tied all the trees together," Robyn said.

"Would Colton be able to touch the living trees from these dead places?" Cairn asked, as he began to realize the implications.

The Chosen hesitated before he answered his friend. He gazed at Cairn with a sad and knowing look in his eyes.

"He could possibly, though it would not be easy," Robyn replied solemnly.

"And ultimately then, the First and the Gem that it harbors?"

Cairn inquired, though he already knew the answer.

Gretchen shuddered visibly at the scholar's words, and the others remained silent for a while, understanding now why Robyn had been so hesitant to inform them of this. It was another threat, another cause for concern, for all of them.

"It is best that we know these things, Robyn," Filaree said, breaking the silence. "If nothing else, it motivates me even more to fight on."

"And me too!" Cairn agreed. "I prefer being more informed rather than less. At least I have an opportunity to do something."

"What of the sisters, Chosen?" Gretchen asked, returning to the original subject. "How much do you know of their situation?"

"Little more than Dav and I have explained already, I am afraid," he replied.

"I believe too that they are there by invitation," the boy said reassuringly. "The Drue surely have lead them in."

"Can they be trusted?" Filaree asked.

"There is no doubt about the Drue's allegiance. They exist for only one reason," Robyn replied.

"How is it that they have come to be?" Emmeline asked. "What type of people are they?"

"They have always been here, though there was little for them to do until the last few tiels. Whenever one of the great trees departed it was their job to secure the area and to protect it until the living trees restored the gaps that the loss of one of their own created," Robyn explained. "The Drue were the only living things who could enter the spaces left behind and not be affected by them. When they were called upon to defend a hollow, there was never a question that it would be in jeopardy. They are quite formidable in their own way."

"Have you encountered any of them yourself?" Filaree asked.

"It would be impossible not to for anyone who enters the Forbidden Places," Robyn answered.

"What are they like?" Emmeline asked.

"Different than you or I, that is for certain," Robyn said. "A bit unusual looking, but quite gentle. Their loyalty is uncompromising, and they have no fear whatsoever. In fact, they would not understand the meaning of the word."

"Fascinating," Cairn said. "We take so much for granted all the time. It never occurred to me that there would have ever been a reason to protect the Forbidden Places. But then again, I do not have the perspective of the trees. I could not have known the danger of negligence or complacency in this regard."

"Dav?" Filaree questioned the boy. "Do you know for sure that the sisters we speak of are guests of the Drue? How much do these shards allow you to see?"

Davmiran looked at her as if this was a profoundly difficult question to answer. He pondered heavily before replying.

"Yes, I am sure now. Until a few moments ago, I merely carried the pouch at my side. I was unaware. They seem not to tolerate my prodding though, even at this very moment. The communication flows only one way. I must learn," he replied dreamily.

"This is new even to me," Robyn said. "When Premoran entrusted the pouch to the boy, he did so with little or no explanation other than that with time the importance of the shards would manifest itself, and now this has begun to happen. Whilst we are guests here, perhaps he will have an opportunity to learn more about what has been bequeathed to him."

"We are all anxious to assist him in that regard," Gretchen said. "The full resources of the tower and its libraries are at your disposal as well," she said graciously, and Emmeline nodded enthusiastically in agreement.

"Sister Bethany will be most happy to aid you in your studies," Emmeline said. "She is most knowledgeable, though her eyesight has been failing her of late," she explained.

"The prospect of freely perusing your library is an exciting one, sister," Cairn said. "I will be grateful for whatever help she is willing to offer. I have studied in some of the greatest repositories of knowledge in the world, but the idea of actually turning the pages of the Tomes that you have here in the Tower is quite thrilling. They are renowned among scholars everywhere," he said respectfully. "I am sure that as Davmiran and I settle into our studies, he too will benefit from his proximity to these great books."

"And I am likewise anxious to begin the charge that was placed upon me by Baladar of Pardatha. We seem finally to have found the refuge that we needed," Robyn concurred. "Perhaps you can supplement my instruction?" he asked Emmeline.

"I will certainly do whatever I can, though I am merely a novice, Chosen," she said humbly.

"A novice perhaps, but definitely one with enormous potential," he answered bluntly. "The boy will benefit from whatever you can share with him."

Emmeline tipped her regal head delicately to the side in acknowledgment of the compliment.

"I have seen no weaponry here. I have also seen neither hide nor hair of a training ground of any kind. Have the sisters never learned how to defend themselves?" Filaree asked.

"There has never been a need, Lady Filaree," Emmeline replied. "But as with all else these days, that seems to have changed as well. Though most of us have never trained in the physical arts, I believe that you may find some who are eager to do so, and I suspect that they will be very fast learners."

"My primary responsibility is to instruct Davmiran, but it will be my great pleasure to work with any of the others who wish to work with me," Filaree said.

"May I ask you a question, young man?" Gretchen asked.

"Of course, sister," he replied. "I only hope that I can give you better answers than I have so far."

"You have told us much already, my son. We had no knowledge before of the fate of the two who left here, and now we have hope," Emmeline said. "Facts are not all that provide succor in a time of need, Davmiran dar Gwendolen."

No one had ever called him that directly before and the boy grew visibly pale at the appellation. Though it was the name bequeathed to him by Baladar, since he had so little recollection of his past, he was unaccustomed to the usage.

"Please call me Dav," he replied almost sheepishly. "The other name seems not yet to be mine."

"Very well then, Dav. I will be less formal henceforth," she replied, seeing how this affected him so. "Dav it shall be. One day perhaps your surname will make you joyful rather than sad. There is much greatness in the line of which you should be proud," she said kindly. "Tell us then, if you can, what you know of the sisters."

"As I said already, I know that Tamara and Angeline are alive, but I cannot tell whether they were drawn into or driven into the Drues' realm, though they have been welcomed. I know also that what they carry is still with them," Davmiran said.

"Thank the First!" Emmeline said under her breath. "You said before that what they carry none need save one. Can you explain that any further?" she asked.

"No, sister. I cannot," he answered her. "I barely remember saying it."

"So you do not know what it is that they travel with?" Gretchen asked.

"Yes, sister. I think I do," he answered, surprising them all once again.

"If you know my child, is it likely that others know as well?" she prodded.

"Others?" he questioned her.

"Yes. Aside from those of us here in Parth, is it possible that their commission has been discovered by the enemy?" she asked bluntly.

"That would explain their presence with the Drue," Robyn replied for him. "I think it likely."

"And you, Davmiran?" Emmeline asked him directly.

He closed his eyes once again and seemed to be concentrating deeply. A slight tremor coursed over his body and it was visible to them all. Filaree started at the sight of it and she put her arm around his shoulder.

"It is more than likely, Robyn," he said, opening his navy blue eyes wide and gazing at the Chosen. They shone deeply in the bright sunlight that streamed over them all. "But they are safe for now," he said in a tone that made them all instantly confident.

"That is good news indeed," Gretchen said, and she sighed with relief.

"They will travel the paths that none dare tread, though I know not what their destination will be," Dav explained.

"We do not know either," Emmeline confessed. "Tamara though it best that we remained unaware."

"She was wise to do so," Robyn said. "Their quest is fraught with danger, and the fewer people who know of their destination, the easier it will be for them to continue on in secrecy."

"Would someone please tell me what it is that they are doing? Every one here seems to know but me!" Filaree asked, frustrated by this point.

"You are not the only one in the dark, Filaree," Cairn said. "I also do not know," Cairn confessed.

Emmeline nodded her head immediately. She required no assurances from either the Lady Filaree or Cairn of Thermaye that they would protect the information, for she knew in her heart that they would.

"For tiels untold, the sisters of Parth guarded an ancient scroll which we kept in a vault here in the tower," she began. "The scroll is a map of sorts, though it certainly is not an ordinary one. We believe that it contains directions to the First, though we have never actually unfurled it and studied it ourselves," she said somberly. "I had been understood from the beginning of our commission that it was here for us to protect, not to analyze."

Tamara was instructed to remove it from the Tower by Oleander and Liam,"

Gretchen added. "Until that day, our guardianship of this parchment was what united us in purpose here," Emmeline recalled. "It was not easy for us to relinquish it, though it was done so without question."

"We have only recently focused our attention upon the development of our skills in other areas," Gretchen explained. "We had been quite content with our previous responsibility," she concluded somewhat sadly.

"Alas, those were simpler days it now seems," Emmeline concurred with her sentiment. "But, now we realize that our skills are needed, and the sisters have adopted their new purpose with ardor."

"Needed indeed," Robyn said under his breath.

"I am confused," Filaree said aloud. "Forgive me if I am not understanding this clearly, but are we not on a Quest for the very thing that you said you had a map to?" she asked.

"We are," Cairn agreed. "Was it just a matter of timing that brought us here after it had already been spirited away?"

"Timing?" Robyn asked skeptically. "The fabric weaves of its own...."

"Yes, we know that," Filaree interrupted him, though not wishing to sound annoyed or to be rude. "But, maybe we should pursue those two women then, instead of spending time here preparing ourselves and Davmiran to search for something the location of which we have no idea whatsoever," she said.

"Filaree makes a valid point. If you know where they are," Cairn addressed both Robyn and Davmiran, "...why should we not go after them. Would not the possession of a map of this sort give us a substantial advantage?"

"I never said I knew where the sisters were. I merely said that they are in the hollows. The area is so vast, it would be virtually impossible to locate them," Robyn explained.

Filaree and Cairn simultaneously looked at Davmiran, hoping that his response would be different than the Chosen's was.

"Do you have a sense of where they are?" Filaree asked him.

"No more so than Robyn, I am afraid. But perhaps if I learn how to communicate better with the shards, if such a thing is possible, in time I might learn their whereabouts," he replied.

"Then I suppose here is where we must remain for the time being, unless of course one of you can figure out where they went rather quickly," Filaree responded somewhat disappointed. "I just hope that what we need has not slipped through our fingers only to fall into the hands of another."

They all knew her meaning, and it was not a thought that passed any of them by during this conversation.

"Are you the 'one' who needs this map?" she asked Davmiran directly.

"Again, Lady Filaree, I do not know," Davmiran answered sadly. "I am sorry that I cannot be of more help," the boy said dejectedly.

"She did not mean to criticize," Cairn reassured him. "But the opportunity of obtaining directions did seem so compelling"

"It is not your fault that you know not where the women are. Forgive me if I spoke rashly and without consideration. But as Cairn so aptly said, it was compelling indeed," Filaree replied. "I actually was looking forward to the beginning of our training sessions more than you might imagine before this thought arose," she said to Davmiran, and she was smiling once again.

"As was I, my Lady," Davmiran replied graciously. "I hope that I will not disappoint you."

"If your prowess with a sword and bow even approximates your other 'talents', I will not be disappointed," she laughed.

"Well then!" Gretchen said with finality. "It seems we have covered much ground here this morning, and it is high time that you met the rest of the sisters," she concluded as she rose from her chair. "I can think of no better place to do that than in the dining room over breakfast."

"And I could not think of a better idea!" Robyn replied.

"I had not realized just how hungry I was until you mentioned it," Filaree said with an expectant grin upon her pretty face.

"I am beyond hungry! Though I am accustomed to fasting, I did not choose to do so this day," Cairn said as they all stood up to follow the sisters out of tower.

Robyn lagged behind so that he could walk side by side with Davmiran, and they both allowed the others to file out before them. He put his strong arm around the boy's shoulders and hugged him affectionately.

"You handled that like a master," he said to him out of earshot of the rest of the group. "I had hoped to spare you, but I see now that I was unnecessarily concerned."

"Are the Drue strong enough to keep him out of the hollows?" Davmiran asked.

"Yes, for now," he replied. "But his power is growing as that of the Lalas fades. May the Gem of Eternity light the way for those brave sisters, wherever they may be headed," Robyn replied. "I am more concerned right now about how he knew of the sisters' flight. They were driven into the Forbidden Places most definitely. There are only a few possibilities to speculate upon, and each is harder to imagine than the next."

"It could not have been anyone here who gave them away," Davmiran said with certainty. "I sense only loyalty and faithfulness among the sisters."

"Further conjecture will only unsettle us all now," Robyn said. "We have too much to do in too short a time. We cannot waste it worrying unnecessarily. In time, we will learn who has betrayed them."

"And us!" the boy added and Robyn somberly nodded in agreement. "What could the sisters be doing with the map?" he asked. "Where could Oleander have possibly asked them to take it that would provide it with more protection than the Tower of Parth did? I thought this was a sacred place, supported by the trees. Have things weakened so much so soon?" he questioned sadly. "And who has constructed this unusual shield all around us?"

"The trees have grown fragile, Dav. Unfortunately, they most certainly have. Maybe the Lalas are worried that they can no longer guard it with certainty here, and thus they had them carry it to a safer shelter, though I can think of only a few such places. As to the shield, it bears a familiar touch and I have my suspicions, but until I am certain, I will not venture to speculate out loud. I do know, with no uncertainty, that we must begin your training at once! Time is running short. I have never felt this as poignantly as I do this very moment. You have much to learn before we leave here."

"Yes, I know too. I feel so anxious inside, as if I am standing upon the edge of something, but I cannot see into the darkness ahead. Each step seems so incredibly important ," he replied reflectively. "And Robyn..." he said a bit more anxiously, "... the ring is no longer silent either."

"How does it speak to you, Dav?" he asked soberly, while attempting to hide his surprise.

"In images; bits and pieces, though unlike the shards. I cannot quite explain it. The shards present images to me too, but the ring speaks as if it was me! It guides my thoughts while the shards simply show me things. Does that make any sense?" he asked.

"Yes, in a way. While you lay unconscious in Seramour, I joined with your ring myself in Pardatha. I think I know what you are saying, though I was not fully conscious either at the time. I knew then that it was not mine to keep and that it rightfully belonged to you. But it harbored tremendous power, and it guided me in the way it is guiding you now, I believe. Take comfort in it. It will serve you well in the days to come."

"I am fortunate that you were picked to be one of my teachers," he smiled and squeezed the older man's arm.

"I am fortunate as well," he replied earnestly.

"Are you going to join us or not?" an impatient voice shouted from the hallway. "I do not know about you..." Filaree said to Davmiran and Robyn, "...but I must put some food into my body soon if I am going to be able to train anyone in the near future! Do you two think you could hurry it up a bit?"

"Patience, my Lady, patience!" Robyn replied. "We are right behind you! I know better than to cross you when your belly is empty," he yelled back, as he guided Davmiran out the door.

Chapter Twenty-four

"Get up!" Fobush ordered. "Though I would like to leave you here, as you well deserve, I swore allegiance many tiels ago to your parents, and out of respect for them, I cannot! Now get up off of this floor and walk with me through these doors, or by the First, I will carry you like a child over my shoulders!" he yelled.

Kettin stood up slowly and sheepishly in the corner of his bedchamber.

"Put this on. You look foolish in your sleeping gown. It is bad enough that you have dirtied the family name with your actions. At the least, when you leave here, do so with a bit of dignity," he said disdainfully, and he threw a tunic to the cowering young man.

Kettin turned his back on the general and like a small child, he slipped what he was wearing over his head and put the fresh clothing on. Fobush kicked a pair of boots over toward him and tossed a cape and a belt his way as well.

"Hurry up!" he commanded. "If you wish to stem the flow of citizens out of the city, you must do so immediately or there will shortly be no one left. They have physically deserted you as readily as you deserted your principles it seems. In the absence of your 'surrogate'..." he found if difficult to utter Margot's name, she was so distasteful to him, "...they have also abandoned their allegiance to you as quickly as you did your own honor," he said scornfully.

Kettin finished putting on his clothing and he walked over to his dressing table in the corner. He pushed the implements around with his hands until he located the box, opened it, and then slipped his ring upon his index finger. Desperately, he rummaged through the other items searching for something that seemed to be quite important to him.

"We have so little time left. What are you doing?" Fobush asked with angry impatience.

"My medallion! I must find my medallion!" Kettin cried.

"Rings and necklaces? Those are the things you are thinking about now?" he asked, astonished at the young Duke's foolishness.

"I have to find it! I cannot leave without it!" Kettin said, growing more frantic with each passing moment.

He was pushing things off of the table now and tossing them carelessly to the ground. He broke a frame and a porcelain container in the process, and he was flinging papers and documents in all directions. Suddenly, his fingers clasped a blackened silver amulet from which a heavy chain dangled, and he lifted it up gleefully before his eyes. Like a man possessed, he quickly placed it over his head and let it hang upon his chest. Immediately, the color returned to his cheeks. His back was to Fobush at this time so that the man could not see how his eyes darkened and how his expression changed. Surreptitiously, he slipped a small dagger that lay upon the table under his cuff and then he turned toward the door.

"Ah," he sighed to himself. "I am ready now," he said in a still frightened voice, though the look in his eye belied a different emotion. Fobush was still so exasperated by the young Lord's behavior and so preoccupied by the tumultuous events of the day that he paid scant attention to his expressions.

"I suggest that you speak to those who still remain as quickly as possible. Perhaps you can persuade some of them to stay at least. If not, you may find yourself the ruler of a barren city, if you are even able to continue as the ruler at all," he said contemptuously.

"That is a good idea. You have always advised me well, Fobush," he replied thoughtfully, as he turned around. "I must have lost my senses before. You know that I have not been well? The illness has taken its toll upon me. I scarcely recognize myself."

"Forgive me, Kettin, but I have little patience left for this. Muster whomever you can whilst you still can, and spare me the explanations. They are too little and too late for me," he replied derisively.

The young Duke grabbed a voluminous black cape from the nearby wardrobe and flung it around his shoulders. He walked toward the other man and smiled as if he had behaved honorably all the while, and had not cringed in the corner like a frightened animal only moments ago.

"Surely you understand, Fobush? I have been through so much. For the sake of my parents, will you not stand by my side?" he pleaded. "It has been so difficult for me."

"You shame the memory of your father and mother!" he answered him abruptly. "Your actions these past weeks were unforgivable. Invoking the names of those more noble than yourself will not alter how I feel. The damage is irreparable. You are wasting your efforts here." By this time, Kettin stood directly beside his Master at Arms. "When this episode is over, I shall turn in my resignation and seek other service. I can no longer serve the house of Dumas."

Kettin feigned dismay and drew his cape tightly around himself.

He hung his head as if Fobush's words had physically stricken him.

"I never thought I would hear this from you, of all people," he replied. "Can it be so? Would you abandon me at my weakest moment? I have sinned, I admit it. I have committed grievous actions against my people and against you!" he lamented, though he eyed him craftily all the while. "But I can change. It was that woman, Lady Margot! She is to blame," he continued. "Will you not reconsider? Give me another chance?"

He seemed so forlorn and so pathetic that it was almost cruel to be so harsh with him. Fobush was a retainer to whom loyalty had always been endemic, and it pained him to have made the statements he made. Though he had always been honest and forthright, he was mindful of the sentiments of those he commanded and of those who commanded him. His mind was awash in confusion, and he was suddenly unsure of what was the right thing to do. Kettin has sidled up to him like a young colt to its mare, and he looked at the elder man closely. The medallion glowed silver-black upon his chest, though Fobush was too preoccupied to notice.

"What have you to say? Can I count upon you as always?" he appealed earnestly. "Please Fobush, I have never needed you as much as I do this very moment. Do not forsake me," he pleaded. "Think of the people! Think of Talamar! There is much damage to repair and as usual, you have shown me the light. Will you not now stand by my side and guide me as you have e'er done?"

Kettin smiled slyly, though Fobush did not see him do so. The old soldier's mind was consumed with thoughts of duty and commitment, and he was suddenly awash in feelings of guilt. He thought of the boy's father, the late Duke, and his years of service to the family. He felt the hand of his frightened Lord grasp him around the shoulder and he was touched by the sentiment. He raised his eyes to the young leader, and he was about to acknowledge his acceptance of his responsibility and to reconfirm his loyalty. He had decided to help him one more time. Maybe Kettin could still redeem himself and regain his honor. Perhaps it really was not altogether his fault.

Fobush was completely unaware of Kettin as he silently withdrew the dagger from the folds of his cloak, never suspecting the treachery that was to be his fate. His thoughts were upon the young man's welfare and his own sense of duty and sacrifice. He had no opportunity to defend himself against the assault. With deadly accuracy and no remorse, Kettin plunged the cold, sharp blade deep into the old man's heart, and then he twisted it sharply to make sure that he would not survive. Fobush slumped into the Duke's arms, as his life blood poured out from the gaping wound in his chest. In shock and disbelief, he looked into the eyes of his killer. Kettin backed away as soon as he was certain that the wound was fatal, and he carelessly let Fobush's limp body fall to the floor.

"So trusting. So easily fooled," he said aloud. "All these months, so easily fooled," he said, and he shook his head mockingly.

Kettin straightened his cape and tunic and looked into the polished glass that hung upon the wall. He ran his fingers through his hair and stood before the mirror admiring himself, while never once even gazing at the man dying beside him upon the carpet.

"This truly was enjoyable. I will miss this," he remarked as the image in the polished glass before him began to quiver and fade.

Kettin's features blurred as if his face was merely a tablet that had been wiped clean of the markings upon it. Within seconds, the transformation was complete; the illusion was terminated. Sa'Tisfied, Margot turned her head away from the mirror and toward Fobush just in time to witness his final gasp of breath, and then she smiled an evil and gratified smile. She opened the large door of the nearby wardrobe and with one hand, she grabbed the collar of the Duke's shirt and dragged him out and to the side of his now dead aide. She let go of him and he collapsed heavily upon the rug. His lips were cracked and bleeding from the gag that was stuffed into his mouth, and his wrists were blackened and bruised, burned and cut by the coarse ropes. His eyes were opened wider than it seemed possible and panic was written all over them.

"Thank you for giving me your city, my love," she said in a sugary-sweet voice. "And your soul," she hissed. "Now it is time for you to share your parent's fate."

She bent down and kissed him on the cheek and the terror in his eyes enhanced her pleasure even further. Margot backed away from the two bodies and gazed out of the window. Kettin thrashed and bounced upon the floor, but he might as well have not been there as far as she was concerned. She could see the last of the people still fleeing the city, and she watched with an evil glee as the looters and scavengers began to pilfer what remained in Talamar. They scurried around, filling their bulging sacks with candlesticks and teapots, jewelry and flatware; all of the coveted implements that seemed so valuable to their owners only days ago, and had now been fecklessly abandoned in their haste to escape.

"They think the Knights will save them," she scoffed. "Let them run to Avalain. It will not be long before it too succumbs. I could not have asked for more! Now they have truly given their city to me, and I so appreciate the gift!"

She raised her right arm and summoned a ball of yellow fire and hurled it into the corner. It quickly ignited the heavy draperies that hung upon the walls and began to spread slowly across the thick, woolen carpets.

"Farewell, my love," she mocked Kettin as she shut the door behind herself. "Stay warm!"

She turned around and stood and faced the doorway before walking down the hall, and she ran her fingers around the thin gap between the wood and the stone of the wall. As she did so, she fused the frame shut with a hot, blue light that emanated from her fingertips. By the time she emerged into the open space of the courtyard, she was thoroughly pleased with herself.

"This will be most enjoyable," she muttered as she walked toward the grove of polong trees that had supplied the castle with oil year round. "I so love the irony of it all," she said as she incinerated the first tree with a ball of yellow fire. The oil laden tree burst into flame and exploded in an ear shattering boom that shook the entire courtyard. It rained burning droplets of fire upon everything in a two hundred yard radius. Those few thieves who still remained in the city nearly jumped out of their scabrous boots at the sound. "What has sustained this city for so many tiels shall now be the means by which it dies," she laughed. "A fitting end to Talamar."

One by one, she ignited the trees that lined the yard, and each one mushroomed with fire, sending flaming oil high into the air all around. Whatever else the oil fell upon too erupted into flame, until fire could be seen everywhere. By this time, no one remained within the city to extinguish the fires so they burned out of control and spread with a rapacious speed.

She bent down upon one knee and raised her face to the sky. The medallion around her neck glowed with an intense black light and illuminated her entire head.

"I claim this place in the name of Colton dar Agonthea, Lord of Darkness, Master of Destiny! May you join the other dead places upon this earth. Let this be Talamar's first step on the pathway to dissolution. No one will live here ever again!" she bellowed.

The fires burned brighter and the buildings collapsed upon

themselves in a cauldron of ruin and destruction. The heat was unbearable, but Margot felt nothing. The earth trembled with the fall of each edifice and the sidewalks cracked and flew apart. Black smoke rose high into the air, and it blocked out what sunlight still illuminated the dying city. What had once been the castle tower now lay in ruins before the broken and incinerated gates. Papers blew everywhere, flying up and down as if immune to the fires, and the dust of death choked the breath from even the lowliest of beasts who still remained amidst the devastation.

Well done, Margot, well done, a voice boomed inside her head.

She immediately fell to the ground prostrate, with her arms and legs extended.

It is a shame you failed previously in your attempt to capture the sisters, it continued in a sugary-sweet voice. *Such a hollow victory it must be for you here,* he said as if genuinely saddened for her.

"Yes, master. It is. I am sorry I failed you before. They escaped into the pit and were assisted by the beasts within," she explained in a feeble voice.

Was that an excuse, Margot? he asked, as innocently as could be.

"No, Master. Just an explanation is all. I have no excuse for not carrying out your orders," she replied as she cowered before his words.

Her entire body ached to please him. She could think of nothing other than making him happy, and knowing that she was unable to do what he had asked her to do literally caused her physical pain. She cringed beneath it.

No excuse at all, he replied so kindly, though the malevolence was just below the surface.

"No, Master. No excuse at all," she sobbed, frightened and drained.

You have given me Talamar, Margot. That will suffice for now, he said in a satisfied tone.

The elation that coursed through her body at his praise was immeasurable. She was ecstatic and so thoroughly mesmerized by him that she could barely breathe.

You will not let me down me the next time, will you? he asked, and his voice caressed her soul like a velvet glove upon her skin. *There are others who clamor for the chance to replace you. If not for the disappointment it causes me, they would savor another failure on your part, knowing it would be your last,* he said so calmly and soothingly that the tone veiled the mortal threat the words represented.

"Never again, my Lord. Never again," she promised, and she savored even his reprimands.

Never again, he repeated. *Now, see to it that nothing remains alive in this dreadful place. I do not want there to be even a kernel of life here after you leave. Do you understand me?*

"Yes, my Lord. I understand perfectly well. It will be my pleasure," she answered him, still spread eagled upon the ground.

Rise, my little one. Rise, he said, and her body began to ascend from the ground. *Float upon my air, use my breath, partake of my power,* he instructed her.

Filled with the rapture of him, she raised her arms and let the power inundate her until it began to shoot from all of her extremities in bolts of white fire, crashing and exploding into what little remained standing until the entire city was in ruins. She dropped to the ground in a standing position, still filled with his essence, and she basked in the glory of her accomplishment, though she was already beginning to feel the bitter pangs of his withdrawal. She tried to hold her breath and maintain what she could within her, but it was rapidly fading now. The disappointment was so great that she doubled over and almost collapsed to the ground, as she retched uncontrollably.

A deep depression consumed her spirit the moment he was gone, and she desperately surveyed the devastated landscape in order to elevate her mood once again. Breathing deeply, she relaxed her body and fought to accept his absence. She reminded herself of his words and that eased her pain, though the memory petrified her as well. She would not leave until she was certain that nothing breathed and nothing moved; absolutely certain!. Fulfilling his commands was all that mattered. Talamar would soon be no more, a mere blackened smudge upon a heap of rubble.

"I will find you," she vowed as she stood solitary amidst the debris. "You have caused him to be angry with me, and that I cannot bear. And when I do, even the Drue will not be strong enough to protect you!"

Margot spat upon the ground, threw her crimson cape over her shoulders, raised her arms once more and unleashed a whirlwind of white fire and unspeakable destruction that marked the final death knell of Talamar.

Chapter Twenty-five

"It is a sad rhyme, father. There seems so little hope and so much peril in Sidra's declaration. Yet we must carry out her request nonetheless," Caroline explained.

"If there is no chance of you succeeding, why must you try?" he asked, though he already knew the answer.

Caroline simply smiled at him and squeezed his arm tenderly.

"It is not that there is no chance. The words are not all doom and gloom, though they are not particularly encouraging. We still must determine exactly what she wishes us to do. We cannot simply ignore this," she responded.

"You speak as if Sidra knew you would accompany him all along," Conrad said, referring to the elf beside her. "Why must you be a part of this too?"

"Because I am, father. Sidra planted these ideas in his mind and then covered them with other memories. If we had not met, they may never have surfaced again," she replied. "Only one such as I could have helped him to remember. It was meant to be. What a twist of fate that you arrived at our doorstep," she said to Dalloway. "It was as if Sidra knew of my abilities and guided you here."

Her father mumbled something to himself under his breath, but before Caroline was able to question him, Dalloway began to speak and she turned her attention to him once again.

"How were you able to restore my memory? One moment my mind was a blank tablet, and the next moment I remembered everything as if my past was lurking behind a door and you just opened it for me," Dalloway asked, still somewhat dazed.

"I taught you how to speak from within, like the animals do, without words. All your memories were there, but they were disordered and they could not surface. Other things obscured them. Once the thoughts became clear, we merely had to organize them so that you could consciously remember them once again," Caroline explained.

"You make it sound so simple," Dalloway replied.

"For me, it is not difficult. What is trying is to have to absorb so much of another living thing's life, particularly when the memories are painful ones. With the animals, it is much simpler and clearer. Happiness and sorrow are more basic feelings, directly related to pleasures and pains. Today I have learned that with humans, that is not always the case," she said.

"So I am more complicated than the animals?" he asked jokingly, and Caroline grinned.

"A bit more so, I would say. The layers of thought and memory are thicker and deeper. I am glad that I did not have to venture too far in order to find what Sidra intended me to. She was protecting you from having your thoughts stolen by one more unscrupulous than I, so it was good fortune that I intuited the proper path sooner rather than later." Caroline said.

"Stolen?" he asked.

"Yes. What she has asked you to do it so important, and it would be dangerous for us all if it were to be discovered by the wrong people," Caroline explained. "Her words were marked in a way that I cannot explain. It was like following a far away light in a dark passage, though I was continuously bombarded by stray thoughts and memories. When I located her message it obscured all else," she continued.

"You were able to maintain your own identity, daughter. That is not how your mother described her experiences," Conrad related with intense interest.

"I have much experience, though not with humans, father. I have perfected my art," she replied.

"I should have known better than to doubt you, Caroline. My fear had been ruling my heart. You are a very strong girl," he said.

"Woman, father. I am a very strong woman," she replied assuredly.

"Yes, no doubt. You are quite a strong woman, and I am quite the proud father," he said, and his eyes clouded with tears. Stifling his emotions, he asked, "Knowing now to what lengths Sidra has gone to protect this message, what have your efforts revealed?"

"It seems that a map that has been tainted or poisoned in some way has disappeared from the place that it had been kept safe for many, many tiels."

"A map, you say? What more did she say about it? Did she describe it?" Conrad asked, and he was growing more and more curious by the second.

"No, other than to refer to it as 'blighted'," she replied. "Dalloway, you are an elf of royal descent. You are more likely to know what this reference signifies. I sense that you have knowledge of the histories. My education and experience is limited. What does this mean to you?" she asked.

"Though I am no scholar, I do know that there are many places in the Tomes that refer to maps and charts and the like. My mother often read passages from the great books to me as a child. She is a very wise and learned woman. I cannot recollect them all though. But, what I do remember was that the Quest was always paramount in the chapters she preferred, so they almost always had to do with that subject," he said. "One such chapter that I do recall quite well spoke of a parchment that was inscribed with directions to the First. I do not think that my mother ever believed it to be real, but merely a metaphor or a hope, and I also believe it was not merely what it appeared to be. Whether it was defiled or contaminated in some way I do not know. In that particular story, there was something not right about it, and it was not that it was inaccurate or misleading."

"Your description of this item bears a striking resemblance to how Sidra represents it in your memory. Could this be what she wants us to find?" Caroline asked. "A map that leads to the First?"

"That would make sense," Conrad said. "You said that it was blighted. That could mean many things. It could carry a poison upon its surface, it might lead those who follow it to an unholy place, or she could simply feel that it is destined to cause problems in some other way," he speculated.

"What could be worse than having such a thing fall into the Dark Lord's hands if in fact it is accurate and will lead its owner to the One Tree?" Dalloway asked, and he shuddered at the thought.

"I suppose," Caroline said, thinking aloud. "The adjective describes the map, but I sense that the blight refers to the trouble that follows those who possess it. And, she said that the sisters carry it. Who are the sisters?"

"Sisters?" Conrad asked. "Can you be more specific? I must hear the entire text. Share this with me, Caroline. I am still in the dark here. I know Sidra. Perhaps I can help to interpret it," he said, surprising both his daughter and Dalloway with this information.

"You know her?" Caroline questioned. "I thought you only knew of her. How do you know her?"

"It is a long story, my child, best left for another time," he replied. "Suffice it to say, I know the woman and I know her well enough to be of some assistance here."

Caroline raised her eyebrows questioningly.

"Do not think for a moment that I will forget to ask you again about this," she answered. "For now though, we do have more important things to focus upon. The message that she implanted in his mind was in the form of a poem."

"That is always how Sidra speaks. That is nothing unusual," Conrad said knowingly.

Again, Caroline lifted her eyebrows at her father's words.

"Always, father?" she asked, and immediately continued with the recitation of the poem:

> *"'So much you can, so much you can't,*
> *Choose those things you must.*
> *How loud you rave, how loud you rant,*
> *We all return to dust.*
> *Do what you may along the way,*
> *Be brave, be strong, be true.*
> *"Tis not enough, idly by to sit*
> *When destiny beckons you.*
> *Seek it now, the blighted map,*
> *Pluck it from their hands,*
> *Lest it fall forever lost*
> *Upon the daemon's chest to land.*
> *The sisters of the sacred place*
> *know not what they do,*
> *Forgive them the words their actions speak,*
> *They are noble, through and through.*
> *Lost in a moment of what he needs;*
> *"The well at the end go seek!",*
> *Not all can be arranged just so,*
> *The Drue find, the Drue keep.'"*

Caroline finished reciting and she looked anxiously at her father.

"What do you make of it?" she asked.

Conrad barely hesitated before offering his explanation.

"True to her form!" he smiled. "Defiant and confusing at the same time. The sisters can be none other than the sisters of Parth. Sidra admired then always. She spoke of Parth in beautiful rhymes. I think that she even visited there once or twice, though she would never admit it," he smiled. He was more animated than she had ever remembered him to be, and it was clear that his recollections of her were fond ones. "The map she speaks of must be the one we guessed; the one that bears the directions to the First."

"Do they intend to hand it over to Caeltin D'Are Agenathea? Why?" Dalloway asked astounded. "I know of these women. They would not do such a thing willingly."

"No. Listen closely," Conrad instructed. "The well at the end has to be the one in the dead city of Odelot."

"Are there no other wells? How can you be certain that is where they are headed? And they are to drop it down the well then?" Caroline asked.

"Certain, my daughter? I am not certain of anything. But, that is the only one that has always been referred to as the 'Well at the World's End'. Sidra too is from Odelot originally so she would most definitely know of it, though her memories are bitter since its demise. But surely Colton must know this as well by now, and she fears that he will be waiting for them at the bottom. Thus it will fall into his hands when they release it. That must be what Sidra is alluding to and what she fears."

"Someone told these sisters to do this. The poem states it thusly. They are innocents and they have been misled. By whom and why?" Dalloway questioned.

"I cannot tell from the context who 'he' is. It must have been someone they respected and trusted. The sisters of Parth have guarded this parchment since the beginning," Conrad explained. "They would unlikely release it from their custody voluntarily unless..." he hesitated.

"Unless?" Caroline asked.

"Unless the directive came from a Chosen or a Lalas itself!" he said softly. "You surprise me more and more, father. You seem to know so much about the outside world. Why have you kept this side of you secret from me all these tiels?" Caroline asked.

"For fear that you would become too interested in things that were happening beyond our home," he confessed. "I sought to protect you from harm and to keep you here."

"You have, father. You have. Thank you. But it is not necessary any longer," she replied.

"I know that now, Caroline," he said, and he gazed deeply into her eyes.

She smiled and dipped her chin respectfully, and then paused contemplatively for a moment.

"Who are the Drue?" she then asked. "Is it the sisters they will keep, or have they already found the map and is that what they will not relinquish?"

"This, my dear daughter, I do not know," Conrad replied. "But I am certain that Sidra would not send anyone on a hopeless quest.

She is not frivolous in that manner, but deadly serious when it comes to things of import. Before that reference, do you see how she defies even the trees? 'Not all can be arranged as so'," he repeated. "If a Lalas sent them on what she considers to be a misguided mission, it would take someone with Sidra's confidence to question them and even think that it should be thwarted."

"Is her strength equal to her confidence?" Dalloway asked. "What I remember of her now leads me to believe that it is."

"I, too, would be surprised if it was not. Sidra is not one to idly boast. Nor is she one to cower in the shade of a Lalas' might. She is quite unusual," he said admiringly. "Few deal on equal terms with the great trees. She is most definitely one of the few who does."

"So where do we find these sisters? If they are going to Odelot, perhaps we should try to get there before they do?" Dalloway suggested. "It would do us not good to go to Parth now and seek them out. It must be too late for that."

"How long would it take them to reach Odelot? That is, if they could even make it there. The one thing we cannot decipher is the last line. I hope it is not crucial to all of this," Caroline replied. "Who or what could the Drue be?" she asked again.

"Odelot should be our starting point regardless, Caroline. We can back track from thence, if necessary. At least we know that is where they hope to go and have been instructed to go," Dalloway said.

"That would make the most sense to me," Conrad concurred. "If we leave immediately and we ride during the daylight hours only, it should take us no more than seven days to get to Odelot. We cannot travel at night through the wilds any longer."

Both Caroline and Dalloway looked at him with their eyes bulging out of their heads.

"We?" his daughter asked incredulously. "You intend to go with us?"

"Did you really think that I would let you go without me? Would I not be welcome?" he asked.

"Father, I would like nothing more than to have you accompany us. I just never thought you would leave here," she said.

"Until now, I never thought either of us would leave here. We have accepted so easily the fact that this quest is ours to assume. None of us questioned it," Conrad replied. "Besides, If you leave, what have I to stay for?" he asked sweetly, and Caroline bowed her head humbly once again in response.

"You are right, father. The decision came so naturally that I did not even recognize it as a choice that I had made," she said. "But we cannot leave at once regardless. There is packing to do, and I must let my animal friends know that I am going away. Some of them would never forgive me if I left without a word, they are so accustomed to my communications," Caroline said.

"We must provision ourselves carefully, though it should not take too much time to make our arrangements. The wilds will offer us no sustenance, and it will remain as cold and snowy on the way as it is here for a while, at least until we make some progress southward," Conrad said. "Tomorrow morning is soon enough. You should say your farewells this evening, Caroline."

"Do you know which paths to follow to Odelot?" Dalloway asked.

"Yes, I do, my boy," he replied. "I shan't have too much difficulty finding the place, I suspect. I also suspect that the medallion that Sidra gave you, which has already proven to be more than an ornament, will help us again."

"You amaze me, father!" Caroline said once more, and she leaned over and kissed him on his scruffy cheek. "If we are to leave at first light, then I do indeed have much to do! I cannot sit here and chat with you two any longer," she said as if they were all old friends. "But please, feel free to continue yourselves," she smiled, happy and surprised that her father seemed to have finally accepted Dalloway's presence so completely. It even appeared to her as if he was growing to like the elf. "I will return shortly and we can confer then on what we will need to bring with us."

As Caroline left the room, she glanced back and saw the two men with their heads bent, sitting next to one another and staring intently at the medallion on the floor before them while Conrad drew symbols in the dust all around it.

Chapter Twenty-six

Beolan led the ranks of anxious men out of Crispen and across the narrow bridge that spanned the water surrounding it. Without looking back again, he continued on until he reached the road that would take them to the pathway that wound its way up to Silandre's mouth. The cheering and shouting had ended a while ago and a sober hush had descended upon them all. They rode in silence from that point on, side by side, the elf and the dwarf, with their troops also marching as if they all hailed from one nation with one common goal. The sight of elves and dwarves striding together into battle, armed and ready, unhampered by discord or disagreement was one not often seen, and it too was an episode that would remain forever in the minds of those left behind.

As the two physically disparate armies drew closer to the mountain, the sound of the cascading water grew louder and it calmed them all with its unceasing melody as it had done for the inhabitants of Crispen for countless tiels. Even the dwarves who naturally feared the clear blue liquid, derived solace and comfort from the falling waters of Silandre, and they marched toward it with no trepidation in their hearts.

The sun was high in the morning sky by the time they reached the plateau beneath the final ascent to the entrance that they would be using to gain access to the caves. The armies of both nations fanned out quickly and filled the entire space after Beolan and Maringar turned to face them. Far below them now lay the city of Crispen, and the polished quartz facades of its buildings gleamed brilliantly in the daylight. The maze of canals and waterways that crisscrossed it appeared like an intricately designed spider web from this vantage point, sparkling blue amidst the pure white lambency of the towers. It was truly a magnificent sight to behold.

Behind and above the heads of the two young leaders was a gaping hole in the slope of the stone. Flanking it on either side coursed two azure streams of water that originated high overhead and crashed into churning pools of white froth far below, and then ran in countless rivulets toward the city. One narrow path led up to the opening, and from where they stood it appeared a curved and painted, brown stripe drawn upon the lush green foliage that grew voluminously upon the cliffs.

The two warriors had planned their strategy the evening before, and they were determined and unflinching in their desire to begin the crusade. A group of the strongest of the dwarves would enter the caves first, led of course by Maringar. It was their responsibility and great honor to clear the opening of all debris and to enlarge it so that ampler numbers of warriors could enter together thereafter. One of Beolan's fears was that the Armadiel would be able to dispatch small groups of them easily and continually, and they therefore decided it would be most prudent to assault it with numbers initially, hopefully forcing it to remain preoccupied, and thus pressuring it into a defensive position. In order to do so, they required a larger space within which to maneuver than now existed just inside the entrance. The elfin bowmen would take up positions within the entryway as soon as possible and provoke the Armadiel, thus giving the skilled dwarves of the Thorndars, accustomed as they were to the harder granite of their more southern mountains, the opportunity to tunnel through this softer limestone in a number of directions at once. If they were able to progress more quickly than their enemy expected, they could hopefully encircle it before it realized what had happened.

They needed to be able to attack it continuously and forcefully, and to bombard it with all the weapons at their disposal. It was imperative that the dwarves and elves together inflict as much damage upon the beast as quickly as they could. If they were successful in their efforts to cut off its ability to retreat, they could pound away at it from all vantage points. That was the only way they could hope to force it to undergo the transformation whilst it was still in their presence. Beolan and Maringar planned to wait for that precious moment to attack; that one instant when it would be vulnerable to their assault. If the affliction was great enough, it would need to shed its damaged outer skin regardless of its circumstances, and they would thus be there to strike when that happened.

Maringar motioned to the group of dwarves he had selected to accompany him on the initial foray, and they immediately stepped forward in unison, with their picks and axes strapped tightly across their backs and their studded leather helms drawn halfway down over their protruding foreheads. The heavy boots they wore pounded the hard surface in unison as they marched toward their leader. The first line of men carried tall posts swathed in hemp and saturated with polong oil. Maringar saluted Beolan before turning his horse toward the gaping hole in the rock. He walked slowly into the darkness and quickly disappeared from view while his men followed closely behind him. A small contingent of elves with particularly long bows fell in right after with Beolan at their head, and they too were soon gobbled up by the darkness.

Once inside, they set their deep into the soft soil of the entryway and ignited them, thus drenching the space in light. Maringar scanned the surfaces closely and then led his teams to the perimeters where they immediately set to work. They fanned out in all directions in teams of two, and the first in each line began to chip away at the stone. Great piles of rubble were quickly forming behind each of the stone cutters, and these piles were gathered up in nets of tight mesh by their partners and then dragged back to the opening where the larger less pliable pieces were carted away. The remainder was dumped upon the stone floor in piles equidistant from one another and left there for a purpose yet to become apparent.

Strangely and surprisingly, they encountered no resistance, though the noise they made was loud and persistent, and they made great progress in a matter of hours. The strength of the dwarves was formidable and their efforts were unceasing. The cacophonous melody of picks against rock filled the entire space. The chamber was almost double in size by the time the second group of elfin warriors took up their positions.

The tunnel that lead deeper into the mountain had been circumvented up until this point. The majority of the dwarves concentrated on the areas to its left and to its right, seeking only to widen the chamber at first. A pair of them though, on either side, tunneled deep and straight, and they began to create a passage wide enough for two soldiers to walk side by side down. It was through these passages that they eventually hoped to encircle the Armadiel when they finally encountered it. As more room was cleared, more warriors entered, and they assembled in neat and precise rows behind the laboring dwarves, whose numbers too grew as the surface space upon which they could work was expanded.

Beolan had anticipated having to keep the beast at bay while the dwarves tunneled, but his concerns were for naught. They saw and heard neither hide nor hair of the Armadiel. Even the odor which had been so strong and obvious when he had been here only a day ago seemed to have abated. The air that they breathed today was not impure as expected, and the rock itself was as inanimate as it had always been in the past. It yielded to the labors of the dwarves as easily as they could have hoped.

Maringar walked back from the front line in search of his Elfin friend. He was as surprised as Beolan at how easy it had been to enter and to begin the task that they both assumed would be costly at the least. He found him standing with a group of bowmen behind a pile of rock and pebbles that a pair of dwarves were quickly shaping into a protective barrier that sat atop an almost translucent tarpaulin that they had placed upon the surface earlier. The bottom of this covering was studded with countless polished rocks that looked like tiny marbles imbedded in it. These makeshift walls were being erected throughout the rapidly widening space behind which the elfin bowmen took up their positions.

As Maringar approached, he smiled to himself as he watched his men instruct the elves as to how to maneuver their newly created shelters. They seemed surprised when the now formidable pile of rubble about six feet thick and just as high slid forward so easily when pushed upon from the back. It glided before them with very little exertion on their part despite the great weight of the debris. Furthermore, they could move it from left to right just as effortlessly. It required only a slight touch in order to shift its position.

"How is it that such weight does not hinder the movement?" Beolan asked with wonder as Maringar approached.

"The cloth upon which the walls sit has been meticulously created. The bearing balls distribute the weight so evenly that it remains a fraction above the surface, and therefore nothing hampers its movement," he replied.

Beolan pressed slightly upon the compacted rubble before him, and the entire wall moved in response.

"Ingenious! You are masters at this art," he said, impressed.

"We understand the composition of our environment, as you do yours," he explained. "Such an understanding allows us to work with the elements rather than against them."

"You think much as we do," Beolan said.

"Is that such a surprise to you?" Maringar asked, and he smiled at his friend questioningly.

"No longer a surprise. Now, it is more of a confirmation," the elf replied.

"I see it as an affirmation of our common purpose," Maringar said, and the elf nodded in agreement.

"We have much to teach one another," he responded.

"And we shall have the opportunity sooner than we ever imagined," Maringar said.

The elves had quickly learned how to maneuver their protective barricades, and they advanced as fast as the dwarves were able to dig. They had their long bows ready and strung, prepared to defend their burrowing friends, though no enemy had yet shown itself before them. The sharp eyes of the elfin warriors missed nothing, even in the dim and flickering light of the cavern.

"It is just a matter of time before he attacks. The beast will not wait forever. Neither will he run from us. He thinks himself invulnerable," Beolan explained.

"And well he might have been for all we knew had we not read that passage as closely as we had," Maringar commented.

"I only pray that we are correct in our interpretation. Should we be wrong, it will cost us dearly," Beolan warned. "The great books are not manuals. We can only be hopeful that what we read into the words is what was intended. There is no certainty when it comes to what is yet to be."

"We would attempt to defeat him nonetheless, would we not, regardless of what the books have revealed to us?. At the least, we will do so with hope in our hearts now. What better motivator could urge us forward?"

"You are wiser than your years, Maringar, and you seem always to know the right words to say. I am fortunate to have met you," Beolan replied earnestly. "Now let us find this monster before he finds us. When I was here last, everything seemed different. It was so hot that I could barely stand it. And there were other things so wrong that it pains me to recall them all. Perhaps he has retreated deeper into the mountain."

"That will only make the job of surrounding him more difficult. We must draw him back out then," Maringar replied.

"My thoughts exactly!" Beolan concurred. "He did not reveal himself to me the last time, but I was stealthy and cautious."

"He must be aware of our presence here now. The sound of the picks and axes upon the stone could not be more obvious."

"I doubt not that the beast knows we have come. He is no dolt for sure, and certainly not easily fooled into complacency," Beolan said.

"Then let us take the initiative whilst we still can. The more time we afford my men to dig and yours to advance, the better our chances will be later," Maringar replied. "It would be best if we were the attackers rather than the attacked. If we do not challenge his presence, he will choose the where and when of his approach, and our plan to encircle him will be for naught."

The two young leaders were of one mind once again. They each gave brief instructions to their men and then joined one another before the opening to the main tunnel. Beolan had already drawn his blade and he held it loosely in his left hand. Maringar too had unsheathed his dagger and he brandished it before him in the semi darkness.

"What shall we use to light our way? Though my vision is good at close range, it is not good enough to navigate this tunnel in the dark," Maringar said, not wishing to have to sacrifice the use of his free hand to a torch.

"My sight is quite sharp even at a distance, but I agree completely. It would only handicap us if we could not both see equally as well. We are the seekers in this foray, not the sought," he said. "I am no wizard, but my race is blessed with some natural talents," Beolan replied, and he removed what looked like a small cloth sack from his pocket and hung it over his neck by the strings that were attached to it. "I did not come unprepared," he smiled, and then effortlessly conjured a modest orb of light within it that burned blue and bright. "This should suffice."

"More than adequate," Maringar readily concurred.

They walked side by side with still a slight bit of room between each of them and the walls. The height of the tunnel was considerable despite the narrowness of it, and the floor was smooth and free of debris. It wound downward slightly, and then after a short while, it began to widen. All the evidence of the Armadiel that Beolan witnessed before was gone. Silandre was as he remembered it from days long past. The rock was cold and hard and the only odor was that of the mountain; natural and organic. There was nothing threatening in the air and no manifestation of the beast's presence anywhere.

"It has erased all signs of itself. A ploy, do you think?" Beolan asked.

"It must not want us to know where it hides, though that is no surprise. It is not as bold as I would have expected though," Maringar replied.

"Guileful, I would surmise. I had hoped it would have been less attentive to such things, and thus less careful. A beast with as much power as legend attributes to this one seems not to be taking it for granted," Beolan said worriedly.

They continued to walk upon the path as it veered left and right, while all the time they were aware that they were descending with each step. Time passed as they moved deeper and deeper into the mountain, and still they saw no indication that the beast was near. Cautiously they kept to the path, and the minutes turned into hours.

"We have left the others far behind," Maringar observed after a while. "And still no signs."

Just then, a gust of humid air wafted through the tunnel directly into their faces.

"I spoke too soon," the dwarf said, and his senses were immediately on alert.

"Be on your guard. We must be prepared to withdraw before we are embroiled in a battle prematurely. We want him to follow us. It would serve no purpose if we were forced into a battle this deep in the mountain," Beolan said, though he knew they were of like minds already.

"Extinguish the light then," Maringar suggested. "We can be lures without being targets."

Beolan heeded his comrades advice, and in an instant they were enveloped by total darkness.

"Stay close to me. We do not wish to lose each other now," Beolan said.

The air was growing hotter and damper with each new step that they took. Furthermore, the odor that had turned the elf's stomach the last time he was here was beginning to reach their nostrils once more.

"This is wretched," Maringar whispered, and he covered his mouth and nose with a gloved hand.

"It will get worse," Beolan warned.

Maringar took another step and his heavy boot slid out to the right almost causing him to topple over. The surface had become so slippery that he had trouble righting himself. He reached out to the wall for support and he quickly discovered that it too was dripping with slime. He withdrew his hand and found it covered with a sticky substance that made it difficult for him to even separate his fingers from one another. After wiping it on the rough leather of his jerkin, he was finally able to clean it. The elf's soft boots offered him better traction than the studded soles of the dwarf's own.

"Be careful not to get any of this on your face or in your eyes," he warned in a hushed voice.

"What is this stuff? Slippery and sticky at the same time!" Maringar observed.

"The residue of evil, I fear," Beolan commented balefully. "The beast cannot be far behind."

"Did you feel that?" Maringar asked suddenly.

"Yes," Beolan replied as the vibration abated. "A tremor, perhaps."

"Like no other I have ever felt then," Maringar said.

Another shudder rippled through the rock underfoot and both of the men stood totally still until it passed.

"That was stronger than the last one. And this putrid smell is stronger too. Be on your guard!" Beolan warned.

A sound like a bellows makes when one is feeding a fire with air could be heard in the passageway. It wheezed and gasped over and over again and grew louder with each intake and expulsion. Maringar shifted his dagger into the hand that still stung from whatever had coated it a moment before, and then he wiped his eyes with his clean one. They burned and teared.

"It comes," Beolan said. "Get ready!"

The walls and surfaces seemed to expand and contract with each pulsating vibration. The stone itself appeared as if it was breathing in and out. A viscous fluid coated all the surfaces and made it extremely treacherous and difficult to maintain a footing upon. And the odor! It was almost unbearable. Sounds coursed through the stone; horrible sounds as if the rock itself was crying out in anguish. Like lightening streaking across a darkened sky, the Armadiel infiltrated the stone surrounding them, and it spread its nightmarish essence throughout the heart and soul of the mountain.

Maringar stood close to his friend as they both prepared to run back up the path toward the assembled warriors. They knew that they could not wait too long once the beast began its pursuit, but they needed to induce it to follow them, and if it did not get a taste of its prey, it might just decide to sit back upon its heels and wait for them to return again. They did not want to have to repeat this excursion, so they waited and waited until the heat became so strong and the conditions became so appalling and horrific that they could not stand it any longer.

"We must go!" Beolan said urgently. "Now!" he insisted, but Maringar did not respond.

He could feel his presence beside him, but the dwarf did not move.

"Maringar? It is time!" he said. "We cannot risk another moment!" he said frenetically.

Beolan felt the ground shift beneath his feet in nauseating waves that caused him to reach out his arms in order to stabilize himself. As he came into contact with Maringar's skin, he retracted his hand in horror. The dwarf was burning up and he could feel that his body was coated in the same slime that oozed from Silandre's stone. Beolan knew immediately what was happening, and he quickly rekindled the small orb of light, only this time he focused his efforts upon it more intensely. It burned blue and steady. He pulled it from around his neck, breaking the cords as he did so, and then he thrust it against his friend's body. The blue light flared brightly and began to expand out of the small casing that housed it, and it adhered instantly to Maringar and began to spread over his entire body. Wherever it came into contact with the slithery coating, the thick liquid immediately fell away in heavy droplets. One force fought the other, but alas, this time the light was not to be the victor. No sooner did a drop fall to the stone floor when another, heavier wave washed over him and threatened to douse the light completely. Extinguished and defeated, the casing fell noiselessly to the ground.

Maringar looked at him with eyes wide and full of terror. He attempted to speak though he was clearly in agony by this time. His body was pulsating and his features were distorted from the battle that now raged within him. The expression upon his face was so painful to witness that Beolan could barely stand it.

"Go!" Maringar finally managed to say in a tormented gasp. "Leave me! We cannot both be lost so soon!"

"I will carry you if I must! It shall not be the victor before the battle has begun!" he shouted, and he reached out his hand to grasp his friend.

A waft of rancid air struck him in the face like a slap from Sedahar itself, and what emanated from Maringar's mouth next was the most chilling sound Beolan had ever heard in his life.

"He is mine!" the beast hissed through the dwarf's contorted lips in the most heinous and bloodcurdling voice imaginable. "He is mine, and so too will you be soon!" it said, as the rock upon which they stood rose up around Maringar as if it was alive, and embraced the dwarf in two horrifying arms of black and shimmering, liquid stone.

Chapter Twenty-seven

"Is it not colder than usual for this time of year?" Alemar asked Teetoo, and she put another branch on top of the fire. "I am accustomed to low temperatures, but this feels wrong."

"Yes. The winds are too strong. They bring with them a moisture that chills the air unnaturally," he replied.

"From the south it comes," she said, as she held up her palm and felt it blow against her naked hand. "From Sedahar?"

"From Sedahar, I fear," the Weloh said to her, as his saucer-like eyes glowed curiously in the dark.

"How far are we, do you think?"

"Another two day's ride, no more," he answered.

"We cannot just ride up to the gates and announce ourselves. We must plan what we will do," Alemar said with an acerbity in her tone that was so alien to her character.

"There are no gates, Alemar," Teetoo began to explain. "None have been so bold nor so reckless as to try to gain entrance into the Dark Lord's home voluntarily. He has not erected walls to keep people out, but merely to keep them in."

"Reckless? Has no one ever assaulted him on his own ground?" she asked.

"No one," he replied.

"Then you and I shall be the first ones to do so?" she asked, and a spark lit her voice momentarily. "Ah, to be the vanguard of such an effort!" she said, though the sarcasm had quickly returned.

"It is quite a responsibility indeed," he answered her solemnly, disturbed by the mood that dominated her words and actions.

"Teetoo?" she asked earnestly. "Are we mad? Do we really have a chance? What weapons can we wield against his dreadful power?" she asked, and her face was sad and disconsolate once again.

"Of course we have a chance, however remote it may appear to be, Princess. Much will depend upon us and much upon him. He will not be expecting any such assault for just this reason; it has never happened before. We bring with us the element of surprise," Teetoo said. "And remember, we are not seeking to topple him from power alone and unassisted. Our aim is to free Premoran, not to kill Colton dar Agonthea!"

"And if we could?" she asked.

"Kill him?" he replied.

"Yes. Rid the earth of him once and for all."

"It is beyond our power to do that, I am afraid. A force greater than what we possess would be required. He has grown too strong."

"Elsinestra was correct then. Nothing short of dissolution will destroy him," she said almost despondently. "So how can we ever be victorious? We will require more than surprise alone I suspect. Are we fooling ourselves?" she asked again and then she hung her head down.

"The boy must find the Gem," Teetoo replied. "The answer lies there. Victory for us will not mark the end of the war. We can alter the pattern in the weave by our actions, but we alone cannot complete the cloth."

"So we just fight on despite the fact that we really cannot do anything ultimately to help? If it is all up to Davmiran, why do we bother then?"

"What has brought this heartsickness upon you, Alemar?" he asked her sincerely. "Since we left Seramour, you have been so negative. For brief moments your enthusiasm returns, and then you sink deeper into this dejection. Things have not changed all that much in such a short while. What happened to the victorious warrior I met some weeks ago who ascended into the Heights with confidence and optimism spilling forth from every pore in her body?"

"I do not know, Teetoo," she said seriously. "I must have left it in Seramour. A malaise has enveloped me and I cannot shrug it off. I fear for the earth. I fear so desperately for the earth that it hurts me day and night," she replied. "And I am angry. I despise Caeltin! He is so cruel and so evil. I do not understand how a soul could be so black and uncaring. And the fact that his is, casts a shadow across all that I do. As we departed the Heights, this darkness grasped hold of my heart, and it has not let go since. Why is this happening? Have I been possessed?"

"It is hard not to hate him, though it will do you only harm if it does not motivate you to fight on. He is despicable. He cannot love. Pity him instead."

"Pity one such as he? To what end? I would rather hate him," she said sullenly.

"Then hate him, but do not regret it. If you choose to feel so about another, than accept those feelings and embrace them. If your abhorrence of him is a choice, use it as best as you can. If you let hate have you and you allow it to darken your soul, then you are indeed possessed. If you view it as a proper reaction to something abhorrent in nature, something your essence cannot tolerate without recoiling, then it will not dominate you."

"I guess it is a choice, now that you put it that way. You are right," she said, as she nodded her head. "It is not the feeling itself, but how I respond to it that matters. Thank you, Teetoo. I feel much better already. Sometimes I forget what I can restrain and what I cannot."

"You are a woman of great self control and of great emotion. It is sometimes hard to balance those two characteristics, yet they make you so unique and so vital," he said admiringly. "A soul as alive and generous as yours must learn better how to defend itself against evil's devastation."

"To feel is to suffer. What is the alternative? I would have to be as cold as a stone in order not to be sad as a result of my reflections," she replied, confused.

"Sadness is not bad in and of itself, Alemar. It is your response to that which feels so unfair that is crippling you now. Yet you are allowing it to do so, and to affect moments yet unborn as well. There is no logical relation there," Teetoo explained.

Alemar contemplated his words deeply.

"You are so right, Teetoo!" she then replied. "The future looks sad to me because I have been viewing it through a darkened glass. But it is not yet upon us, so why look at it in such a skewed manner?" she asked herself. "I see this darkness lingering upon the edge of my emotions, the perimeter of my consciousness, and it angers me. I want it to be gone, but it persists and it taints all of my thoughts."

"This is the effect he has upon you. It is purposeful and difficult to combat. But you must do it nonetheless," Teetoo said. "You cannot allow him to influence your actions, despite the awareness of his evil presence."

"I must! And I will try. I promise," she replied sincerely.

"Good. Then it is time for us to discuss how we are going to accomplish our objectives. I have hesitated until such a moment. Are you sure you are ready?" he asked. "If you remain so negative, it will be fruitless to try and devise a successful plan with you," the Weloh said, ever the pragma'Tist.

"Yes. I cannot say that my mood has changed entirely. But it will. I really do see your points. Either I must govern my own emotions or constantly be a victim of them. And, I have never been a very good victim," she smiled. "In fact, my resistance has been at its best in situations where I have been most imperiled," Alemar replied, forcing herself to shake off her uneasiness.

"Like all heroes," Teetoo said quietly.

"What did you say?" she asked, uncertain if she heard him correctly.

"I said that you are like all the other heroes I have known," he answered her earnestly.

"I am not a hero, Teetoo. I have done nothing to warrant such praise," she said, scoffing at his words.

"I beg to differ with you, Alemar. You may not realize it, but your actions in the woods of Lormarion are already being sung by the bards all over the land. You are considered to be the one who has single handedly reunited the elfin kingdoms, rescued the legions of Iscaron from perpetual suffering and rid the forest of Colton's hideous army all at the same time. Argue with me if you wish, but these deeds sound very much to me like the actions of a hero," Teetoo explained. "Your...."

"Did you hear that?" she asked him suddenly, interrupting his praise, and the two of them immediately crouched down defensively with their backs touching so that they could see all around them.

"Yes, I did. Someone or something is approaching," he replied, and his entire body took on a slightly different color; a bit paler as if the blood had receded from his extremities.

The Weloh's arms elongated silently beside him and the translucent filaments reddened slightly in response. Alemar felt the soft, almost down-like surface brush against the skin of her arms, and her entire body tingled momentarily. She lifted her bow silently from off of her own back and then quietly slipped an arrow into it.

"Have you a sense of what it is?" she whispered.

"Not human. I would know that by now. Not animal either," he said, sniffing the air silently. "Elfin I think."

They then both heard a thrashing in the trees to the east and it was clear that whomever was approaching no longer felt the need for stealth.

"Who goes there?" Alemar shouted. "Declare yourself!"

"It is us, Princess!" a deep and familiar voice called out. "Giles and Clovis," the blonde haired elf yelled as he strolled out of the woods leading his huge stallion by the reins.

Princess Alemar stood up immediately and walked toward the source of the voice.

"What are you two doing here?" she asked, exasperated. "How did you know where to find me?"

"Though your friend left little or no marks, your trail was rather easy to follow," Clovis kidded her.

"I will keep that in mind the next time I decide to go off without you both," she replied. "I asked you not to come. Why have you disobeyed me?"

"Did you? I must not have been listening when you said that," Giles said innocently.

"Nor I," Clovis echoed his friend's words as he too emerged from the cover of the trees.

"Unfortunately, it is too late now. We are here!" Giles said matter-of-factly, and he turned his hands palms up like a young child.

"Yes, I can see that," Alemar replied, feigning annoyance, though in her heart she was glad to see them both.

"This will complicate our mission," Teetoo said emotionlessly. "We were counting upon surprise to be a substantial advantage for us."

"Oh, do not worry about us," Giles replied. "We can be as quiet as mice," he said, as he noisily climbed down off of his huge white stallion, with his various weapons clinking and clanging as he moved.

"Yes, that is obvious, Giles. I am so much more confident now that you have reassured me of this," Alemar said sarcastically, though she was smiling inwardly all the while.

The large blonde elf was busy fiddling with a spear that he had removed from a secure spot upon his saddle. He seemed to have weapons hanging everywhere. He aimed it away from the group and pressed upon the shaft. With incredible speed, it almost tripled in length, and then he brandished it before him as if he was testing its weight and balance before retracting it once again.

"Put your toys away, Giles. Now that we have found them we have other things to talk about," Clovis said to his companion. "We were unable to merely sit idly by and await your return to Seramour, Princess. Both of us would have gone mad not knowing how you fared. You should have known that. It was cruel of you to leave us so," he said earnestly.

"I left you both for a reason. Teetoo? Explain it to them please. They seem not to take my concerns seriously," she said.

The Weloh, who had stood up earlier when Alemar rose to

greet her friends, closed his eyes for a short moment and a slight tremor ran over his body. His arms returned to normal and the filaments disappeared completely from view as if they did not exist at all, and then he prepared to address the two new arrivals.

"We are not going on a journey of recreation and relaxation," he began. "It is crucial that we move stealthily and draw no attention to ourselves. Once we arrive there, our enemy will have the advantage of strength and we will need to balance the odds as best as we are able to. The fact that our approach will be unexpected will mitigate that somewhat. But if we are discovered on route to his stronghold, it will greatly imperil our chances of success," he said.

"We found your trail quite easily, Princess," Giles jibed. "Noise alone is not the only evidence of your travels that you must conceal then," he said sincerely.

"Yes. It seems you are correct in that respect, Giles," Alemar replied. "And I thank you for bringing this to our attention. We did not, though, expect to be tracked by anyone coming from the direction of Lormarion as yet. Though your point is well taken."

"Did you really think you could leave us so easily without even a word of farewell?" Clovis asked. "What did you expect us to do? Do not tell me you are surprised that we came after you. You should have known better, Princess."

Alemar blushed, shook her head slightly from left to right and then smiled.

"I should have known better, dear Clovis," she agreed.

"If we can maintain the secrecy of our journey, the addition of your friends to our ranks may be a boon to us in the end."

"You mean we can stay?" Giles asked jokingly.

"You may stay," Alemar replied like a mother addressing her children, and the two elfin warriors simultaneously sighed in affected relief.

"Very well then," Alemar began. "Now that you are here it is necessary that you know where we are headed and what we intend to do. Do you wish to tell them, Teetoo, or shall I?"

"Be my guest, Princess," the Weloh replied, and he stepped to the side.

The Princess then briefly related to them their destination and purpose, though neither seemed surprised or concerned throughout her telling. When she finished, both Clovis and Giles shrugged their shoulders as if they had just been invited upon the most innocent and harmless of journeys.

"How long will it take us to get there?" Giles asked nonchalantly.

"Is there no one to fight?" Clovis inquired. "We are merely going to sneak in and free the wizard and then leave?"

"That would be the most ideal of all results," Teetoo replied. "But, I fear it may not be that simple."

"We are going to Sedahar, you buffoons!" Alemar said lovingly, though impatiently. "What greater peril could you envision than walking directly into Caeltin D'Are Agenathea's very own home? Do you think he will sit lazily by while we release his brother, his most coveted of prisoners, from his captivity and run away with him?"

"Did I say that?" Giles asked Clovis.

"No. I did not hear you say anything like that," Clovis replied.

"For a moment there I thought I was going mad," Giles continued.

"Stop it, you two!" Alemar said exasperated, though she could not help but laugh. "This is serious."

"Everything with you has become so serious, Princess. We sought only to lighten your load a bit," Clovis replied.

"Well, you have succeeded. I only hope that Teetoo does not get the totally wrong impression of the two of you," she said.

"Princess?" the Weloh interrupted. "If I could have caused you to laugh previously, I would have too. Your friends have succeeded where I have failed, and for that I am grateful," he said, and he bowed slightly to the two men. "She has indeed been in a perilous state of mind these past few days. And now it seems that your presence has changed that. Apparently, you bring something to this equation that was sorely needed. The fabric weaves of its own will once again. It is a shame that you did not spend more time in the Heights this past month. I think that I would have enjoyed getting to know both of you better."

"I was never too fond of being that high up in the air," Giles admitted. "One visit was sufficient for me. Besides, the woods of Lormarion are spectacular. I enjoyed my time there. Eleutheria has no such forests, " he said.

"Where Giles goes, I go," Clovis explained. "In fact, most of the trouble that I have encountered in my life is the result of exactly that," he said, and he slapped his friend heartily upon the back.

"Regardless, we shall all have the opportunity to learn more about one another now," Teetoo said.

"Can you really fly?" Giles asked, He was never one to withhold his curiosity for the sake of propriety.

"Yes, I can," Teetoo answered him, and he was not offended in the slightest by his boldness. "But you know that already. You saw me do so the day we met."

"I confess, I did," Giles replied. "But I needed to ask you myself nonetheless and hear you say it in your own words. Is it incredible?"

"When I do not take it for granted, yes, it is incredible," Teetoo smiled.

"I don't think I could stand being way up there without my feet on solid ground. The thought of it starts my stomach jumping," Giles said.

"You are a woman, Giles!" Clovis said, making fun of his companion.

"Excuse me?" Alemar chimed in. "'A woman'? And that was meant to be an insult?" she said indignantly. "We have truly been apart for too long. I need to put the two of you back in your rightful places!" she chas'Tised them both.

"That is precisely why we are here, your Highness," Clovis said smiling. "We missed your discipline and direction."

"See what has happened to us in your absence?" Giles asked with puppy dog eyes. "We have lost all of the refinement and good manners that people have come to expect of us."

"The two of you are impossible!" Alemar said, and she laughed aloud. "Behave yourselves, the both of you, before I take a switch to your backs!" she kidded.

In just a few short moments, Alemar's exuberance and spirit had returned. Her two companions had succeeded in removing the persistent shadow of doubt and consternation from her brow that she could not shake off by herself. What Teetoo had begun, Giles and Clovis completed.

"Come, sit." Teetoo beckoned to them. "You must be hungry."

"They are always hungry, Teetoo," Alemar said, as Giles and Clovis moved toward the fire with anxious anticipation.

"Good. Let us eat together then, and we can discuss how we are going to accomplish what we need to. Our options have been enhanced by your arrival, and thus we must reformulate our strategies," the Weloh said as he sat down once again.

As they ate, they talked. Teetoo related to them what little he knew of Sedahar, mostly from recollections of the many conversations he had about it with Premoran.

"It actually changes shape and color depending upon his mood?" Alemar asked.

"Yes. It is a city that is alive in that way. Whether it is chimera and appearance only, I cannot answer," Teetoo replied. "After he was defeated at Pardatha, he destroyed it completely and utterly. We heard the sounds of Sedahar's destruction way off in the west. Premoran knew what his brother was doing then. They have this link still between them and though it causes him great anguish, he cannot break it. Since then, Colton has rebuilt it once more."

"This bond that you speak of," Clovis said. "Will it help us to know where the Dark Lord is once we locate Premoran?"

"Yes. It could. Premoran was almost always aware of where Colton was. In fact, it tormented him to know," Teetoo replied.

"Do they influence one another through this link? Is it such that they can reach out to one another?" Clovis continued his questioning.

"Premoran was always concerned about that. He felt that he had to remain forever vigilant in the event that Colton attempted to manipulate him or influence him against his will. Though my friend is amazingly strong physically, and strong of will as well, so is his brother."

"You did not answer my question fully, Teetoo," Clovis prodded. "I asked if they could influence one another and you replied merely how Colton could influence Premoran. What about the reverse?"

"I know that many tiels ago, Premoran had tried to ease his brother's anguish through that bond. What he encountered when he touched Colton's soul, he was never able to speak to me about in any detail. Needless to say, it must have been a hideous experience. He failed miserably in the attempt and as far as I am aware he never tried it again," Teetoo related.

"You know him very well, Teetoo," Alemar said. "This must be so difficult for you."

Teetoo turned his face toward the Princess, and his huge eyes were wide open and unblinking.

"Most difficult, Princess," he replied solemnly. "Though I feel it more profoundly than others do, in reality, the repercussions of his imprisonment are arduous for us all."

"Maybe he needs to try once more to get into this madman's

head," Giles said. "At least, it might serve to distract him. We could surely use that to our advantage once we arrive there."

"It is a good thought, Giles," Teetoo replied. "Anything that would take Colton's attention away from the perimeters of his realm would serve our purposes. But I am certain that Premoran is quite weak now, and in such a weakened state, it could be even more dangerous for him."

"Is there a way you can communicate with him? I have heard you say that you know he is alive. Thus, you are not merely guessing. Your knowledge comes from some sort of connection the two of you must have," Alemar said.

"You are not related by blood like he and Caeltin. There is no bond of that kind between you both. Have you a special means of transmitting or receiving feelings or thoughts that is unique to your race?" Clovis asked.

"No. I am quite intuitive, though I generally attribute it to my heightened sensory perceptions," Teetoo replied, and he was thinking deeply now himself.

"Has he never given you anything that bears his mark?" Clovis questioned. "A knife, a pendant, a coin perhaps? I know that often items such as these are more than they appear to be."

"Like the diadem that was given to Robyn by Iscaron in the final battle? Or the light that Wayfair bestowed upon me before we went into the Caves of Carloman?" Alemar recalled.

Teetoo looked confused momentarily, which was so unlike the Weloh. His big eyes were half closed in thought and his head was cocked to the side as if he was trying to remember something that kept eluding him.

"Yes, that he has. I do not know why this has not occurred to me sooner," he finally said somewhat surprised. "I have a token he bestowed upon me many, many tiels ago. I wear it always," he said and he pushed the sleeve of his shirt over his slim, almost opaque wrist in order to expose it to the others.

By the expectant look upon his face, he seemed as if he was uncertain whether he would actually find it there or not. It was nothing more than a rather small polished piece of blonde wood cut in no particularly discernible shape, but it glowed with an inner fire that they could all easily see, and Teetoo was visibly relieved by the actual sight of it. The token was strung like a bead upon a thin silver thread and it slid loosely around his thin wrist even as he spoke.

"It was a gift," he explained, and he was clearly straining to recall this information. "Premoran gave it to me a long time ago when he and I first met, actually," he remembered. "Though not a shard by any means, he told me that it was a part of what remained from one of the Lalas who had departed. He told me to wear it upon my person always as a symbol of luck, but he never told me anything more about it. In fact, we never spoke of it again," he said, and that now obviously seemed odd to him all of a sudden. "Curiously, I had not thought much about it. As far as I had been concerned at first, it was an ornament, a piece of jewelry, that so many in your world cherish beyond measure. Such adornments have not the same meaning for me. I was grateful for it at the time, but I paid no attention to it since. Actually, I had forgotten about it completely. I cannot even remember seeing it in a very long time, though I obviously never did remove it from my wrist," he continued, and he was examining it now as if he was looking at it for the very first time.

"And you never thought it odd that it glowed so?" Alemar asked.

"I have been totally unaware of even its presence upon me, so frankly Princess, I never noticed that before this very moment," Teetoo replied calmly.

"You are so nonchalant about this. Do you treat all such fortunate discoveries the same way!" Giles asked, surprised at how tranquilly the Weloh was handling this finding.

"You do not know me well, my friend. I express my emotions differently than you do yours. Honestly, what causes me more surprise is that I have remained so unaware of it for so long, and until you all questioned me about it, I did not even remember that I wore it on my own person," he repeated, still so bewildered by his new awareness.

"Teetoo?" Alemar asked him seriously. "Do you think that this bracelet is more than it appears to be?

"I am certain, Princess," he said with a new recognition, yet he remained still sedate and unmoved.

"It must be like a seed that one plants deep in the frozen ground. Such an item can remain dormant almost indefinitely. When the first thaw comes, it awakens and its essence begins to manifest itself," Alemar said. "Premoran is a wizard of the highest order. We should not be surprised that he has placed such things within the world."

"I am merely disappointed with myself, Alemar, for having

forgotten about this for so long," the Weloh replied.

"Your lack of awareness must also be a part of his plan," she responded. "The object remained safer on your person if no attention was drawn to it inadvertently."

"Most definitely," Teetoo concurred. "Though I feel rather foolish having harbored it and yet not having made any attempt to utilize it."

"Foolish? I understand that emotion. How different are you really from us, Teetoo?" Giles questioned him, smiling.

"Perhaps not as different as I have thought," he replied, smiling in return. "This is fortuitous nonetheless, despite how fatuous it has made me feel to have been so unaware. As Alemar so aptly suggested, I had to wait for the thaw to come."

"The time had to be right. Without a doubt, there was intent in that, Teetoo. It should not cause you needless concern. What is really important is that you have discovered it once more. Now we must determine its true purpose," Alemar said.
"You are correct, of course, Princess. My feelings about it are rather irrelevant at this point," he shrugged.

"Now that you have found it, do you think you should try to use it in some way. We are not yet sure that it is anything more than a pretty, polished piece of wood. Maybe you should attempt to communicate with Premoran through it?" Giles asked.

"Let us not be too hasty. We do not know who may be watching him, and it would harm us rather than help us to give ourselves away before we even arrive at the enemy's gates. We must be extremely careful. An attempt at communication through this relic would necessarily affect the weave, and Colton may very well be waiting for just such an event in order to track down the originator of it. He knows that his brother has friends, though I doubt he could fathom the depth of their loyalty to him," Teetoo said. "Regardless, we must wait. We cannot risk revealing our position or our intention."

"I, for one, will not bicker with you over this. After seeing the undead rise from the depths of the frozen Sea of the Righteous and march to war, I do not question those who understand these things better than I do," Clovis said.

"Aye! Neither do I," Giles concurred. "If you and Alemar agree that now is not the time to use this bracelet, who are we to disagree?" Giles said.

"I do agree with Teetoo," Alemar said. "We must wait until we know that it is safe for us and for Premoran before we try to commune with him. Besides, I think that this token has already provided you with some sense of his whereabouts. How else would you know with such certainty that he is in Castle Sedahar and that he is still alive?" she asked.

"Exactly!" Teetoo said. "And I do know both of those things without any incertitude. This limited knowledge must suffice for us now until we can be sure it is prudent to attempt to gain more."

"How then do we plan to rescue Premoran from Sedahar, Teetoo?" Clovis asked bluntly, as he and his companions stared raptly at the Weloh.

Chapter Twenty-eight

"I am so excited. I have dreamed of Avalain my entire life!" Stephanie said, and in her enthusiasm she pinched Preston sharply around the waist.

"Ouch!" he screeched. "That hurt, Steph!"

"Sorry, Preston!" she giggled. "I really did not mean to do that. Forgive me?"

"Of course I do. Just don't do it again!" he replied, and he rubbed his side and grinned at the same time.

"We are going to have to get you a horse of your own if you keep this up," Elion said smiling too. "We cannot afford to have an injured dwarf by the time we get to Avalain."

"I promise! I will be careful. But I would not mind riding by myself by now. Not only do I feel bad for the poor horse that has to carry a double load, but frankly, the back of the saddle is not the most comfortable part," she said.

"As soon as we get to the city, I will make certain that you have a mare of your own choosing for as long as you require it, Stephanie," Queen Esta said.

"Thank you so much, your Highness. It has been so long since I had anything of my own, I have nearly forgotten what it is like," the girl replied.

"Recent events have dealt many of us a difficult hand," Elion said. "And still, we are most fortunate compared to some, I fear."

"I did not mean to complain, Prince Elion. It really has not been that bad for me. I was never beaten and I always had something to eat. My mother and I did not go hungry. And we still had a roof over our heads," she explained. "But I do miss my father," she said sadly.

"He was a truly nice man, Steph. And a noble one too. We have all lost so much lately," Tomas said.

"Do you miss Trevor and Safira?" she asked him.

"I do, very much. Those days seem so long ago," he mused dolefully. "It seems almost like another life. I never realized how peaceful it was before."

"Before?" Stephanie asked.

"Before Colton came to Pardeau and blackened the land with his evil. Before he killed my aunt and uncle. Before the trees began to die," Tomas replied.

"Hey, you two! I know how hard it must be for you both, but come on now! If not for some of these terrible things, we would never have met. I would still be wandering around in the Thorndars, hiding from my father and embarrassed about how I look! The sorrow and pain cannot just go away, but we do have some things to be thankful for," Preston said.

"Indeed we do," Tomas replied, and he smiled warmly at the dwarf. "The fabric weaves of its own will, Preston. I am not one to regret the past, but sometimes I do miss my family."

"And so do I, Tomas. But I do feel as if all of you have taken their places, at least for now," the young dwarf replied. "I guess it is easy for me to say, because I can still go home and find my mother and father and brothers right where I left them."

"My mother would not recognize me if I was standing next to her at this very moment," Stephanie remarked. "I guess that she cannot be too sad if she does not really remember anything."

"Perhaps someday her memory will return to her, dear," Esta said. "Sometimes, when things occur that are so shocking and so upsetting, the mind simply shuts down. She has been through a lot. When things get back to normal, so may she."

"Normal? What would that be like?" Preston asked rhetorically.

"Until the Gem is found, nothing will ever be normal again," Stephanie said.

A hush descended upon the group after those words, and they all walked in silence through the thick woods. Elion led the way and Esta followed closely behind him and gave him directions every now and then, suggesting he turn left at a fork in the road and right at a particularly large boulder that blocked their way. As the terrain became more and more familiar to her, the journey progressed rather quickly. Stephanie held onto Preston and Tomas rode beside them both, though no further words passed between them for quite some time.

"We are not far now," Esta said in as cheerful a tone as she could muster. "We should reach the city before night falls."

It was difficult for her to return to Avalain without Marne by her side. Since the death of her husband, Marne had been her confidant and her friend. Now, with Filaree absent as well, Esta suddenly felt the weight of all of these losses more profoundly. She tried as best as she could to conceal her sadness from the others.

Tomas urged his horse forward and caught up to the Queen. He trotted beside her and kept pace with her majestic mare.

"You need not be concerned about your daughter. She is safe now," he said to her quietly, as if he knew what thoughts were plaguing her mind.

Esta turned her regal head toward the handsome boy and gazed deeply into his green eyes.

"Is it a gift, Tomas, that allows you to read my thoughts?" she asked sweetly.

"I did not need to peek into your mind to understand how concerned you must be for Filaree. It would be natural, would it not?" he replied.

"It is your timing that I so admire, I suppose. You seem to provide solace when it is most needed," she said. "Indeed, I was worried. We speak of our losses, each one of us, and mine are no greater than any of the others. We must speak of our gains as well more often than we do," she remarked.

"Preston seems ever to remember the bright side of things," Tomas smiled.

"His spirit is so full. It is a pleasure traveling with him. His personality is uncharacteristic of his race. The dwarves that I have known have been so serious and so morose. I always attributed it to the fact that they spent so much time out of the sunlight. Preston on the other hand, is a joy to be with."

"He is indeed," Tomas agreed. "We felt an affinity from the first moment we met."

"What do you know of my daughter?" she finally asked.

Tomas hesitated for a moment.

"I know that she is not presently in danger. Though she was before when we were threatened as well, she is no longer. In fact, I sense something that I am unable to clearly understand that is providing her with protection now," he replied, and he was concentrating intensely with his eyes only half opened.

"Go on, Tomas," Esta urged.

"I have little more to say, your Highness," he said frankly. "But, they are all safe for now; my brother, Robyn, Filaree, Cairn and Calyx as well. They have found a place where they can rest. I sense much power within and much power without."

"What do you mean by that?" she asked.

Elion slowed his own mount down in order to join the two of them. The path had widened and the trees were thinning out as they neared the perimeter of the forest that surrounded Avalain.

"May I join you, or am I intruding?" he asked.

"You could not intrude upon us, Elion. We have no secrets from you," Tomas said sincerely.

"Tomas was reassuring me about my daughter and the others, Elion. I was basking in the comfort of his intuition," she admitted, and a sa'Tisfied smile turned her red lips up slightly.

"Have they contacted you in some way?" Elion asked anxiously.

"No, not directly. It is hard to explain, but I see images in my mind's eye, and I just know that they have found the place that they had been seeking. Though they had been called to Pardatha originally, it was never the final location where my brother was to be educated."

"Things happen as they should," Elion said.

"As we hope always," Esta concurred, and she nodded her head.

"Hey, you guys!" Preston called from behind. "What's going on?" he asked.

Tomas turned his horse around and waited for Preston and Stephanie to catch up to him, and Esta and Elion did the same. They were nearly out of the woods altogether and there was now room for them all to ride abreast.

"We are well-nigh at Avalain," Esta said to them all.

"Oh my!" Stephanie gasped. "I cannot believe it! Avalain!" she repeated, and the way she said the name it sounded almost magical.

"It is a beautiful city indeed," Elion replied.

"As beautiful as Seramour?" she asked.

"You are asking that question of the wrong person, Steph," Tomas said. "Ask me instead. I can be more objective," he laughed.

"Why? When were you ever there?" she questioned him. "I thought you went directly to Pardatha when you left Pardeau with Cairn and Calyx. Isn't that what you told me?"

"I never have been there. But I have seen the city nonetheless," he said mysteriously.

"What are you talking about, Tomas?" Preston chimed in. "What trick are you playing on her now?"

"No trick, Preston. Through Ormachon, I have seen many things that I have not experienced directly. Avalain just happens to be one of them," he answered.

"It cannot be the same as actually being in the city," Esta remarked. "Avalain is more than buildings and landscape."

"And so is seeing it through my bond-mate's eyes, so to speak," Tomas replied. "In fact, in that manner I see depths to the city that many others will never see. A Lalas' perception is not quite the same as ours."

"Despite what you say, I am sure you will be even more impressed by the actuality of it regardless," Esta responded quite confidently. "And by the way Stephanie my dear, to answer your original question, Avalain is quite remarkable. Though I am a bit biased, it stands with Seramour in its beauty. You will soon see for yourself and then you may judge."

"Me, your highness? I have barely been beyond the borders of Pardeau. Seramour is but a dream to me too," Stephanie said. "I am not the one to make such a judgment."

"I meant only that you will judge Avalain, Stephanie. It need not be in juxtaposition. Beauty is a quality that exists independent of comparison. Am I not right, Elion?" Queen Esta asked.

"Absolutely!" he concurred. "They are two entirely different cities in all respects, yet both stand out as pinnacles of their craft."

"And both cities bear qualities that rival all others in their hearts," Tomas added. "Cities do have hearts, you know," he said.

They emerged from the stockade like line of tall pine trees onto the ground surrounding the city. They were all almost shocked to see Avalain looming before them so abruptly. Though the trees of the forest had thinned out considerably at the ground level as they neared the city, the tops of them remained thick and they obscured almost everything from view above and beyond eye level. They had been given no hint that they were as close to it as they actually were.

The city was enormous. The massive spires of the castle gleamed in the sun, and the pale white walls surrounding the entire expanse gave the appearance of impregnable permanence. They were constructed out of huge blocks of carved and polished granite perhaps fifteen feet thick. A large swath of open space fifty yards deep surrounded the entire city, and it sloped slightly upward as its green grass neared the stark walls. No openings or gates within eyesight interrupted the continuity. The group had arrived from the southeast, and the main entrance to Avalain was more westward from where they now stood. Esta led them in the direction of the gates.

When what is now the kingdom of Altair was no more than a confederation of small towns, the village that was the home of the fledgling House of Avalain emerged as a dominant force in the countryside. It gained its power and prominence by virtue of the incomparable skills of its fighters, coupled with an intense desire on their part to utilize these inherent skills for the good of the many, not merely the welfare of the few. The primary reason for Avalain's ascendance was the noble heart of its leaders, not simply their physical prowess.

The city grew quickly into a secure center of commerce and trade, and the House of Avalain prospered. A great Lalas flourished in the nearby woods and it bonded with the young King, a pattern that it would follow during the many tiels to come. The Knights of Avalain emerged as the premier fighting force in the entire area, and though Avalain never had imperialistic aspirations, the knowledge that the Knights' loyalty to the royal family was unequivocal compelled every town near and far to accept its guidance and seniority. This order of the Knights was so morally pure and so fundamentally righteous that none even thought to question its allegiance. And thus Avalain grew, both in size and stature.

The finest craftsmen were drawn to the city and they plied their skills on all aspects of the city's growth. Each monument and each public structure was a work of art. When it came time to design and build the castle for the royal family, the best of the best in all trades lined up to volunteer, anxious to leave their mark upon what they knew would be one of the most beautiful cities in the world. They were honored to be chosen to participate in the construction of Avalain.

"Do you see what I see, Elion?" Esta asked the elfin Prince, and her brow was furrowed with concern.

"You are referring to those tents up ahead?" he asked.

"Yes. There are hundreds of them. Who would be camped so outside the walls of Avalain?" Esta asked, though she did not expect an answer. "Do you see any banners flying above them, Elion? Your eyes are far sharper than mine."

"It appears that you have guests from Talamar in residence, your Highness," Elion said, scanning the horizon with his eyes. "The colors alone seem to indicate that."

"Talamar? That is odd indeed. What reason could bring all of these people from there to here? Our two lands have not been on the best of terms of late," Esta said questioningly. "Put up your hoods until we know what we are dealing with here. It is best if we do not announce ourselves so obviously yet. Ride with care. They may not be friendly."

"It looks more like an assemblage of commoners rather than an organized entourage," Elion observed, as he covered his head with the brown hood of his cape. "The tents are strewn around in a haphazard manner, and I can see no headquarters marked nor even any guards or soldiers."

"But they are definitely Talamaran?" she asked again while tucking her hair inside the folds of her tunic.

Tomas, Stephanie and Preston followed suit, and they too concealed their identities from the crowds, though anyone with a keen eye could tell that a dwarf rode with them by the heavily studded black boots that stuck out conspicuously from under his long mantle.

"Most definitely! I can see the crest of the House of Dumas upon at least two of the tents now," Elion replied.

As they rode closer to the outskirts of the group and turned around a bend in the thick wall that surrounded the city, it became clearer just how many people were actually gathered outside of the gates. Perhaps half of Talamar it seemed was in abidance! Not only were there tents and people, but children, animals, household items, carts, donkeys and all manner of personal possessions were littering the ground as well. These people were clearly not here for a simple visit. They had taken up residence outside of Avalain.

"I see no arms amidst the people here," Esta observed now that they were all close enough to view things. "Keep your words to a minimum and follow closely behind me. Take care not to get separated by the crowds."

As they rode slowly by, they could hear bits and pieces of conversations and discussions.

"Have we no more wine?" an overweight matron asked a boy who bore a striking resemblance to her, though he was much slimmer in stature. She was reclining upon a makeshift lounge chair that appeared to be much too flimsy for her bulk, and she was fanning herself furiously with an elaborate, feathered fan though it was not at all hot out. "It is almost suppertime. What are we going to eat tonight? I cannot bear another evening of gruel. Is there nothing else you can get for us?" she whined. Her gown was too elaborate for the circumstances, though it was none the better for wear.

"It is gone! I swear it. Totally gone!" a young man said to an older gentleman who stood beside him, in a tone of disbelief. "I could not even tell where the gates had been! It was as if it had never existed."

"He brought this upon us, that wretched, spoiled boy!" another aging man commented as they walked by.

"It was our own fault, grandfather," a handsome, dark-haired young man replied. "What did we do to stop him? Nothing! We did nothing."

"What could we have done?"

"Fight, grandfather! We could have resisted. I am glad to be gone from there. It was a shameful way to live."

They maneuvered their horses gingerly between the crowds, careful to keep their faces concealed. They did their best not to draw attention to themselves, and amidst all the tumult, it was less difficult than they had expected to remain inconspicuous. Their ears and eyes remained open nonetheless.

"Everything is lost. Everything! How am I going to live this way?" another porcine woman lamented from the middle of a squalid campsite. "Where will we get money from? Our oil is gone, our house is gone. I don't even have a decent dress to put on!" she said to the younger girl who was standing beside her and holding a squirming toddler.

"But you must pay me mistress. How will I feed my own son otherwise?" she replied.

"Pay you? How am I to pay you?" she asked in an astonished tone.

"Then I must seek work elsewhere," the maiden answered downcast.

A small group of men who were sitting around a spitted and roasting rabbit exchanged angry words with one another as the Queen and the others sidestepped their campfire.

"His father was a good man. How was I to know?" one said defensively.

"You worked in the castle! When was the last time you saw him? Did he ever get out of that big bed of his?" another asked.

"It was the woman from the south. She was the evil doer! Duke Leonard's son was just a pawn. He was never a leader. It all started when that ambassador from the south arrived," a short, stout man said, and he cursed under his breath.

"It's too late for regrets now," they heard one of them say as they walked on past.

The conversations they continued to overhear were all too

similar to one another. If they did not hear incessant complaints and gripes about having to live under such trying circumstances or about the lack of food of their liking, they heard tales of shock and surprise over the destruction of their city. Though no discussion of resistance of any kind was mentioned by any but a few, they were certainly bold enough now in their criticisms of each other's inaction. Many of the younger people were not quite so disappointed as the older ones, it appeared to them by the words they overhead. A spark of hope still burned amidst some of the youth of Talamar, though it was by no means a bright light shining in the darkness. Rather, it was merely a flicker, though it was surprisingly still alive despite Margot's attempt to snuff it out entirely. One thing that all their comments had in common was a disdain for the woman called Margot.

"She did not make friends during her tenure in Talamar," Preston commented.

"Nor did she try to!" Elion replied. "It seems she accomplished what she went there to do in any case."

"Why would anyone want to destroy a city?" Stephanie asked. "What good would that do her?"

"Destruction and devastation is what he seeks, Steph," Tomas explained. "It brings the physical place one step closer to the void."

"And it brings the problem of all these refugees to the gates of Avalain!" Esta said, as she surveyed the vast numbers of people who had taken up temporary residence everywhere. "This will strain all of our systems to the limit. To have an entire population un-housed and unfed before winter sets in upon us? How can we focus upon the Quest when we are forced to deal with issues such as these. Colton must know how difficult this will be for us all here."

"And there may yet be elements within this population who are loyal to the Dark Lord!" Elion observed. "They will attempt to infiltrate Avalain, as they did Talamar. We must be careful, your Highness."

"They will have little success here in that regard," Esta replied boldly. "The people of Avalain are strong of spirit. They would not succumb so easily to his overtures. Let him try to still the hearts of my people!" she said defiantly.

"Besides, your Highness, you are here now!" Stephanie said proudly, and Esta dipped her head gratefully in response.

As they neared the mighty gates of the city, they could see a group of mounted Knights standing guard before them. Parsifal's silhouette was unmistakable and Esta spurred her horse onward as soon as she recognized him. Lord Markal stood beside him on his large dapple gray steed, flanked by four other Knights of Avalain and one very tall, dark haired stranger whom no one recognized at first though he rivaled even Parsifal in stature.

The crowd parted reluctantly as this new group of riders cantered toward the entryway, cursing and complaining as the dust flew all around them. When Parsifal noticed the skirmish in the bunch, he turned his horse around to face it and initially he waited patiently for the swirling clouds of dirt to settle down, having grown accustomed to dealing with the many petty disputes that constantly arose among the refugees. This was different though, he recognized rather soon thereafter. Few of the Talamarans had arrived on horseback, and even fewer dared challenge the Knights at the gates.

"Be on your guard!" Parsifal said warily.

Queen Esta was so anxious to be home, that for a moment she forgot that she had not announced herself, and she led her war horse directly toward the assemblage of guards at a quickening speed. Elion, Tomas, Preston and Stephanie followed closely behind, and their presence caused an unmistakable stir in the crowd. Parsifal drew his sword, as did the others standing beside him, and he stepped forward to meet this newly arrived contingent. They formed a redoubtable wall before the gates that only a martyr or a fool would ever attempt to breach.

As she neared the waiting group, she threw back her hood and let her long,
dark braid fly out behind her in the wind. Her porcelain skin stood out starkly against the blackness of her hair and her eyes sparkled brightly in the sun, though she soon was enveloped by the swirling debris.

"Hail, noble Knights!" she yelled through the gray haze as she approached.

Parsifal recognized the voice immediately despite the tumult and dust that accompanied her advance and still obscured her countenance from his view. He leapt from his horse and bent down upon one knee awaiting her arrival. As she approached, he bowed his head respectfully before his Queen. Esta reined in her horse directly in front of him and it rose up upon its hind legs before stopping. She too jumped from her mount, though gracefully and regally as always, befitting her rank.

"Rise, Sir Knight!" she said to Parsifal with great affection, and the huge warrior stood before his Queen with his head still bowed, though his eyes were locked upon her face. "It is good to be back home," she exclaimed as she took his large, gauntleted hand in her own.

"It is good to have you home, your Highness," he replied. His blue eyes were as piercing as anyone's could possibly be, belying the intensity of emotion that his voice did not contain.

Lord Markal too had dismounted and moved to greet the Queen as well.

"Welcome, your Highness. It is so good to have you back amongst us again," he said sincerely. "I apologize for this," he then said, as he swept his arm before the large and motley crowds that seemed to be everywhere that there was a square inch of ground to erect a tent upon. "They sought refuge and I know that you would not have wished us to turn them away entirely. We have not allowed any inside the city, though."

"Who speaks for them?" she asked her Master at Arms.

"The Duke's former right hand man, Sir Fobush, your Highness," he replied.

"I remember him. He was a good man. This cannot be pleasant for such a one as he," she said. "Send someone for him. He and I must speak."

"As you wish, your Highness. He was particularly disappointed that you had not yet returned to the city. He was quite anxious to meet with you when he arrived," Lord Markal replied.

"He knew of my absence then?" Esta questioned.

"Word spread, your Highness. It was impossible to keep it secret after a few days had passed."

"Ah yes. Of course," she replied, though the comings and goings of those in Avalain was rarely of interest to Talamar. "Well, fetch him then and he will have his opportunity to explain what has occurred and to give us his thoughts on his people's future. As I said, he always struck me as a noble man. It is sad that fate has caught him too in his master's duplicitous web, though it was inevitable at some point."

"He was not as fortunate as we to serve a leader as honorable as you, my Queen," Lord Markal replied and he bowed humbly. "I will send for him right away," he said and then he dispatched a runner immediately to locate the man. "It is good to have you back, my Lady," he said again as he turned toward her. "You were sorely missed. Your absence, unannounced as it was, was rather difficult to explain to a worried population. It was no less arduous for me as well," he confessed. "Sir Parsifal informed us of Mistress Marne's heroic demise. We all grieve with you," he then said earnestly.

Queen Esta dipped her chin in acknowledgment and fought back the tears that, unbidden, filled her eyes.

Another Knight stepped from behind the others and slowly walked forward until he was standing beside Parsifal. His eyes were bright and attentive, and he looked adoringly upon the Queen.

"Sir Etan," Esta said approvingly. "You look well. Avalain appears to have been the right prescription for your health."

"Indeed, your Highness," he said, and he bowed low before her. "Thanks to you."

"And no thanks to the demon's surrogate, the Lady Margot," she replied with disdain.

Sir Etan blanched at the mention of her name.

"No, your Highness. No thanks to her," he replied disgustedly.

"It seems we have a situation on our hands, Lord Markal," Esta said diplomatically. "Have you made arrangements to deal with it?" she asked.

"We have begun to organize the Talamarans, my Queen, though they seem so reluctant to work even for their own benefit. There is a group to the north digging ditches for latrines and another group foraging in the brambles yonder for nuts and berries, and yet another organizing a council of sorts to administer the masses in the absence of the Duke. They have only just arrived two days ago, your Highness," he replied almost apologetically.

"What is the news of Duke Kettin?" the Queen asked.

"According to all accounts, he perished within his city, your Highness," Lord Markal replied.

"Has that been confirmed?" she questioned, though she was neither surprised nor particularly saddened by the information.

"Yes, your Highness. It has been confirmed," the Master at Arms said, though he offered no further explanation at the moment.

"I see," she said. "Only two day ago," she commented to herself as if the timing was significant in some way.

Esta surveyed the situation pensively for a moment before speaking again. She could not help but notice the crowds gathering upon the ramparts as the news of her return swept the city. She was beloved by the people of Avalain, and they were one and all overjoyed to hear of her safe return. But hearing of it was not sufficient for a population so enamored of its leader. They needed to see her with their own eyes in order to be sa'Tisfied once and for all, and she could see them now as they jockeyed for space atop the massive walls.

"Elion! Tomas! Preston! Stephanie! Join me," she beckoned to her friends who were still sitting on their horses a few paces behind her.

They had been drawing the gazes of all of those in the area even while the Queen addressed them. It was not a common sight to see an elf and a dwarf riding side by side into Avalain. Parsifal had already acknowledged their presence with a subtle nod of his majestic head and a warm smile, whilst Lord Markal looked upon them with many questions marking his expression.

They each dismounted, Preston helping Stephanie to the ground, and they walked a few paces until they were standing beside the Queen. She extended her arms and encircled them as best as she could, indicating clearly to all those present just how devoted to them she was. This one gesture spoke a thousand words to the people who were looking on from the gates as well as to all of those within the city who had assembled upon the walls.

"It is humbling to have amongst us such a noble contingent," she said loud enough for all to hear. "My friends here, all of the most noble of blood..."

Stephanie gasped audibly as Esta spoke, and she blushed a deep crimson while Preston beamed from ear to ear.

"...found me in my time of need and rescued me from the clutches of a very evil woman and her cohorts. Had it not been for them, I would likely be a prisoner of the Dark Lord in Sedahar by now, held hostage in order to coerce my daughter, Filaree, to forsake the path she has been called upon to follow," the Queen continued, as a great cheer arose from the populace gathered above them. "As you have been told, my dearest friend Marne, died in service to the crown. She gave to me willingly the most precious of gifts, the gift of life, by virtue of her sacrifice," she related sadly. "Her name shall be inscribed into the Book of Heroes and henceforth her day of birth shall be commemorated by celebration throughout Avalain!"

Esta closed her eyes and bowed her head. She was silent for a moment, while everyone else around her held their breath until she began to speak again.

"Sir Parsifal was as stalwart as ever; a beacon of virtue and loyalty in my hour of darkness and want," she said, and she stared directly at him. "Together, and with the help of a Lalas fast and true, we have returned to Avalain! Welcome them as you do me!" she proclaimed, and she included both Parsifal and the others in her gesture.

Trumpets blew and cheers rang out everywhere, so deafening in their volume that they would have undoubtedly drowned out anything else Esta could have wanted to say.

"I can hardly hear myself think!" Stephanie yelled into Preston's ear.

"Neither can I, Steph. What an amazing way to come to Avalain!" Preston said.

"Who would ever have imagined?" Stephanie replied.

Tomas and Elion stood beside one another, but their expressions were more pensive that the situation seemed to dictate. Esta noticed them, as did both Preston and Stephanie a moment later. The Queen did not wish to cast a shadow upon the happiness of her people, so she did not acknowledge their concern openly. Rather, she walked to Tomas, grasped his hand in her own and squeezed it knowingly. She glanced at Prince Elion briefly but meaningfully, and then she urged them to follow her. Dipping her head down momentarily and feigning an abundance of emotion at the crowd's enthusiasm, she whispered to them both so that no one else could hear, "Need I be concerned too?"

"It is best that we enter the city as quickly as possible, your Highness," Tomas said in a calm and steady voice.

"Ah, yes," she replied at once. "I understand."

Esta handed the reins of her horse to an attendant and then she beckoned to the others to do the same. She swept her cape behind her regally, maintaining her composure all the while, and raised her head high into the air. The crowds continued to cheer and cheer, and she refused to do anything to limit their delectation. Slowly and steadily, without a hint of concern marring her beautiful features, she led her friends through the broad gates of Avalain.

Chapter Twenty-nine

Will you come to his aid?

No, he answered simply, without any hint of emotion in his tone.

What will become of them?

The fabric weaves of its own will. We must wait and see.

We have intervened before. Why not now? The Dark One seeks the map, yet he strays.

Yes, he strays, he replied, clearly dismayed. *And I grow weary.*

Your Chosen is vulnerable and yet you will not assist him?

I cannot. Some sacrifice is necessary if our goal is to be reached. It is greater than the parts, he related coldly. *We must exert our influence where we are sure to have the most impact.*

A difficult decision. Has the other the shards still?

Yes, though there will yet be more that must be gathered, he said sadly. *He does not yet have the eleventh.*

I cannot sense it. My reach has been limited. Who will retrieve that now?

That is uncertain, he replied and then he paused before continuing. *The sapling thrives outside of the circle.*

Will it choose?

In time perhaps. In time.

Chapter Thirty

"What shall we do, my Lord? If the crowds continue to grow, it will be difficult to maintain an orderly viewing," Grogan said.

"It is not for us to limit access to the tree. Just the sight of it brings hope to all who visit. We are no more than its steward now," Baladar replied soothingly. "Perhaps it will choose soon. Then its bond-mate will instruct us."

The Lalas, the seed of which Tomas planted before he and his friends departed Pardatha, was thriving in the fertile soil beside the River of Tears. It was so beautiful that it humbled anyone and everyone who gazed upon it. No longer small, it towered over the bushes and shrubs that grew in its vicinity, and it dwarfed nature's boldest attempts at competition. Lush, silver-green foliage dominated the branches. Beautiful, platter shaped leaves, intricately veined and paper thin, graceful beyond measure, bowed and fluttered in the wind, and responded to even the slightest of breezes. The gusts rippled through them creating waves of motion up and down the delicate offshoots. The bark of the trunk resembled finely tooled silver, darker at its thick base and lighter and more burnished as it reached out over the branches, until it was almost translucent by the time it terminated in a myriad of web-like tendrils that hung so exquisitely from the tips. It illuminated the entire area within which it grew whether the sun shone upon it or not, and it radiated an inner light that was both remarkably beautiful to gaze upon as well as profoundly comforting to bask in.

"They come from everywhere, my Lord," Grogan said while staring out of the large, leaded windows at the throngs assembled on the plain below. They wore the colors and carried the banners of every village, town and city across the land.

"As they should. As they should," he replied, and he nodded his head in acknowledgment. "They will respect the tree."

"But will they respect one another, my Lord? When it was just the citizens of Pardatha, I was more confident. But now, they arrive from all corners of the earth," he replied. "I can no longer vouch for their behavior."

"We cannot impose rules here, Grogan, providing no threat exists for the city itself. The tree will make its own in time. I understand your concern, but you must have faith. You need not fear for the Lalas," he replied convincingly. "It is a great privilege for us to be able to see it each morning when we wake and each evening when we retire. Everyone else who so desires must have this opportunity as well."

"I would be remiss in my duties, my Lord, if I did not assure those who come here a safe viewing," Grogan said.

"Very well then. You are correct of course. You may station guards around the tree, but make sure that they are inconspicuous, and that they do not impose upon the crowds," Baladar agreed, though reluctantly. "Until it chooses, all are free to congregate around it. I hope the presence of our militia will provide a sufficient incentive for them to remain civil. "

"It is so beautiful, my Lord," Grogan said adoringly, and he was staring out through the glass once again. "I cannot imagine it causing anything but happiness in any who are near it."

"Indeed," he agreed. "Would that the others could see it now. Surely their hearts would fill with joy at the sight," he said with a faraway look in his eyes. "Now you must go," Baladar said, as he regained his concentration. "Advise your men of our decision."

"Yes, my Lord. At once," he replied. He saluted to Baladar respectfully and left the chamber.

Baladar stood there for a moment and watched his trusted friend walk down the wide hallway. He listened as the clicking sound of his boot heels upon the stone floor faded into the distance. Soon, there was nothing but silence to be heard, and he walked back into the room, slowly pushed the heavy door closed, and then he carefully and fastidiously set the seals. He sat down at the large, wooden table that dominated the center of the room and leaned heavily into the cushions of the high-backed chair.

The sun streamed through the tall, leaded glass windows that formed the easternmost wall of the chamber and ran almost entirely from the ceiling to the floor. It illuminated the intricacies within the noban planks from which the massive table had been hewn so many tiels ago. Baladar absentmindedly ran his fingers over the natural designs in the wood, but his mind was elsewhere.

"Tis a new dawn, he thought to himself. *Why is it that I feel so melancholy? The tree thrives, but still there is no news of the twins. Oh Briland! I miss you today,* he reflected on his beloved, deceased wife whose memory was never totally gone from his consciousness. *How you would have adored this tree.*

He fidgeted with the heavy gold ring that he wore upon his index finger, twisting it around and around. It was totally silent within the room, and he was suddenly so tired that he practically dozed off to sleep for a moment.

What harm could it do if I rested briefly, he thought to himself. *It seems these days that there is little more for me to do than greet visitors and maintain civil order. The difficult tasks have been assumed by others, and I do not even know where they are anymore.*

He closed his eyes and slid the ring back upon his finger so that he would not drop it in the event that he did fall asleep.

Curious, he mused. *My ring is warm. Far warmer than usual.*

He pulled it off and lay it on the wood before him. There was no mistaking it; it glowed ever so slightly!

There is surely meaning to this! It has been dormant since the boy left, he recalled Tomas' departure along with the others. *And now it has come to life once again! Just what I have been hoping for,* he thought, and he shrugged off his former drowsiness as if it had never existed.

His excitement was mounting steadily as he reached for the small, suede pouch that hung from the inside waistband of his tunic. He untied the braided cord and loosened it as quickly as he could, and then he spilled the contents upon the table. A handful of gems of various and disparate colors glinted and glittered as they rolled in different directions until they each came to rest within a few inches of one another. He reached for the ruby one first and placed it to the right and toward the back of the large ring. He then picked up the sapphire stone and placed that one at the back left corner. Next, he slid the green one to the near right corner, and finally, he carefully picked up the black stone and completed the square by placing it on the left in the front.

Immediately, the ring began to glow more brightly and the rune engraved upon it began to expand off of its surface and take shape in the air above it. Thin tendrils of white light inched their way from the now suspended image to the stones, and as each ribbon of light touched a colored stone, the gem burst forth with its own vivid color and sending it back up the thread of light and to the ring in four rapid and intense explosions. The ring was now hovering high above the table, enmeshed in a web of multicolored rays that spun and wove themselves together around it in intricate and delicate geometric patterns. As the movements gained speed, the colors merged and blended, and they began to spin in harmony with one another, where at first they appeared independent and apart. They moved so quickly that Baladar had to fight so as not to become completely mesmerized by the motion.

So I am to be drawn back into the weave after all, he thought with no small amount of excitement. Not since he had called the boy's teachers to Pardatha and he had cast the spells of protection upon the unconscious heir had the gems reacted so.

Baladar watched closely as the images formed in the air before him. First, a tree appeared. It resembled the young one on the banks of the River of Tears below, but it was distinctly different. It was much larger and older. Its image was as sharp and defined as if he was standing right before it.

An ancestor perhaps, or an glimpse of the future, he speculated as he looked for identifying signs.

The area around it did not look at all familiar to him. He could not see any water in the vicinity, and the trees surrounding the Lalas looked like miniatures in comparison. Then he realized that they were not small at all, but that the other was just so incredibly large! It dwarfed everything nearby. Before he could focus more closely upon it, the image grew blurred and changed.

A city came into focus with towers and spires that rose high into the air, piercing the clouds as they ascended. The stone of the buildings was dark, yet it was quite beautiful to look upon. It too was unfamiliar to him in appearance, but there were flags flying from the tops and he tried desperately to bring them into focus. He saw a black gryphon on an emerald green background on one banner, and then he saw a bolt of white lightening splayed across a dark blue field on another. Others were flying as well beside these two, but each of the images upon them was as unknown to him as the next. His gaze was drawn to the walls and beyond, where he saw thousands upon thousands of people surrounding them in all directions. He was elated by the vision and he felt light and carefree.

He lurched forward in the chair, suddenly staring at dark swirls of smoke rising in thick spirals from a burning ruin as the figures changed once again. All that remained was a charred mass of rubble and thousands of dead and dying bodies strewn everywhere. Weapons lay broken upon the ground and he could hear the sounds of people crying though he could not find them in the devastation. He opened his mouth to scream someone's name, but no sound ushered forth because he could not recall the name he wished to shout. He watched in sadness as he visually scanned the battlefield, hoping desperately to find the person he sought, though frightfully worried that he had come to some terrible harm and that he would never see him again. Still all the while, he did not know whom he searched for. A cloud of dust rose from the ground, obscuring everything completely, and he fanned the air with his hands in an effort to clear it so that he could continue his hunt.

Once he regained his focus he was looking at a completely different picture than the one he had been viewing only moments before. A piece of paper or parchment was fluttering back and forth in the still air as it slowly descended toward the darkness below. Hulking buildings framed the area, but they were lifeless and in disrepair. Baladar felt great trepidation once again and he wanted to reach out and grab the object before it was lost forever. He could see the glow of many eyes looking on from above and they were motionless and seemed unaffected by the loss. He wanted to warn them, to tell them to save the thing that they calmly watched fall, but he could not. His heart stopped beating as the paper floated silently down, and he had a compelling and unremitting urge to cry.

Mist obscured everything as the images shifted once again. He watched intently trying to peer through it and straining his eyes in the process, hoping for it to lift so that he could see what lay hidden within its billowing thickness. A chill ran over his body and then a feeling of foreboding engulfed him, taking the place of the sadness and sorrow that had previously consumed him. He stared intently despite feeling a strong impulse to avert his eyes. Like a child looking through spread fingers at a grisly scene, he watched as a figure formed in the fog.

A man shrouded in black from head to foot was standing with his back toward him, and Baladar immediately felt a wave of nausea wash over him. Fighting the compulsion to wretch, he kept watching. He could not see the person's face, but he stared as he raised his arm and reached out for something in front of him. The figure grabbed for what Baladar feared was the parchment, but instead he now clutched in his gloved hand what looked like a branch of a tree. He drew it toward him as he bent down upon one knee.

Suddenly, another figure came into focus beside this other, horribly ominous one. The second one was smaller in stature than the first, and Baladar smiled involuntarily at its appearance. It too was clothed from head to toe in a garment that obscured any identifying features from him, but just seeing it before him generated a feeling of buoyancy and well-being. It too reached out and took hold of a branch from what he could now clearly see was a tree looming in front of him, and this figure too bent down upon one knee before it. He heard chanting and humming everywhere as if some kind of ceremony was taking place. Each of the figures lifted his free hand to his forehead and was about to pull the hood back and reveal himself, when the tree's branches spread out over them, and partially concealed them from Baladar's view. Just before the second figure disappeared completely behind the veil of leaves, his fingers clenched the fabric that covered him and he slipped it from his head.

"Davmiran!" he gasped out loud as he saw the boy's blonde hair fall out from the folds of his cape.

The boy turned to face him an instant before the darkness of the foliage overtook him, and the last thing that Baladar saw was Tomas' green eyes, swollen with tears, as they stared back at him. His young face was anguished and stricken with sorrow. A loud cracking noise immediately ensued, and the branches upon which the thick foliage hung crumbled to powder all over the kneeling boy, blanketing him and concealing him from Baladar's view.

He had no time to think or to react. A brilliant white light blinded him from somewhere behind the massive trunk of the tree, and he was forced to cover his own eyes in response. The crackling sound grew louder and louder, assaulting his ears as well. It sounded as if the whole world was coming down around him. A pounding noise like the beating of a very loud drum distinguished itself amidst the cacophony of sounds, and then he heard voices shouting desperately. They were familiar and he cocked his head sideways to listen more closely. He could see nothing now as his eyes were completely besotted by the intensity of the light, but he craned his head in an effort to understand.

The hammering grew louder and more defined, and the noises gradually became more intelligible. He rubbed his eyes and his vision began to slowly clear. The room started to take shape before him once again, and he could see his ring lying beside the gems which were glinting in the sunlight that streamed in from the windows.

"Lord Baladar! Unlock the door. Let me in!" he could hear someone yelling amongst the continual banging upon the thick wooden slab.

Slowly, he rose from his chair, leaned forward and swept the stones back into the suede pouch. He lifted the ring which was still warm and placed it upon his finger. His mind was flooded with the visions from before, and he replayed them so that he could remember as many details as possible, though he knew that some had already faded and were lost forever. He struggled to recall as much as he could. Grogan was worried about him, and it was cruel to delay him any longer.

As he walked to the doorway the thought struck him, *I must go to the lake!* It was almost as if someone had directed him to do so. With a determined look in his eyes, he released the seals and opened the door. Grogan burst in to the room, anticipating trouble.

"My Lord! We have been standing here for quite some time. Is everything all right?" he asked anxiously.

"Yes, quite all right. You have no need to worry. I must have dozed off and I did not hear your entreaty," Baladar explained. "I am truly sorry to have caused you such concern. It seems that I am more fatigued than I realized. Is anything wrong?" he asked.

"No, Lord Baladar. As long as you are okay, everything else is fine. I only wished to advise you that the guard has been posted as inconspicuously as possible as you so directed," he said.

"Thank you, Grogan. I do not anticipate any trouble in any event, but you are correct. It is the prudent thing to do under the circumstances," Baladar replied. "And now, I think that I will go for a ride and mull all of this over. It is difficult to gain perspective when I am holed up in the castle all the time. Our responsibilities have multiplied since the others departed, and I have much to consider."

"As you wish, my Lord. Do you wish me to accompany you?" he asked.

"No, Grogan. That will not be necessary. I need some time alone. I shall return before night fall," Baladar responded.

"As you wish, my Lord," he said as he bowed his head slightly, though it was clear by his tone of voice that he disapproved of his master's decision.

Baladar often in the past wandered out into the woods to commune with the spirit of his wife and her Lalas, and Grogan knew how important those moments were to him, though he was always disquieted and vexed until he returned. Fortunately, it had been a long time since he had done so, much to the relief of the Master at Arms.

"Shall I have your horse saddled and readied?"

"No, thank you. I will do that myself. I have so little to do these days, it will be my pleasure," he said.

"With the crowds gathering daily around the young tree, you may one day recall these moments of leisure more fondly than you do so now, My Lord," Grogan said with a wry smile.

"That may be, Sir. If so, you must remind me of my words so that I do not complain and sound foolish," he replied warmly.

"That is a promise, my Lord," Grogan said, and he smiled.

"Good. I will hold you to that!" Baladar replied as he ushered him out of the room. "Meet me here at sundown and we will discuss the more permanent arrangements we must make regarding the future of the tree."

"Yes, my Lord," Grogan replied, bowed respectfully, and then left the room.

Chapter Thirty-one

The passageway opened abruptly into a cavernous space. It was illuminated by strips of light that were suspended in mid air all around. Neither Tamara nor Angeline were able to determine what these bright bands were made of. Every strip was about three feet in length, and they hung high above their heads in symmetrical rows. As they walked into the chamber and looked up, each one virtually disappeared. From beneath, they were invisible, yet as soon as they gazed at any one of them from an angle, it became visible again.

"These are fascinating!" Tamara commented as she stared all around. "How is it that they seem only to have substance when looked upon from certain directions?" she asked Etuah.

"What you see is an illusion," she replied simply. "Behold!" Etuah said, waving her long arms back and forth.

As she did so, the lights that were so geometrical seconds before and seemed so fixed in space, broke up into thousands of swirling, luminous pinpoints that flew in all directions, caught in the whirligigs created by the Drue's hand motions. They floated high and low, and as the gusts of air reached further into the chamber, more of the objects that had appeared to be stationery and solid, disintegrated instantaneously and flew randomly and directionless around the room, while they sent clouds of light of different intensities everywhere.

"We try to create order where we can," Etuah explained. "Though there is no real need, it still comforts us."

As they walked deeper into the cavern, the Drue moved her arms again, and the pinpoints of light reassembled in what appeared now to be torch-like shapes that began to adhere to the walls all around them.

"Are you more at ease with these?" she asked the sisters.

"I was not uncomfortable before," Tamara said, wide-eyed. "However, whatever you choose is fine."

"I thought the other lights were just beautiful, but it really does not matter," Angeline agreed as they continued moving across the flat, hard floor.

"Our time together is limited. We must begin as soon as possible," Etuah said, changing the subject a moment later.

Tamara looked at Angeline before speaking once again to their host.

"You have said that we cannot stay here, that we do not have time. And you say we must begin. You know so much about us. It is not as if I do not trust you, Etuah," Tamara said to the Drue, "I truly do, believe me! But, you are confusing me. Who told you we would be arriving here? You said that the Lalas know, and therefore, so do you. But did they also tell you about the map?" she asked bluntly.

Etuah had stopped walking and turned to face the two sisters. When she stood sideways she was practically invisible, much like the lights that they saw before. Now, as she stood before them, they could see her clearly. Her garments trailed out behind her like streamers or filaments in the wind, though not even the slightest of breezes wafted through the cavern. Her skin was so pale and her limbs were so thin that she appeared waif-like despite the fact that she was taller than either of the other two women. The glow that engulfed her came from within her body, as if the blood that flowed through her veins was itself iridescent.

"You cannot stay here," she began to explain. "A part of you will die if you stay here. The hollows cannot sustain you for long. There is no life here, and if you remain between you will never be able to leave. The hollows claim those eternally who abide here longer than they should, or who cannot withstand the intrusion upon their souls," she said.

"How long do we have?" Angeline asked.

"That depends upon each of you somewhat," Etuah answered. "I do not know your strengths yet," she replied, and she eyed them both closely.

"A day? A Week?" Tamara continued to press her.

"Perhaps a few days. It is uncertain," Etuah said, avoiding a more definite response. "Perhaps less. I told you before that the Lalas advised us of your arrival. It was an unusual communication. We do not confer with the trees; we share things sometimes. And even that is sad for us as well as for them. We arrive when they are no more." Etuah opened her bulbous eyes even wider than usual as she stared hard at Tamara. "It was necessary this time," she said.

"If the trees are guiding us and protecting us , why need we fear?" Angeline asked in a voice that sounded more ethereal than usual.

Tamara turned to her friend and looked her directly in the eyes. Before she had an opportunity to question her, the Drue spoke again.

"The Dark One seeks the map as well," Etuah replied simply.

"And more…"

"How could he have known that we had taken it out of Parth? Was he even aware that it was in the Tower to begin with?" Tamara asked.

"Somehow he became aware," the Drue woman replied ominously.

Both Tamara and Angeline gasped at her words. Neither of them quite understood the full implications of them, but they were quick witted enough to realize what she meant.

"One of the sisters told him? That cannot be possible," Tamara said with conviction.

"Absolutely impossible!" Angeline agreed.

"He was advised nonetheless," Etuah said. "It was not a coincidence that lead one of the Possessed to your trail. The options for betrayal are few."

Tamara pondered her words for a moment.

"Though Parth harbored the parchment for hundreds of tiels, that fact was almost as well kept a secret as the location of the First itself," the Drue said.

"Yet this betrayal led us to you!" Tamara reasoned. "We would never have found you had we not been forced to seek shelter."

"The fabric weaves of its own will," Etuah replied.

"Often, yes," Tamara agreed. "But this time?" she questioned.

"What are you saying, Tamara?" Angeline asked her friend, confused.

"I do not know for sure, sister. I am bewildered as well. Etuah tells us that we were deceived. She tells us that perhaps one of our own trusted sisters told Colton of our journey. That seems unlikely to me. But, surely someone gave us away. The Lady Margot did not simply stumble upon us in the hills. That was not the first time she and I had met, but she had no reason to track me, sister!" Tamara said. "And we ended up here, in a place we would never have found otherwise. So whoever betrayed us, regardless of their intention, assisted us enormously, it now seems!"

"Assisted us? She almost killed us!" Angeline replied.

"But she did not, sister. And now we are here, sound, though perhaps not altogether safe," Tamara said. "Etuah tells us that we can journey to Odelot through the hollows," Tamara continued to think out loud. "So, despite Margot's efforts, and despite the fact that she was sent by someone to intercept us, it is still possible that the betrayer helped us instead!" the stout sister concluded.

"You are a wise woman," Etuah said. "It is no wonder you were chosen."

Tamara looked at her askew once again. Her use of the word 'chosen' was ambiguous enough this time that she did not reply directly to it.

"Do you know the truth, Etuah?" she asked.

"You ask me that as if 'the truth' was something tangible; a fact that we need only discover. I know what I know. We were advised of your arrival by the trees. I cannot tell you when they determined you were in danger," she said.

"If they wanted us to come here, then why did they not just instruct us so?" Angeline asked. "You told me that Liam and Oleander were forthright with you before. And they knew that evil woman was after you. Why play these games with our fate and the fate of so many others?"

"I cannot answer that. I only hope that if what we suspect is true, there is a greater purpose here that we do not comprehend now. It is not our fate that is the issue, sister. Surely the fabric weaves of its own will, but the yarn is set and the loom still must be warped somehow. I believe that the cloth is the result of both free will and determination, not one or the other alone," Tamara said.

"We must hurry now," Etuah interrupted. "We are almost there. Time grows short. Perhaps one day you will learn what you call 'the truth' about this. Now though, there are other things to be concerned with."

Etuah grabbed both of the girls' hands and pulled them forward. Her fingertips adhered to their skin in a way that was not distasteful at all, but rather, quite compelling. Her long legs moved fast, though it seemed as if she was merely gliding along at a leisurely pace. Tamara and Angeline rushed to keep up with her. They were crossing this large, open space that was now illuminated by the countless torches that hung upon the far walls. The floor was flat and hard and when they looked up, they could not see a ceiling above, however it could have been lost in the darkness.

A large arched opening appeared before them after a short while and Etuah headed directly for it. Once inside, the path sloped downward steeply.

"Come," the Drue urged.

She sat down abruptly and pulled them along with her. They immediately began to slide down the passage. It was honed smooth by someone or something, and they moved easily and quickly through it. It grew wider as they moved further on, and every now and then, smaller tunnels split off from it, but these other passageways all seemed to head in the opposite direction. The three women veered right and left somewhat, but they appeared to be heading straight ahead for the most part. Etuah's body glowed again in the absence of any other light sources, and it illuminated the area as they made their way deeper into depths of the earth.

"What is this that we are in?" Angeline asked as they glided along.

"It is where a root once was," the Drue replied.

"A root?" Tamara questioned.

"Yes. We are nearing the heart. The roots were larger here."

"The heart of the tree?" Tamara asked.

"Yes. Though the Lalas is no more, the space remains intact," Etuah said. "You must prepare yourselves now. You have felt it already, though you may not know it. But it is far more difficult to enter this space. Do not allow your feelings to overcome you. Be strong," she warned them.

Nothing could have prepared either Tamara or Angeline for the shock that they felt the moment the passage ended and they found themselves standing once again beside the Drue woman in this massive, new space. Angeline gasped audibly and Tamara reached out to her to comfort her. She too wanted to cry, but she fought the impulse as hard as she could. Neither of them could explain the profound feeling of sadness that suddenly engulfed them. It was so deep and so total that they could barely keep their heads upright. The weight of their emotions was almost unbearable, and they sought out each other for solace, though even that did not help. Angeline fell to her knees and wrapped her head in her arms.

"You will grow accustomed to the feeling," Etuah said with compassion in her voice. "It will never leave you whilst you remain in the heart, but it will ease."

"This is the saddest thing I have ever experienced," Angeline sobbed. "The feeling of loss is overwhelming. It seems so tragic, and I cannot stop myself from crying, yet I do not know why!"

"It is tragic, sister," Tamara said, as she stared at her friend through her own tear streaked eyes. "What could be more tragic than this? It feels as if life itself has been stilled."

"A part of life has been taken from the whole. What you are experiencing is the absence. As well, you are reliving the passing. Thus, you suffer twice," Etuah explained. "I told you that the hollows are the closest a living thing can come to the void. And you two have the great misfortune of being alive here. Your living spirits are imbued with the same essence that the Lalas who resided here personified. Thus, you can sense what once was and what is no more. That is why the pain of sadness is so intense. You feel the change; you recognize just how much has been obliterated. The lost ones see in this only a chance to end their anguish. They see the nothingness that remains and no more. That is what they crave."

"I cannot bear this any longer. You must help me, Tamara," Angeline pleaded. "My heart is breaking. I have never felt such sorrow," she said, and she laid her head down upon the hard ground.

"Take my hand, sister," Tamara said.

She reached out and grasped her friend's fingers tightly and assisted her to her feet once more. Though she too was suffering more intensely than she could ever have imagined, she found the inner strength to calm herself, and she thereby attained a place of peace within the turmoil of her spirit. With confidence and tremendous self control, she shared that place with her friend, as she coaxed Angeline gently though forcefully, into the same shelter that she found. She breathed a relaxing breath and opened herself to the tormented sister fully and selflessly until Angeline too gained solace from her efforts, and until she too achieved a spiritual equilibrium once more. But oddly, something was no longer the same with her. Tamara perceived a subtle difference in Angeline that she could not fully understand.

"Abide with me until it passes," Tamara said to her while holding her hand tightly. She simultaneously tried to determine what it was that had changed in her friend.

"Thank you, sister. Thank you so much. I could not have withstood that anguish much longer," she said gratefully.

Etuah looked on approvingly, and she nodded her head back and forth upon her long, thin neck.

"You are all that they said you were," she commented.

Tamara looked at her askew yet again, confused by the Drue's words.

"Me? Are you referring to me?" she asked, distracted still by the disturbing difference she sensed in her friend.

"Yes. I was advised of your strength," Etuah replied.

"Advised?" she questioned. "My strength?"

"Few others could have recovered so quickly from the effects of this place while assisting another concurrently. Yes, they have chosen well."

Before Tamara had an opportunity to ask another question, four other Drue emerged from behind a tall, black obelisk that stood in the middle of the chamber. They looked very much like Etuah, but slightly different in height. Two were considerably taller and two were a bit shorter than she was. The two taller of the group had long hair, or what appeared to be hair, streaming down their backs. It was almost translucent, much like their skin, but it gleamed and glinted in the semi-darkness, and added to what was already an altogether otherworldly appearance. Etuah walked toward them and extended one of her long arms. The others did the same until the suctions on the ends of their fingers touched one another. All of their lips colored slightly and stood out starkly against their pale skin, and both Angeline and Tamara felt the tenderness between the group of Drue as they reunited.

They spoke to each other in a language that neither of the sisters could understand. Shortly, they all walked up to the women and formed a circle around them. There was no threat implied by this action, and the sisters stood quite still while they waited for the Drue to introduce themselves. A moment later, each extended one long arm toward Tamara and Angeline, who continued to hold each other's hands the entire time, until the suctions adhered to their skin.

A rush of feeling swept over them, and they could hear the Drue speaking through their touch. By the time they removed their fingers from the girls, both Tamara and Angeline knew their names, their sexes, and much more about them than they had ever expected to learn or be told. History, family relationships, births, deaths, their fears and hopes, loves and hates, and even their most personal of concerns were communicated. Suddenly, their sorrow was easier to bear. Though it did not abate entirely, it settled into its own place in their psyches, and there was once again room for other emotions. They both found themselves sighing audibly with relief.

"My kindred shared with you as the Lalas do with us," Etuah explained. "We will be with you and you with us now forever, for good or for evil, as we are with all the Chosen who have visited with us in the hollows."

By this time, Tamara decided to ignore the references to the Chosen that Etuah kept making. She was obviously not going to stop from speaking so, and there were certainly more important issues to contend with at the moment.

"Welcome," one of the group said in a deeper voice than Etuah's. "Though you already know now, I am Petuah. This is Hewlo," he said as he pointed to the tallest of the four.

"My name is Behani," the third Drue spoke out in a melodious tone.

"And I am Uhani," the remaining figure said while smiling. "It is not often that we have guests. Usually, the Chosen are here before us. It is a rare occasion when one comes after the shards have been removed."

"You are strong of character," the one called Petuah said directly to Tamara. "It did not tax us greatly to shelter your spirit from the pain."

Tamara and Angeline had barely a moment to rest in the last few hours. Everything was happening so quickly. It seemed like days ago that they were sitting on the hilltop somewhere far above where they currently stood. They listened intently to the Drues' words, but they had some practical concerns as well.

"Forgive me if I say anything inappropriate, but would it be possible for us to sit down somewhere and rest for at least a few moments?" Angeline asked. "I do not think that I can continue to stand here for much longer. I am so tired."

"Of course," Etuah replied immediately. "Follow me," she said, and she began to walk toward an alcove in the wall.

The other Drue followed behind the sisters while chatting amongst themselves in their odd sounding tongue, which both women now surprisingly now understood as if they had spoken it their entire lives. There was no question that the language was one they had never heard before today, but as they listened, they comprehended everything. Tamara and Angeline felt entirely comfortable with them.

"You learn faster than some of the others have," Hewlo said.

"They are more receptive," Behani noted.

"And less defensive," Etuah said.

They all crossed under a smooth archway and then emerged into another chamber that was smaller and lined with long, sponge-like cushions. One of the walls was carved into shelves and laden with canisters and cartons.

"We are not so different as you might expect," Behani said as she noticed the sister's reaction to what they saw. "We too eat."

"And we sleep as well," Hewlo said.

"I hope I did not offend any of you," Angeline said after she realized that her expression must have betrayed her surprise.

"Offend? You have been most gracious," Hewlo replied. "Many from above find our appearance difficult to look upon. You seem to find only our eating habits noteworthy," he smiled. "Please. Sit. They are most comfortable," he said, as he pointed to one of the sponge cushions.

Angeline and Tamara both accepted the offer quickly, and they reclined upon the nearest of the seats. They were extremely pliant and they found themselves sinking deep into the soft seats.

"I do not have the same feeling here as I did before. Is that due to your influence or the fact that we left that other room?" Tamara asked.

"A bit of both," Etuah replied. "Though having left the heart is the primary reason. Unfortunately, you must return there as soon as possible."

"And you must prepare to leave here as quickly as you can," Petuah said. "It is not safe for you, despite the fact that you seem to be more resistant than most to this space."

"We are not immune," Angeline said. "Maybe Tamara here is dealing with it better than I am, but for me it was quite difficult. It still is," she conceded. "But I must confess that the sensation is now more strange than it is frightening or sad."

"I am not as disturbed as you, sister," Tamara said. "Though the feelings are not pleasant, certainly."

"You cannot understand just how awful they were then, sister, if you characterize them that way. You are fortunate indeed," Angeline shuddered.

The Drue began to open some of the canisters on the shelves with their suctioned fingers, and they prepared something that looked as if it was to be eaten. Sure enough, within moments, Uhani removed some thin, platter shaped stones from one of the crevices, which adhered to the tips of her long fingers. She reached them out to Hewlo who poured the contents of one jar onto each and then another and another. Behani stretched her arms upward, extended her fingers and grabbed a number of translucent goblets from another shelf. She then poured a liquid into each of them from a long tube that protruded from a hole in the wall.

After handing a full plate and a goblet to each of the women, the Drue all sat upon the floor with their thin legs wrapped impossibly around themselves. Using their fingertips once again, they began to eat, lifting the food from the plates and sucking it into their pursed lips.

"We have utensils for you if you so require," Hewlo said. "I imagine it would be rather messy if you tried to eat with fingers that terminate the way yours do," he commented as he handed them each a small ladle carved from a white colored stone.

"Thank you," Tamara said, never the shy one, and she began to eat almost immediately.

Angeline was a bit more reluctant to taste the odd looking food, but Tamara seemed to find it so pleasing that she too shortly began to eat.

"Is it far to Odelot?" Tamara asked, wiping a drop of the sweet substance from her chin and licked her finger.

"Distances are measured differently in the hollows than above. It is difficult to answer that question," Etuah replied.

"It will take you a good deal of time to get there," Petuah said.

"Odelot was abandoned many tiels ago. Our brethren protect it the parts of it that they can. But, you must pass through areas that are not as well sustained in order to get there. One such place will only soon come under our protection," Uhani said.

"Another tree has died?" Tamara asked. "Do you know its name?"

"No. Not yet, but soon. It is one of medium stature. It calls itself Mintar and its Chosen is Carlisle. The heart is not so great as this one, but there is no one to remove the shard," Petuah said matter-of-factly. "We cannot enter as yet."

"It is the eleventh," Etuah said, as if that was meaningful, and the others all nodded solemnly.

"The Lalas has been wavering for a while. It is not a surprise to us," Behani said. "Yet, we are helpless."

"The world does not yet know. Neither does its Chosen," Hewlo said sadly.

"Is there nothing to be done?" Tamara asked.

"Done?" Etuah asked. "Why would one want to do anything? The tree has made this decision. We can only protect the space afterward, once the shard has been secured."

"Shard!" Angeline said. "The tree's essence?" she asked, having learned about these things only recently.

Etuah nodded to Angeline, but her eyes were upon Tamara as if she had only just realized something, and her recognition was mirrored by the other Drue.

"You have not been informed, of course. You could not have known," she then said to Tamara. "We are unaccustomed to this order of events. The Chosen e'er arrive before we do."

"And always just after the Lalas departs," Uhani said.

"It is fortuitous nevertheless," Hewlo said immediately.

"Most definitely," Behani agreed.

"I believe that she has the strength," Uhani said.

"There is no doubt," Petuah affirmed.

"I knew that she was exceptional immediately. But this is most irregular!" Etuah said.

"Did they suspect?" Petuah asked.

"No. I do not think that they did. It is quite remarkable!" Etuah replied.

"I am sure that they could not have known," Hewlo agreed. "When one of their own departs, they must keep their distance. It would be too dangerous otherwise."

"Yet she is here. Who then is responsible?" Uhani asked.

"A combination of freewill and determination, I surmise," Etuah said, and she winked in Tamara's direction.

"This changes everything. When will you leave?" Petuah asked.

"Soon, though I had not thought the moment was yet upon us," Etuah said, more contemplatively than before.

Until a second ago, they were all talking about Tamara as if she was not present, and it took her until then to realize even that she was the subject of their conversation.

"I will accompany you as far as I am able to," Etuah began to explain. "I cannot enter however until you have gathered the shard. Once that is done, you may pass, and then the others can approach and begin their work," she said to Tamara whose jaw had dropped almost to her chest.

"Me? You want me to gather the shard from a dying Lalas?" she asked, exasperated.

"Of course," Petuah replied. "That is surely one of the reasons why you are here."

"How am I to do that? I know nothing about shards and hearts and dying trees," she said. "Besides, we are here because we were chased here by the enemy who would have gladly killed us has we not come upon you or you us," she said to Etuah.

"If someone wanted to help us, it was to protect the map! It can only be coincidence that a tree is dying at the same time that we arrived."

"Unlikely," Etuah replied. "Most unlikely."

"There is little to know about retrieving the shard," Petuah said, ignoring Tamara's protestations. "What is most crucial is that you are able to enter the heart and remain rational. And it is quite clear that you are. Either one can or one cannot."

"So very few can," Uhani said.

"Once you are inside, you remove it and bring it back out with you," Hewlo said as if this was something she did everyday.

"What do I do with it if and when I am able to recover it?" Tamara asked, though she had not yet fully accepted her role in this venture.

"Return it to the heir, of course," Petuah said "It is the eleventh."

Tamara was once again dumbfounded. She stared at Petuah as if he had said the most outrageous thing she had ever heard in her entire life.

"The heir?   The heir to what?" Tamara asked. She was growing more stupefied with each new declaration. "How can I return anything to anyone when I first have to take this parchment to the end of the world and cast it down the well? What else am I expected to do? Take on the Dark Lord himself in his castle in Sedahar?"

The Drue stood there contemplating her words. They seemed not to understand her sarcasm, and they considered her last question as if she really expected an answer from them.

"First you must see that the shard is safely returned to the boy," Uhani said.

"The boy? What boy?" Tamara asked. "I am confused. Am I supposed to know who you are talking about?"

"The heir of legend, sister. The one who the great books say will find the Gem. Bethany has spoken of him more than once, though I know you never paid much attention to the histories," Angeline said.

"Oh, that boy! Now I understand!" she said exasperated, without exhibiting any true recognition of who they were actually referring to. "First, I am to gather this shard and then we are to travel through the forbidden places all the way to the dead city of Odelot to dispose of the map. After that, I will simply go and find this mythical character who is going to save the world according to the Tomes and everyone else here, and then give him the shard from the dead Lalas. Have I missed anything?" she asked.

"No. I believe that you have stated your tasks in the proper order," Petuah replied seriously.

"And then Angeline and I have permission to attack Colton dar Agonthea?" she asked incredulously.

"If you think it wise. But you must do that alone if you choose to pursue that endeavor," Etuah replied, somewhat perplexed by Tamara's questions.

Tamara began to laugh, and even Angeline looked at her oddly at that point. She laughed until she was bent over and could barely catch her breath. She laughed until the tears streamed down her face and her eyes grew red and swollen. She laughed until she could laugh no longer. The others stood there and watched without saying another word and without making any attempt to stop her. Even after she finally regained her composure and dabbed her tear-streaked face with the sleeve of her tunic, the Drue remained assembled around her expressionless. Angeline walked to her side and placed her arm around her shoulders.

"So much has been thrust upon us so quickly, it is difficult to absorb it all," Angeline said in support of her friend's behavior.

"More than you can imagine!" Tamara said seriously now. "I am sorry, truly sorry for behaving so. I could not help myself. This all just seems so incredible," she explained. "Do you think that we are going to be able to do all of this? We are simple sisters from Parth. Until I visited Oleander, I had never even been outside of the county in which I was born!"

Tamara shook her head in order to clear it before speaking again.

"This heir?" she finally said. "How do we find him, assuming of course that we can retrieve the shard and after we dispose of the map?" she asked. Her tone of voice was beyond the point of disbelief by now.

"Etuah will not be able to assist you either. Her time will expire after she has secured the heart," Hewlo said.

"Either? Are you saying that I must do this alone? And what do you mean by 'expire'? You mean she will die? What about Angeline?" Tamara was becoming agitated. "What is going on here?" she asked, and her concern was mounting precipitously.

"Angeline shall remain with us," Petuah said calmly. "She will take Etuah's place here."

"What did you say?" Tamara asked, as her head snapped in Petuah's direction.

She was thoroughly shocked by his words. She looked at Angeline who appeared to be quite calm, though her features were becoming a slight bit blurred in the odd light of the room.

"He said that I am going to stay here, sister," Angeline said. "Do not be frightened for me. I think I knew that the moment that I stepped into the hollows."

Her hair had loosened itself from the braid that had bound it, and it streamed out behind her as if the wind was blowing it, but there was not even the slightest breeze to be felt in the chamber.

"I belong here now. This is as it should be. 'The Drue find, the Drue keep', sister. You have not studied your books well," Angeline smiled.

"No, Angeline! It cannot be! What will you do here?" Tamara asked.

"I will do what the others do," she replied. "Only the Chosen come and go from this place. All the rest of us remain."

"We were all like you at one time," Uhani said to Tamara.

"Like us?" Tamara asked.

"Yes--human, elf or dwarf. But now we are all Drue," Hewlo said. "The change comes quickly once the role is accepted."

"Angeline will be safe here," Behani said kindly. "Our numbers are finite. When one of us leaves, another must take his or her place. It is so ordained."

"And if someone new should arrive, then one of us here must go," Etuah said.

"How did you first get here then?" Tamara asked, still astounded by this turn of events.

"We were not necessary until only recently. The trees flourished and spread throughout the land for thousands of tiels. When the first Lalas died, our services were required," Petuah explained.

"Who were the original ones?" Tamara asked. "If you were all from somewhere above before, how were the first of you ever chosen for this role?"

"We assembled slowly and gradually. All of us stumbled upon the forbidden places unwittingly, or so it seemed. Remember, the spaces in between did not exist until the first tree departed," Uhani said.

"Your families and friends did not know what happened to you?" she asked.

"No. They must have thought that we came to harm

somehow, and simply disappeared," Petuah replied. "The only regrets that we all have is that we could not put them at ease."

"We learned soon after our small group was formed that the hollows can only sustain a finite number of us. Though there are others of us, our numbers are limited. When someone new arrives who is not already Chosen for other purposes, they must replace one of us who is already here. We do not choose," Behani said.

"No. Neither those who come nor those who go," Etuah said.

"How is it decided then?" Tamara asked.

"The fabric weaves of its own will. But, when it is time for a change, we all know," Hewlo said. "As more trees die, perhaps our ranks will increase. We cannot hope for such an occurrence for it could only indicate a greater need, precipitated by an even greater loss."

"Do not fear for me, sister. They have given me a purpose which I embrace with all my heart," Angeline said. "I am ready for this. It seems so right to me."

Tamara hugged her friend tightly. She could already see the transformation beginning, and though it saddened her to think that she would be losing her friend forever, she believed Angeline when she said that it was something that she welcomed.

"Are you certain Angeline, that this is something you want to do?" she asked.

"More certain than I have ever been about anything else in my life. Even more certain than I was when I first entered Parth and became a sister," she admitted. "Believe me, Tamara. I would not lie to you."

"I will miss you, sister. What shall I do without you?" she asked tenderly.

"You are so strong, Tamara. Far stronger than I ever was or ever would be. I will do my part here," she replied.

"Will I ever see you again?" she questioned her friend.

"That will not be possible," Uhani answered for her.

Tamara's heart skipped a beat.

"How will I know that you are alright?" she inquired pleadingly.

"You need have faith, dear sister. This is how it must be. I could never return now even if I so wished," Angeline replied, and she opened her arms wide and purposely drew attention to her body.

Her skin appeared to be getting pallid and translucent even as they spoke, and her eyes were suddenly more rounded and luminescent. She glowed with a pale though obvious inner light. Angeline reached out her hand and touched Tamara affectionately on her arm, and in the dimness it seemed as if her fingers had already grown considerably in length.

"Will you remember me? Will you still know who I am after I am gone?" Tamara asked.

"Yes, sister. I will remember you always. You are the one who brought me here. I shall e'er be grateful," Angeline replied in a voice more ethereal than ever before.

"Promise me, Angeline!" Tamara said.

"I promise," she replied, and they embraced affectionately.

Her body felt thinner and frailer to the touch, but Tamara sensed a profound energy within it as well, and that served to comfort her despite the heaviness she felt in her chest. She kissed her on the cheek.

"May the First protect you and keep you, dear sister," Tamara said, and she forced herself to step back a pace, hoping that the distance would help her to maintain her composure.

"I will be safer than I have ever been, sister," she smiled. "May the Gem of Eternity guide you through the darkness always."

"You are my best friend, Angeline. I will miss you so much," she said, as she fought to hold back the tears she vowed to herself she would not shed now.

"And I you," she responded, choking on her emotion as well. "But this is where I belong. Your destiny lies elsewhere, and this fact is beyond our control. We must accept what we cannot change," she replied, and Tamara reluctantly nodded her agreement.

"I am proud of you, Angeline. I will always be so proud of you," Tamara said sweetly. "You will be in my heart forever."
"As you will be in mine, sister. Forever," she replied with unbridled emotion.

"And you Etuah? What will become of you after I remove the shard?" Tamara asked, forcing herself to turn her attention to the Drue woman before she broke down entirely.

"I will die," Etuah replied calmly. "I have lived a long life, Chosen. No one should mourn my passing."

This was all happening too fast. Tamara was so overwhelmed by the events that she could barely maintain her perspective. She looked from one of the Drue to the next, searching for solace until her gaze rested once more upon Angeline.

"What am I to do then?" she asked. "How will I find my way to Odelot without you, Angeline? And how will I ever find the heir?" she asked, momentarily losing her confidence.

"I will guide you through the nethers, and I will set you on the right path through the forbidden places. You will find the dead city if that is what you wish," Etuah replied with no doubt in her voice.

"But what of the boy? How will I locate him?"

"That will be the simplest task of all for you to accomplish," the Drue said. "You merely need to return to Parth once you have relinquished the map. He is there now in the Tower with his companions, and he will be there when you get back," Etuah said. "They await your return, though they know it not yet."

"When must we leave here, Etuah," she asked.

"As soon as we can. This space cannot sustain both Angeline and I after her transformation is complete. If we do not leave before that, it will be impossible for me to leave at all. I shall die here."

"Then what are we waiting for?" Tamara asked, as she tried to sound optimistic. "If I have to say goodbye to my sister once more, I will probably die here as well," she said. She smiled endearingly at Angeline, despite the tears that were building up in the corners of her eyes and blurring her vision even further.

"Please help us to gather the few supplies we will need. Time grows short. We must hurry now," Etuah said with an urgency that they had not heard in her voice before.

Tamara watched while the five other Drue glided off to carry out her request, and included among them now was Angeline as if she had been one of the guardians since the beginning of time.

Chapter Thirty-two

Maringar could only watch from within his imprisoned body as his friend attempted to free him from the beast's possession. Beolan slashed out with his dagger, but there was no enemy to strike that a blade could harm. But in his frustration and fear, he swung nevertheless. The walls of the cavern were alive, and the ground upon which he stood heaved and buckled.

Silandre resisted with all of her might, but the Armadiel infiltrated the stone despite her efforts. Long fingers of rock reached out from above and below and threatened to engulf the elf as he jockeyed for space, leaping deftly from left to right. The walls themselves expanded and contracted with each breath of the beast. Maringar stood helplessly by and watched, incapable of moving even an inch on his own. It felt as if his insides were being consumed by a ravenous invader, and he wanted to scream, but even that he was unable to do. His mouth moved involuntarily, and the beast used his body mercilessly.

"Surrender to me, elf! You cannot win. I can give you eternal life. With me you can become a part of your beloved mountain!" Maringar's voice said.

"You bring nothing but death and defilement to Crispen! You are the instrument of the Dark Lord, and nothing more!" Beolan shouted, as he leapt upon an escarpment to the side of him and drew an arrow from his quiver and set it to bow. "Show yourself, coward!" he yelled, but the demon only laughed through the mouth of his captive friend.

Beolan stood with his back to an earthen wall, and he sought shelter from the stone into which the Armadiel had insinuated itself.

"Have you no strength of your own, beast? Must you always use another's body?" he shouted in an effort to distract him and keep him off guard.

"I will use yours soon enough, little one," he replied, as the dwarf's lips mouthed the beast's words. "Shoot me here if you want. Kill your friend. Perhaps you will hurt me too," the Armadiel prodded him.

"You come and get me!! Maybe hiding in an elf's body would make you feel safer than in a dwarf's," Beolan teased it, hoping to give him a reason to leave Maringar alone.

Three hands of stone rose up from the ground before him

and grasped his ankles. He cringed in pain as they dug into his skin. The walls were contracting and expanding more violently now. Beolan shouldered his bow and smacked the flat side of his dagger against the rock as hard as he could, seeking to loosen the grip that was tightening around him. Sparks of power flew as the elfin metal met the stone, and he was able to fend them off for the moment as he leapt out of their way to another sheltered alcove.

The Armadiel continued to speak through his prisoner's lips, but his friend's body had remained stationary the entire time.

"Resist, Maringar! He has not captured your soul!" Beolan shouted. "Coward! You are a coward, just as we were told. Have you no body to fight with that you have not stolen? The Dark Lord's puppet seeks a puppet of his own? Your master has taught you well."

"No one is my master!" the voice bellowed from Maringar's mouth, its anger obvious.

Beolan touched upon a raw nerve, and quickly realizing it, he sought now to capitalize upon his discovery.

"Everyone is your master if you must use them so! Why will you not reveal yourself then? Stand before us! Have you no pride? Must you hide inside of another?"

Silandre creaked and groaned as it resisted the beast's advances, and
Maringar's face writhed in agony. Cracks and fissures appeared upon the rock walls and the earth beneath their feet shifted and shook violently. Boulders tumbled to the surface and sent clouds of dust and debris into the cramped space, and great fissures appeared in the stone floor. The ground trembled and shuddered from the impact of the falling rocks.

"You are just a tool of the Dark Lord; another of his pawns. He is using you for his own purposes. Do you know why you are here?" Beolan asked while walking backward all the time and now drawing the Armadiel with him. Maringar's body walked stiffly in pursuit.

"To destroy Crispen!" it replied. "To possess the water and the rock and claim it for my own forever."

"You are a fool if that is what you believe!" Beolan shouted as he inched his way back down the passage.

The earth shook even more violently all around and the walls and ceiling closed in upon them like a vise. The stone moaned louder and shifted precariously under the pressure that the beast was exerting upon it from within.

"What would you have me believe then, elf?" Maringar's lips moved. "That I do not govern my own destiny?"

"You do his bidding and you do not even know it!" Beolan continued, inciting it and coaxing it all the while.

His tactics were working, as the ego of the snake was even bigger than he had imagined. As he suspected, the great power of the beast was matched in intensity by its pride and arrogance.

"Your destiny is to serve Caeltin d'Are Agenathea as is the case for all of those who ally with him. Did you think that you and he were partners? Did you presume that you were his equal?"

"I have my purposes, he has his!" the beast replied, still unconvinced.

"Ha!" Beolan snickered. "You do only what he wants you to do and no more. Do not flatter yourself," he taunted. "Has he not even told you of the key?" he asked as ambiguously as possible while seeking to gather any information that he could from the unsuspecting monster.

"The key to what? The key to power no one need advise me of," it replied, misconstruing Beolan's question. "If it is a key to conquering this mountain, then I know more than he could about such subjects, and there are no doors in Crispen that I require a key to open, little one!" he stated arrogantly.

At least Beolan now knew that the Dark Lord did not inform it of his true purpose in resurrecting it. And thus, he could safely obviate the prospect that the key was in the Armadiel's possession. He smiled inwardly, as the image of his father's face passed across his mind's eye. Relieved, he tucked the new information into the back of his mind for the present and focused once again on more pressing matters.

The cracks in the walls were becoming more numerous, and Beolan was quickly growing concerned that the sides of the passage would soon cave in on them if the rock continued to deteriorate in this manner. He needed to carefully weigh how far to push the beast before its anger brought the entire mountain down upon them. He was trying to lure the monster back down the passage way in the direction that they had come from originally, hoping that the dwarves had burrowed fast enough so that they could come upon him from behind and surround him as planned, and in that he was succeeding. He jumped from his stony perch to another and then to another, and each time Maringar's possessed body slowly followed him.

"Silandre will not surrender to you, usurper," he chided him. "This mountain has a soul of its own. It is elfin too, just like me!"

"It has already given itself up," he replied confidently. "The resistance has practically ceased."

"Never! You are wrong. Just as you let the Dark Lord delude you, so have you allowed your arrogance to blind you to the truth. Silandre is still alive," Beolan said. "She is older than you, Armadiel. She is as old as time itself. Be on your guard."

An inhuman growl roared from Maringar's mouth. The beast was growing frustrated by the baiting, and the elf recognized that.

"You will be crushed like an insect in the dwarf's body. Has your master not warned you? Silandre will collapse upon you before she surrenders!"

"I cannot die like that, little one. Let the entire mountain come down upon me. I am not afraid," it responded. "I am not afraid of anything!"

"If his body dies, then you will suffer with it. Caeltin knows that. He sent another to do his dirty work once before. Silandre will trap you, like it trapped him," he warned. "Take your chances if you are foolish enough not to heed my warning."

"And why then would you tell me this? To assist me? Do you think that I am so simple?" it asked, but Beolan thought he sensed a note of doubt in the response.

"Because I would rather have you as an ally than an enemy!" he said, as he leapt out of the way of another falling stalactite. "Because I feel sorry for you. I have witnessed the fate of those who give of themselves to Caeltin. Though you have come here to kill me, I can still show mercy."

"I am your enemy!" he bellowed. "Your kind and mine cannot live together! I will consume your soul and the souls of all others like you. We are opposites. Death to you is life to me!"

"And what of your master? Has he not told you what he wants of you? We are more alike than you and he are," Beolan said with as sincere a tone as he could muster while cringing privately at the thought.

"He is not my master, little one!" the monster hissed. "He released me. That is all."

"Do you wish to die then? Is death better than captivity?"

Beolan asked, as he continued to retreat down the corridor. "Death is life, you say? Do you not know what death means to him? It is not what you think, Armadiel!"

"What I think, little one, is that you are trying to confuse me. She who imprisoned me is dead. He killed her. Your great trees are dying! That much I know. And your mountain will die too. I shall become the potency that guides it! It will be my instrument and it will resound with my tune!"

"You do not know what the Dark Lord seeks, then," he said, as if some great secret had been kept from him. "Has your ally not told you of his deepest desires? Has he not shared the truth with you, since he is such a friend?" he continued to mock it.

"Power! We both seek power! I attain it by consuming the lives of those like you," the Armadiel snickered.

"He seeks only death and dissolution! Dissolution, beast! Dissolution!" Beolan shouted. "Know you not what that means for you?" he asked while feigning disbelief.

"What is this word you speak of to me?" he replied. He had become curious now.

Maringar's possessed figure was slowly and stiffly walking down the path, steadily following Beolan all the while as he spoke.

"Caeltin d'Are Agenathea has no interest in you. He is using you. If you hinder us here we cannot fight against him elsewhere. What bargain did you make with the Dark One? He did not respect you enough to tell you of his deepest desires? We cannot help to prevent him from destroying the world if we must fight you as well."

"Why should I care what he wishes? Let him enjoy his power in his realm, and I will savor mine. He offered me Crispen."

"And yet, it was not his to give. What did he really do for you? Or are you doing it all for him?" Beolan asked. "If he wins, you will perish too! Just like all the rest of us! Dissolution spares no one and no thing!"

"He cannot kill me. And neither can you, little one," the Armadiel said.

"You truly are a fool, beast!" Beolan scoffed at it. "I can hear him laughing at you all the way from Sedahar!" he teased. "Listen and you will hear it too!"

"No one laughs at me!" it replied, and its ire was growing steadily.

"He is laughing. And so am I! He deceived you so easily! "

Beolan jeered.

"I said, no one laughs at me!" it roared and the chamber shook all around them. "Even you, little one," it hissed threateningly.

Long arms of rock shot out from the walls and the floor menacingly in all directions, though they did not touch Beolan. The beast now sought only to impress the crafty young elf with his might. His pride compelled him unwittingly to seek Beolan's respect.

"Are you dumb then?" he pressed him. "You do not know what dissolution really means? Go back to school, beast, if you know what's good for you. Quit this mountain and learn what your fate will be. Dissolution means the end for us all, you included! That is what he craves. That is all that he desires. Power is a means. Dissolution is the end."

The Armadiel was growing tired in Maringar's body. It was feeling the fatigue of its host, and it knew that the dwarf's body could not sustain his presence much longer. And, it was also growing confused by Beolan's constant questions and persistent jibing. It contemplated resuming its own shape and showing this brazen young elf the true and fearsome form of the Armadiel, and then putting an end to him.

"Your friend is dying, little one," the monster warned him.

"Only cowards kill the unsuspecting, beast. Let him live. Show me that you have courage after all," Beolan said.

"Show you my courage? To what purpose?"

"Because I doubt that you possess it. Because I think you are scared and you could not bear watching me die whilst I still believed that!"

"You doubt my courage?" it bellowed. "Behold!" it said, as Maringar's exhausted body collapsed heavily to the floor of the cavern.

Right before Beolan's eyes, an enormous being sprang to life. It rose from the rock as if it was growing out of the stone itself. Countless black scales covered it from the top of its head to the tip of its tail, and each one gleamed and glinted even in the semi-darkness of the cavern. Though it was referred to as the Snake of Recos by some, it looked more like an animal than a serpent. It had two arms and two legs that terminated in long, sharp, menacing claws instead of benign fingers and toes, and it stood erect at least twelve feet in the air. Its head was huge and sat precariously atop a muscular neck that seemed to elongate and contract with each of the heavy breaths it took. The nose was broad and the nostrils were wide. Its eyes were almond shaped and very large, and when it blinked, the eyelids seemed transparent. The black pupils stared at Beolan even from behind the lids. Its mouth was well formed and human looking, and it seemed oddly out of place on its face. Behind its thin lips were two rows of pointed teeth, though none were large enough to appear dangerous. The tail was the only other characteristic that looked to be reptilian aside from the scales, and it moved back and forth threateningly across the floor, as it slowly swept from left to right. It was quite long and it reached nearly to Beolan's feet as it arced across the surface, causing him to step back cautiously in order to remain out of its reach.

Beolan found it difficult to breath for the stench of the beast was almost unbearable. Its body seethed with a menacing power, and the rock walls of the cavern mimicked it, sucking the air out with each compression and filling the chamber with the most putrid and suffocating smell Beolan had ever inhaled. He covered his mouth and nose with a scarf that he pulled from his pocket, but it did nothing to prevent the odor from reaching his nostrils. He saw that his friend was still breathing, and thanking the First, he bent down and placed his gloveless hand on the dwarf's burning forehead.

You are on fire, my friend. I am not a practiced healer, but I know I can help you somewhat, he reflected quickly.

Beolan sent what healing energy he could to his friend, and he felt him stir if only slightly. He helped him to his feet and put his arm around his shoulder.

"He will not die! I left him soon enough," the Armadiel said, as he easily read the elf's thoughts. "Courage, you say I lack? Observe then how I let my enemies live," it boasted. "I can kill you both later if I choose to. I have no fear of you, little one," it said, as tentacles of stone danced around Beolan, skimming his ankles and causing him to cringe at the touch.

"You are truly magnanimous, beast," Beolan said, though he was completely repulsed by the appalling feeling of violation. "It is a shame that you were not strong enough to defend yourself against Caeltin's domination."

The Armadiel roared again, only this time it was his own lungs that generated the sound, and it was so loud that it almost burst Beolan's eardrums.

"I am ruled by no man!" it howled.

"Then why are you here? What do you want with Silandre and Crispen?" he asked.

"The water, little one. I want the water," it replied. "I crave it. It is among the purest in all the land. That was the deal that I made."

"There are other well springs in other places where no one resides. Surely one must be just as good. Why must you destroy my land?"

"What do I care for you and your people?" it replied. "The source here is limitless."

"It is not limitless. It freezes in the winter. The falls turn to glistening icicles, and the lakes become so hard and thick you can build upon them. You are one who covets the warmth, are you not? The legends speak of you so," Beolan said.

"Your legends speak of me?" it asked. Its black eyes opened wider than before and rolled upward in satisfaction.

"Perhaps I am mistaken," Beolan said. "When our books refer to the Armadiel, they describe it as one who thrives in the water, not upon it. They speak of a beast who moves gracefully beneath the surface."

"That is me, little one. I prefer the water to the land," it replied. "The legends describe me correctly," it said, and it puffed its chest out and elongated its neck proudly. "But the water here runs deep."

"I see," Beolan replied knowingly. "He did he not tell you then of the extent
of our weather changes here, I should have guessed. For half of our year, the water does not flow and the snow falls without a break."

"Snow?" it asked as if the word were unfamiliar.

"Yes, snow. It is like frozen rain that falls heavily from the sky, though it accumulates everywhere upon the surface and does not melt away until the spring. The higher up the mountain we climb, the deeper it gets and the colder the air remains."

A shiver ran down the spine of the beast and it shook the entire chamber.

"Here within the caves, the air gets so cold that when I breathe, the moisture in my breath freezes as I exhale. I cannot even come up here in the depths of winter. I would die. Are you accustomed to the cold?" he asked innocently, knowing that the Armadiel was born in the molten depths of the earth.

"Cold?" the Armadiel repeated as if this word too was unknown to it.

"Sedahar is warm. It is in the south. Perhaps Caeltin forgot how different the weather is here," Beolan replied innocently.

The beast snorted his derision and everything shook once again. Maringar lifted his head weakly and looked at Beolan. He nodded to indicate that he was alright, and the elf acknowledged him with relief.

"You did not lie to me, beast. My friend lives," he said to the Armadiel.

"Why need I lie to you, little one? I told you that my courage is great and that I have no fear of you. Have I not proven that?" it asked, and it seemed as if it was almost seeking Beolan's approval. "There will be time enough later to dispose of you both if I so choose."

"The legends depict you accurately. Your courage may indeed match your wisdom," Beolan replied.

The beast appeared to be almost smiling to itself, childishly flattered by the elf's praise, and distracted enough not to realize that he was leading him further and further down the path. It was so preoccupied by the praise that it paid scant attention to what was happening around it. Beolan could hear a different sound now resounding throughout the passageway, that of picks striking stone, and he knew that he was getting closer to the others, but the demon was deaf to all but Beolan's flattery.

"Are you courageous enough to leave us be? Could you walk away from Crispen now? Do you fear the wrath of the Dark Lord?" he asked.

"I told you, little one, I fear no one," it replied. "But why should I leave? I am enjoying this. And I will enjoy it even more when I destroy you and your city as well. I can depart later if what you tell me proves to be true."

"You will ne'er be allowed to leave. You made a bargain with him; Crispen for your freedom. If you do not destroy us, he will send you back to whence you came. And if you do, he will never let you leave here. You will die once again in this mountain, only this time it will be for all eternity. He wishes to rend the whole cloth, and put and end to the weave forever."

"He is not so powerful as that. You give him more credit than he is due," the Armadiel replied. "Your fear should be of me, little one. You and yours will not live to contend with the Dark

Lord. I will see to that. You have captured my attention but your words cannot change what I must do. "Tis a shame that your scribes will ne'er have the opportunity to write the legend of the Armadiel and the mountain it conquered in your books."

Maringar and Beolan had finally retreated to the point where they had overtaken the burrowing dwarves. They could practically hear them behind the walls. As planned, the tunnels had been dug around and behind the main passage that Beolan, Maringar and the Armadiel had been walking down. With the cooperation of Silandre, the rock and soil responded to the picks and axes willingly and practically fell away at their touch, thus allowing them to progress at greater speeds than even they anticipated.

As the elf and the dwarf emerged into the larger chamber where they had planned to converge, they came to a halt. There was now only a thin wall of rock on either side of the cavern that kept their fellow dwarves and elfin bowmen separated from them and the beast. The barricades of rubble had been rolled into place right up against it and the men waited anxiously behind the last row of dwarves. The timing was as perfect as they could have hoped. Once the stone was breached, they could begin their attack.

"The fabric weaves of its own will, Maringar," Beolan whispered to his friend. "We have come far enough now."

"Just in time, it seems. The demon grows restless," he replied weakly.

"I have enjoyed our little talk immensely, but all things must come to an end at some point," the beast hissed. "He has given me life once again. I am afraid that what you have to offer cannot match what he has already done, and what he can yet do. We are too different, you and I. Sadly, I am more akin to The Dark One, and that is why, although it is truly a pity little one, I must kill you."

Beolan stood with his back against the wall and pressed the palm of his hand to the surface. He could feel the vibrations behind it, and he knew that the men had accomplished their task. He signaled to Maringar to assume the same stance on the opposite wall. The Armadiel had been so distracted by the conversation and it was so enamored of the moments of flattery that it never even sensed the presence of the others in the adjacent passages.

"I can offer you one final opportunity to renounce him and to leave Crispen," Beolan said. "This will be your only chance to prevent the sundering and save your own life."

"Or you will shoot one of your arrows at me? Or perhaps your friend will hit me with his axe?" the beast snorted derisively. "Though it pains me, the time has come, little one...."

The floor began to vibrate violently and the Armadiel rose high upon its powerful hind legs. Its black scales shimmered dangerously in the near darkness. Beolan watched in horror as its tail pierced the rock surface as if it was a piece of parchment and disappeared underneath them. The ceiling and walls pulsed with the beast's potency as it they were alive. Maringar and Beolan both pressed themselves tightly against the walls and removed their weapons from their scabbards. With gloved hands, they grabbed the blades and pounded the hilts hard against the stone.

Silandre responded willingly to their caresses. The thin sheet of rock that remained between the tunnel that they now stood in and their waiting soldiery shattered and fell away in a cloud of dust, and revealed two wide openings to the left and to the right of the demon in its wake. The dwarves had performed their tasks masterly, and as soon as the holes were clear of debris, the elves pushed the easily maneuverable barricades forward through them and into the chamber and formed a semicircle in front of the Armadiel. From behind their defenses, they began to rain elfin arrows upon the beast. Out of the darkness of the tunnels, more barricades were thrust forward, and perhaps four dozen additional elves emerged and proceeded to deluge the Armadiel with arrow upon arrow. In the meanwhile, Beolan and Maringar retreated quickly behind the foremost defensive position. They acknowledged with pride and no small amount of relief the efforts of their countrymen . Though the plans were well conceived, they did not know until that very moment that they would be just as well executed.

"We could not have asked for more," Maringar said to his comrade.

He was still exhausted from the abuse that his body had suffered, but the adrenaline in his veins was keeping him alert and aware.

"I had expected no less from your brethren," Beolan replied.

The dwarves had cleared large areas just before the tunnel walls on either side of the passageway. They were able to accommodate at least fifty elves and twenty dwarves in each. While the former were busy chipping away at Silandre's stone and preparing for this moment, the other fifty or so armed elves had made their way into the tunnel from the main entrance. Now, almost two hundred warriors with bows raised and axes ready proceeded against the beast.

The Armadiel roared in anger. It had been so thoroughly taken by surprise, that it took more than a moment for the beast to fully understand the nature of the threat. Immediately, it needed to protect itself, and it had no time to concentrate and plan a counterattack.

"Do not cease the barrage!" Beolan yelled, loud enough for it to hear his voice.

Knowing that it had been deceived by the elf enraged it even more, and it lashed out in fury without contemplating the impact of its actions. Sharp spears of stone fell heavily from the ceiling all around it and bounced off of its hard scales. Most of the arrows too fell harmlessly to the surface at first, though a modest number did insert themselves into the small spaces between its armor and its broad belly, causing it to shriek in pain. It swung its taloned fingers back and forth, and knocked the shafts out of the air as they flew at it from its front and sides.

A moment later, yet another contingent of elfin warriors began their assault from behind the Armadiel this time. They had traveled deep into the mountain and emerged at a point well to the rear of the beast. Their weapons too now added to the monster's travail. With lightening speed, the elves of Crispen unleashed onslaught after onslaught of silver tipped arrows upon the monster, never giving it even a moment to rest and organize a response. It howled in frustration and swung its tail dangerously back and forth, shattering rock and stone and sending sparks flying everywhere. But the attack continued relentlessly.

Beolan walked to Maringar's side, making sure to remain well hidden behind the many partitions, and he whispered in his ear, "Will you able to do this, my friend?"

"Most definitely!" he replied without any hesitation. "I think that the only way I will ever rid myself of this terrible feeling of filth and disgust that the beast has left in me is to kill it!" he replied. "It will not be enough to witness his death from afar."

"Then we must ready ourselves. The opportunity may come at any time. It has been awake and aware for quite a while now, my conversation intrigued it so."

"That was as well done as any man to man combat I have ever seen," Maringar praised him.

"Thank you. The beast was most receptive. I even think it liked me."

"It liked you alright! It liked you enough to have you for dinner, though not as its guest I suspect, 'little one'," Maringar chided him.

The black scales that covered it all over were darkening in color as the torrents of arrows continued to pummel them. Their inner gleam faded as time wore on, and they began to assume a duller, flatter color.

The Armadiel swung around and thrashed out wildly at everything that the warriors sent against it. They refused to rest even for a moment, and with Beolan and Maringar coaxing them to pursue their attack without any break whatsoever, the beast had no opportunity to relax. It was being assaulted from all sides and from all angles. Arrows were dropping down on it from above, as some of the elves arched their shots deftly and had them fall on its head and back, while others aimed at its chest and face. Small contingents of dwarves rushed the beast in sporadic waves and hacked away at the plates of armor on the back of its legs, while nimbly avoiding the thrashing tail each time.

An emboldened dwarf leapt over the demon's tail and sought to strike at the beast from below, but he was caught in one of its clawed hands. Instantly, the Armadiel pierced the warrior's heart with a sharp talon, and the dwarf turned grey as stone. It released the dead fighter, and as the immobile body hit the surface, it crumbled to dust. Two more dwarves leapt into the fray and they began to hack away at its hind legs. The beast flicked its heavy tail first to the left and then to the right so quickly that the brave fighters had no chance to even sidestep it. The first dwarf was flung into the wall with such force that its back was shattered by the impact, while the second was caught under the foot of the beast and squashed to death mercilessly.

Immediately, two more dwarves rushed in to replace those who had fallen. With a fierce rage, they pummeled the monster with their sharp axes, but this time they retreated before it had a chance to strike. Another then dashed across the heaving stone floor with a pick in one hand and its heavy hammer in the other. Unnoticed at first by the frenzied beast, it inserted the sharp, diamond tip of its pick between two scales on the back of its leg and swung its hammer hard and true. The armor gave way and two black scales fell to the ground. The Armadiel screeched in response and swiveled around supplely, but it was too late to catch the nimble dwarf. It had already made its way back to the shelter of one of the barricades.

"It is beginning to tire," Beolan said, as he noticed that it was breathing more heavily than before. "Do not waver now!" he urged. "We must force the transformation upon it."

Despite the casualties, they fought on without respite, heeding Beolan's words and trying not to give the beast a moment to do anything more than defend itself from their attacks. In response, the Armadiel's tail surged deep into the stone floor once again and this time the entire chamber shuddered, but its eyes were not as bright as before and its movements were a slight bit slower now than previously.

An arrow struck it in its eyelid, and though it quickly pulled the shaft out and broke it in half, the eye began to swell. The few areas where it was vulnerable were being targeted as heavily as they could be by the attacking armies, and though they all knew it would never ultimately succumb to this type of assault, both the dwarves and the elves were cognizant of the ulterior motive of their continued onslaught. At some point, the beast would need to rest and then it would try to replenish itself.

A fissure suddenly appeared in the rock upon which they all stood. It was only about a fingertip in width at first sight, but as the floor shook and throbbed, it grew wider. Maringar noticed it first, and he drew Beolan's attention to it right away.

"It runs from one end to the other, it seems," the dwarf said. "Do you think that the beast can cleave the entire mountain?" he asked.

"I do not know the extent of its ability, nor of its power. But the cleft grows even as we speak. We have to get it to remove its tail from the rock!" Beolan said.

"If you show yourself, that will no doubt enrage it even more. In its misguided way, the Armadiel thought you were its friend," Maringar said.

"Misguided indeed! I do pity it, but I wish to see it dead and gone from Silandre and Crispen as surely as I would if it was Caeltin himself!" Beolan replied.

Without another word, Maringar pulled his dagger from the scabbard at his waist and lofted his axe in his other hand. He dashed from behind the rocks while shrieking a dwarven war cry at the top of his lungs, and he waved his weapons dangerously above his head. A flurry of elfin arrows accompanied his advance, along with another charge upon the monster's rear by a quartet of dwarves.

The Armadiel's big eyes were half closed and its head lolled heavily upon its now contracted neck. Many of the scales that protected it showed signs of damage, though only two had fallen to the surface. It continued to bat away the metal tipped shafts that rained down upon it, though with less speed and dexterity than previously. Many of the barbs penetrated its defenses, but they only bounced harmlessly off of its black armor. The beast's powerful tail remained thrust deep into the stone, and the reverberations could be felt everywhere. The chasm in the floor of the chamber was widening steadily.

When it saw Maringar, its helpless captive of only hours ago, rushing toward it with his weapons raised, its concentration lapsed momentarily. Distracted by the multifaceted assault as hoped, as well as by the attack upon its pride, its tail withdrew involuntarily from beneath the surface. The vibrations ceased immediately. With lightening speed, Maringar attacked, and the beast swung its tail around in order to intercept him. Dropping his dagger, he nimbly ducked and pivoted and then extended his razor sharp axe above his head with both hands securely holding the handle. The Armadiel's tail swept over the honed metal of his weapon. The blade sliced clean through three of the beast's bottom scales due to the immense force of the monster's own action. Black blood poured from the wound and sizzled as it splattered upon the surface. Maringar had been knocked to the floor by the impact, but he was unharmed. He rose quickly and grabbed his axe before scurrying back to the defensive lines. The Armadiel howled from the unexpected and unfamiliar pain. It knew instinctively that it now needed to renew itself, and quickly!

Its eyes clouded over and it drew in its arms. Its big head sunk down upon its chest and the now wounded tail wrapped itself protectively around its legs and lower body. In the dim light, the black scales glowed eerily and seemed to be changing before their very eyes.

"Well done, my friend!" Beolan said, and he slapped the dwarf sharply upon his back.

"The time approaches," Maringar said to Beolan. "By the First, let us pray that our interpretation of the ancient texts is correct. If so, we must strike the deadly blow when it is most vulnerable. I doubt we will have a second chance."

"I am right beside you!" Beolan replied as the two warriors leapt forward in order to approach the beast.

Maringar had replaced his axe in its sheath and he now held the thick dagger with his two strong hands. Beolan left his bow behind and he too held his long, thin sword with both hands. Side by side, they walked toward the monster. It still stood before them, though it barely moved. Only its heavy breathing indicated that it was still alive. They watched as the color of its skin began to change, beginning at its head. The black scales started to turn pale and almost translucent. At the same time, its eyes closed completely and each breath that it took became slower and less frequent. It seemed to be totally unaware of the presence of the two warriors. Its skin started to fall away from its head and neck, and soon it hung limply all around. Softened scales fell to the ground everywhere. But, almost as fast as they peeled away, new ones formed, and the new ones were once again deep black and luminescent. There appeared to be no more than fifteen seconds between the shedding of the old skin and the formation of the new.

"The heart is where we must strike if we are to be successful," Beolan said.

"I am ready" Maringar replied.

They watched the transformation with bated breath, awaiting their one moment to attack. The shoulders of the beast were now exposed, and in a matter of seconds they were armored and invincible looking once again. Its skin hung all around it in heavy folds by this time, as the shedding progressed. Soon, the protective armor had faded and fallen away almost to the beast's chest.

"Prepare yourself!" Maringar said, and he raised his dagger in the air.

A large piece of skin and scales fell to the stone surface, and as it dropped away it revealed a bony section of chest hidden beneath it. Maringar lunged with the speed and force of a man possessed, and he sliced the beast's thorax down the middle, breaking his dagger in the process on the hard bones of the monster, while leaving a deep gash in the demon. Black blood poured form the wound, but the scales were quickly reforming above it. Beolan followed closely behind, and with both hands grasping his sword, he thrust his weapon as far as he could into the Armadiel's body. He twisted it violently, hoping to rend the Armadiel's heart with one swift shove, but he was unsuccessful. The black blood, though dripping from the wound itself, was not the blood of a sundered heart.

"Help me, Maringar!" he yelled.

The dwarf had been watching closely, though he had no useful weapon in his hand any longer.

"I have not the strength to drive my blade home!" Beolan said.

They both saw the scales rapidly approaching the wound that they had just made. Maringar lifted Beolan in his muscular arms and thrust him upward and into the body of the beast. This effort gave him just the right amount of leverage he needed to manipulate the sharp blade that he held. Pushing up himself with his own strength as well, he now had enough momentum to reach and pierce the Armadiel's throbbing heart. Vigorously, he shoved his ancient blade deep into the demon's organ. Torrents of jet black liquid rained down upon the two of them, pulsing and shooting everywhere, and Beolan and Maringar both collapsed under the weight of the beast's coursing essence.

"We have to get out of the way," Maringar yelled, and with a second wind he lifted Beolan once more and carried the exhausted elf back a few paces.

The blood continued to pour out of the body of the beast, and by this time it had covered the floor in an ever spreading pool of slippery liquid that was slowly seeping into the cracks of the surface. The monster's eyes were still closed and its skin fell away as if it was still shedding, though no more new scales appeared to be forming any longer. The massive legs of the Armadiel were beginning to buckle at the knees, and its entire body was shriveling like a deflating balloon before their very eyes. It leaned backward upon its tail momentarily, and then it collapsed hard onto the wet surface.

With their two heroic leaders looking on, the other dwarves and elves who had remained behind the barricades now stepped forward and massed around the dying demon in silence, watching with jubilation and relief. Suddenly, the crack in the middle of the floor, cleaved by the Armadiel's tail only a short while ago, began to increase in breadth. The chamber shook violently and the floor heaved once more as Silandre's stone jaws opened wide. They drew the beast into them and consumed it completely and forevermore.

Pale and broken scales, along with fragments of bone and pieces of ragged skin shot high into the air. A black and bloody mist spread throughout the cavern only moments before an earsplitting groaning sound assaulted the ears of everyone present. As they watched, the gaping cleft in the rock floor clamped violently together, accompanied by a incredibly loud crash that seemed to reverberate endlessly off of the walls and ceiling and was certain to be heard all the way in the city of Crispen itself. The entire mountain trembled and shook as Silandre voraciously digested the final remains of the beast that had so arrogantly sought to posses it.

Chapter Thirty-three

"I need to speak with my brother, Robyn. The ring keeps talking to me. I cannot stop it," Davmiran said to the Chosen beside him.

They were standing in Dav's small room talking. The others had long ago gone to sleep and dawn was fast approaching.

"Can you understand what it is saying?" he asked.

"Most of the words are indecipherable. Occasionally I recognize one or two. The only thing that I am certain of though is that it keeps repeating the name 'Tomas'."

"Do you know where he is, Dav? Are you able to communicate with him in any way?"

"No. I have no idea where he might be. As for your second question, I have never tried. But, there is no doubt that now I must."

"Come with me then," Robyn said and he motioned to the door. "This is not the place to do it. I will find Gretchen and ask her to take us to the tower. That would be a more conducive environment for such an important endeavor, and a more secure one."

"What do you fear, Robyn?" Davmiran asked, surprised at his friend's concern. "Surely nothing bad can come of me finally talking to my brother!"

"No, it is not merely the encounter with Tomas that concerns me, though events of this magnitude will impact upon us all," Robyn replied sincerely. "But, any attempt to even utilize the rings would definitely generate an energy that we would not want anyone else to notice."

"Anyone like Colton you mean?" Dav asked.

"Yes, or perhaps one of the Possessed who have been tracking us and the others," he said.

"The others? You mean my brother and his group?"

"Yes. But not them alone. The sisters who left here before we arrived have been followed too."

"They are safe now. But Robyn..." the boy said, looking into the other's eyes, "...they are no longer together," he said.

"The sisters?"

"Yes. They have separated. I have been meaning to tell you this, but it did not seem all that important," he said with his eyes half closed. "I cannot sense the second one clearly any longer.

Before, the shards provided me with images of the two of them, and now I see only one whom I can recognize for certain. Tamara, the stout one, travels with a Drue. The other seems to be there at one moment and then not at the next, and even when she is present before my mind's eye, her image is vague and unlike what it was before."

"But she is still alive and unharmed?" Robyn asked.

"Yes, definitely. No harm has come to her."

"That is good at least. Why they have separated, I do not know."

"With both the ring and the shards communicating with me, this is all getting very confusing. And tiring!" Dav said. "They speak to me differently, yet they speak nonetheless."

"They are both powerful relics though they are of diverse origins. I am more familiar with the derivation of the shards power than of the ring's," Robyn confessed.

"The ring feels more like an old friend. It comforts me, like a good conscience and seems to give me advice. When the shards speak, I feel as if I am reading a book whose pages are not in order. The story jumps forward and backward and forward again arbitrarily."

"We must work with both of them, Dav. We must work hard. While we are in Parth, we have an opportunity to do that. Though I am convinced that neither the ring nor the shards are anything more than tools for you, they are of tremendous importance, and learning how to make the most use out of them is crucial."

"I agree, Robyn. The ring seems to be more efficacious. I can use it to help me and enhance my own abilities. The shards tell me things and allow me to see things that my eyes alone would not, but they do so in images, not words. Yet, even the images feel incomplete somehow. I sense a yearning in the shards," he explained. "They reach beyond me. It sounds so odd, does is not? The ring itself has a voice, and though I do not recognize it, it feels as familiar as an old shoe."

"Odd? No," Robyn replied. "I would not expect anything less. But it is clear that you are learning from them both already," Robyn commented with satisfaction. "I am not unfamiliar myself with the ring, as you know. I can only assume that the silver one that your brother possesses is similar in nature to yours. I could be wrong, though Dav, and they may be totally different. But, in any case, I am sure that I can help you to utilize its power. It was quite an experience for me that last time in Pardatha, and it was also incredibly draining," he recalled. "Does communication with it tire you at all?" he asked.

"I cannot say that I have communicated much with it. Rather, it speaks to me. I would like very much to learn how to speak back."

"That is one of the first things we will work on then. That is if Filaree and Cairn are willing to share you with me," he smiled. "There is also much that you could learn from Cairn. He traveled with Tomas for quite some time. Their friendship is strong. He is also familiar with his strengths, and he knows his personality. Though you were the one he was called to Pardatha to assist, he spirited him out of his home when the enemy had already located him and escorted him all the way to the city," Robyn reminded him. "And by the way, thoughts of the shards are never too distant from a Chosen's mind, though they remind us always of the losses that they are the results of. Nevertheless, we must examine and understand them as well. They may prove to be more potent and more useful than the ring itself, " Robyn said.

"Although they remind us of the losses, they also represent what can never be lost," Dav replied.

"Yes, that is true," Robyn agreed, and he nodded. "As we begin, we will both learn more. Though I am to be your teacher, that fact does not preclude me from gaining knowledge in the process. And it is important too that we learn about the nature of this shield that surrounds us."

"Does it worry you?" the boy asked.

"Anything that prohibits me from moving freely worries me, Dav. But I do not sense anything evil about it. It even has a vague familiarity to it."

"It is here to protect us, at least for now, not to harm us. But it is quite impenetrable!" Davmiran said, impressed still with the power of it.

"Quite. I have tried many times to breach it, and I cannot. I feel comfortable with it around us, though I am unaccustomed to being restricted by anything so completely. I am also very anxious for you to learn how to communicate through the ring. But, you must be very careful. The results of your efforts are surely going to be unpredictable at the least. I hope that the shield does not restrict your attempt as well."

"I do not think it will affect those efforts. This barrier's protection is much more corporeal in nature. The ring does not require a spatial continuum in order to transmit thoughts. That much I have learned already from it," Dav replied. "Who do you think has placed this protection around us? Have you any suspicions?"

"I know of only a few who are capable of such things. The trees of course could have been responsible, but I am convinced that it does not stem from them. It feels altogether different. Premoran alas is also an unlikely choice right now. He himself is under great duress."

"He is alive. The shards tell me that," Dav said.

"I feel it too, though his power is weakened by his imprisonment."

"Who else then, Robyn?" the boy asked, and he scrutinized him closely.

"There is one other who has always lived just outside of convention. Though her loyalty to the earth is unquestionable, she is somewhat of a renegade, and always has been," Robyn said.

"And you are not, Robyn? You must understand her well then," Davmiran said with a smile.

"Yes, I suppose many have thought of me so. But not in the same was as Sidra."

"Sidra? I am unfamiliar with the name. But that is no surprise. There is so little that I remember."

"Most people are unfamiliar with that name, Dav. I highly doubt that even if you regained your past, any knowledge of her would have been a part of it. She has remained quite reclusive. But, her power rivals that of any Chosen I have ever known."

"She is not bonded?" Dav asked.

"No. She declined when the offer was made many tiels ago."

"Declined? How unusual," the boy said contemplatively.

"No one had ever declined a request like that before. And no one has since. Sidra is different," he said, with a definite fondness in his voice. "She claimed that she was unable to bond with the Lalas who chose her because they were too different. It caused quite a stir at the time," he recalled with a smile.

"You obviously admire her," Davmiran commented. "You knew her well? Was it her rebelliousness or is there more about her that you are not telling me?"

"You are quite intuitive for one so young, you know? Either that or I have lost my ability to conceal my inner feelings," Robyn said, and he grinned at the boy. "Oh, yes, there is much more about her that I am not telling you. And, I do not intend to tell you, young man," he smiled again. "But I did admire her strength of character. It was not easy to deny the tree."

"How is it that you are so familiar with her?" Davmiran asked, with a suspicious look in his big, blue eyes. "Which Lalas was it whom she denied?"

"How did you guess?" Robyn asked. "I really have become that easy to read?"

"No. It was not a guess. I carry the shards, remember? Images come to me all the time," he said. "Was it difficult for you in the beginning knowing that you were not Promanthea's first choice?" he asked bluntly.

"No. Actually, I was surprised when Sidra declined him. But I was overjoyed at the same time. It was my good fortune. How could I have been disappointed? I never really thought of myself as a second choice, but rather just another choice," he said.

"I suppose," the boy replied, unconvinced. "Did you ever discuss it with him?" Davmiran asked.

"My feelings about Sidra? No. I found no reason to. But he harbored a bitterness for her that I felt for quite some time," Robyn recalled. "Perhaps bitterness is the wrong word to describe his emotions, but he was hurt by the rejection in a very human way," Robyn said, as he remembered those days from long ago. "It was not his pride that bothered him. Rather, I think that he felt that he had lost a great opportunity, and he regretted it profoundly, therefore his thoughts about her were negative. I was bonded shortly thereafter, and the beginning of our relationship was the only time I can recall when Promanthea concealed things from me," he explained, though his voice had suddenly become strained. "Sidra left Tamarand and never returned again. She moved up north near Eleutheria and lived a totally reclusive life. I have been told that she still resides in the hills somewhat near the city, though no one I know has actually seen her in countless tiels. One thing I can be certain of is that she must now be at least as formidable a woman as she was a maiden."

"What is the source of her power?" the boy asked.

"It is uncertain. She is not of the counsel, though I know that Premoran and Calista had conferred with her in the past, as had the others over time," Robyn explained. "I think that they all realized later that what she did was for the best. She just could not be bonded to a tree. Though her power is of the earth, it is different than any other I have experienced."

"Was she from Tamarand originally? Has she family there still?"

"No, to both questions. She was from Odelot, and she came to Tamarand alone after her own city's demise. She hid her bitterness toward Colton well from most people, but not from me. I sensed her pain as well as her immense hatred. She never spoke of her losses, but they must have been great," Robyn related.

"And you think that she is capable of creating this?" Davmiran asked, referring to the shield.

"I know that she is. I just do not know why she would intervene now when she has never done so in the past," he said.

"The times have changed. Calista is gone. Premoran is a captive in Sedahar. The trees themselves are dying. When else would one of power make a stand?" Dav asked.

"True. Very true," Robyn contemplated. "This shield certainly has her mark upon it. It is as unconventional as she is," he smiled.

"Do you think that she knows something that would cause her to assist us now in such a manner?"

"That we are imperiled in some way? That without her help something terrible would happen to us," he replied, looking deeply into Davmiran's blue eyes. "That the danger is so grave that it requires her attention and assistance. Nothing short of that would have motivated her to act I fear, so I venture to guess that she does. She has lived apart for a long time."

"Is this what you believe?" Davmiran asked him sincerely.

"If it is in fact she who has done this, she is buying us some time, Dav, time that we would not have had without her intervention. We must utilize it well. We may not have another opportunity to work and learn in such safety," he answered gravely. "Sidra would not get involved unless she felt it was totally necessary. At least not in such an obvious manner. Though her enmity for the Dark Lord was beyond measure those many tiels ago, it never prompted her to intervene before. She has left these things to the trees and the Chosen."

"Speaking of Lalas, Robyn, have you communicated with Promanthea recently?" Davmiran then asked, as if this question followed naturally after the others.

"I have not had the opportunity," he replied, and he looked away from the boy.

"Oh. I see," he said, though it was clear by his tone of voice that he did not believe Robyn's words for a minute. "We have been quite busy of late," Davmiran commented, seeking to ease the sudden tension that filled the air.

"Some other time perhaps, we can discuss this in more detail, Dav," he then said, knowing that it was unfair of him to expect the boy to settle for such an obviously false explanation. "There are some things I need to sort out first," he replied defensively.

"You seem reluctant about it. Is that normal for a Chosen?" he asked.

"Reluctant to talk about this subject or to commune with Promanthea?" he asked, but he did not wait for an answer. "What is normal today, Dav?" Robyn replied earnestly. "To be honest, the last time Promanthea and I spoke, I felt as if he was keeping something from me, and it disturbed me so much that I have avoided him since," Robyn confessed. "I had that feeling only once before with him as I just told you, and he was so totally unwilling to discuss his behavior then that there was no point in me continuing to ask him about it. This time as well, he made it clear to me that it was not a subject that he wished to address."

"You were hurt, Robyn?" he asked.

"Yes, very hurt. You cannot imagine the intensity of the bond between a Lalas and its Chosen. This rejection was more difficult to bear than if he had been my own father," Robyn explained. "The hurt is so strong that it feels almost physical and I cannot dwell upon it. It would consume too much of my energy."

"I am sorry," Davmiran said sincerely. "Though I am not a Chosen and I am unbonded; I carry the shards, remember? Maybe I can help you deal with this, Robyn."

"Thank you. I will certainly consider your offer more fully later," he replied gratefully. "Perhaps you are right. Until now, I have tried not to remember how it felt when last we conversed, and that in itself has not been healthy for me. Fortunately, my mind has been on other matters most of the time, and ..."

"Robyn, I need to speak with my brother," Davmiran said again, interrupting Robyn in mid-sentence with an urgent tone in his voice. "I must not wait any longer."

"Let us go then," he replied recognizing the exigency, as he pulled the heavy door open for his friend.

Tomas was sitting in his room staring out of the window across the rooftops of Avalain. It was early morning and the sun was rising still. It cast a welcoming light in all directions, and it dissolved the darkness and turned the night into day. He and his companions had settled in quickly after arriving to the shock of having virtually the entire population of Talamar camped outside the gates. Queen Esta was a marvel at statesmanship, which was not a surprise. Her grace and demeanor suited itself to leadership, along with her other qualities, particularly her strength of character. The people of the city truly loved her and were comforted by her return, and they looked to her for political leadership as well as moral guidance.

In a short span of time, the camps were fully organized. Her army assisted those Talamaran's who chose to remain, in constructing temporary housing and facilities that would be more than adequate to last them until the spring thaw. They could then decide better where they wished to take up a more permanent residence. Being displaced so abruptly afforded them all few immediate choices.

The mere presence of the Knights of Avalain was more than enough of an incentive to keep their guests behaving properly. Talamar had never been a city of fighters. The people adhered to the rules imposed by the guards, and though many of them were reluctant to work as hard as their circumstances required, for the most part they complied adequately.

Tomas, Stephanie, Preston and Elion were left to their own devices for the first few days. Queen Esta had a lot to do upon her return and they did not wish to interfere, nor did they wish to impose upon her when she was being pulled in so many directions at once. They settled in to their rooms without much difficulty, and they each enjoyed the luxury of good food and a good bed for the first time in a long while. They also took this opportunity to wander the broad streets of Avalain and marvel at its beauty. In addition, there was so much for them to discuss and to plan that the days went by very quickly.

The ring that Tomas wore around his neck had been bothering him of late. It seemed always to be trying to talk to him, to communicate with him, but whenever he grasped it and attempted to focus upon it, the feelings disappeared. Nevertheless, its presence against his skin was constantly one that he was completely aware of. Now though, he felt compelled more often to lift the ring in his hands and examine it, though he was unsure of just why. It beckoned to him, but it did not reveal anything. He thought perhaps that one of the council was trying to reach him, but when he tried to determine who if any it was, without unnecessarily generating a link, he realized that it was not a Chosen who was the source of this feeling. The ring itself was stirring.

From the moment he retrieved it from the sapling's heart until this day, he felt its latent potency. He wondered if there were things his uncle Trevor would have wanted to tell him if he'd had the opportunity. Surely he must have known it was there all along. Maybe he even planted it there all those tiels ago when the tree was still tiny, knowing that it would be safe until the day Tomas retrieved it. The myriad of questions would never all be answered, and Tomas felt the emptiness in his heart that this longing to know generated. But it was not simply a longing for knowledge that weighed so heavily upon his soul. He felt the sundering of his links to the past; the seemingly systematic disruption of his history and his heritage, and he pined for the memories that he would never be able to have.

Despite the fact that he wore the ring always and that it surely and certainly evoked feelings and memories of his legacy however ephemeral and nondescript, he never looked upon it as a weapon or an independent source of power. Rather, it seemed to be an extension of his own self in a way. The heat that it generated was comforting, not disturbing, and he was forever aware of its presence. Today though, it burned with an uncommon intensity.

Tomas was concentrating so thoroughly upon this that he barely was aware of the soft knocking upon his door.

"Tomas? Are you awake?" he finally heard Elion's muffled voice sound through the heavy wood.

He turned from the window and hastily made his way across the thickly carpeted floor.

"Come in," he said, while opening the door for his friend. "I was lost in thought and I did not hear you. Have you been standing here for long?" he asked.

"No. Not really. I thought perhaps you were resting, and if so, I did not want to disturb you," Elion said. "I was just about to turn and walk away. Is everything okay?"

"Yes. Why do you ask?" Tomas replied.

"No particular reason. You just look preoccupied, that's all."

"Well, to be honest, I am. You knew that, didn't you?"

"I suppose," Elion replied. "Though I did not realize it until now. Is there anything you want to talk about?" he asked.

Tomas walked back to the leaded glass window and sighed. With his back to Elion, he started to speak.

"I have worn this ring around my neck since the moment I left Pardeau. Until I used it to link with the Chosen before we got here, it has been nothing more than a comfort to me. I felt its warmth and I felt its power, but it never impinged upon me in any way."

He then turned around and faced the elf.

"It is beckoning to me now, Elion," he said seriously. "I do not know what it wants because it does not speak in words to me, but images flood my thoughts. Sometimes I feel as if they are my own memories that I should somehow recall," he explained.

"Can you describe one to me?" Elion asked. "Maybe I can help."

"You know that I never met my parents? I was removed from their home as a newborn and I did not know of them until recently. Yet, I have been seeing faces and locations, rooms and buildings, that I believe have something to do with my family. My aunt and uncle told me what they felt was safe to divulge, but these images could not be stemming from anything they said," Tomas said.

"How do you know that it is the ring that is provoking these experiences? Maybe you are just longing for your family, and you are therefore imagining what they and their surroundings might have looked like," Elion replied.

"I have seen my brother's face, Elion," he said soberly, and he looked the elf directly in the eyes. "His blue eyes were staring straight into mine."

"Now Tomas, I do not mean to cast doubt upon what you believe you have seen, but how hard would it be for you to picture your brother? After all, you are twins!" Elion said.

"He has a need to contact me, Elion. I just know it!" Tomas said. "It is not my imagination. And I do not know how to use the ring to facilitate this."

"You had no problem communicating with the other Chosen. What is the difference here? Can you not just use the same method as you did then?   That is, if you are certain that it is Davmiran who is beckoning you."

"I am sure, Elion. I am quite sure. And I have tried to respond. Something is interfering with my efforts. I wish I could be more specific, but it just feels as if each time I reach out to and then through the ring, the link that I know is there is severed before it is even completed."

"Then you must try a different way," Elion said. "Or maybe from a different place. How long have you been attempting to communicate with him?"

"For the past hour or so," Tomas replied.

"Was tonight the first night that you tried?"

"Yes, It was. I never though it was safe to attempt it before. And besides, I did not initiate it either this time. The ring did. "

"I think we should go find Esta and ask her if there is a place in the castle or elsewhere in Avalain that she thinks would be more secure than here. Maybe someone *is* trying to prevent you from reaching him," Elion said. "You know that there are others who want very badly to stop you from ever talking to your brother, let alone meeting him. Caeltin's reach is quite extensive. It would not surprise me if he was behind your problems."

"It would not surprise me either. In fact, I would have expected it of him if we were still out on the road. I just did not think that he could do anything to us here in Avalain," Tomas said dejectedly.

"Neither did I, but things are changing every day. We have to be careful wherever we might be. You and your brother are so important to all of us."

"I will not endanger him. If the Evil One thinks that he can reach my brother through me, he is mistaken," Tomas replied adamantly.

"I think he is probably more concerned that you will reach him yourself, Tomas," Elion surmised. "He has two of you to contend with now, when before he thought there was only one. He must have been quite surprised when he found that out!"

"Davmiran and I cannot be together. That would be foolish of us," Tomas said.

"I agree. But if you two could confer with one another, perhaps there is no harm in that."

"I suppose," Tomas replied.

"What is troubling you?" Elion asked earnestly.

"My brother and I are like two lost souls. He has no memory of his past, and I never knew of mine. We are all that is left of our family and of our history, and yet it is too dangerous for us to even meet," Tomas confessed.

"It is best that you do not spend time in the same location. There is no question that Caeltin would be overjoyed if he could dispatch the two of you at once. But if you are able to talk to Dav in some way, that may ease your concerns, and maybe in time you will also be able to be together."

"The time will come," Tomas replied. "But it is not now."

"Ironic, is it not? I found Davmiran and brought him to my home away from the city that he was supposed to be awakened in. And Cairn found you and brought you to the city your brother was supposed to be in. Does anything ever proceed as planned?" Elion asked.

"According to someone's plan perhaps."

"As long as it is not Caeltin's," Elion remarked. "In the meanwhile, I think we should find another location within the city where we can try to use the ring and find out once and for all if the two of you can actually communicate through them."

"Should we really consult with Esta about this? I imagine that if anyone knows where it would be safe for us to go in this city she does," Tomas said.

"On second thought, I think she has enough to contend with right now. Besides, I do know where we can go," Elion replied.

"You do?"

"Yes, I am sure of it! When Filaree arrived at Pardatha she was accompanied by a loyal and devoted knight, Cameron, for whom she had more than a common affection," he recalled cheerlessly. "I told you the story of his courage and of his sad demise."

"Yes, I remember, though she herself had never spoken to me about him. The Queen told me that they were friends since they were children," Tomas recalled. "There were many tragedies that occurred that fateful day. And many courageous warriors," Tomas said to Elion, and he emphasized the elf's own role in the victory before the gates of Pardatha.

"Perhaps, Tomas. But I never felt courageous. I did what I had to do under the circumstances, and I was very scared," he said candidly.

"Who ever said that heroes were not allowed to be scared?

And, is not the definition of a courageous person exactly what you just described? A person doing what he or she has to do under the circumstances regardless of concern for oneself?"

"I suppose," Elion said modestly. "But in any case, my point in bringing this event up was that Cameron and Filaree had a strange and meaningful encounter in the woods just outside of Avalain before they got anywhere near Pardatha. There is a place called the Winding Woods that I believe is still protected."

"By the Lalas?" Tomas asked.

"No, but by less sentient trees than Lalas, though safe nonetheless. At least, safe from the Dark Lord's eavesdropping."

"How can you be sure?" the boy asked.

"Filaree told me a story when we were together in Pardatha about her father and another from Avalain named Pembar. Her father had known him well many tiels ago, and she and Cameron had to pass through the Winding Woods on their way to meet Baladar."

"I remember hearing it too, now that you mention it," Tomas recalled.

"This forest, though dangerous in its own right, was a haven as well. I am sure that it would be a safe place to communicate with your brother from. Filaree said that the thousands of trees that make up the woods live and act as one, and that once you step foot within the borders of the Winding Woods, you are in its world and no others can influence you."

"Nor can they assist you!" Tomas added as a warning.

"Why would we require assistance? We intend only to enter for a brief moment and then to leave the way we came. We are not trying to cross through them, as she and Cameron did," Elion said.

"Did Filaree not have a token which she wore around her neck to identify her?" Tomas asked.

"The black tree?" Elion acknowledged.

"Yes. The item that her father had given her."

"Do you think that we need something like that just to go in there and come right back out?" Elion asked.

"How am I to know, Elion. But can we take the chance without knowing for certain?" Tomas asked.

"How badly do you need to speak with Davmiran?" Elion inquired seriously.

"The need is dire," he replied seriously.

"Then what other choices do we have? The risk is greater for us all if Caeltin is able to eavesdrop upon you. If we feel that the place is unsafe for us, we will leave at once. Let us venture in carefully and not too deeply."

"Or if another whose allegiance we cannot vouch for interferes," Tomas said with a strange look in his eyes.

"One of the Possessed, you mean?" Elion asked, confused by the boy's use of words and his lack of specificity.

"Perhaps," Tomas replied, though it was clear from his response that the Possessed were not the ones he now feared.

"Who else did you have in mind, Tomas?" the elf asked.

"There are many now whom we can no longer trust. The Dark Lord's reach has grown longer of late, and he has touched and befouled some of those whose fealty we never questioned before. It is hard to determine exactly where the enemy lurks," the boy said ominously.

"Even in Avalain?" Elion asked, surprised.

Tomas looked intensely into Elion's eyes. There was a sad and worried expression upon his face that deeply disturbed him, and that made the boy look many tiels older than he was.

"Few allegiances cannot be sundered by his evil," Tomas replied. "It is best that we trust as few as possible."

"If you suspect something or someone, please share your concerns with me. I cannot help you if I am kept in the dark," Elion said.

"I have no one specific in mind," the boy replied. "I just think that we should be more careful now than ever before. The influence of the trees is waning and we must be prudent. The Lalas have concerns of their own, and ours and theirs may no longer always be parallel."

"You frighten me sometime, Tomas. Was I not the one to begin this conversation by advising you that we should watch our backs? How long have you felt this way?"

"Since the day you carried me into the cave. The feeling has never fully left me."

"More the reason we should seek the shelter of the Winding Woods. It is as independent as any place on earth.," Elion replied.

"Do you know where the entrance is?" Tomas asked.

"Yes," Elion answered knowingly. "I believe that I do. It will take us some time to get there though. We have to cross through Chilmark first."

"Is that a problem?" Tomas questioned.

"It should not be. The plains are usually safe, although these days, nothing is for certain any longer."

"How long will it take us to get to the woods?"

"If we ride fast and do not stop on the way, it should not take us more than three hours or so. That should leave you enough time to do what you need to do, and we can still be back by nightfall. Six hours round trip traveling time and an hour for you and your brother sounds about right."

"I cannot imagine needing more time once we arrive. That is, as long as nothing unforeseen delays us," Tomas replied.

"Do you sense something?" Elion asked apprehensively.

"No. I do not. But as you said before, things these days are unpredictable. I hope the woods welcome us."

"Unless the trees therein have been unduly influenced since Filaree was last there, they will not refuse us," Elion said with confidence.

"I have no doubt that they will allow us to enter. But, will they also allow us to leave?" Tomas asked ominously.

"We will soon find out, Tomas," the elfin Prince replied.

"The sooner the better then. The ring is burning a hole in my chest, Elion."

Tomas grabbed a cloak from a peg on the wall and tossed it over his shoulders.

"Let us go," the elf said, and he led Tomas out the door.

They walked down the wide hallway to the staircase at its end. It wound down a number of flights and then opened up into a common room on the ground level of the castle. A few people were milling about, but no one that they recognized. Together, they crossed the broad floor and exited through a doorway onto the courtyard. The palace stables were close by, and in minutes they were saddling up their horses for the journey to the Winding Woods. Tomas paused for a moment, reached inside his tunic and then clasped the ring tightly in his palm. He closed his eyes and allowed the warmth it generated to permeate his entire body. Just as suddenly, he released the delicate silver band and climbed into his saddle.

"Are you ready, Elion?" he asked his companion.

"Are you, Tomas?" the elf replied, and the boy nodded solemnly. "Good. I needed to know that.

"This meeting has been long overdue and many times

postponed. It has never felt right. Now the moment is upon us and I yearn for it so," he confessed.

"May the First guide us and protect us," Elion said, and they both spurred their mounts onward.

Tomas said something in response, but his words were lost in the rush of the wind as they sped out the stable doors and across the cobbled streets of Avalain.

Chapter Thirty-four

The thick woods gave way to scrub and brush, which made it difficult for them to conceal their whereabouts from anyone or anything that might have been passing passed overhead. But, the flat terrain and lack of physical obstructions were more conducive to swift travel than the dense and tangled forest from which they recently emerged. The sky was streaked with grey clouds that pulsed with an odd lightning unaccompanied by the thunder claps of natural storms. There was a heaviness to the air that they could not attribute to the intense humidity alone. It seemed more tangible than mere moisture, and far more menacing. The group of four lead their horses carefully and determinedly across the plains, in the direction of Sedahar.

"Did you see that, Teetoo?" Giles pointed overhead.

"Long before you did, I suspect," the Weloh replied.

"What do you think it was?" Clovis inquired.

"I am uncertain. But, you can be sure that whatever travels here uncloaked does so only with the Dark Lord's consent," Teetoo said.

"Except for us," Giles said.

"Yes, except for us," Teetoo concurred.

"I feel so exposed. How are we to maintain the secrecy of our arrival if we have to travel so openly?" Alemar asked.

"I am not leading you totally unprotected into the jaws of evil, Princess. It seems that Premoran's gift to me has powers beyond those of communication," Teetoo explained, and he revealed the brightly glowing bracelet on his wrist. "I believe that this is masking us somewhat. Have you not noticed that what little life we have encountered since we left the forest has barely been aware of our passage here?"

"I did, actually, Teetoo. But I paid it little mind. I assumed that these creatures were simply unafraid or unconcerned," Alemar replied.

"I found it strange that they allowed themselves to be nearly trod upon!" Clovis remarked.

"Inured to the realities of Sedahar?" Teetoo commented.

"Maybe," Clovis said. "One would still think that life had meaning for them."

"Here, just the opposite is the case," Teetoo said ominously.

"Are you saying the he and his spies cannot see us nor sense our presence?" Alemar asked.

"To an extent, yes. If he suspected our arrival, others more astute would be searching. He cannot see us because he is not looking."

"And if he was?" Giles asked.

"Need I answer that?" Teetoo replied.

"How long do you suspect we will be able to proceed in this way?" Alemar said.

"As long as the bracelet's power conceals us," the Weloh answered. "Do you have the map, Princess?"

They could see a structure towering in the distance but no matter how hard they tried to focus their eyes upon it, it remained blurred and nondescript. Even the incredibly sharp eyes of the Weloh could not pierce the obfuscation. She withdrew the rolled parchment from her knapsack and handed it to Teetoo. Giles and Clovis flanked Alemar protectively.

"Do not expect things here to be as they appear elsewhere," Teetoo warned them as he unfolded the thin parchment. "Most is artifice and sham. The truth is hard to glean from deception."

They all felt quite vulnerable as they marched across the plain, but other than the clouds that streaked quickly overhead and the scurrying of an occasional small animal, nothing else moved.

"As I had hoped, his eyes are elsewhere," Teetoo commented. "One as arrogant as Colton would not feel as if he needed to guard his own home. But we still must locate the entrance."

"Let's hope that the eyes of his generals are elsewhere as well," Clovis said.

"Generals?" Teetoo questioned. "He has no generals. None save the Dark Lord himself wield power in his realm."

"What of the Possessed?" Alemar asked.

"Outside of Sedahar they can exert themselves. Within the boundaries of this horrid place, no power is effective except his own unless he so wills it," the Weloh replied.

"Lucky for us, I guess," Giles said.

Alemar spurred her mount forward and left the custody of her friends in order to ride beside Teetoo for a while.

"Can it be..." she asked, "...that he has left Premoran unguarded?"

"Anything is possible, Princess. We will not know how he

keeps him captive until the moment we find him. What we do know is that he is alive and that he is a prisoner."

"It is hard to imagine that a Lalas once grew somewhere near here. It all looks so hopeless."

"And when one dies, what emotions are evoked?" Teetoo asked.

"Hopelessness," Alemar replied immediately. "Does that mean we are nearing where it once was?"

"Perhaps, Princess. All here is hopeless beyond measure. We must examine the map closely for the signs if we are to find the opening," Teetoo said and he turned his sharp eyes upon the ancient map. "There are symbols of power upon it. We will not be able to find anything that remains from before, so we must find the locus of this power if we wish to find the entrance."

"Do you think that Premoran can sense the bracelet that you wear?"

"I do not know, Alemar. If he can, then he will know already that we approach. Whether that is a good thing or a bad thing, I cannot determine."

"Hush, you two!" Clovis admonished them as he rode to catch up. "Something is afoot. I see movement ahead."

An eddy of dust rose in the distance and they all stopped advancing in order to try and determine its origin.

"Another!" Teetoo pointed to the left of the first one they spotted.

"And yet another!" Alemar remarked.

"What are they?" Giles asked.

They stared at the puffs and swirls, and before their very eyes the shapeless mists began to coagulate into hideous forms.

"What do you see?" Teetoo asked Alemar in a strange tone of voice.

The Princess stared ahead and tears flooded her eyes.

"I see my brother," she replied. "He is in agony. I must help him!"

"And you, Clovis? What do you see there ahead?" and he pointed to the same swirling fog that Alemar had just described.

"My mother! She crying out to me. Can you not hear her too? She calls my name," he said pleadingly.

Alemar restrained him with her hand as she quickly realized that it was a chimera that she saw. Kalon was dead. She forced the sorrow away and focused upon her companions.

"Hold, Clovis. Abide with me. What you see is not real," she said reassuringly.

While she comforted Clovis, Giles leapt forward on his horse before she had a chance to detain him.

"Ariel? Is that you?" Giles asked as he swiftly broke away from the group. "Can it be you?"

"Stop, Giles!" Teetoo ordered him while reaching out with lightening speed and grasping the reins of his horse out of his hands.

"I must go to her! She needs me!" he replied and he tried to snap the leather straps away from the Weloh.

"It is illusion, Giles. There is nothing there! Take hold of yourself!" Teetoo said. "All of you! Listen to me! We have crossed into Sedahar. Nothing is real. Come closer to me!" Teetoo ordered them and he raised both of his graceful arms. "Take hold of me. Touch me!" he instructed them. "The power of the bracelet will help you to see through this deception."

Alemar was the first to obey. She sidled up next to the Weloh and placed her palm atop his right forearm.

"Dust!" she exclaimed. "It is no more than a cloud of dust!"

Clovis followed suit immediately after and he too took hold of Teetoo's extended arm, but Giles was too captivated by the semblance of his young lover to break free of the compelling urge to touch her. He walked forward in a daze.

"Giles, no!" Alemar shouted.

He turned his face to the Princess briefly, but the look upon it was confused and uncomprehending.

"She is dead, Giles!" Clovis yelled. "It is not Ariel that you see!"

"Ariel?" Giles said again, and he ignored his friends. "I am coming, Ariel."

"Stop, Giles! Stop!" Alemar screamed.

Giles turned toward her quickly, and she saw in his eyes that he was totally lost. Without hesitating any further, she leapt forward, letting go of Teetoo's arm. Images of painful and hurtful things appeared everywhere. Long lost friends, dead relatives and sorrowful visions began to form in the inky mists that swirled all around, but she ignored them. With determination, she reached her friend's side, and then she quickly and tenderly took his hand in her own.

"Come, Giles. What you see is untrue. You must ignore it.

Ariel is dead, Giles. She cannot be here!" Alemar said.

"Ariel? But she is there right in front of us. You see her too, don't you? Tell me you see her too!" he pleaded.

"I see only evil and delusion, Giles," the Princess said, as she stroked his arm.

While Alemar was gently guiding Giles away from this vile seduction, Teetoo and Clovis joined them.

"What you long for the most and can never have is what Colton wishes you to see. That is what Sedahar is about, Giles; longing and pain, illusion and disappointment," Teetoo said. "And cruelty!"

"Come, friend!" Clovis said. "Ariel was a good and loving woman, but she is gone, Giles. What you see here will only rekindle the fire that burns your soul still."

Giles shook his head back and forth as if he was trying to clear it.

"Concentrate, Giles. See this place for what it really is," Alemar said.

Looking distraught and confused, he rubbed his eyes hard with the knuckles of his hands and squinted at the images before him.

"Ariel?" he said once more with a heavy heart, but even as he did so, the illusion began to fade away. He looked at the others standing beside him, and he smiled the half smile of a realization reaffirmed. "I thought for a moment it was really her," he said dolefully. "Stupid me," he said, and the others sighed with relief.

"The power here is strong, and your love for her must also have been exceedingly strong. Do not fault yourself. Had your love not been true, these visions would not be haunting you," Teetoo said. "Come now. We must continue on. Though the bracelet may conceal our movements, it obviously cannot protect us from the traps that death and yearning have prepared for us."

They walked through the visions of pain and suffering, across the barren plain that sustained no life; a precursor to dissolution. Their heads hung low from the weight of the emptiness that surrounded them. In the distance, the tower of Sedahar loomed, but it was still blurred and indistinct. The sky flickered and pulsed with errant energy. The air was odorless, and no matter how deeply they breathed it in, it did not refresh them nor sa'Tisfy their need. They found themselves constantly gasping for more. It seemed almost as if they had entered a tomb that had never been breached before, and they felt as if they were being violated with each step that they took.

"What shall we do with the horses?" Clovis asked. "We cannot leave them outside once we find the entrance," he said.

"What choice have we?" Giles asked. "They can forage here whilst we find Premoran."

"There is nothing here for them to forage," Teetoo commented. "We must direct them back toward the woods."

"They will understand," Alemar said. "I will send them on their way when the time comes."

"How will we return then if they are not here for us when we come back?" Giles questioned. "After we free the old man it will be hard for us to hide."

"They will not survive here anyway even if we bade them stay. Besides, once we have left them, the bracelet will no longer keep their presence secret. Not only will they give us away if they remain outside the gates, but they will surely meet an even swifter demise," Teetoo said.

"Their chances are best if we let them try to return to the forest," Alemar agreed.

"We are almost there. Do you see the symbol glowing more brightly?" the Weloh asked, and he held the map up before them.

They all looked ahead at the massive white tower that still seemed so unclear and ill-defined. It seemed enormous, far larger than they had ever imagined, and it looked so impregnable and daunting from their vantage point. The walls were sheer and smooth, and no windows interrupted the imposing surfaces. It was a forbidding place and it nearly sucked what little breath they still had remaining within them out of their tired lungs.

"Over there!" Teetoo shouted. "There is a mark upon the ground," he said, while pointing to the right of them. He folded the parchment and carefully put it inside the folds of his clothing. "We will need this once we descend," he said to Alemar.

She nodded to him and strained her eyes in order to see what he was referring to.

"The place that is not blurry? Yes, I see it. It is all that I can see clearly," Alemar said.

"Follow me," Teetoo instructed them, and he dismounted from his horse. "Send them away now, Princess. Firstspeed!" Teetoo said as he handed his reins to Alemar who had already slid gracefully from her saddle.

Alemar spoke into the ear of her horse and it whinnied in response. She removed its bridle and saddle and motioned to the others to do the same. Then she carefully took them from Teetoo's mount as well.

"Bury these as best you can," she said to Giles and Clovis.

She whispered to each of the animals. They looked as if they understood while pawing the ground expectantly.

"Go now!" she said aloud. "Stop for no one or nothing!"

The horses bolted off in the direction that they had come, raising clouds of dust and debris behind them as they ran.

"Will they be safe?" she asked Teetoo.

"We can only hope," the Weloh replied. "But we have no time to worry about them now. That is most definitely the entrance," he said as he pointed ahead. "Follow me quickly. If the horses are noticed, it will not be hard to trace their movements back to us."

They all ran behind Teetoo for the one patch of clarity that distinguished itself in the distance, as the sky above churned and seethed violently. They could see the hole in the surface of the earth. It was difficult to tell which seemed more menacing to them; the tower of Sedahar or the passage that led beneath it.

"Brace yourselves!" he warned as they approached. "The instant you step down into one of the Forbidden Places you will feel like you have never felt before! Are you ready?" he asked.

They nodded in response.

"Go then, Alemar. Enter!" he said to her.

She immediately descended and disappeared into the darkness below. Giles followed quickly, not wanting to leave Alemar alone for even a moment, and Clovis scrambled down behind him. Teetoo scanned the horizon for one final moment with a sad and far away look in his eyes. He took a deep breath that rippled across his slender back, and then he stepped deliberately into the gaping orifice.

Chapter Thirty-five

The snow was still falling and the air was so cold that they had to cover their noses and mouths to stop the moisture in their breath from freezing as they exhaled. They had draped their horses in heavy blankets and made sure that they rested them as often as necessary so that they would not collapse from hypothermia. Thick puffs of cloudy air blew from the horses nostrils in rhythmic bursts. They stopped frequently, and warmed a few cups of water over a small flame. Then they drank it slowly and deliberately while letting the animals partake of it as well.

"It is unbearably cold!" Conrad said, as he rubbed his gloved hands together briskly. "I cannot remember a time when this waterway froze over completely like this," he said, indicating the rocky terrain ahead. "The falls always kept the water flowing no matter what the temperature."

"Save your breath, father," Caroline said. "If we cannot find shelter soon, we will need all the body heat we have."

"We have not come this far to die of exposure!" Dalloway said. "We will find a place to rest," he said determinedly.

They rode in silence for another hour or so, hoping that the sun would break free of the dense clouds that obscured it. Soon, it would be setting altogether and then they would really feel the worst of the cold, particularly as the evening winds began to sweep across the riverbed.

"Look, Caroline!" her father shouted, and he shattered the silence with his exclamation. "Is that not a footprint?"

"By the First, it is!" Dalloway said.

"It is a fresh one too," Caroline said.

"What type of animal left it?" Conrad asked.

"A cat of some kind I think, by the looks of it," she replied. "That would be good, Father. The cats speak more clearly than some of the less intelligent beasts."

"Should we follow the prints then?" Dalloway asked excitedly.

"We do not want to scare it further away, though it could barely hear us coming in this storm. The cold will dull its senses. Besides, our smell will not travel on this wind," Caroline said.

"I hope those paw prints are not just frozen in the ice and the feline is long gone by now," Dalloway said.

"No. The snow would have covered them if they had been

here for more than a few minutes. It has been falling unflaggingly for a while now," Caroline observed. "The animal must be nearby. I will try to find it," she said, and she urged her tired horse forward by whispering in his ear.

"Do not stray too far, daughter. If you get lost in this storm, we may never find you again!" Conrad warned.

"Rest the horses for a moment then. I will find my way back if you do not move," she said to them and then she disappeared under the cloaking snow before either of them could respond.

"Be careful!" Conrad shouted into the blowing flakes, but his voice was swallowed up by the blistering wind and muffled by the blowing snow.

The two men dismounted and laid a heavy blanket upon the cold, cold ground. Dalloway pulled a pouch from his saddle bag, untied the strings and sprinkled a small amount of a fine powder around the edges of the cloth. It glowed subtly in the gloom of the afternoon and quickly generated enough heat to melt a small amount of snow on either side of it. The two thirsty travelers greedily scooped up the warm water and sucked it from their cupped hands. Dalloway then filled a small flask with more of it and walked to the horses so that they could partake as well. As quickly as he could, he returned to the blanket and languished in the little bit of warmth that the particles he distributed were generating.

"Enjoy it whilst you can," he said to Conrad, who had joined him on the blanket. "It will not last for long before this abominable cold extinguishes it."

"I hope Caroline does not chase that bloody cat too far. It will be darned difficult for her to find us in this storm if she loses her way."

"She will find us. Our thoughts travel despite the coldness," Dalloway said confidently.

"Yes, I suppose she will. But the First knows what else she may encounter out there! These parts are uncharted and I have a very bad feeling about them," Conrad replied ominously.

"I think she is safe for the time being. What would be out and about in this storm anyway?"

"That is exactly what I am a feared of," Conrad replied.

As if his worries had come to life by virtue of his words, a startling wail shattered the monotony of the storm's cadence. Both men jumped to their feet and drew their weapons, though they could see but a few feet into the blowing storm.

"Caroline?" Conrad shouted. "Are you near?"

"Your voice will not penetrate the denseness. Waste not your breath. She will return," Dalloway said in a calming voice.

"What was that, do you think?" he asked the elf.

"An animal lost to the storm, I hope."

"'Twas not the cat whose prints we saw here. It must be larger than that for us to have heard its scream," Conrad said.

"Aye. So it must."

They stood vigilantly, but there was nothing they could do. They could not leave the spot that they agreed to meet at, and neither of them would fare better than Caroline if only one of them ventured out to find her. The minutes felt like hours as they waited.

"There is goes again!" Dalloway said. "Did it sound further away to you?"

"Yes. Maybe it is lost too. Just as long as it does not find Caroline before she finds it!"

"I doubt it could take her by surprise, Conrad," Dalloway said reassuringly.

The wind was blowing harder now and the snow rose in gusting spirals everywhere. They could barely see their horses who stood only a few feet from them.

"We had best hold onto their reins, or we may lose them," Dalloway shouted over the mounting clamor of the storm.

He stepped off of the blanket and reached for the leather straps that were by then standing almost straight out from the side of his horse, having gotten caught in the blowing wind. Conrad did the same, but with their weight no longer securing the cloth that they had been standing upon, the wind lifted it and carried it away before either of them could reclaim it. The phosphorescent particles sparkled and died, their light and warmth snuffed out quickly under the new snow, and they found themselves standing beside one another and struggling to maintain their own footing.

"We will miss that blanket!" the elf yelled.

"My thoughts are on my daughter, Dalloway, not some bloody blanket!" Conrad replied.

As if she heard him, at that very moment Caroline came bounding through the blowing snow and nearly crashed into the men and their animals.

"Thank the First!" Conrad yelled.

"Follow me! Quickly!" Caroline shouted at them without

another word. She turned her mount abruptly and waited anxiously. Once they had jumped into their saddles she leapt away and they immediately took off after her without waiting for an explanation.

Running closely behind her, Dalloway cried out, "Did you find it?"

"Yes," she yelled back. "And if we do not hurry, it will all be for naught. We are not safe out here any longer!"

"We were never safe in this storm!" Conrad exclaimed.

"It is not the storm that threatens us now, father," Caroline said, and her voice rang with terror. "The animals have spoken to me. The Possessed seek the source of the power. Sidra's medallion may be the beacon that will lead them to us as well!" she shouted.

"Then let me throw it in the snow!" Dalloway yelled back and he grasped the thong that hung around his neck.

"No!" Caroline screamed. "No! Whatever you do, do not give it up. It is all that we have to protect us. We will need it in the hollows!"

"The Hollows?" Conrad shouted back as they dashed through the blinding snow.

"Yes. The entrance is up ahead. See how the ground slopes down over there? Make haste!" she warned and she raced forward.

The sky grew darker very quickly and the wind stopped dead in an instant. The flakes ceased to fall and silence replaced the previous clamor of the raging storm.

"Hurry! I see it now. Follow me, quickly!" Caroline said as she pressed her horse unremittingly onward.

The distinct sound of heavy hooves pounding the hard ground sounded somewhere behind them, rapidly growing louder, but none looked back. The earth trembled with each step as their pursuer approached, and the air crackled with power. Caroline leapt from her horse and grabbed the bridle of her father's horse almost simultaneously. Dalloway, too, dismounted in an instant and stood with them.

"I must send them off on their own. They cannot enter with us," she said almost frenziedly, and she spoke to the animals briefly. The horses wasted no time before dashing into the distance in three different directions.

"Come! Quickly!" Caroline ordered them. "Quickly!"

She stepped down into what looked like a black pool amidst the interminable whiteness and disappeared instantly. Conrad and Dalloway followed her without hesitation.

Chapter Thirty-six

They crossed the plains of Chilmark faster than they could have hoped. Nothing slowed their progress, and their horses were well rested and strong when they set out initially from the gates of Avalain.

"I see the edge of the woods ahead," Elion said. "We are almost there."

"I see it too," Tomas replied. "Is there an entrance? It appears almost like a solid wall."

"There must be a way in. We will have to search for it when we get closer," Elion answered.

They rode nearly into the stockade-like perimeter, but as they feared, they were thwarted by the density of the trees and there was no apparent entryway.

"There is so much brush and so many trees, we cannot fit between," Elion observed.

The ring was burning upon Tomas' chest.

"Were we followed, do you think?" the boy asked, and he looked behind himself warily for a moment.
"I doubt it, Tomas. No one saw us leave. Besides, I do not think too many could have crossed the Chilmark that fast. And even if they had, it was pretty barren. I suspect we would have noticed at some point, if anyone was tracking us," Elion said as he too gazed over his shoulder at the barren plains of Chilmark.

"Look, Elion!" Tomas said in surprise, as he returned his attention upon the woods before them. "We turned our heads away for only a second, and the trees have rearranged themselves!"

"The Winding Woods, Tomas!" Elion answered, as if that was enough of an explanation for the extraordinary phenomenon. "Remember what Filaree said."

A narrow passageway opened up in front of them and it was flanked by trees on either side. It was barely wide enough for them to ride single file, and Elion took the lead.

"Follow me and stay close. Who knows what the trees have in mind? We should try to make sure that they do not separate us!" Elion warned.

"We should try? And how do you suggest that we accomplish that? We are not in control here."

"It was only a suggestions, Tomas," he replied while looking left and right anxiously as he proceeded down the path.

"Just do not lag behind."

They had walked no more than twenty yards into the woods when Tomas looked behind them.

"I hate to say it, but we might as well be as deep in this forest as we could be. There is no longer a clear way out!"

Elion too looked back and he saw that the trees had filled in the space to their rear as if there had never been a path at all.

"How do they move without us seeing them do so?" Elion asked. "Are they really there? Could this be illusion?"

"They are there. They are just very quick. We cannot keep our eyes on them all at once. They probably perceive us as a threat and they are just being cautious."

"I wonder what we can do to let them know that we mean them no harm."

"I do not know if they are as sentient as you believe, Elion. They respond defensively, but it may merely be a reaction to our intrusion. Even the simplest of beasts responds to stimuli. It seems to me that this entire forest does behave as if it is a single entity, not thousands of independently growing things. That is the wonder of this place, is it not?"

"Filaree seemed to think so," Elion replied. "Do you think it is leading us to any particular point?"

"If what I said is correct, then it is most likely leading us away from any vulnerable areas if such places exist here," Tomas said.

"And I suspect that we are the only vulnerable things here."

"My sense of direction is quite upside down," Tomas observed after a few more minutes of riding. "Now I understand why no army or invader has ever ventured into these woods. Avalain has a very secure border on this side of the Chilmark!"

"How far do you want to walk before you contact your brother?" Elion asked, reminding Tomas of the reason why they came here in the first place.

"I think it would be best if we let the woods answer that for us."

"We could wander this way forever, Tomas. We could not find our way out now if we tried."

"No, you are right. A masterful defense!" Tomas observed, more impressed with the Winding Woods than he was fearful of the possible consequences of having entered them.

The landscape did change as they walked. Many different

types of trees appeared before them and behind them. They crossed through a thick grove of fragrant trees laden with succulent fruit and then through a dark section where the ground was barren of all debris except for a soft covering of pine needles that muffled the sound of their steps. The path that they were being led down crossed over many small rivulets of sparkling water and an ever changing terrain. Though the sky pierced the treetops in places, the ground seemed to be illuminated by its own source of light. It was much brighter on the surface than it should have been considering how dense and copious the treetops were.

"Are we making any progress, do you think?" Tomas asked after they walked for another twenty minutes or so.

"It is hard to tell. We cannot look back and determine how far we have come. I am just hoping for a sign of some kind. As you said before, maybe the woods will bring us to a point where we feel we belong."

As the elf spoke those words, they turned the corner of a small bend in the path and came up against a solid wall of trees. Both of them focused their attention ahead and then they waited for an opening to appear so that they could proceed forward, but no such opportunity presented itself.

"We have reached an impasse!" Elion observed.

"Most definitely!" Tomas concurred as he looked to their rear and saw that the trees had completely filled in space behind them, leaving them both very little room to maneuver.

Their horses were stamping their feet impatiently, practically dancing within the limited area in which they now found themselves.

"Now what?" Elion asked.

"It was your idea to come here, Elion," Tomas reminded him. "What do you suggest?"

"Maybe this was not such a bright idea after all," he replied sheepishly.

Suddenly, leaves began flying in all directions around them and the air took on a colored hue as if they were gazing through a green tinted glass. They both found themselves swatting leaves from the air before them like they were swarms of attacking insects that were threatening to overwhelm them, yet no wind could be felt. The surface upon which they stood was quickly piling up with loose foliage, frightening the horses, and causing them to rear up nervously as the debris quickly mounted around them. An earthy odor permeated the atmosphere;　heavy and strong. They could practically taste the leaves and the pine needles in each breath, and they felt as if the essence of the trees was entering their bodies through each and every pore.

Through the chaos of the moment, they could see the leaves rustling visibly in a big tree directly in front of them, causing it to bend and dip toward them, yet still they could feel no breeze passing through. Then, to the right of it they heard yet another sound of foliage in motion, but the air remained as calm and still as possible. The branches began to creak and the leaves rose and fell in response, as if the trees were carrying on a conversation in a language all their own. This cacophony grew louder and louder until they could barely hear themselves think. Surrounded as they were by a ring of trees, they sat upon their jittery horses and watched cautiously and listened carefully to the music of the Winding Woods.

Abruptly the sound ceased, and the leaves and debris that had been swirling everywhere, fell to the ground and lost all their animation at once. The wall of pines visibly swayed left and right and then parted revealing a massively large, craggy old tree behind it. All was now as still as could be, and Tomas and Elion respectfully awaited the forest's next move. They stared intently at the huge tree that stood before them.

A slender tendril broke free of the tangle of branches and bark that covered the ancient tree, and it floated gracefully through the air toward Tomas. He sat perfectly still and did not flinch as it curled around his neck and slid across his face. Elion was about to raise his voice in concern, but Tomas calmed him with a look. The green strand slithered down the front of his shirt and curled around the ring that hung there. It lingered upon it for a moment before withdrawing from his tunic. It then hovered for another second in front of his face, touched each of his eyelids tenderly with its soft, rounded tip and then floated back to the main body of the tree.

They could both hear a rustling sound again coming from all directions as if the trees were chattering loudly. As soon as the noise stopped, the path upon which they stood widened considerably, though the movement of the trees was again impossible to detect. If they looked to the right, all was still, and when they returned their gazes to the left once again, all was rearranged. Even if they looked in opposite directions from each other, the movement still occurred outside of their range of vision.

Tomas raised his finger slowly to his lips, and indicated to Elion that he should remain silent. They had both given up their efforts to spot the motion, and they stared instead at the old, gnarled tree in front of them. Tomas reached into his shirt and grasped the leather thong upon which the ring hung, and he pulled it out. Gently, he released it and let it hang exposed upon his tunic. They both sat up straight in their saddles and waited.

The foliage had arranged itself in such a way so that they now stood in the middle of a circle open only at one end, surrounded by a solid row of dense pine trees, backed by graceful, incredibly compact willows, which were in turn backed by enormous trees of all different kinds that shot high into the sky and overhung the entire area. They formed a canopy over them and sheltered them protectively. Before the two visitors loomed the aged tree. Elion was staring at it raptly, and for a moment he swore to himself that he saw the image of a face concealed amidst the thick and wrinkled hide. He looked quickly at Tomas, who smiled and nodded to him. Tomas bowed his head and raised his right hand in salute, whereupon the space that existed before them closed as the trees seemed to spring to attention, completing the circle and obscuring their view of the tree beyond.

"It is safe to dismount now," he said to Elion. "We have been accepted by the forest. You were right. It will be secure for us here."

"I had my doubts for a moment there," Elion admitted. "Are you sure?"

"Yes, Elion," he replied with certainty. "There are no signs of evil here. Though these trees are not as aware as the Lalas, they recognize the difference between good and evil."

"Tomas? Did you see the face too?" Elion asked.

"Yes. I did," he replied, and the elf sighed with relief.

"I thought I was imagining it. Filaree told me that the old legend about Pembar mutating into a tree in his final years was true. I just did not believe her until today!"

"There is little left of the man anymore," Tomas said.

"Oh? How could you tell? I merely saw the image, but I felt nothing unusual," Elion asked curiously.

"Did you notice how indistinct his image was? When the filament touched my eyes I think he tried to communicate with me, but he was unable to. He could not manage the thought process needed for speech any longer."

"He recognized the ring though. It was clear that he knew just where to find it."

"The relic emanates power all the time. Many could locate it. But he did accept us because of it," Tomas said.

"Something tells me Tomas, that you would have been accepted here with or without the ring," Elion said.

"We should get started," Tomas said, changing the subject. "I have waited my whole lifetime for this moment," he replied.

"And you must wait still longer!" a strange, female voice spoke out, shocking them both.

Elion drew his blade from his belt and stood protectively beside Tomas, while brandishing it before him.

"Who said that? Where are you? Show yourself!" the elf demanded.

"I am right here behind you, Prince Elion. Have no fear of me," she replied.

Tomas and Elion turned around, and like the trees which seemed to be in one place for a moment and then gone or relocated without any sign of movement, a woman appeared right before their eyes seemingly out of nowhere.

"Did you not sense me, Tomas?" she asked, as if she knew the boy well.

"No," he answered simply, but he kept eyeing her curiously all the while.

"Strange," she muttered to herself. "I expected you would have recognized me after having spent so much time with the Chosen from Tamarand," she said, referring to Robyn. "You can put that knife away. You will not need it against me, my fine young Prince."

"Who are you? Why are you here?" Elion asked, still suspicious. "Be careful, Tomas! I am mistrustful of people we do not know who use our names so familiarly," he warned.

"I am Sidra," she replied and then she waited a moment to see if recognition appeared upon their faces. "Now you too can speak my name," she smiled, revealing her large, white teeth.

"The name is unfamiliar to me," Tomas said. "You know Robyn dar Tamarand?" he asked.

"Yes. And he knows me. I am disappointed he did not speak of me to you. It would have saved me some time."

"He did not," Elion replied cautiously. "And how do we know for certain that you are a friend of his?"

"You must take my word for it! I would not lie. Can you not sense that for yourselves?"

"She speaks the truth, Elion," Tomas said while still staring closely at her.

"How did you get here?" the elf asked. "Why should we trust you?" Elion questioned. He was still not willing to take any chances until he was certain she was indeed a friend.

"Because I tell you that you can!" she replied, and her patience was clearly waning. "My time here is limited. There are things I must say to you, and I cannot waste precious moments on explanations. Pembar has been generous enough to allow me to intervene myself. The Winding Woods might otherwise have dealt with you both in a different manner. He sensed the danger as well."

The woman was tall; taller than both Tomas and Elion. Her hair was long and black and it hung loosely down her back. It was woven with tiny, fragrant white flowers, the odor from which permeated the entire area. She was not a delicate lady, though she was quite beautiful in her own way. Her hands were broad and her fingers were masculine and tipped with short, white nails. The features of her face were rather bold. Her nose, though long, was well formed and her nostrils flared as she spoke, like a mare out of breath. Her black eyebrows were thick and seemed almost as if they were painted across her forehead. Bright green eyes sparkled beneath them, and they stood out conspicuously against her whitest of white skin.

"It is not wise for you to contact your brother now," she said to Tomas. "The eleventh shard is not yet secured."

"Do you know what she is talking about, Tomas?" Elion asked him.

"I know of the shards, Elion. This one though, I do not," he replied.

"I can protect you for a time, but the Dark One will know if you communicate with one another. You must not," she stated emphatically.

"Sidra? Have I pronounced it correctly?" Tomas asked with a respectful tone, and she nodded in response. "We have come here because the need was great, or so I thought. How can we know that what you say is correct? I do not mean to say that you are speaking anything but what you believe to be true, but how can we know that you are right?"

Sidra walked up to Tomas and placed her hands upon his

as he sat atop his horse. She gazed deeply into his eyes.

"Look at me, Tomas," she said. "It would be a grave mistake if you were to attempt to speak with Davmiran now. He is less experienced than you. He does not have the skills that he needs to protect himself and to protect that which he will require for the Quest. Not yet. He is like a candle in a storm, and the winds of Sedahar are blowing his way. I have sheltered his flame for the time being, but I cannot do so forever. He and his friends are safe for now. But his yearning for contact with you is dangerous. He is not strong enough to resist it. But you are."

"What single shard is so vital?" Tomas asked. "Why does it matter to Dav and to me?"

"It is all that can protect the Chosen from death," she replied without answering the question directly. "It is the eleventh."

"The Chosen? There are many Chosen," Elion said.

"Yes, and the great books are ambiguous. Are you versed in the Tomes?" she asked Elion.

"My mother is as knowledgeable as anyone, and she has passed much onto me," he replied. He was listening intently to what Sidra was saying, but he was still hesitant to accept it all.

"My brother is not a Chosen," Tomas interrupted them.

"No, Tomas. But you are," Sidra replied in a solemn voice. "And one day he may be," she said, and then she began to recite a poem from the books:

> *"The sleeping child shall awaken soon,*
> *his senses shall all be attuned*
> *to the other, whom he has yet to greet.*
> *To the other, and should they ever meet*
> *the Gem will burn with fire anew,*
> *and the trees will pass, all but a few.*
> *The trees will pass, all but a few.*
> *The Chosen shall die in the darkness alone*
> *bereft and far away from home,*
> *his body turned to ash and bone.*
> *A stepping stone?*
> *A stepping stone."*

"I have heard this before. This is but a part of a longer poem," Elion recalled.

"Yes, there is more to it. But this is the portion that

concerns me. The Gem cannot reveal itself now. Not yet. We are not ready. You and your brother are not ready," Sidra said. "You cannot risk a meeting with him at this time."

"Do you think that I am the Chosen who will die?" Tomas asked, and his green eyes seemed distant and fragile.

Sidra hesitated for a second before speaking.

"Honestly, Tomas, I do not," she replied. "But we cannot count upon my intuition here. You must assume that you are as vulnerable as any of the others."

"And the shard? You did not answer me precisely before," Tomas said.

"Premoran has entrusted the shards to Davmiran, as was expected. But there is one more that he knows he must obtain. Colton too knows this and he cannot gather it himself, though he craves it, as you can imagine. The hollows are forbidden to him. He needs his brother still for that, so he has thus far allowed the wizard to live."

"Allowed?" Tomas questioned her.

"Yes. I believe that he would have killed him already had it not been for the shard," she replied. "Although his arrogance is great, he would not toy with his brother this long for that reason alone. He is well aware of Premoran's strength. A fool he is not."

"The eleventh shard," Tomas said to himself.

"Yes, Tomas. But it is much more than a number. The shards hold within them all that was, and they point therefore to all that can be," Sidra explained.

"Why is this one so important?" Elion asked.

"Without it, the Gem can never be approached by a Chosen," Sidra replied. "It completes the key."

"My brother has the others," Tomas stated knowingly.

"Yes," Sidra said. "But Premoran was captured before he was able to retrieve the final one."

"He could not have known which Lalas was to depart next," Tomas said, contemplating. "Does Colton?"

"No. But the tree has only precious moments left now. He will know soon which one it is," Sidra responded.

"How?" Tomas asked apprehensively.

"He will be told," she replied frowning, and Tomas blanched visibly.

"And Premoran is still his captive," Elion said darkly.

"He is," Sidra confirmed

"What has this to do with me now, at this moment?" Tomas asked.

"As the Tomes suggest, the Gem will reveal itself in some way when you and your brother reunite. Whether the two of you must meet physically or not for that to occur is undetermined. But, we cannot take that chance. For the Dark One to discover this, and potentially the location of the Gem thereby when the shard is still vulnerable would be unacceptable!" she asserted.

"What can we do then to help?" Tomas asked.

"You must return to Avalain! You have no other choice now. I can shelter you there and protect you from him, as I have sheltered and protected your brother and his instructors in Parth. And, you must contact the others, the Chosen, and advise them of what has transpired here. Let them know of the shard, if they do not already. Use your ring for that purpose," Sidra said.

"How do you know that we can communicate?" Tomas asked, surprised by this revelation.

"There is much that I know, Tomas. The how of it is unimportant," she replied. "What is important is that you remain in Avalain until it is safe for you to leave. This is the time for others to act in the world, Tomas, not you. Colton Dar Agonthea will seek you out, and he must not find you yet."

"Yet?" Tomas repeated.

"At some point, you will confront one another. It is inevitable," Sidra said. "But it is better that it be when you are ready. And your brother as well. He will have his hands full with the two of you and your friends, I surmise," she replied, and then she smiled for the first time.

"How long must we remain hiding in Avalain?" Elion asked.

"You are not hiding, my bold young Prince. You are preparing. The fabric weaves of its own will. Allow it to incorporate you into the pattern in its own time.

"Be not so hasty," she continued. "The Dark One knows the prophecy as well as I. Fortunately, he requires the shard before you can be of use to him," she said to Tomas.

"Tell the Chosen to beware! There is mischief and betrayal afoot. Tell them to trust no one outside of the circle that has already been drawn. No one!" Her voice was adamant. "The Lalas must not know that we conspire!"

"Why don't you tell them this yourself?" Elion asked her.

"I choose not to speak to those who serve the trees in that way," she replied almost curtly.

"You are speaking to me," Tomas stated matter-of-factly.

"I must," Sidra answered. "And I have spoken to the Chosen of Tamarand. But it pains me greatly. One day, you will understand," she said, and she indicated by her tone that today was not that day. "I believe that they can help if they so desire. This will test their loyalty like nothing before," she said.

"Their loyalty to the Lalas?" Elion asked.

"To the earth!" she answered forthrightly.

"Is there a difference?" the elf questioned.

"There may be, Elion. There may be," Tomas replied sadly.

"Quickly now, you should not linger here any longer. Pembar has risked enough already. Once you return to the city, go to the chamber in the castle behind the library. You can access it by removing one of the books from the top shelf in the upper left corner facing the door. In the back there is a latch. Spring it and the panel will slide away. Within that room you will be safe. Contact the Chosen from there."

"How do you know of such a room in the castle?" Elion questioned her, surprised again by the extent of her knowledge.

"Esta will tell you how I know. I have not the time. Go now," she said, and she pointed behind them.

When they turned around, the pathway was already spread out before them. The trees had reassembled, revealing or creating a passage that lead all the way to the outskirts of the Winding Woods. They both climbed quickly onto their horses' backs.

"Perhaps we shall meet again, Tomas. And we too, Prince Elion," she said, and she bowed her rugged head to them both. "Heed my words! Speak of this only to those whom you must, and to whom you can entrust this information without fear of treachery, " she said

"Farewell, Sidra. And thank you," Tomas said, and he bowed back to her respectfully. "We will abide by your admonitions."

"Make certain that you do, young man!" she smiled again. "Farewell Tomas Dar Gwendolen! Farewell, Elion, Prince of Lormarion. Ride with the wind!"

They turned their horses and started to walk away, urged on by a strong breeze that blew steadily and purposefully into their backs. Simultaneously, they looked over their shoulders, but as they both suspected, Sidra had vanished already and all that remained for them to gaze upon where the pathway had been a scant second ago was a solid wall of stalwart and unyielding trees.

Chapter Thirty-seven

Etuah and Tamara quickly made their way down the broad passage that led away from the others. The sister was profoundly saddened by the leave-taking, and though she harbored no fear for Angeline, she already missed her immensely.

Things have become so complicated, she thought to herself. *How am I to handle all of this? Shards and maps, Drue, forbidden places; it all feels so overwhelming. I have to keep my wits about me!*

"You are strong of character," Etuah said as if in response to her thoughts. She turned her graceful head almost halfway around in order to look back at her.

"I do not feel strong, Etuah," Tamara admitted.

"Much has changed for you in a short time. It would have been difficult for anyone."

"Will Angeline be alright?"

"She will thrive," the Drue said with conviction.

"And you, Etuah? How is it you can accept what you must do so easily?"

"It is not as easy as you may think, Chosen. But I do accept what I must do. I am honored to lead you," she replied.

"And I am grateful," Tamara responded. "But why do you still call me 'Chosen'? I am not bonded. I have a difficult time accepting the appellation."

"Be that as it may," Etuah replied simply. "There are only a few who could gather a shard. In that respect at least, you have been chosen."

Tamara walked on for a while and silently contemplated all that had transpired since she first came into contact with Liam in the woods outside of Parth. It seemed like a century ago, yet she felt like the same person she was before, only more alone now than ever. Angeline's absence from her side was painful. "What is so important about this shard? You said it was the eleventh. Is that meaningful?" she asked.

"Very," Etuah replied.

"Why?"

"It completes the configuration. The heir requires eleven. He would never be able find the Gem without it," Etuah explained. "You must retrieve it before Colton does."

Tamara's head spun around as if it was on a spring.

"The Dark Lord knows of this too?" she asked

incredulously.

"Certainly! But he does not know which tree will depart next. Not yet. But he will know it is Mintar soon," Etuah said calmly.

"And he will try to get there before we do?"

"Most definitely," she continued. "But he cannot enter the dead spaces any more than the lost ones can. Doing so now would destroy him and yet leave the world intact. His spirit would never find the peace he seeks."

"So how will he be able to get it?"

"He must use another for that purpose, or simply wait for another to recover it and then take if from them."

"Another? You mean someone like me?"

"Perhaps. Or someone else under his control. Regardless, you must forsake your original pursuit and return it to Parth immediately, once you have gathered it. It would be unsafe to do otherwise."

Tamara was wondering if there could possibly be anything more terrifying than the thought of being pursued directly by Colton Dar Agonthea!   Having the Lady Margot chase her was bad enough! When she left the Tower she thought that by having the map in her possession she was a target. Now, she would have both the map and the shard!

"Why, Etuah? Why me?" she asked.

"Because you are able. There is no other explanation. The fabric weaves of its own will. It is not for us to choose what tests of spirit life will present to us," the Drue said. "Only how we respond to them."

They had been walking for about two hours by this time and the passage had narrowed considerably though it was still smooth and uniform in shape.

"We will be leaving the safety of the tunnels soon. Once we step into the nethers, you must be on your guard. When you look upon the lost ones do so with your eyes only, not with your heart," she warned.

"I thought you told me the last time never to look at them?" Tamara asked, confused.

"I did. But that was before I knew how strong you are. Besides, you were not alone. Angeline could not have withstood the pain and sorrow of the experience then. You will see what has truly become of them as you now must, and about what price they will pay eternally for their weakness and their transgression against the earth. This opportunity may not present itself to you again."

"A lesson of sorts?" she questioned.

"Of sorts," Etuah concurred. "Though I had not looked upon it that way. I see it as an opportunity. You already know right from wrong, Tamara. For some, it might be a lesson."

They walked in silence for another thirty minutes or so, and Tamara continued to think about all she had been through recently and all that still lay before her. She reached inside her cape just so that she could feel the map in its case and reassure herself that it was still safe. Soon she would have something else to guard that was surely at least as important as the map itself from the way Etuah described it. She shook her head in wonder, still amazed that this was really happening to her. Without even realizing what she was doing, she surrounded herself and the Drue as well in a protective nimbus of pale, white light. It glowed subtly as they stepped up and out of the passage into the nethers, and it reflected eerily off of the pock-marked walls. Etuah looked at her with satisfaction and nodded to herself.

Voices bombarded them from all directions. Pleas and supplications, cries and whispers, and screams and terrified, sobbing laments burst upon their ears and then faded, only to be followed by other, even more harrowing sounds. Faces pressed against the walls, the rock of which seemed almost transparent, and these faces were more horrible than any ghouls the worst nightmare could ever have fathered. Damp, warm air drifted over them and whistled down the tunnel. Tamara looked upon the lost souls and listened to them emotionlessly, as if she was not really present. Etuah ignored it all.

"They are afraid of your power," Etuah observed. "I do not need to warn them. They see that they cannot approach you."

Tamara had still not realized that she had conjured anything at all. She looked at Etuah without understanding for a moment until recognition hit her.

"My fear must have triggered something," she apologized. "This was involuntary."

"It gives me comfort to hear that. Your instincts are good. They will serve you well. Follow me," she then directed. "We must cross here quickly. Despite your strength, our presence can be detected more readily in this place. Particularly now that we are surrounded by your energy."

"I am so sorry. Have I jeopardized us?" Tamara replied,

concerned that her lack of training and control may have endangered them both. "Will the Dark Lord know we are here?"

"It is possible. But you have made my job much easier nonetheless. We will make much better progress now that you have intervened. They will not harass us," she said, referring to the lost ones.

"Somehow, it does not feel any safer to me. How far must we travel before we
reach the Lalas?" Tamara asked, worried that they could be waylaid any moment now by Colton.

"We will be past here soon. The passage will widen and then we will be closer to the surface. We should make very good time," Etuah said, seemingly unaware of all that was going on around them.

"Will they ever find peace?" Tamara asked while looking around the chamber.

"No, never! Do not feel sorry for them. One cannot be coerced into his arms, though some had not the strength of character to help themselves. They all went willingly. They now seek the end of the world too. That is their only chance for escape from the circle of time."

"How sad for them," the sister said.

"Save your compassion for those who deserve it. For most, it is not as easy as you might suspect to give yourself to him. You could never have made such a choice. Your nature would not allow it!"

"So you think that all of these lost souls were flawed to begin with? Was there no hope for them ever?"

"Perhaps for some. For others, no, but they are all weak Look upon them, Tamara. See the anguish. If you have never seen this degree of evil before, see it now. Remember it! What we Drue do in the hollows, you and your friends must do above ground. Hold back the evil! Keep it at bay. It will never disappear as long as life goes on, but you must be forever vigilant. You must guard the earth and protect it against those who wish to defile it."

"How can we ever win if evil cannot be destroyed once and for all?" she asked.

"A state of perfection will never exist in this world. Do not be fooled by those who say that it will! As long as there is life, there will be good and there will be evil. If you seek one without the other, whichever seems to triumph will simply fragment, and the cycle will begin anew. Colton has seen this! He knows that there is no way to end the battle short of total annihilation. That is one reason why he seeks dissolution. We must learn to live with both extremes and be thankful for those whose hearts and souls are strong," Etuah said.

"This is a far different way of looking at things. I had always hoped that one day...."

"One day there will be peace. One day good will prevail and evil shall recede. You will play a part in that if you remain steadfast and do not succumb to despair when the darkness seems so impenetrable. It will not last. All on earth is defined by its opposite and finds meaning within that context! Look at these faces! Remember them. They will help you to understand the face of goodness too."

Tamara stared from one agonized face to another. She saw what they had done to themselves by choosing the path of darkness or by having darkness seek them out and allowing it to poison them. None were innocent. Some could have taken a different path when the fork presented itself. They were the guiltiest ones; those for whom there was once hope!

"Choice! Guilt and innocence is all about choice!" Tamara said. "Whether they knew it at their moment of decision or not. But I do pity those who could not help themselves. They seem suddenly not so shameful."

"And there are many such. Remember though that the havoc they wreak hurts just as much! The fact that the evil is pure and without doubt, and was embraced without a conscious decision to do so is not cause for redemption! They are guilty for their actions nonetheless, if not for their nature!"

"Is it not their nature that determines their actions?"

"To an extent, Tamara. But we must defy evil regardless."

"Can one be both evil and innocent?" she asked, perplexed.

"Look upon them. Do you see an innocent face amongst them? The ones who did not consciously choose may have hearts as black as pitch. And they will commit horrendous acts. They cannot help themselves, perhaps."

"How can we condemn them then?"

"For the sake of the earth, we must confine them. Judgment we will leave to others. Their actions speak for their souls, and it is the affects that they have upon the world that are their measure. We must evaluate our response thereupon. This is the perspective we must assume if we hope ever to make the world safe again."

"And what of Colton? I want to believe that he could have chosen otherwise. I want to believe that he is guilty."

"Never doubt his guilt! As evil is to good, so is Colton to the earth! Though they be the opposites that define each other, he is but an example. It may be that in him, the rule is broken! The earth will survive without this demon, this icon of iniquity!"

Tamara was unsure of what she was feeling, but she knew that she would forever look upon things differently from now on. Things were not as simple as she had always thought. Her mind was unaccustomed to deep thoughts, and now she could not stop herself from thinking. As she walked, she contemplated these issues over and over again in silence.

She had been so immersed in thought that she barely noticed that they had left the nethers some time ago, and that they were heading up a steep incline in another passage totally unlike any she had been through before. The odor of Lalas was unmistakable, and as soon as it reached her nostrils, the aura that surrounded them vanished.

"Oh!" she said, startled. "My body reacted before I even made the decision. All of a sudden, it felt wrong to have this around us."

"No explanations are required," Etuah replied, and she drew deeply on the scent. "How sad and how lovely. It is not often that I am able to experience it. Usually, all signs of life have vanished by the time we arrive."

"Knowing that the tree is dying, I can hardly bear this," Tamara said. She was suddenly breathing in fits and starts. "Is he still alive?   And what of his Chosen?" Tamara asked, already profoundly disturbed by what she was seeing and feeling.

"Behold!" Etuah said and she held her long, thin arm outstretched before her.

Lying upon the soft ground about twenty yards ahead of them was the body of a large man. It sat there motionless and unprotected.

"This is awful! Is that Carlisle?" Tamara asked. "Is there nothing to be done?" she said, almost frantic with concern.

"Nothing, sister. It is too late for him. The tree itself will depart soon, and you must be ready. Now Tamara, you must go on without me," she said.

"Without you? You mean I have to go in there alone?" she asked, though she knew this before.

Etuah nodded.

"How will I find the shard?"

"I cannot answer that, but I am confidant that you will know how. Go, sister. The time has come," she said. She extended her arm toward the heart and her long, knobby fingers stretched almost double their ordinary length.

Tamara looked at the Drue closely.

"Will you be here when I return?" she asked.

"I will."

"And then?"

"And then I will enter and secure this place from the lost ones."

"And then?" she asked again.

"And then I too will depart, Tamara," she replied. "And so must you, for other places as well," Etuah smiled.

"I will see you again then," Tamara stated with certainty, and that thought gave her courage and hope as she walked past the fallen Chosen. She glanced back momentarily at Etuah and nodded soberly.

She looked at Carlisle's face as she passed him by, and impulsively, she leaned over and picked up his bow and quiver. Carefully, she laid the quiver across his chest and stuck the end of the bow as deep into the ground beside him as she could. Briefly, she kneeled upon the soft ground next to the Chosen and placed his hands over the quiver. They were already cold and the tears came to her eyes unbidden at the touch. She rose and walked past him, while choking back the sorrow.

The surface upon which she stepped was strewn with rubble, branches perhaps, or fallen rocks, she was uncertain, and she created a small light in her palm so that she could walk forward without tripping in the gloom. She looked back once again, only this time she saw Etuah standing there in the distance with her hair and garments streaming out from her body as if a strong wind was blowing at her. A soft and peaceful glow surrounded her and her eyes were bright with anticipation. No sign of fear or regret marred her beauty. Suddenly, Tamara understood the true meaning of sacrifice.

She is so strong and so noble. This will not be for naught, she vowed, as she stepped cautiously into the sacred chamber ahead.

Chapter Thirty-eight

"We must move quickly," Teetoo warned. "This place is not safe."

"Why? What do you fear?" Alemar asked. " I thought that no enemy would dare pursue us whilst we are in one of the Forbidden Places."

""'Tis not the enemy outside that concerns me, Princess. These places are so named for a reason," the Weloh said.

"Forbidden? Yet, we are here," Clovis said.

"Prepare yourselves. It takes a person of strong constitution to endure the sorrow that will greet you," Teetoo explained. "It may be that we are permitted to enter at all only because of Premoran and his token that I wear, but nothing can insulate us fully from the impact of this place."

Suddenly, a wave of nausea washed over Alemar and she doubled over in response. Clovis went to assist her when he too almost collapsed from the weight of his grief. Giles was leaning against the packed earth of the tunnel wall and he was shaking his head back and forth as if in a stupor.

"Fight it!" Teetoo said. "I have been in these places before. It is not easy, but you can do it," he urged them all.

"I feel as if my whole world has ended," Alemar sobbed. "I can barely breathe."

"I am so cold," Clovis said, and his body was shivering noticeably. "My heart has turned to stone!"

"Aye! Mine too," Giles said. "What manner of place is this?"

"It is the space that remains," Teetoo said. "We are in the emptiness left in the wake of the Lalas whose roots passed through here at one time."

"It is dreadful!" Alemar said. "How are we to fight this feeling?"

"Accept it for what it is and keep it from crippling you. This is as close to the void as you will hopefully ever come!" Teetoo explained.

"Is this what death will feel like?" Clovis asked.

"Death would be more welcome than this," Giles said.

"Here you feel the pain of collective loss. It is amplified because the Lalas was connected to life so intimately that it is far more intense than anything an individual could feel."

"The regret I perceive is insufferable. Did the tree love the earth so much?" Alemar asked with tears in her eyes.

"More than anything else," Teetoo responded. "Though it chose to depart, that choice did not mitigate its sorrow," he explained. "Walk with me. Hold your heads up!"

They struggled to obey his directions, and slowly they each pulled themselves together and followed the Weloh down the dark passage. It twisted and wound its way through the earth, descending all the while. The further they walked, the less they were able to see, and they tripped and stumbled constantly, but they did not stop again for quite some time. The motion of walking seemed to keep them from collapsing upon themselves in total despair.

"We must review the map, Alemar," Teetoo reminded her. "Soon, we will have choices to make. We cannot afford to take the wrong path."

"The light, Alemar! Take out the light!" Giles said hopefully. "Can you do that in here?"

"Can I, Teetoo?" Alemar looked to him for reassurance. "It will be impossible to see this without it."

"Colton would not dare to pry into this place with his own senses. He knows the dangers thereof. It should be quite safe. The light may help us in many ways," Teetoo replied and he nodded his delicate head.

Alemar reached into her blouse and grasped the finely woven chain upon which hung the delicate cocoon of silver that encased a simple looking object. She held it before her and at her urging it exploded with light.

"It makes me feel so much better just to see it shine," Clovis said while breathing deeply. "It is like a reminder of how beautiful things can be."

"A much needed reminder," Giles concurred euphorically.

"Spread the parchment out on this surface here," Teetoo pointed to a flat area in a crevice in the wall.

They all huddled around it in a semi-circle, shoulder to shoulder, and stared at the markings.

"We must avoid these areas at all costs," Teetoo said. He traced a line across the left side of the map with the tip of his index finger. "These passages lead through the nethers. We cannot traverse them without being observed. We also cannot get too close to the heart. The feelings you are experiencing would only intensify if we were to draw closer."

"This must be castle Sedahar itself," Alemar said, and she reluctantly placed the tip of her finger over a blood red design on the top left of the parchment. "Odd. It is warm to the touch," she commented, and then she removed her hand quickly as if the feeling was offensive in some way.

"The routes to it look like veins in the skin," Giles observed.

"Some are red and others are black," Clovis added.

Alemar went to trace her finger down one of the red ones, but as soon as she touched it she recoiled. She then attempted to follow one of the black lines, and it did not bother her at all.

"A warning if there ever was one!" Giles chimed.

"So which one shall we choose? There is more than one painted in black," Alemar asked the group.

"Bring the light closer," Teetoo instructed.

The Princess removed the chain from around her neck and placed it practically on top of the map. As she did so, the map began to glow in some places while it simultaneously dulled in others. It appeared now as a three dimensional image, and the various lines wove over and under one another. Alemar gasped in response.

"Do you see the breaks in the lines now?" Teetoo asked.

"My eyes just are not good enough," Clovis admitted. "I can barely see the lines themselves."

"I saw them before, but it was obvious none of you did. Without the light, even I would not have known which ones rose and which ones fell. Look more closely here," Teetoo pointed to one of the thin, black markings that wound from the bottom of the parchment nearly to the top.

"I see it!" Giles said. "There is a mark perpendicular to the line. What does it mean, do you think?"

"That the passage is most likely blocked!" Clovis said impatiently. "What else could it signify?"

"I suppose," Giles responded sheepishly.

"Here too. This one is blocked also," Alemar noticed, as the markings became clearer and more defined. "And this one," she pointed.

"Here as well," Giles said.

"Are they all dead ends then?" Clovis asked as he strained his eyes in vain to see.

Teetoo scrutinized the map closely.

"No. There is but one that leads without interruption to the castle," Teetoo observed and he laid his graceful finger upon it. "This one!"

"So we have our answer!" Alemar said. "Does it take us too near the heart?" she then asked, remembering Teetoo's last admonition.

"No. It stays safely away," Teetoo replied. "Look here! This is where the tree was once centered. And here is Sedahar. This pathway leads us around the nethers and into the outlying root work. You can tell by the smaller striations that crisscross it. It then heads straight for the castle, though it may be rather narrow as it nears it."

"The others all terminate quite abruptly after the blockades. I thought that all the trees were connected. These passages all end before Sedahar," Alemar said. "Did they ever extend further, do you think?"

"When the tree lived, it stretched itself as far out as it could. It was remarkable that it actually came as close to Sedahar as it did. I suspect that this passage has another's hands upon it, " Teetoo explained. "An actual meeting of the two, Colton and the Lalas, would have been cataclysmic! After the tree departed, Colton must have sealed all the burrows off, large and small."

"All but one it seems," Alemar observed.

"This one must be shielded in some way or he would have found it as well when the Lalas died. There is surely some great magic at work beneath the plains of Colton's domain that he is yet unaware of," Teetoo said while contemplating this turn of events.

"I hope that it continues to work whilst we are here," Giles said.

"I second that!" Clovis agreed.

"Without the map, we would have been wandering in this maze forever," Alemar said.

"And without the light, we would never have been able to see what we needed to on the map," Giles said.

"The cloth weaves around us," Teetoo reminded them all. "Fate and coincidence, destiny and luck; there is so much that we do not understand," he mused aloud.

"Shouldn't we start moving?" Alemar suggested. "We still have quite a ways to go."

"Yes, Princess. You are so right. We have such a long way to go," Teetoo replied.

She stood up with the map in her hand and started to walk

forward, while she turned it back and forth to make sure that it was properly oriented. Then she strode determinedly ahead.

"This is the way. Follow me!" the Princess said.

Teetoo immediately caught up to her and walked by her side while Giles and Clovis took up the rear. It was not difficult to travel down the tunnel now that it was illuminated, and nothing hindered their progress except some occasional debris and a fallen rock or two. They made good time. The feelings that they had suffered previously were rapidly abating the further they walked from the heart of the Lalas, and according to the map, they were traveling directly away from it. But it was the blacker heart of another, more fearful place they would soon be entering that dominated all of their thoughts now.

Chapter Thirty-nine

"It is Mintar!" Colton said aloud. "Mintar, my beauties!"

He was sitting upon an obelisk of polished black stone that rose from the center of the smoking ruins of Talamar, waiting for the answer that he knew would reveal itself to him soon. Below him, prostrate upon the scorched earth, lay the forsaken women, the Possessed, motionless and silent. Now that it had come, Colton gazed out toward the western horizon through his black and shining eyes. Invading the thoughts of the women carelessly and without shame, he engraved the image of the dying Lalas and its location upon their minds.

"Soon, another of the trees will be gone. But this one is different! It harbors something that I want much more than any of the others did!"

He slid off of the high pillar and floated to the ground. Before he reached the scorched earth, his legs extended and he landed softly and quietly amidst the perfectly still women, as if they were not even there. His crimson robes settled softly around him, and they caressed his perfect body like a soft brush upon his hair.

"They deceive and conspire too, my beauties. They had been so self righteous, so judgmental, these 'great trees', but they are so no longer. They have accepted their fate, and now it is my turn! It is our turn!" he said, while barely moving his sensuous lips.

Colton extended his arms and the dust rose in thick clouds from the smoldering surface beneath him. It swirled around for an instant, and then it began to coalesce. In moments, the semblance of a huge tree loomed before him, though it was grey and deathly in appearance; a mockery of the Lalas that he had just named. He moved the fingers of his left hand slowly and the apparition erupted. It burst apart in all directions and rained ash and detritus everywhere. The debris from his conjuring covered the women in a blanket of grey death. Colton laughed gleefully with his mouth wide open. His laugh became a wail and the wail became a howl, as the horrific sound rolled across the barren plain and increased in intensity as it spread throughout the countryside. It reached into the towns and villages, and cottages and homes of anyone who still remained anywhere within miles of Talamar. Like a scream ululating through a silent, summer night, the Evil One's laughter invaded the unsuspecting hearts of all who heard it, and it turned them into cold stones in their pounding chests.

"Rise, Margot! Come to me!" he ordered and he curled his index finger at one of the women.

Immediately, a prone body clothed in red, liquid-like garments ascended from the darkened surface, her body still stiff and unmoving.

"Go to Sedahar! Fetch my brother and lead him to the site of the dying tree!" he commanded. "I will be waiting there for you when you arrive."

Her body now floated before him, perpendicular to the earth once again, but still not in control of itself, though her wide open eyes stared at him adoringly.

"He shall retrieve the shard and it will be mine at last!" he hissed. "Take this..." he said, and a small orb of black stone appeared in the air before her. "Use it to unlock his chains and to hold him captive while you bring him there."

Margot's arm rose involuntarily and her stiffened fingers plucked the ebon object from where it floated. She concealed it within the folds of her cloak. Her eyes were locked upon his face and her breath came to her in gasps and spurts. The sheer ecstasy of being chosen for this was almost too much for her to bear, and she struggled to breath and not swoon in response to this honor. Though the sharpened talons of fear gripped what remained of her human soul, even this unmitigated terror now felt like a privilege bestowed upon her, and she rejoiced in it as well.

"Go! Go now, my beauty," he said while he nodded his head slowly up and down. "But be wary of him! He is conniving and manipulative!" he warned. "He will not go willingly." The hatred flared in his black eyes, and they burned red with passion. "I want you to succeed where you have failed before. I want you to rejoice in my satisfaction as if it was your own," he said sweetly once again.

She was once again in control of her own movements, and she bowed deeply before him, though she never took her eyes off of him for even a moment. She wished only to breath in his scent, to inhale what he exhaled and to retain whatever of him she was able to. Her rapture had no boundaries now and she nearly burst from the empowerment of it. The thought of pleasing him in this way was overwhelming.

"Do not be fooled by his captivity. He is still strong. Pay no heed to his words. The orb will bind him to you through me, and he will not dare to touch it. None dare touch it without touching me! If he tries to break free, it will kill him, so do not provoke him. I need him to remain alive," Colton said. "He must remove the shard. He has no choice. It is his destiny to do so. The tree cannot depart until the shard has been taken from its heart, and he could not suffer it to remain in between, neither here nor there. He is too soft, too compassionate," he mocked. "Once he has it in his possession, lead him from the empty space and I will be waiting."

Colton bent over, raised his hand and caressed her head. She could barely breathe. The sensation was so intense that it touched every part of her body, and she could not tell the difference between the pleasure of it and the pain. She was afraid that she would be consumed by his power, it was so vast and all encompassing. As he removed his fingers from her hair she settled down upon the earth beneath her. A coal-black stallion with hooves of chiseled stone and a tail and mane of crimson fire ascended from the ashes and settled upon the ground next to her.

"Ride, Margot. Ride!" he commanded, and she floated up and onto the beast's broad back.

The flames framed her body in a hellish shroud as the horse rose off of the surface in total silence. At a nod from its master, it bolted off toward the south and left behind it a festering trail of fiery death that slowly burned itself out in the torrid midday sky.

Chapter forty

"The medallion glows beneath your shirt, Dalloway. It must be a sign," Caroline said. "Take it out so we can see," she suggested.

Dalloway grabbed the necklace and let it hang freely upon his shirt.

"Where in the world are we?" he asked, as he looked around at the earthen chamber that they had climbed down into. "And what was that pursuing us before?"

"We are in a place that is dying; a place that once was something and will soon be no longer," Caroline replied dreamily. "Can you not feel it?" she asked.

"I feel only emptiness, daughter," Conrad said.

"Emptiness and sadness and loss," Caroline said. "Yes, father. That is how we all feel. There is no hope left here. It has been lost with the tree that will shortly be no more."

"What kind of a horse was that chasing us?" Dalloway asked again. "Was it even a horse?"

"'Twas no horse borne of this earth," Conrad said.

"It frightened everything that lives upon the plain. I had never felt such fear in a living thing before," Caroline said, and a shudder ran over her body. "Even this place seems a relief in comparison."

"I wonder where it was headed," Dalloway said.

"I would not wish to be the object of its pursuit!" Conrad said. "You said it was searching for the source of the power? That it was one of the Possessed?"

"That is what the animals feared. Let us just be thankful that we have alluded it. If we were not its prey though, I too feel sorry for whomever it seeks," Caroline said.

"A Lalas lived here once?" Dalloway asked, anxious to change the subject.

"It lives still, though barely," she said regretfully. "These spaces will be all that will remain of it," she said regretfully. "But take heart! It has sheltered us from the monsters above who pursue us. They will not enter here."

"How can you be sure, Caroline?" her father asked.

"Because the animals told me so. Even they will not come near this place any longer. We must be careful not to lose ourselves to despair. Keep Sidra's token in sight. Its warmth will aid us in many ways," she explained.

They followed Caroline as she walked down the twisting path.

"Where are we going?" Dalloway asked.

"To the heart," she said and she continued to descend into the gloom.

"Why?" Dalloway asked. "What good can we do for this tree?"

"I do not know, Dalloway," Caroline replied. "I do not know why we are here at all. I only know that had we remained above ground, we would not have survived. Colton's hounds are near and he cannot be far behind himself. Besides, my friends above told me we must seek the heart. What else can we do but heed their suggestions. They led us here just in time, did they not?"

"Yes, certainly they did! But, can we travel down here safely, daughter?" her father asked. "Have your animal friends told you any more about this place?"

"There was little time, father. I learned what I could. Besides, none of them have ever been down here themselves, though some of the burrowing ones had come close at times. I felt what they felt, but it was often unclear, and it was always filled with desperation," she explained. "All the caverns are connected in some way. They exist everywhere!" she said. "The Lalas' roots cover the earth."

"We can walk all the way to Odelot then?" Dalloway asked.

"It is conceivable," Caroline replied. "Remarkable as that may sound."

"Why do others not use these places?" Dalloway asked suspiciously.

"Because it causes great suffering and anguish to pass through them," she said. "For all living things, to be in the Forbidden Places is stultifying. It is like stepping into the void; into the blackness of nothingness. And it is hard to bear. For most, they can never recover from even a glimpse of this," she said.

"And for us? Why would it be different for us?" Conrad asked apprehensively.

"Sidra has made it different. She guides and protects us," Caroline replied. "Her mark is upon us."

"Yet she would never come here herself. She avoids the places of the trees," Conrad said.

"How is it Sidra knows so much about the Lalas, father?" Caroline asked as they continued to walk down the winding tunnel.

"It is a long story, and one that has never been recounted to me fully. There is much animosity, so to speak, between Sidra and the trees. That much I know, though 'animosity' may be too harsh a word. Perhaps ambivalence better describes her attitude toward the Lalas. Yet, I also know that they fight upon the same side, despite the fact that they can not always do that side by side," he replied. "She has always retained her independence, and she was never willing to accede completely to their authority. Sidra is a strong willed woman!" he said with clear and tangible admiration. "And we can trust her totally. We may not understand all that she does, but she would not send us into harm's way unless it was necessary."

"Or the better of two evils?" Caroline asked.

"Perhaps," he replied, and he contemplated his daughters words. "Though, I suspect we are here for another purpose altogether."

"Maybe we will learn more when we reach our destination," Caroline said.

"Our destination, daughter? What exactly is our destination? Odelot? The Lalas' heart? Do we even know?" her father asked.

"You tell me we can trust her, and I am willing to do so. Have you really the faith in this woman that you claim to have?" she asked.

"I do, Caroline. I am just not accustomed to tasks with no obvious goals. I am a practical man," he replied as they wandered down the twisted path.

Dalloway's head was hanging particularly low and his pace was slackening even as they spoke, and neither of them had noticed that he had not said anything for a while.

"Hurry! Do not fall behind," Caroline called back to him, realizing now that he must be lagging as the light that he carried was growing dimmer because it was further away.

When the elf lifted his head to gaze at her, she immediately realized that something was very wrong. He had been slowly succumbing to the overbearing depression that was settling down so heavily upon him, and she and her father were too preoccupied with their conversation to have noticed. She quickly walked over to him and put her arm around his shoulder and under his own in order to assist him. He smiled gratefully at her, but the look in his eyes was faraway and weak.

"Father! Help me please. I fear we may be losing him to the tragedy of this place," she said urgently.

Conrad stood on the other side of Dalloway, and together they all walked on. Dalloway could soon barely move his legs, and he was stumbling and falling as they progressed. Had it not been for Caroline and Conrad, he would have crumbled in a heap upon the ground.

"I must help him. He seems so much more susceptible than we," she said, and her eyes were wide with concern. "He must still be weak from before we found him."

"Be careful, Caroline. We cannot afford to lose the both of you now," Conrad said worriedly.

"I will be. He needs me now," she replied. "He succumbed so quickly. I had thought he would have been as strong as we down here. I had forgotten just how seriously he had been wounded afore, and it was stupid of me to imagine he could have recovered fully in such a short period of time. No one should have been expected to bounce back so fast from such an experience," she said, and she was angry at herself for being so foolish as to assume otherwise.

Before another word was said, Caroline had taken Dalloway's hands in her own and she was staring deeply into his half closed eyes. They both fell to their knees facing one another. Shortly, the two of them had gone into in a trance-like state, and Conrad could do nothing more than stand there and prop the elf up so that he would not collapse totally upon the ground. Fortunately, it was only moments before both pairs of eyes opened, and it was obvious that Dalloway was much stronger. His eyes were once again clear and bright, and Caroline, though fatigued, had a look of satisfaction upon her delicate features that required no words to explain.

"He will be fine, father. Thank you," she said, and she sighed audibly with relief.

"Thank you," Dalloway said meaningfully to Caroline, and he squeezed her fingers tightly. "I had not realized how to protect myself before. Now that I know, I will not succumb again. It was inadvisable of me not to ask earlier, but for an elf from Seramour not to understand how to abide with the trees seemed so unlikely to me. My arrogance..."

"It was not arrogance that made you vulnerable, but

innocence. I have spent a lifetime learning how to protect myself from the invasion of outside emotions," Caroline said.

"And I have known Sidra too well and too long to have wandered into the Forbidden Places without preparing myself for the experience," Conrad recounted. "Are you both alright? Can we go on. I think it ill advised to linger here much longer."

"Tired is all," Dalloway replied. "It will pass."

"I am ready. But where are we headed, father?" Caroline asked, staring at a multi-pronged fork in the pathway.

"You are asking me? Are you not the one who communed with the animals? Did they not instruct you?"

"They merely told me where the entrance was and warned me of the danger above. They said to seek the heart. That is all. They have not entered this place before."

"So we have our answer, daughter. Why are you worried?" Conrad asked with a smile.

"Yes, I suppose. But it was such a vague directive. How are we to decide which path to take?" she asked, as she pointed to the three different choices that loomed before them even at that moment.

"The medallion will lead us. Look! When I turn it over, it is almost like a compass, is it not?" Dalloway said. He was examining the back of it.

"By the First, I believe the boy is right!" Conrad replied, and he slapped Dalloway sharply on his back. "Just look at that! Sidra has not failed us after all!"

Sure enough, what had been smooth and polished before with no obvious markings upon it, in the glow of its own internal light, now appeared to be guiding them. A small dot of intense illumination remained steadily pointing in one direction even as Dalloway moved the amulet from the left to the right.

"If we follow the light, I bet it will lead us to where we need to go!" he said.

"I am certain that it will!" Conrad concurred.

They hastened down the path, and at each new fork in the road, they held the amulet aloft and went in the direction that it indicated, winding deeper and deeper into the earth.

Chapter Forty-one

"The path grows narrow and it is much steeper than previously. We have been heading upward for some time now. Do you think we are nearing its end?" Alemar asked, while first staring at the map and then ahead into the darkness.

"It appears to from the drawing," Teetoo said.

"Will we then be in Sedahar?" Giles asked from somewhere behind them.

"That is the plan, is it not?" Clovis said sarcastically.

"What I meant was will there be no transition betwixt the two?" Giles explained himself.

"The point where they meet must be concealed in some way or someone would have found it before this," Alemar said.

"My thoughts exactly," Teetoo concurred. "When we reach the termination we will see. It seems as if we are nearly there."

They walked further on, though it was now difficult to stand erect. The ceiling had become lower and lower with each step. Alemar allowed the light to dangle upon her chest and she kept both of her hands out in front of her to avoid walking into anything. Vines hung down from above and broken branches protruded from the walls in many spots, and they had to walk carefully in order to keep from becoming entangled in them or tripping over them. The pathway turned abruptly to the left just ahead, and she could not see anything beyond it.

"We are changing direction," she observed.

As she rounded the bend, she rubbed her eyes with her fingers and shook her head. Everything was blurry, and she could not distinguish the wall from the ceiling or the floor.

"Stop!" she announced as the others rounded the bend and began to walk right into each other. "This must be the end."

"That does not sound good to me!" Giles said.

"I meant nothing by it, Giles," Alemar sought to reassure him. "But the path we have been on definitely terminates here."

Teetoo joined Alemar, and together they stared at the blurred space in front of them. It was impossible to determine if what they were looking at was a doorway or not. Alemar raised the light before it and withdrew it abruptly, startled.

"Did you see that?" she asked, unsettled.

"Yes. Illuminate it once more so I can get a better look," Teetoo instructed.

She raised her hand again and held it aloft this time. Within the obscurity of the space before them hovered the image of man's face. It appeared to be three dimensional, though it was clearly a chimera or a replica only, suspended in the blurred portal, and not a living person.

"Do you recognize him?" Alemar asked.

"No. The features are unfamiliar. But look at the diadem upon his head. Is that not the symbol of Gwendolen etched upon it?" Teetoo said.

"Clovis? You know the ancient signs. Look at this," Alemar instructed.

Clovis stepped forward and scrutinized the image that hovered before them.

"Yes, Princess. Without a doubt that is the sign of the royal house of Gwendolen," Clovis concurred.

"The heir's house," Teetoo said.

"What could it mean here under Sedahar?" Giles asked, confused. "Is it a warning, do you think? Did not the King and his entire family die by Caeltin's hand?"

"All but one died that fateful day," Teetoo said.

"All but two, I believe!" Alemar corrected him.

"Yes, you are right, Princess. All but two. Nonetheless, I do not perceive it as an admonition, nor as a harbinger, but rather as a reminder," Teetoo said, as he continued to contemplate the image. "There is more here than meets the eye. Look closely there," he said, and he pointed to the space beneath the chin of the figure. Does it appear particularly blurred to you," he asked the others.

"Yes. More so than the areas around it," Alemar agreed. "But it is hard to tell what we are really looking at."

"There is something behind there that I cannot see clearly at all. Bring the light closer," Teetoo said, and Alemar leaned in and pressed the necklace against the opaque surface.

It gave way slightly at the touch, bending inward, but her hand did not penetrate it at all. The surface area where she pressed the relic remained intact, though now it was somewhat concave. Teetoo scrutinized the area closely, but to his dismay as well as to that of the others, he discovered nothing that could help them to pierce the barrier that now stood in their way. Clovis and Giles both began to examine the walls on either side of the blurred area, while Alemar ran her hands over it, and tried to find something that would trigger a response of some sort. Teetoo stood back motionless for a second, contemplating the dilemma.

"Alemar! Extinguish the light for a moment," he said suddenly. "Anyone who wandered in here would have done so with some sort of illumination and would hesitate to remain here without it. Let us see what the darkness reveals."

Alemar willed the light to cease and instantly they were bathed in total blackness. They all stood in silence, unmoving, and they could see nothing whatsoever, as their eyes struggled to adjust, searching vainly for even the tiniest speck of light in the gloom.

"I had hoped..." Teetoo began to say, when a vivid spot of whiteness appeared upon the surface before them. They all turned quickly toward it. In moments, a symbol materialized where the spot began, and it glowed brightly seeming to stand out from the surface in three dimensions. "There is no doubt that this is Premoran's work. Look!" Teetoo said, and he held his delicate arm in the air. The bracelet was gleaming too. "There is a rune upon the bead that matches the one before us!"

"How could he have known we would come?" Alemar asked.

"He is a wizard!" Giles replied.

"Nay. No wizard even could predict the future," Clovis said.

"It is likely that others as well as we could have triggered the lock to appear had they kept their wits about them," Teetoo said.

"But how many keys are there that can open it?" Alemar asked.

"All that matters is that we have one of them!" Giles said.

"Do we, Teetoo?" Clovis asked.

"We shall soon see," Teetoo replied. "Alemar, bring forth the light once more, but allow it to remain dimly light, if you will."

Alemar held the small necklace aloft and willed it to shine. The area was immediately bathed in a soft and warm glow.

Teetoo walked close to the wall and held the bracelet up before the symbol that loomed in front of him. The rune on the small ornament upon his wrist was a mirror image of the one on the portal. He pressed it hard against it and it seemed to fit it perfectly. As soon as the wooden drop that hung from the bracelet touched the area, the juncture waxed brilliantly, and the light seemed to be absorbed by the surface like water by a sponge. It spread rapidly throughout the entire space, streaking it with glowing rays of light from the source to the edges. As each beam of light reached the perimeter of the portal, pieces of it fell away and disintegrated in the air before them, dropping to the ground in small clouds of iridescent matter as if it had been a wall of glass that shattered silently and then disappeared. Soon, the entire portal was gone, and all that remained was a bust of a man sitting upon a thin and delicate pedestal in the middle of the passage. Just behind it stood a solid wall of black rock, and just below it was a plaque with an inscription etched upon it. They all leaned in closely and read the words:

> *So ends the path that honor paved*
> *upon this somber ground.*
> *To be traveled once and ne'er again*
> *by ones not lost but found.*
> *A passage to the darkest place,*
> *the source of fear unbound.*
> *Measure the reason for which you come,*
> *against the risk you take,*
> *Tread lightly upon this accursed ground,*
> *if this be the choice you make.*
> *Who dares trespass into this space,*
> *beware the demon's hound!*
> *Let it rest, awake it not,*
> *no harm will come to thee,*
> *but when the time to flee is nigh,*
> *be sure to set it free.*

"We have the map. This is indeed what we were searching for. We are not lost," Alemar said after reading the words.

"This is definitely the passageway into Sedahar," Giles said.

"Now we now know that we cannot return the way we came," Teetoo said. "This path can only be traveled once."

"Before we go further, have any of you doubts?" Alemar asked. "We are all in agreement as to our purpose and the peril?"

They all nodded without a moment's hesitation.

"What of the 'demon's hound'? Has anyone an idea what this is?" Clovis asked.

"A watchdog of sorts, I would suspect. Caeltin could not have left Sedahar completely unguarded, even if he is unsuspecting," Alemar said.

"Let us hope that his eyes remain focused elsewhere, and that all we have to contend with is a sleeping dog," Clovis said.

"Why must we set if free when we leave? I, for one, do not wish some monstrous beast to pursue us when it is time to go," Giles said.

"There has to be a reason, Giles," Teetoo said. He was repeating the words of the poem over and over in his mind. "We must take the directive seriously. It could mean the difference between our survival and our death!"

"Some things become clearer as you near them. Perhaps we will understand this better once we are inside," Alemar said.

"I agree. We cannot expect to understand everything all at once. Let us find Premoran and free him. Then we can determine what next we must do," Teetoo said with conviction.

He walked carefully behind the sculpture and examined the stone that still stood in their way. The edges were so finely chiseled that he could barely see where they ended and the rock of the walls began. With one hand, he pushed lightly upon the left side of the figure and it immediately gave way. It pivoted as if on a hinge and revealed another passage behind it.

"Come," he instructed in a whisper. "Extinguish the light Princess, and make as little noise as possible. We know not where this 'hound' lingers. Nor any other perils, for that matter."

One by one, they carefully and noiselessly slid themselves through the opening and into the vileness of Sedahar.

Chapter Forty-two

She traveled so quickly across the sky that it took her own breath away. Her legs straddled the broad back of the horse, and she was exhilarated by the experience like never before. Fire streaked from the animal, and it lit up the atmosphere eerily as they sped over the towns and villages dotting the countryside. Margot relished the thought that those below must be cowering in fear at the sight of her astride this frightening beast, blatantly invading their territory without any fear of recrimination. She was swollen with glory and dizzied with hubris. But, somewhere deep within her lay the embers of a fear that she would not allow to ignite; a fear that lurked beneath the surface of her consciousness. It smoldered and sparked, and caused her to gag and shiver, but she repressed it and forced the heavy blanket of her boundless joy to smother it, though it could not put it out entirely.

He picked me, she thought, and her body tingled all over. *I am his sword! I am his Chosen!*

She reached inside her cape and grasped the ebon orb that he had given her. It was hot to the touch, and though it hurt her to keep it within her grasp, she was reluctant to let it go. The pain was almost pleasurable and she shook her head at that thought, confused by this realization.

I will die for him if I must! she thought. *Nothing can thwart me ever again. He has blessed me. I can endure anything for him.*

The beast crossed the land so rapidly that she could barely determine where they now were. The air struck her in the face with such force that she had to close her eyes entirely for a time. And, it was growing cold! In fact, she was shivering all over, and her breath blew out from her mouth and nose in billows of thick, almost frozen fog. She grasped the orb tighter though it felt as if her fingers were afire from the touch. The landscape constantly changed beneath her and the snow soon disappeared, she was traveling with such enormous speed. Shortly, the air became warm and dry and the ground beneath her was flat and barren. The beast upon whose back she rode sped forward relentlessly.

A tower loomed in the distance and she recognized it immediately.

Sedahar! she sighed inwardly, and the recognition both invigorated her once again, though it chilled her to the bone simultaneously.

The animal descended swiftly as the tower drew closer. They were moving so fast that it seemed as if they would crash right into the white stone, and she shielded her eyes with her free hand in anticipation. But, her protective action was unnecessary. The horse reared up before the castle and hovered in the air about ten feet above the ground. It then settled to the surface slowly and stretched its huge legs out in front of itself so that she could dismount. Its mane crackled and burned all around her, and it thick tail pitched fire to the left and to the right as it flicked back and forth. She slid from its back and hit the ground with a thud. No sooner did she regain her footing when the animal rose up and off the surface once again, and then it lifted its chiseled, blackened snout to the sky. Shrieking like no horse born of natural means, it quickly flew off and disappeared faster than her eyes could pursue it.

Standing alone before the gates of Sedahar, Margot was certain she had finally attained the high point of her life, the place of respect and approbation that she had worked for and deserved for so long. She felt like the Dark Lord's Queen who was returning to her home.

One more task to perform for him and he will love me forever! My value will be proven for all to see. None will doubt me again, she thought, as she neared the huge doors that swung open at her approach.

She untied the string that held her cape closed and let it trail out behind her in the still air, like a ruler walking into court. Though no subjects lined the halls to greet her, she imagined what it would be like when next she returned victorious to Sedahar. In her delusion, she nodded to the left and to the right haughtily as she proceeded down the wide hallway.

She knew instinctively where to go. It was not necessary to think about it at all. Though the hallways seemed never-ending and the lavish trappings of Castle Sedahar were awe-inspiring, she barely noticed them. One chamber faded into the next as she made her way to the stairway that would take her down into the depths where Premoran was sequestered; magically shackled and pinned to the foundation wall. A flutter of fear surfaced at the thought of the wizard, and she grasped the orb more forcefully in response.

Margot flung the final door open and stepped across the threshold. A carved stone stairway towered before her, winding into the darkness, suspended over the molten pit that lay beneath the castle.

Bursts of fire erupted from below and shot high into the

hot, moist air. She could feel the craven power everywhere; in the air, in the rock upon which she stood, coursing throughout her body and resonating animatedly in the depths of her perverted soul. Her lips curled upward into a wicked smile, and she screamed like a savage with primal satisfaction into the vast emptiness that surrounded her.

The noise seemed to echo endlessly in the massive space, and it empowered her even more to hear it over and over again. She stepped onto the path and then began the long walk over the burning chasm to the chamber beyond where Premoran was. Her skin prickled and stung from the heat that rose up and over her, but she found it strangely sa'Tisfying. The hem of her garment caught fire and she even allowed that to burn for a moment before snuffing it out with her slippered foot. She felt invulnerable, as if nothing could harm her, and it pleased her to feel the pain as a reminder of her imagined invincibility.

A small doorway appeared in the wall in front of her as she neared the end of the staircase. Margot had no fear of the wizard. He had been held captive for weeks now, deprived of food and water and pinioned to the wall, unable to move. What strength he had left he required just to breathe! He would pose no threat to her at this point. She would remove his shackles from the wall and he would cower at her feet, still bound by them and by her!

I am the arm of the Dark Lord! she thought, and she puffed her chest out before her as she walked.

From beneath the deafening shroud of arrogance that enveloped her mind, she could barely recall Colton's warning. Premoran was no longer her master's nemesis, but rather a cowed and ruined man, kept alive for one reason only. His days were numbered. She only needed to bring him, like a plow horse in harness, to Colton's side, and he would be forever grateful to her and he would honor her as she so deserved. She was the master now!

The door flew open as she approached it and she strode through it without hesitation. It slammed shut behind her and all signs of the entryway vanished as if had never been there. She raised her arm and willed a light to ignite upon the wall beside her. The air was musty and smelled of death, and the room was barren save for a pedestal of stone in the very middle of the floor. The ceiling was incredibly high, and it seemed as if the chamber could have contained the heavens themselves within it. Margot walked over to the seat that Colton had clearly created for himself and she sat down regally upon it, and then she tossed her cape out behind her arrogantly.

In front of her, suspended by five glowing bands of light, the wizard hung from the wall spread-eagled. There was a band around each of his ankles, one around each of his wrists, and one encircled his neck. His feet were barely one foot off of the ground, but just beyond its reach. His beard had grown long and straggly, and his forehead was streaked with sweat and grime. The grey cape that dangled from his shoulders was tattered and threadbare. But his eyes remained open and sharp, and they followed Margot unblinking as she strode across the floor.

She unwittingly gripped the ebon orb inside her cloak a bit harder, and she forced herself to stare back at him. His face was expressionless, though his eyes spoke volumes. His contempt for her was almost tangible.

"How does it feel, old man?" she hissed from her perch in the center of the room. "Last we met, if I recall, you were a bit more dignified. I had forgotten the encounter until now. It seems that seeing you again has rekindled my memory."

Premoran said not a word. He moved not a muscle. But his blue eyes followed her like a Moulant's upon its prey.

"Though I am so enjoying our reunion, we have little time to chat. Your brother wishes me to escort you to his side. It seems he needs your services one final time," she said, and she glanced casually from side to side. "Another one of the cursed trees is dying," she said nonchalantly. "Not quick enough for me. But it matters not. Soon they will all be no more."

Margot rose and walked closer to the wall upon which Premoran hung. She slowly pulled the orb out from under her clothing and held it up before her. It glowed with a menacing inner light, and as if in reply, the shackles that bound the wizard also shone more brightly. Premoran cringed visibly in response, but his eyes never wavered.

"When I place this against the wall, you shall be released from your position, but you shall be bound to the stone still. The shackles will remain upon you, and if you attempt to flee or if you use any of your powers, they will constrict immediately. I will be unable to prevent them from killing you. Once set into motion, they will instantly seek to close the circle that they surround. And, alas, your limbs and neck will sadly be caught in the middle."

Premoran followed her with his eyes as she approached the wall. He watched her as she lifted the black stone, and he hung there immobile and silent. She looked up at his face defiantly, needing to prove her power over him and her lack of fear for him, and she attempted to humble him once more by staring into his helpless eyes. She would not be intimidated by him now. He was vanquished and as weak as any commoner, and she was in control. The power coursed through her veins, and she gazed deep into his defeated eyes as she reached to touch the orb to the stone.

That was the moment he was waiting for. Before she was able to make the contact, he focused what strength he still had and he unleashed a bolt of white light that threw her backwards violently. She hit the wall hard and fell to the floor. Margot needed a moment to regain her breath, and she lay stunned for a second, but she did not let go of the stone.

"I underestimated you, wizard. I will not do so again," she said, and she began to stand up, red faced and humiliated. She straightened her clothing and smoothed her hair. Her pride was all that had been seriously injured, but for someone like her, that was more devastating than a mere physical blow would have been. "You should not have done that!" she said contemptuously, embarrassed by her show of weakness. "You think I am not a match for you?" she scoffed derisively. "I have his power within me!"

She walked slowly across the stone floor. As she neared him, she raised her hand sharply. A blue-white fire buzzed and swirled around her fingers. She directed it toward the wizard's chest. When it reached him, it wound itself around him like thousands of delicate spider webs, and then it began to constrict. Margot moved her fingers gracefully as if directing the motions of a puppet. She desired just the right amount of pain and fear without harming him too seriously.

Premoran gagged soundlessly and his eyes bulged. Margot, driven by arrogance, her head swollen with power, pulled upon the strings a little bit harder in order to prove her dominance over him, and then suddenly, his eyes fell shut and his head lolled to the side. She dropped her arm with a start and cautiously moved closer to the unmoving captive. He was not breathing and his skin was white and pallid!

"Open your eyes, old man!" she commanded, but he did not respond. "What trickery is this? Open your eyes, I said!" she repeated, though her voice now quivered slightly. "Look at me! I will not be fooled by you again."

She dared not touch him, and she was reluctant to get too close to him this time, but it did not seem as if he was faking. Her stomach began to heave as she watched a small line of blood escape from the corner of his mouth and stain his beard as it trickled down. His body hung limp and motionless upon the wall.

What have I done! she panicked. *He cannot be dead! Was he weaker from his captivity than I realized? Have I killed him?*

Her heart was beating faster than it ever had before, racing to catch up to her fear, for she was completely overwhelmed with an uncontrollable, totally encompassing terror! She leaned in closer to him while every nerve in her body tensed and tingled horribly.

He must be playing me for a fool, she thought, but she sensed no life left in him. *This cannot be! It cannot be! You cannot be dead!* her mind screamed.

"Wake up!" she shrieked, and in her fear and frustration, she grabbed him by the shoulders.

His hand shot out and clenched her wrist with the speed of a snake striking its prey, and his clear, blue eyes opened wide and caught her in their gaze. She had no time to react. Emotions overcame her at his mind's touch; regrets and sadness, doubts and fears, and then terror; sheer and unmitigated terror. Without uttering a word, he flooded her body with an unendurable feeling of loss and pain, and she began to fall backward upon the stone surface as if in a dream. As she felt her consciousness slipping uncontrollably away, the chamber was once more bathed in darkness. The light she had conjured went out with the final flicker of her senses.

"Did you think my brother would suffer me to die at the hands of one such as you?" the wizard asked before her mind shut down completely. As she began to fall, he reached out quickly as far as the shackles would allow him to in order to grasp the orb. "This has not the power to kill me! Did he tell you otherwise to give you courage? Has the web of lies caught the spinner of the tale too? Now regrettably, in your hubris you have squandered the moments you had, and it will be too late to return me to your master when you awaken. The tree will be dead and my brother's need for my services will have expired along with the Lalas. Such is the way of evil."

His fingers just barely grazed the black stone as Margot was flung backward and out of his reach. The ebon orb was still securely in her hand, but in that one instant, that one slight touch, Colton recognized his brother's touch and he immediately knew everything that had just transpired. From his perch in Talamar, he erupted with rage like he had never done before. Though Premoran was still bound to the wall with no hope now of escape, the wizard smiled to himself fully sa'Tisfied, before he too slipped into unconsciousness.

As they both faded into the oblivion of sleep, the demon's hound opened its one opalescent eye and stared across the room, unblinking, watching and waiting.

Chapter Forty-three

Tamara stepped as lightly as she could upon the surface. She felt as if she was in a shrine, a sacred place, and she did not want to disturb anything. A faint humming sound resonated in her ears, and as soothing as it was to her, it nonetheless brought her to tears. The smell of Lalas was so strong, but it was a little too sweet, and though it was still incredibly wonderful, it evoked a profound sadness in her. She knew instinctively that it was the tree's last breaths that permeated the air.

Something moved in the far corner, but she was already being drawn so compellingly to the heart that she could not even look in any other direction. Whatever it was seemed so insignificant against the backdrop of Mintar's demise that she relegated it to the back of her mind for the moment.

She could feel the awesome power. It resounded throughout the chamber as she walked determinedly toward the heart. The sense of loss was also potent, and she sighed deeply in response to it. The soil was warm beneath her feet, and Tamara bent down and grabbed a handful of it and brought it to her cheek. Her tears mixed with the rich soil before she unclenched her fist and let it fall back down slowly to the ground. Something was glowing up ahead within the broken shell of the once mighty tree and Tamara walked directly toward it. She felt as if she was dreaming. Each step seemed to be a step out of time.

The dust rose around her feet as they touched the ground, and it swirled and circled about her in slow motion. The humming grew louder the closer she got to the heart. It was mesmerizing, and it added to the ethereal quality of the surroundings and circumstances. Leaves fluttered and settled upon the surface which was already strewn with countless broken branches and twigs; a poignant reminder of the loss, far different from fall's natural devastation, and so stultifying in the knowledge of its permanence and irreversibility. She allowed the small light that burned in her palm to fade as she walked carefully forward. The source of illumination in front of her flared brightly as she neared it, and then it began to pulsate, throwing eerie bursts of light everywhere throughout the darkened chamber.

Tamara's senses seemed to be sharper than ever. Every slight sound, every tiniest movement and every subtle smell was intensified and vivid. She breathed deeply and opened her eyes wide. She was unsure if the humming was growing louder or whether it was simply moving from its source to a place within her head, but it was a hundred times more acute than even moments before. As if she was watching herself from somewhere outside her own body, she lifted her arm and reached for the radiating object sheltered within its cushion of deep brown wood. It was warm when her fingers grasped it, and the sensation that accompanied her first touch was so amazingly unexpected she almost withdrew her hand.

Her mind was flooded with images and thoughts, feelings and emotions, faces, cities, animals and beings of all kinds and shapes and colors, and trees; enormous trees, graceful and wondrous. But, amidst the confusion of this sensory assault, she remained grounded still and something kept her focused. Though no voice spoke to her and no words directed her actions, she was guided nonetheless.

Confidently, she grasped the shard and lifted it out of Mintar's shell. It came free easily, and as it did so, its light went out completely and totally, and just as instantly, her legs felt as if they could no longer hold her up. She tottered slightly and fell to her knees. Using her free hand, she tried to push herself upright, but the soil was soft and gave way under the pressure, and she fell again. Tamara hit the ground with a thud and she lay for a moment upon the warm soil. She sought desperately to right herself and regain her equilibrium. Slowly, she stood up and concentrated so that she would not stumble to the earth once more and chance dropping the precious shard. At the same moment that physical weakness threatened to waylay her body, a surging wave of sadness wafted over her and threatened simultaneously to capsize her soul.

I will not falter! I will not fail! she vowed to herself, and she forced her legs to strengthen and her spirit to rise.

She rekindled a light in her free hand and held it aloft. Though it seemed so pale and feeble in this chamber of death, she held it up defiantly and it became for her a beacon of hope.

Leave, Tamara! Leave quickly! Something evil is loose in this place, she heard Etuah's voice resound inside her head. *And the lost ones come!*

The shock of hearing the Drue's concerned voice propelled her forward more compellingly. As she dragged herself away from the devastated and ruined remains of the Lalas, she felt the desperate and frantic onrush of the millions of lost souls, imprisoned forever by their own tragic mistakes and miscalculations and now searching in vain for release, and clamoring abjectly to fill the vacuum of this suddenly dead place.

A spectral object brushed by her as she left the main chamber and though she could not see it clearly, she knew that it was Etuah. Tamara turned her head around to look upon the emptiness once more and she saw what looked almost like a shimmering, liquid blanket spread itself over Mintar's heart. It covered the entire area where the shard had been and she watched as it appeared to meld with the wood and become one with it. In moments, a massive but totally silent explosion sent millions and millions of tiny, brilliantly blazing particles shooting out in all directions. They adhered to all the surfaces, top and bottom, and left not a single spot untouched by the light. Then they glowed with a blinding intensity before they burned out all at once and sealed and protected the space for all eternity. The lost ones voices were stilled.

Tamara knew that Etuah had completed what she had come here to do, and she said a silent, emotional prayer on the noble woman's behalf before heading for the entrance to the corridor in front of her. For some strange reason, she was not as saddened by Etuah's demise as she had anticipated. It now all seemed so right, and as she witnessed her essence spread throughout the space that Mintar had previously occupied, she felt that the Drue had fulfilled herself and completed her mission in life. She tucked the shard into a pocket in her cape, and with the small light in her palm to illuminate the way, she began to walk to the opening that she hoped would lead her out of the hollows and back to the surface.

Tamara turned quickly to her left, and out of the corner of her eye she was certain she saw a shadow dart across the floor. She needed to take only another few steps in order to reach the opening ahead, and she began to move more swiftly now. She reached her hand inside her cloak and felt for the shard. It was still warm to the touch, and then she remembered the map. Frantically, she searched the folds of her cloak for the container within which the map was hidden. It was nowhere to be found! She must have dropped it when she fell earlier.

Something rushed out from behind the broken heart as she turned to retrace her steps and locate the map. Reflected in the tiny light suspended on her palm she distinctly saw a glistening pair of eyes not more than ten feet away, and they were glinting malevolently in her direction

Chapter Forty-four

"Did you hear that?" Caroline asked, and she stopped in mid step.

"What, daughter. I heard nothing."

"Neither did I," Dalloway said.

"Something moved up ahead," she said, and she cautiously began to walk again.

"It must have been the earth shifting. It is very moist down here now, and the roots are breaking through the surface. Something lives here," Conrad said.

"Are we still following the light?" Caroline asked.

"Yes," Dalloway replied, while looking intently at the medallion.

"Then we must be approaching the heart. Stay close together. We do not know what we will find there," she warned them.

A rush of warm, humid air blew into their faces and the smell of Lalas was unmistakable. But, it was far sweeter than it should have been and it caused them each concern rather than comfort, it was so intense.

"It has never smelled so strong before," Dalloway said. "It is almost as if it has breathed its final breath and soon there will be no more."

The elf's words suddenly seemed dangerously foretelling, for within the next moment, the odor ceased and it was replaced by a cold, fetid stench.

"The tree is dead!" Conrad said coldly.

"Yes. I feel it too," Caroline agreed. "Shh!" she said again. "Did you not hear that?" she whispered.

She motioned with her hand for them to follow her, and she cautiously rounded the bend before them. In the far distance she could see the silhouette of a archway and it was illuminated by a dim light from somewhere behind it.

"We are not alone here," she said softly. "And it is no longer safe!"

"No longer? When was it ever safe in this wretched place?" Conrad muttered.

"When the tree was alive," Caroline replied quickly. "It was safer then, father," she said sadly. "We cannot stay in this place much longer. Hurry. I do not know why we are here, but we must find out soon or we may never be able to leave. We have to reach the chamber ahead. The answers we seek lay there," she said with an urgency in her voice.

"The medallion is brighter than it has ever been. Should I conceal it? It may give us away," Dalloway asked.

"Yes. Put it in your cloak again. We know where we have to go," Conrad said.

A second later, they were enveloped in darkness. As their eyes adjusted to the new circumstances, the aperture ahead began to become clear once more, lit from behind as it was. They approached it with caution, and they did not make a sound. When they were only a few feet from the opening, Caroline motioned to them to duck down and let her go through first. Both Conrad and Dalloway shook their heads vehemently in disagreement, but she was insistent. She was already first in line, so short of physically restraining her and chancing making noise in the process, they reluctantly gave in to her intention.

She stepped cautiously toward the archway and flattened herself against the wall before she reached it. Caroline carefully inched her way close enough to the opening to peek through it. In the middle of the space she could see what looked like a massive circle of broken wood, blackened and dead, and all over the surface lay pieces, large and small, of the dead Lalas. Everything appeared to be coated with particles or powder that sparkled and glinted slightly in the dim light. As her eyes took in the devastation, she realized where she was.

By the First, she thought. *This was its heart!*

She was thoroughly astounded despite the fact that they had been searching for this since they first entered the hollows. It just did not seem actual before, and now, with the shell of the once mighty Lalas shattered and lifeless before her, the reality of it hit her hard. So much was still resounding in the air, and her senses were involuntarily honing in upon the disparate and disjointed memories like a bee to honey. Pieces of the past floated before her mind's eye like a painting cut into hundreds of sections and caught by the wind. They were disjointed and vague. The tree had died, though it had not yet departed fully. Now, it was fading, and fading fast. She was lucky for that. With each moment, the feelings grew less intense and the memories sparked and burned out, one by one. Caroline shook her head and centered herself. The images were far, far away now, floating further into the distance on the fleeting wings of the past.

A sudden movement at the far end of the room caught her attention and served to focus her mind once more fully upon the present. A woman in a long grey cape was standing before another archway, and it appeared as if the light that illuminated the room was coming from something in her hand. She rather tall and she stood erect, but Caroline could not see her face. The distance was too great, and she was facing the opposite direction. Caroline's thoughts linked with hers for a moment, and she knew instantly that she was strong and wise, and infinitely good. Suddenly, the dark haired woman turned and faced the center of the room, maybe in response to Caroline's probing.

Before Caroline had a chance to reveal herself, a figure darted out from behind the rubble and rushed toward the unsuspecting woman by the doorway. Caroline felt a pain shoot through her as if she had been pierced by a knife, though nothing had actually physically touched her. Her senses hurt from the assault, and without thinking, she ran to the woman's defense. She knew without a doubt that whatever was running toward her was evil through and through. She caught up to the two of them quickly, but not before the attacker had grabbed the other woman's leg and brought her to the ground.

Caroline reached its side and entered its mind, and she was repulsed instantly by the vileness she encountered. She felt as if she had climbed down into the pits of Sedahar itself! This beast was corrupt beyond measure, and she cringed as its essence touched her soul. She was falling deeper and deeper into its sick emotions--unadulterated hate, vile desires and depraved past--when she realized that it was an elf she was communing with, an elf from Seramour! She saw the matricide and she saw the treason and she sobbed inwardly at the debauchery that marked its existence. Once, it called itself Ruffin!

Tamara hit the floor hard when she fell and she was dizzy and confused. Her head hurt and she lay prostrate among a pile of dry leaves. Something warm trickled down her face and she brought her hand to her forehead. She was bleeding. It was dark and she could not see anything, but she heard the sounds of breathing nearby. She sat up quickly and almost fainted as the blood rushed to her head. She pushed herself away from the noise, slid across the littered floor, and then rekindled the flame in her palm. To her shock, an elf clothed in the ragged remains of a once grand outfit, lay sprawled nearly at her feet, and a young woman lay unmoving beside him. They both seemed to be unconscious, though they were breathing steadily. The girl's face was tortured and pained, and the elf's closed eyes jumped and twitched behind his heavy eyelids.

Two more figures suddenly rushed out of the darkness on the other side of the room, one with a long bow strung and ready and the other with a dagger brandished before him. They stood menacingly beside the stricken elf and Tamara. The older of the two kneeled at the girl's side and tenderly ran his hand over her forehead. Tamara willed the light to burn brighter.

"She saved me from him," Tamara said. "He came from nowhere."

"Who are you?" the standing one asked.

"I am Tamara, a sister of Parth," she said without hesitation. "Who are you?" she then asked.

"I am Dalloway, son of Treestar and Elsinestra, Prince of Eleutheria," he replied. "And these are my friends, Caroline and Conrad," Dalloway said, and he smiled strangely, though the circumstances did not seem to be such that they would generate mirth. "We were searching for you!" he said.

"Me?" Tamara asked astounded.

"Yes. You must be the sister with the map!" Dalloway blurted out.

Conrad had not picked his head up from his daughter's chest. He was listening to her heartbeat and he was growing paler and paler by the minute.

"So many seem to know of things that I thought were secret," Tamara said and she shook her head back and forth as if mystified. "Is the girl alright?" she then asked.

"She is an empath. She has melded with your attacker. She is strong and knows what she is doing but she has little experience with humans and elves," he explained. "Can you help her?" Conrad asked.

"I can try," Tamara replied and she bent down beside them. "Though I am no healer," she said. She placed her palm upon Caroline's forehead and withdrew it almost immediately as if it had hurt her to touch the girl. Then she reached out again and this time kept her fingers firmly on the girl's skin. "She is burning up." She closed her eyes and summoned what power she could. Then she directed it at the girl. In a few moments, Caroline's features eased and the painful expression upon her sweet face vanished. She appeared relaxed and at peace.

"I do not know exactly what I did for her, but she is at rest now. I cannot wake her though. She seems very far away," Tamara said, concerned.

"Do you know who your attacker is?" Conrad asked.

"No. He came from nowhere. I did not think anyone else could survive down here, so I was careless," she said, obviously annoyed with herself, while she dabbed her own forehead with the corner of her cape. "I am bleeding," Tamara said calmly.

"Let me clean that," Dalloway offered. He pulled a handkerchief from his pocket and carefully wiped the blood from her wound. Then he dampened it and wiped it again. "It is not serious. Just a surface abrasion. Does it hurt much?"

"No. Not really. I am more concerned about your companion than about myself. We will have to carry her if we cannot revive her soon. It is not safe to stay in this place," Tamara warned.

"And the elf? What about him?" Dalloway asked. "Why did he attack you?"

"I have no idea. I suppose he wanted what I carry," she said.

"Perhaps Caroline can tell us when she awakens," Conrad said optimistically. "By the First, I hope that is soon!"

As if she heard him, she began to stir. The elf's breath resumed a more relaxed pattern at the same time, though he remained motionless.

"We had best restrain him. We already know he is not a friend," Dalloway said, as he and Conrad began to bind his ankles.

Before they could finish tying him securely, Caroline sat up with a start and shrieked. She continued screaming violently and thrashing about. Conrad and Dalloway rushed to her side. She sounded as if something was hurting her terribly. Tamara held her hand while she tried to soothe her anguish.

"Caroline? What is it? Talk to me? What can I do?" Conrad pleaded.

She was sobbing uncontrollably and gasping for breath. She was so disturbed that she could barely speak, though she was muttering something about the Dark Lord and murder. Caroline was wringing her hands wildly as if she wanted to wash them of some unspeakable filth that had dirtied them. Tamara placed her palms on either side of the distraught girl's head and held it steady while Conrad continued to ask her questions. Dalloway too was leaning over her and searching for a way to ease her pain and fear. While they focused their attention on the maiden, Ruffin slowly opened his eyes. He reached for the ties that bound his feet and began to cut them as quietly as he could with a black dagger that was concealed in his filthy tunic. Once his feet were free, he adjusted the knife so that the hilt was in his fist and he was about to strike out at Dalloway whose back was nearest to him.

Tamara heard him move and she swung around quickly, though she had no weapon ready with which to attack. She raised her hands defensively and moved instinctively to protect Dalloway. He turned his head around sharply an instant later and found himself staring directly into the deranged elf's eyes. Dalloway simultaneously pulled his knife from its sheath and was poised to strike.

"Mercy, brother, mercy," Ruffin pleaded, while concealing his weapon in the folds of his shirt as he inched closer to Dalloway. "I hail from Seramour too," he said in an overtly affable way.

Suddenly, Caroline broke free of her father's arms, pulled her knife from its case and lunged at the renegade elf with an almost superhuman strength. Consumed with a fury the likes of which her father had never seen in her before, she pierced Ruffin's heart with one fast blow followed by another and another until her father forcefully grabbed her from behind and hugged her tightly to him. She continued to strike out at the air in front of her, thrusting the knife in the direction of the fallen elf relentlessly, and sobbing all the while.

"Stop, Caroline. Stop. He is dead," Conrad said soothingly, trying to console her. The elf lay face down in a pool of dark red blood. "He is dead, my daughter. He cannot harm us anymore." Finally, Caroline relaxed in her father's arms, but she looked at him as if she barely recognized him. "It will be okay," he said, while he brushed her hair back off of her forehead tenderly. "I promise. Everything will be okay."

Dalloway went over to the elf, and with his foot he turned him over so that he was facing upward. His black eyes were wide open but lifeless, and as they all watched him closely now, dark shadows began to swirl around him. They buffeted him back and forth and practically lifted him off of the ground. Within a few moments, his body began to disintegrate as if it had been dead for tiels. Howls and screams could be heard in the distance, and they were quickly becoming louder with each passing moment. Soon, a pile of gray dust that began to slowly billow out from the empty and ragged clothing was all that remained.

"We must go! The lost ones approach! Though they cannot enter here, they have come to claim this elf's soul for their own. Now that his body is gone, his spirit must join them. He has forsaken his other options," Tamara said. "Hurry! Follow me," she instructed, and she started to head for the archway that she was about to walk through when Caroline first appeared. Conrad and Dalloway assisted Caroline, and they moved as quickly as they could to catch up to Tamara. "Wait one moment," the sister said urgently. "I have forgotten something." She rushed back into the room and headed for Mintar's shattered trunk in center of the floor. When she reached it she stopped and scanned the surface quickly. Then, she reached to the right, bent over and picked something up. Hastily, Tamara put it inside her cape before returning to them. "Now we can go," she said confidently when she caught up to the others once more. "I could not leave without the map."

Chapter Forty-five

The air was as empty and lifeless as air could be. Alemar hated the thought of even breathing it into her lungs. She walked beside Teetoo with her arm inside the crook of his elbow. Clovis and Giles followed closely behind.

"Though my eyes tell me that this place is very beautiful, my senses tell me otherwise," Alemar said.

"There is nothing beautiful here," Teetoo replied solemnly. "Sedahar is built upon deception, lies and illusion. It is ironic, is it not, that the one who wishes the world to end has chosen to surround himself with so much of what makes life unique? Art, sculpture and architectural masterpieces? Does this soothe his tortured soul, I wonder?"

"Maybe it reminds him of what could have been," Clovis suggested.

"Why do you say this is all illusory?" Giles asked. "It looks real enough to me."

"It was not built by the hands of man. Colton has created this place by other means, and it is not as it appears to be," Teetoo said sternly. "Pay no heed to what you see. He is a master at seduction, as you learned before."

They wandered through a hallway of white stone walls and polished black floors that appeared to wind endlessly downward now, after having just ascended for what seemed like an interminable period of time prior to entering Sedahar. A mellow light illuminated everything, though its source was not evident. No blemishes marred the surfaces, no angles were askew, no fading of the color or variation in the pattern disturbed the continuity of the space, and this perfection alone distinguished what they saw from reality.

"Is there no one else here?" Giles asked.

"Let us hope not. He originally constructed this place for himself alone those countless tiels ago. He would not suffer another to share it with him. None are his equals here," Teetoo explained.

"Sedahar was for Caeltin d'Are Agenathea a place to rival the one he could no longer tolerate according to the Tomes. He sought refuge here when he parted from the others. And to prove his defiance and contempt, he has built it and destroyed it himself more often than we could count," Alemar related.

"For one who cares so little about life, he seems anything

but indifferent to it," Clovis said. "He does so much in reaction to it."

"And that is what torments him so. He cannot break free from the circle, and he cannot abide within it. In his isolation, he sees life and love more clearly, when all he desires is not to see it at all," Teetoo said.

"And not to feel!" Alemar added.

"How could a living thing not feel?" Clovis asked. "Is that not a contradiction in terms?"

"Exactly, Clovis!" Teetoo said. "Exactly."

They had come to the end of what had initially seemed like an endless corridor, and now they stood before an open doorway. Beyond, it pitch was black. The light from the hallway that they were in did not extend into this space though it seemed as if it should. The darkness consumed the space ahead completely.

"Careful now," Teetoo instructed them as he stepped into the shadows.

The others followed him through the portal and then it took a moment for their eyes to adjust once again. The blackness was so complete that they could not even see their own hands in front of their eyes. For a moment, it seemed almost as if they had lost their vision completely. Then Teetoo's bracelet began to glow. At first, it looked like a bright star in an endless sky of nothingness. But soon its light illuminated the space around it enough so that they could see where they now stood. A long, winding path led into the distance. It was difficult to distinguish where the walls ended and the floor began. Everything here blended together in the darkness.

"The bracelet is leading us to him," Teetoo said. "It grows brighter with each step."

"I cannot tell if we are going up or down," Giles said.

"Neither can I. But I have not been able to determine that since we left the hollows," Clovis said.

"We have been descending, Clovis. But, nothing is as it seems here," Teetoo reminded them. "Pay it no heed. All that matters is that we find Premoran."

They walked and walked, and it was difficult for them to keep track of time. If not for the change in the bracelet's intensity, they could not have determined if they had been making any progress at all. Everything seemed the same no matter how long and how far they traveled.

"Without something to guide you here, you could wander

forever and never get anywhere," Giles said.

"The fate of so many," Teetoo replied.

"Shall I bring forth the light?" Alemar asked.

"No! It is of the trees. Its power could be sensed. We do not dare," Teetoo replied quickly.

"Are there no servants or squires or soldiers in this place?" Clovis asked.

"Fortunately for us, no. He is an untrusting soul. And an arrogant one! He sees not the need," Teetoo said.

"When we find Premoran, how likely is it that he will be guarded?" Giles questioned.

"If he is not surrounded by evil demons, then he must be in a very secure prison. He would not just leave him alone, would he?" Clovis asked. "He needs to eat and to drink. Otherwise he would die."

"Premoran has his own resources upon which he can draw for his survival. Besides, if Colton wanted him dead after he captured him, then he would be dead already. He is here and alive for a reason," Teetoo replied.

"It is unlikely that he is guarded by anything other than Caeltin's own devices. He seems not the type to trust such a job to another," Alemar said.

"He trusts no one!" Teetoo confirmed.

"Then it is logical to assume that something magical binds him, something very powerful and very secure. The Dark One would not risk his brother's escape," the Princess continued.

"I agree, Alemar. And Premoran could not have anticipated what methods and means Colton would have used to keep him captive. I suspect that this bracelet will serve only to lead us to him. I doubt it will do more," Teetoo responded.

"Then how are we to free him?" Giles asked.

"I do not know," Teetoo answered simply.

They continued to walk down the path. It branched off in many directions, and they carefully observed the intensity of the bracelet's light in order to determine which fork to take. Finally, another doorway appeared before them. Teetoo raised his wrist high in the air for them all to see and he signaled them simultaneously not to make a sound. The bead that hung upon the bracelet was glowing more intensely than ever before. He pointed to the door. Premoran was somewhere close behind it.

Alemar was standing next to Teetoo when the

transformation began. She sensed it rather than saw it happening at first. From that point on, she watched awestruck, as if this was the first time she was witnessing it. She noticed his cape lying in a soft pile upon the ground behind him. Then, his back rounded and his arms elongated slightly. From the light of the bracelet, she could see a fine filament appear between the Weloh's arms and the sides of his body. His neck stretched upward and the features of his face became sharper and more chiseled. His ears had virtually disappeared beneath his soft, feather-like hair, and he cocked his head to the side, leaned partway through the doorway and listened intently into the room in front of them.

"Stay behind the portal. Let me go first," Teetoo said in a higher pitched voice than normal.

As he spoke, he turned to face her and she saw that his eyes were covered with an opaque covering that opened and closed quickly now as if he was trying to clear his vision, instead of his usual eyelids. He blinked so fast and so often that she wondered how he could see clearly. He reminded her suddenly of a hummingbird perched before a flower.

"The bracelet, Teetoo!" Alemar said suddenly. "It will give you away if someone or something is in there!"

"Thank you, Alemar," he said, and he removed it from his now thin and bony wrist. It slipped easily over the slender, taloned fingers. "Keep it safe. We may yet require it."

It was too small for her to slide over her hand, so she attached it to the same chain that the silver cocoon hung upon.

"After I am gone, count to five and then follow me cautiously. We may not be able to communicate for a while," he said and then he disappeared without another word.

"That was incredible," Giles said as soon as he was through the door. His jaw had dropped nearly to his chest.

"I never saw anything like it," Clovis agreed.

"He is that last of his kind," Alemar remarked sadly, before taking her place guardedly by the doorway. "One, two, three, four, five!" she said quietly, and then she too slipped through the passage while hugging the wall tightly.

Giles and Clovis followed closely behind her, though it was extremely difficult to see with the bracelet hidden beneath Alemar's blouse. Once inside though, the room was not totally dark. Somewhere, a single, dim light burned, but they could not pinpoint its location. Though they could see its luminosity, they could not begin to determine how near or far from them it might have been. They walked in silence, and stepped as lightly as they could. There was not a sound to be heard. With their backs to the wall, they inched their way deeper into the chamber. As soon as their vision adjusted to the level of illumination, they scanned the room searching for any movement while they slowly made their way around the perimeter.

Alemar noticed something in the middle of the floor. It looked like a high backed chair, but she could see nothing else around it. The shadow that it cast caught her eye and it finally helped her to locate the light which caused it. On the opposite wall of the chamber, a small glowing orb hung suspended. Then, she saw something else. On the wall near where they were headed something was hanging. It could have been a decoration of some sort, though the room did not seem to be one that would have been ornamented. She squinted her eyes, but she was still too far away to see it clearly.

She could no longer tell if Clovis and Giles were still behind her and she was not going to call to them until she was certain that there was no one else in the room. So, she kept her back to the wall and made her way slowly but surely. She thought she heard a whooshing sound in the air high above her head, and she suspected that Teetoo was conducting his own reconnaissance. At least, she hoped that the sounds were coming from him! Alemar was walking with her arms outstretched in opposite directions in order to extend her reach as far as possible. She slid them along the wall, anticipating what she would do should her fingertips encounter anything other than rock.

While the others explored the surface, Teetoo circled the chamber carefully after rising silently to the top of it. It was incredibly high, and for a moment he thought that it would never end. It must have reached right into Castle Sedahar itself, he surmised, as he attempted to calculate the distance from when he first took flight. There was no more light at the top than there was at the bottom. The ceiling was domed, and it appeared to be hewn from solid rock, though it was smooth and polished, unlike like the dulled walls of a cavern. Colton's handiwork was impressive in its scope, if nothing more.

The Weloh's vision was quite keen; better than anyone could have suspected. Still, he was unable to pierce the shroud that blanketed the room. He was cautious in his flight and he had to rely upon his other senses in order to avoid hitting anything unexpectedly. Slowly, he made his way back down to the floor of the chamber, descending in broad circles.

As he neared the bottom, he smelled something odd. It was a human smell, though it was not a healthy one. He hovered over it briefly by stretching the tendons in his wings and bending them in such a way the air held him aloft without any motion on his part. He virtually floated in the air. Since his eyes could still not locate anything or anyone, he honed in upon this odor. Teetoo dropped a little closer to the source, and then he listened carefully. He could hear something breathing about ten feet below him and he was certain that it was the steady breath of a person asleep or unconscious, not of one awake and aware. Carefully, he landed next to it. The unusual light that seemed to be suspended on the far wall did little to illuminate the body that he now stood beside.

Giles was determined to find Premoran. He saw little reason to follow right behind Alemar. If she were to encounter something, he would not be far away regardless. Besides, Clovis was certain to remain by her side no matter what. He wanted to tell them that he was going to go the other way, but he dared not risk speaking after they had a3ready entered the room. So, he chanced leaving them, and he ventured off on his own. His weapons were securely belted to his side so that they would not rattle, and he had nothing more than a small dagger in his hand when he stepped slowly into the gloom. He headed for the oval of light on the far wall. Curiously, it did not illuminate even the area immediately surrounding it. Everything was pitch black, but it hung upon that wall, he could see it clearly, and he knew that someone must have placed it there for a reason.

The fear that Alemar had anticipated she would feel was nothing of the sort. Rather, she experienced a rush of relief and joy as soon as the tip of her finger touched Premoran's warm skin. She knew it was the wizard immediately. His arms were outstretched and he was shackled to the wall somehow, but he was breathing. Alemar stood before him and her head was just about at the level of his chest. She rested her ear against it and listened for his heartbeat. It was strong and rhythmic, though he did not respond to her touch.

Teetoo stood tentatively by Margot's side after having settled to the surface. He hesitated for a second before touching her skin, but then he bent down and felt for a pulse. The woman was alive. A brief wave of nausea passed over him at the contact. She was sprawled upon the floor motionless, but he could not determine the nature of her stupor or how long it would last. He quickly withdrew a thin cord from the pouch at his belt and bound her ankles. As he reached to bring her arms together in order to tie them as well, he noticed the orb.

Giles had made the passage around the room very quickly. His long legs carried him far and fast. He was an experienced hunter, and despite his bulk, he made very little noise when he was tracking something. The oval light that formed his reference point from the moment he had entered the chamber was only about ten feet away. Maybe he could find a way to brighten it when he reached it, or carry it to his friends wherever they might now be. It was odd though, how it shone, almost as if it was alive.

Alemar took a small skin filled with kala sap from the folds of her cape and placed it against Premoran's mouth. She squeezed it slowly and let the rich liquid coat his lips. Then, she reached into another pocket and retracted a parcel of powder that Elsinestra had given to her before they left Seramour. It was crushed Lalas leaf, and she was saving it for just such a moment. She reached up, pulled the wizard's lower lip down slightly and pried his jaw open. Standing on her toes, she sprinkled the contents of the pouch onto his parched tongue.

The wizard opened his eyes with a start. Rather than looking relieved, his expression was uncommonly disturbed. At first, Alemar assumed that he was simply surprised and unsure of who had come to his aid, or still disoriented from his long travail. He was looking past her toward the middle of the room and he was trying to say something, but he was still not fully coherent.

Teetoo leaned over and reached out his still taloned hand toward the black stone. The woman's fingers were holding it so tightly that it must have been very dear to her. Her fingers were clenched around it as if in a death grip. He was about to grab it when her body stirred, and he quickly retracted his arm. Slowly and silently, he lifted off of the ground and hovered about ten feet above her once more.

Alemar was trying to release Premoran's arms from the magical ties that bound them, but it became clear to her very quickly that they were not going to give way from her efforts alone. She could do nothing to sever them.

"You cannot break them, Princess," Premoran said weakly. "Only the orb can set me free."

"The orb? Where is this object then. Tell me and I will bring it to you," she whispered.

"It is on the floor yonder, held by an evil woman," Premoran said.

Clovis had been right behind Alemar all of the time, watching her every move protectively. He heard the wizard's words, though he did know what orb he was referring to. He wished for nothing more than to be able to locate it and bring it to Alemar. Silently, he slipped away and headed to where Premoran had indicated that the evil woman was.

"I will fetch it and convey it to you," Alemar said, relieved that he was strong enough to speak. "I will return as soon as I can."

"No!" he said adamantly. "None can touch it safely save those possessed already!"

"What can I do then to help you?" she asked.

"Leave here immediately! There is nothing more to do. My brother will return eventually and he cannot find you here. Or better yet, kill me so that he will not even have the pleasure of torturing me. I have succeeded in thwarting his plan; the shard has been removed. The earth no longer needs me, and neither does he. I am now expendable," the wizard said.

"We have come to set you free! We cannot leave. Teetoo would never leave you!"

"Teetoo? He came too?" Premoran said tenderly. "I had hoped he would find me, but I had not expected such a perfidious form of imprisonment. Alas, he cannot set me free any more than you can. He must not try!" Premoran said anxiously.

"We have come all this way. There must be something we can do," Alemar
said, as she wiped his brow with the corner of her cape.

"You are not alone here. My brother sent one of the Possessed to bring me to him. I was able to prevent her from completing her task. But I could not kill her. She lies over yonder somewhere. Beware of her," he said feebly. "He needed me for the shard! He knew of the tree's death," he said as if to himself.

"What tree, Premoran? I do not understand," Alemar said.

"He knows more than he should, Princess," the wizard said somberly.

Teetoo squinted his powerful eyes and tried desperately to pierce the gloom. The figure below him was moving now and he dropped down just a little bit closer. She noticed the binds upon her ankles and she quickly untied them with one hand, while in the other she still clutched the round, black ball. He could vaguely see her silhouette, though he could not see her face or her features. He could hear Alemar's voice nearby, and then he heard the wizard speak!

Margot stood and frantically looked all around her, but she could barely see anything either. Her head hurt and she was a little dizzy, but otherwise, she seemed alright. She heard voices and she recognized Premoran's. She sensed another presence and she flailed her arm in the darkness like a blind woman. The thought of rekindling a light so that she could see occurred to her, but she was reluctant to give her location away to whomever had entered the chamber. Fear gripped her heart and it clenched its debilitating fingers ever tighter as she realized what she had done. She forced herself not to panic, and she persuaded herself that perhaps she still had time to rectify her error. She had to move quickly.

The orb was still in her hand. He had not been able to steal it from her. But, she remembered the wizard's words vividly now. He would not die by resisting her. She had not the power to kill him. In a way, that was a blessing, or perhaps he would be dead already, she had been so foolish and so impetuous. But he was still bound to her! If he could have broken her master's grip, he would have done so by now.

Teetoo watched closely as the woman moved. He could now see her silhouette inching across the dark floor. His body tensed and he retracted his wings so that he could dive with as much speed as he required. He rose silently in the air and hovered like a missile poised to strike.

"I will find the others," he heard Alemar say. "They must know that I have located you."

"Be careful. The Possessed one lives," Premoran warned.

Alemar backed away from the wizard slowly and carefully. She heard something move a few feet in front of her and her mind was furiously debating what she should do. She gripped the chain that hung around her neck and waited for the right moment.

Clovis stealthily tiptoed across the floor. He saw the shadow stand and he watched as it approached the place where he had left Alemar and Premoran. Silently, he followed behind it with his dagger drawn and ready.

Alemar was standing perfectly still and barely breathing as the figure approached. She could see a shape in the gloom coming closer. Then she heard something that sounded like an arrow shooting through the air. She willed her necklace to shine, and instantly it illuminated the chamber with a brilliant, blindingly bright light.

Teetoo dove and in an instant he hit Margot square in the chest. The woman shrieked, stunned by the light and seriously injured by the Weloh's blow. She fell sprawling upon the floor. Teetoo rose again, and prepared to strike once more. The black orb was still in her fingers and she lifted it and held it in front of her. The shackles that bound Premoran to the wall glowed menacingly and he cringed visibly in response.

Before Teetoo could attack again, Clovis leapt deftly and threw his heavy body directly on top of her. He hit the crazed woman with his fist sharply on the side of the head, and she crumbled. With lightening speed, he reached out his hand and pried the stone from her grip.

"No!" the wizard screamed. "NO!"

The blood rushed to Clovis' head. He felt as if he was about to explode, and then the darkness closed in upon him. Premoran fell from the wall heavily onto the floor. The magical chains that had held him secure were gone. As abruptly as they disappeared from his limbs and neck, they reappeared on Clovis', pinioning him to the stone floor mercilessly.

Alemar was at his side instantly, while Teetoo hung in the air a few inches above Margot's still body, guardedly.

"Do not touch him," Premoran shouted feebly from the distance. "It will bind you as well!" he warned.

Alemar could do nothing but watch her friend die, helpless and grief-stricken. In her heart, she knew that Clovis' life was forfeit the moment she looked upon him. The magic shackles glowed brightly and it was clear that they were constricting as each second passed. Clovis was unable to move, pinioned as he was, and all he could do was stare into Alemar's face. It was difficult for him to speak.

"A fair trade, Princess, me for the wizard," he gasped, while looking at his shackles. The circlet around his throat was getting tighter and tighter. "Is he free?"

"Yes, Clovis. He is free," she replied, and she had to fight the impulse to take his hand in her own and try to comfort him.

"You must get out of here or all will be for naught," he said. He was choking already on his own words. "Where is Giles?

Is he safe?" he asked. The heartfelt concern for his friend during his own final moments was almost too much for Alemar to bear.

"He is fine, Clovis," she lied. "Rest easily," she said, as fear for her other dear companion rushed through her anew.

"Please go. You have to go," he urged her, though he could barely speak.

"I know," she answered. A heavy tear fell from her cheek and landed upon his face. It mingled with his own and slowly trickled to the ground beside him. "Dear Clovis," she sobbed, and she caressed him with her words since she was unable to offer him anything more. "Dear, dear Clovis," she said sweetly.

He smiled back at her endearingly, as the color that still remained in his cheeks paled and faded.

"Have I made you proud, Princess?" he asked weakly.

"Very proud, Clovis," she answered him. She leaned in as close to him as she dared without touching his body. "Very, very proud," she repeated.

Clovis smiled and closed his eyes, and Alemar watched the light go out from them forever. He exhaled heavily and his head lolled to the side. He was no more.   The glowing bands had closed upon themselves and Clovis was caught in the Dark Lord's heinous grip. Instantly, his body turned to powder as they abjectly stood helplessly by and watched, heartsick and shaken to the core. Alemar reached out and grabbed a handful of his dust and placed it in the pouch that had so recently held the life-giving Lalas leaf. She pulled the string taught and held it up before her.

"You will have a heroes burial when I return to Eleutheria. That I promise you!" she vowed solemnly, and she brushed away the tears that streaked her face.

Premoran raised himself from off of the ground weakly. His body was stiff and sore, but his mind was still as sharp as ever.

"We must leave here as quickly as we can," he said.

"What of this woman?" Teetoo asked from the distance. He had been watching the still unconscious Margot protectively, though all the while he wanted so badly to be able to rush to his old friend's side. "She lives still."

"Let her remain. My brother will deal with her failure more harshly than we could. Death will not save her anyway. Her soul is forfeit for all eternity."

"Will he come for us?" Alemar asked.

"Eventually, Princess. But, we can be of little use to him

now," Premoran said. "It is too late. The shard has already been removed. He will lick his wounds and take out his vengeance upon his own, I suspect. Woe to those who have given themselves unto him and who still live!"

"Where is Giles?" Alemar said nervously, only just remembering that he was still not with them. "Teetoo? Do you see him anywhere?"

Giles had been too far away from his friends to see clearly what was transpiring in the gloom before Alemar rekindled the light. His eyesight was bad to begin with, and from this distance, he could only hear some faint mumbling across the room. He climbed onto a promontory that extended out below the light on the wall that he was trying so hard to reach. It was curiously warm and pliable, but it supported his weight easily. Even though he was right in front of it now, the light still did not project itself at all. He reached up and ran his hand across it, looking for a way to dislodge it from the wall and carry it over to the others. His fingers came away covered in a viscous, clear liquid which he immediately rubbed off on his pants. He stared deeply into the luminescence and it seemed to him again to be almost alive, and that thought sent a chill running through his blood.

What a strange kind of glow lamp, he thought, but his contemplation was quickly interrupted.

He turned around abruptly and looked into the shadows of the chamber when he heard what sounded like a missile shooting through the air, followed by a thud. Then, a burst of bright, bright light blinded him. He could not see anything! He rubbed his eyes and squinted, but all he was able to discern was a jumble of flashing colors. Blindly, he jumped from the perch upon which he was standing, and his boot got caught on something hard and metallic. He tumbled to the floor just as a gust of hot air hit him from behind. He pressed into the wall to steady himself and it gave way slightly as he put pressure upon it. As his vision returned to normal, he saw figures moving and he knew that there was a scuffle going on, but he could not see that far.

Damn these eyes of mine! he cursed himself.

He heard people talking quietly, and he was sure that one of the voices was Alemar's.

A bolt of white light streaked across the room and hit the far wall, opposite from where they had first entered. It was followed by another and then another. The rock facade began to crack and fall in huge pieces to the surface. Suddenly, great chunks of stone were crashing down from the ceiling, and dust was rising everywhere. Giles jumped onto the step in order to avoid a falling piece of debris and he leaned back against the softness of the wall once again. The light still glowed weakly above his head.

"Giles? Giles?" he then heard the Princess calling him. "Where are you?"

"Here, Alemar! I am over here!" he shouted back and he walked forward a few steps. He waved his hands in the air as his vision cleared. He could see them near one another, and they were huddled over a body that lay upon the floor.

Alemar and Teetoo stopped still in their tracks and stared at the elfin warrior aghast! Giles was standing upon the huge snout of a hideous beast whose one eye gleamed eerily just above his head, and he seemed to be totally unaware of his predicament. Premoran was hurling huge bolts of white light at the far wall, and he continued to batter it with his magic relentlessly. Layer upon layer of stone had fallen away already, and with the next barrage, a small doorway finally revealed itself.

"Follow me!" the wizard yelled, still unaware of Giles situation, and he began to run toward the opening. "The doorway will not remain passable for long."

"The demon's hound, Giles!" Alemar screamed.

"What did you say, Princess?" Giles screamed back. He could barely hear her with the noise of the falling rock echoing throughout the chamber. He slipped slightly and he reached out behind him to steady himself. His eyes followed his hand and he turned to face the wall. To his great shock, he realized for the first time that he was staring into the lambent eye of a massive animal! He froze in his place and held his breath, but the beast did not move.

Is it sleeping or waiting to pounce upon me? he wondered watchfully.

"The demon's hound, Giles! Beware the demon's hound!" Alemar shouted again.

Then it struck him. The words of the poem came back to him in a rush:

Who dares trespass into this space,
beware the demon's hound!
Let it rest, awake it not,

no harm will come to thee,
but when the time to flee is nigh,
be sure to set it free.

"Come, Giles!" Teetoo called to him from his place next to Alemar. "Run! We must flee!"

Flee! Giles said to himself. *It is time to flee!*

Giles searched frantically for a chain or cuff or something that could possibly be holding the animal captive and keeping it from waking up. He jumped from the snout upon which he had been standing, and he scrutinized the surface next to where he could now clearly see the hound's thick neck extending through the wall. To his great relief, he saw a heavy braid of iron lying upon the floor. He picked it up and traced it to a hole in the side of the chamber into which it disappeared. The other end looped around the snout of the captive animal.

I tripped upon this before, he thought fleetingly. *Now, if I can only break it.*

He rifled through the many weapons from his belt until he found the one he was looking for. He removed the leather thongs that bound it securely to his pants and raised his stout war hammer before him. He brought it down hard and fast upon the woven, metal cord. Sparks flew everywhere but the leash remained intact. Again he hit the iron braid with little or no result. The hound was breathing steadily though infrequently now and its solitary eye stared blankly outward, unmoved by the activity occurring right before it.

The others had made their way to the doorway and waited for their companion to join them. They could see him hammering away at something, but the falling rubble was partially obscuring their view.

"You must hurry, Giles," Alemar shouted urgently over the din. "I could not stand to lose you both," she muttered fearfully to herself.

Once more, Giles lifted the weighty hammer high into the air and with both hands, he brought it down heavily upon the leash. This time, he could see the braid begin to give way. He knelt down beside it and pulled it apart forcefully. Using all the strength he had, he gritted his teeth and tried to wrest one section away from the other. The leash squeaked slightly as the pieces strained against one another, and then it separated completely. He quickly tossed the broken section toward the wall and let the other end dangle on the floor beside the hound's thick neck. Then, he looked over toward Alemar.

Immediately, the monster blinked its solitary eye and shook it massive head from side to side. The stone encapsulating it fell away and crashed to the floor. Slowly and ponderously, it lumbered out of its captivity. Giles was mesmerized for a moment by the sheer size of the animal as it emerged from the wall, but he was no fool. He rose from his kneeling position and began to run toward his friends. He loped across the floor as quickly as he could, as the beast contemplated its newly found freedom. It shook its head back and forth, opened it huge jaws and growled a deep and virulent growl.

As soon as Giles caught up to the others, Alemar ushered him promptly thorough the still sturdy opening that Premoran had uncovered, and she followed closely behind him. When Giles did not see Clovis among them, he glanced curiously at the Princess. She looked at him in a way that spoke more than her words could have, and then she placed one of her delicate hands upon her heart. He turned from her and walked sorrowfully on. Teetoo bounded through the opening a second later, but Giles barely noticed the Weloh. Premoran stood alone for another moment and surveyed his former prison for the last time. He saw Margot's body stir slightly where it lay in the middle of the floor, just before he stepped through the doorway himself. He turned and motioned with his hands and the opening collapsed upon itself. Its closure sealed them out, while it sealed Margot and the beast in.

Colton's hound saw the woman's movements too. As fast as lightening, it pounced across the floor and was upon her. Margot knew she was doomed. Still, there was no mistaking the sheer terror that they all heard in her scream. It echoed down the corridor and continued to reverberate for some time in their minds as they fled from the crumbling edifice that was Sedahar.

List of Characters, Items and Places

A

Acire. Lalas tree. Tenth tree to die. Theran's Bondmate.

Adrianna. One of the forsaken women. Colton's evil worker.

Alemar. Elfin Princess of Eleutheria. Daughter of Whitestar and Aliana.

Aliana. Elfin Queen of Eleutheria. Whitestar's first wife. Alemar's Mother.

Aliceo. Alemar's great, great, great, great grandmother. Iscaron and Kala's daughter.

Aliya. Queen of Crispen. King Bristar's wife.

Angeline. One of the twelve Sisters of Parth.

Armadiel. Snake of Recos.

B

Baladar. Ruler of the city of Pardatha in the Thorndar Mountains. Husband to Briland.

Behani. One of the Drue.

Beolan. Elfin Prince of Crispen. Bristar and Aliya's son.

Bethany. One of the twelve Sisters of Parth.

Blodwyn. Chosen of Lalas Lilandre.

Briland. Chosen of Lalas Snihso. Lord Baladar's wife.

Brimgar. Daggerfall Thorndar dwarf. Maringar and Preston's father.

Bristar. Elfin King of Crispen. King of the Mountain Elves. Aliya husband. Father to Beolan.

C

Cairn of Thermaye. One of the three called to educate Davmiran.

Calipee dar Tamarand. Baron. Laord of Tamarand. Robyn dar Tamarand's father.

Calista. Lady of the Island. One of the Council.

Calyx Moulant. Cairn's friend and protector.

Carlisle. Chosen of Lalas Mintar.

Caroline. Daughter of Conrad and Sophia.

Carthane. Lalas tree. Paras'Bondmate.

aryssa. Sea Elf.

Colton Dar Agonthea. The Evil One. The Dark One. Lord of Sedahar. Premoran's brother. Called Caeltin D'Are Agenathea by the Elves.

Connor. Chosen of Lalas Catalan.

Conrad. Father to Caroline.

Courtney. One of the twelve Sisters of Parth.

Crea . Chosen of Lalas Wayfair.

Crispen. Kingdom of the Mountain Elves.

D

Dahlia. One of the twelve Sisters of Parth.

Dalloway. Elfin Prince of Seramour. Youngest son of Treestar and Elsinestra.

Dashiel. Chosen of Lalas Nemaroe.

Davmiran. One of the twins. Tomas' brother. Garold and Lewellyn's son.

Dorothea. Duchess of Talamar. Wife of Leonardo.

Drue. Protectors of the Hollows. Came into existence after the death of the first Lalas.

E

Edmond. Chosen of Lalas Xia.

Eleutheria. Ice City. Kingdom of the Northern Elves.

Elion. Elfin Prince of Seramour. Eldest son of Treestar and Elsinestra.

Elsinestra. Elfin Queen of Seramour. Treestar's wife. Elion, Fallean and Dalloway's mother.

Emerial. Elfin Queen of Eleutheria. Whitestar's second wife. Mother to Kalon.

Emmeline. One of the twelve Sisters of Parth.

Esta par D'Avalain. Queen of Avalain. Filaree's mother.

Etan of Balstair. Knighted by Margot, forsaken by Colton.

F

Fallean. Elfin Prince of Seramour. Second son of Treestar and Elsinestra.

Farrow. Lalas Tree. Bondmate of Harton.

Filaree par D'Avalain. Princess of Avalain. Daughter of Esta. One of the three called to educate Davmiran.

G

Gretchen. One of the twelve Sisters of Parth.
Gwendolen. High Kingdom. Kingdom destroyed by Colton. Birthplace of the twins.

H

Harlan. Goodheart Discoverer of the darkening.
Harton. Chosen of Lalas Farrow.
Hollows. Forbidden places.

I

Iscaron. Ancient Elfin King of Eleutheria. Kala's husband.
Ishdomar. Lalas tree. Third tree to die.

J

Jocasta. One of the twelve Sisters of Parth.

K

Kalon. Prince of Eleutheria. Half brother of Alemar. Whitestar and Emerial's son.
Kettin. Lord of Talamar. Son of Leonardo and Dorothea.

L

Lana. Princess of the Sea Elves. Daughter of Windstorm.
Leonardo. Duke of Talamar. Husband of Dorothea.
Liam. Chosen of Lalas Oleander.
Lilandre. Lalas tree. Bondmate of Blodwyn.
Lormarion. Kingdom of the Southern Elves.

M

Marathar.Lalas tree. Bondmate of Pithar.
Margot. One of the forsaken women.
Maringar. Daggerfall Thorndar dwarf. Eldest son of Brimgar Daggerfall. Preston's brother.
Markal. Lord. Master of Arms in Avalain.
Marne. Loyal friend and personal aide to Queen Esta.
Merala Da. Capital city in the Sea Isles.

Mira. Nursemaid who raised and protected Davmiran.
Mintar. Lalas tree. Bondmate of Carlisle.

N

Nemaroe. Lalas tree. Bondmate of Dashiel.

O

Odelot. The Dead City.
Oleander. Lalas tree. Bondmate of Liam.
Ormachon. Lalas tree. Bondmate of Tomas.

P

Paras. Chosen of Lalas Carthane. Became sick and broke his bond with Carthane. Went to Praxis.
Parsifal. Leader of the Knights of Avalain.
Pembar. One who mutated into a tree. Resides in the Winding Woods outside Avalain.
Percepton. Protector of the Forest of the Winds.
Phero. Chosen of Lalas Relamon.
Pithar. Chosen of Lalas Marathar.
Premoran. Wizard. One of the Council. Brother of Colton. Keeper of the shards.
Preston. Daggerfall Thorndar dwarf. Son of Brimgar Daggerfall. Brother of Maringar.
Promanthea. Lalas tree. Bondmate of Robyn dar Tamarand.

R

Relamon. Lalas tree. Bondmate of Phero.
Rella. One of the twelve Sisters of Parth.
Robyn dar Tamarand. Chosen of Lalas Promanthea. One of the three chosen to educate Davmiran. Son of Baron Calipee.
Rose. One of the twelve Sisters of Parth.

S

Safira. Wife to Trevor. Raised Tomas.
Sedahar. Colton's home.
Seramour. Treetop city in the Kingdom of Lormarion. Home to the Southern elves.

Sevilla. One of the twelve Sisters of Parth.
Sidra. Sorceress who declined to be bonded with Promanthea.
Silandre. Mountain in Crispen.
Snihso. Lalas tree. Bondmate of Briland.

T

Tallon. Town of the Chamber of the Roots.
Tamara. One of the twelve Sisters of Parth.
Teetoo. Weloh (last of the race of winged humans). Friend to Premoran.
Theran. Chosen of Lalas Acire.
Tiel. The equivalent of six years.
Tobias. Chosen of Lalas Torenth.
Tomas. One of the twins. Chosen of Lalas Ormachon. Brother of Davmiran. Son of Garold and Lewellyn. Raised by Trevor and Safira.
Tomes of Caradon. Recorded history of the land as well as premonitions for the future. The Great Books.
Torenth. Lalas tree. Bondmate of Tobias.
Treestar. Elfin King of Seramour. King of the Southern Elves. Husband to Elsinestra. Father of Elion, Fallean and Dalloway.
Trevor. Husband of Safira. Raised Tomas.
Trialla. Evil sorceress in league with Colton.

V

Violet. One of the twelve Sisters of Parth.

W

Wayfair. Lalas tree. Bondmate of Crea.
Whitestar. Elfin King of Eleutheria. King of the Northern Elves. Husband to Emerial. Father of Alemar and Kalon.

W

Windstorm. Elfin King of the Sea Isles. Brother of Elsinestra. Father of Lana.

X

Xia. Lalas tree. Bondmate of Edmond.

Gary Wasssner was born and bred in New York. He is a Phi Beta Kappa graduate of Harpur College, SUNY Binghamton. He has a Masters Degree in Philosophy with a concentration in ethics and 19th Century Continental Philosophy. He joined his family's business many years ago and is currently the President and senior partner of Hilldun Corporation, a commercial finance company in New York City.

Mr. Wassner resides in New York with his wife, Cathy. He has three sons, Brien, Cristopher and Cole; four dogs, Trevor, Zoe Rose, Diesel and Marylin Monroe; and one cockatiel. As a family, they travel the world extensively from the North Cape of Norway to Moscow, and from Italy to the Caribbean island of St. Barthelemy.

He is currently a moderator and administrator for Science Fiction and Fantasy World (www.sffworld.com) for which he also writes book reviews. Recently, he was a conference panelist at the World Fantasy Convention in Minneapolis where he read from his *GemQuest* series.

He has completed the fourth book in the series, *The Revenge of the Elves*, and has begun book five.

See next page for title recommendations.

The Twins
(Gary Wassner)
Book one in the GemQuest series.

The Awakening
(Gary Wassner)
Book two in the GemQuest series.

The Road to Kotaishi: Part 1
(Kevin Radthorne)
A lyrical fantasy novel set in a mythic Asian world.

The Road to Kotaishi: Part 2
(Kevin Radthorne)
The first part of the spic adventure concludes.
A lyrical fantasy novel set in a mythic Asian world.

Queen's Champion: The Legend of Lancelot Retold
(Cris DiMarco)
A haunting retelling of the classic Arthurian story.

Bones Become Flowers
(Jess Mowry)
The mysterious voodoo culture in Haiti intrigues an
American humanitarian.

Immortality
(Jennifer DiMarco)
A mysterious maze holds the promise of immortality.